Praise for Hybrid:

"I thoroughly loved reading *Hybrid* by Dr. Bria[n] ... written suspenseful thrilling novel will keep you on your toes ... what happens next. Move over Michael Crichton there is another medical thriller novelist on the block!"
— Gather

"This novel grabbed me from the first page and I just couldn't stop reading. It is terrifying and intriguing and I was drawn to the author's use of modern technology to give the plot a sense of realism."
— Simply Stacie

"*Hybrid* is a slick, tight thriller which when you step back and think about it, is scarily possible. I couldn't put this book down... If you like Michael Crichton or Dean Koontz, this is the book for you!"
— The Bibliophilic Book Blog

"This book is both exciting and suspenseful. It is the type of book that keeps you on the edge of your seat and makes you want to keep reading from the beginning to the end."
— Dad of Divas

"From the first page, I was hooked and could NOT put it down until the ending forced me to.... *Hybrid* is AWESOME! Any fiction you read this year has to include this mind-blowing book from Brian O'Grady."
— True Crime Book Reviews

"This book is absolutely fantastic.... You do not want to miss this book. Make room on your book shelf, your night stand, your coffee table or your Kindle... and get this book! It's worth every penny spent and every second of your time."
— Outnumbered 3 to 1

Hybrid

Hybrid

Brian O'Grady

The Story Plant
The Aronica-Miller Publishing Project, LLC
P.O. Box 4331
Stamford, CT 06907

Print ISBN-13: 978-1-61188-059-5
E-book ISBN-13: 978-1-61188-060-1

Visit our website at www.thestoryplant.com

First paperback printing: March 2011

First Story Plant Printing: October 2012

Printed in The United States of America

Acknowledgments

Writing a novel obviously requires a great deal of time, and no matter how much I would want the world to simply stop and let me "finish this chapter," it continues to spin on. The grass grows, the paint on the fence begins to peel, and children become young adults. Life is about balance; writing a novel is about indulging a burning desire that does not recognize balance. For all those who "picked up the slack" while I was locked in a room alone so no one would disturb my aura, I thank you for this great indulgence.

To Shannon, Brian, and Erin – the time I spent writing *Hybrid* was yours.

I would also like to apologize to all the people that I forced to read the various versions of my musings. I know some of you suffered in silence out of a sense of misguided loyalty, while others, Jerry, simply suffered.

I would especially like to thank Doug Burns, Christy Bates, and Dalice Lewis: it was your professionalism, talent, and humanity that created the success that gave me the opportunity to write *Hybrid*.

Of course I would like to thank my publisher, editor, critic, and guide: Lou Aronica. Despite the fact that you are a New York Yankees fan, an irredeemable character defect in most educated circles, I appreciate your patience, experience, and expertise, but mostly your foresight in creating a vehicle for others to succeed.

To my wife Margaret: without you, nothing has meaning.

To Margaret; here's a little sex.

Chapter 1

From: amanda.flynn@home.com
Sent: March 5, 2015, 2117 MST
To: v.induction@cdc.org
Subject: Viral outbreak

Nathan A. Martin, M.D., Director of Special Pathogens, Centers for Disease Control, Atlanta, Georgia:

Dr. Martin, we met seven years ago at the Tellis Medical facility. I'm sure you remember, although I can't discount the possibility that in your tenure at the CDC you may have detained so many people that my name is only a distant memory. Let me refresh it; you and your medical team held me for three months under the pretext that I was a public health risk after I had been exposed to a virus in the jungles of Honduras. Ultimately the United States Army intervened and I was released over your objections.

You visited me on three separate occasions. During our first two conversations you openly lied to me about several things, the most important of which was your true intent. Our final meeting was cut short when you nearly asphyxiated yourself. Perhaps now you remember that it was me who saved your life.

I am contacting you not because I trust you, but only because I have no other options, and I hope that the health and welfare of the American people mean more to you than your pursuit of me. A situation has arisen that requires your immediate attention and intervention. The virus that you named EDH1 has resurfaced in the city of Colorado Springs.

I realize that taken at face value this is a fantastic statement and that your first inclination may be to ignore it but, as the only survivor of this virus, I am in a unique position to make it.

While I was being held in Tellis, one of my many frustrations was the fact that none of your staff would actually listen to what I had to say. Your investigations were misdirected from the start; the answers you sought could not be found in any of the preprogrammed forms and questionnaires that I was forced to endure. To fully understand what happened in that Honduran jungle, you needed to be there or, failing that, listen to someone who was there.

So, for the health and welfare of the American people, for your understanding, and for my own piece of mind, I am going to set the record straight.

I was a part of a Red Cross disaster response team sent to Tela, Honduras, after Hurricane Michael. Tela is a coastal city, but due to the heavy storm damage it could only be reached by helicopter. With a platoon of seventeen Honduran soldiers, our team of fourteen was ferried in by helicopter. Shortly after we arrived, a local woman, covered in blisters and suffering from a gunshot wound, brought EDH1 to our camp. Later, we found a second group of soldiers, all infected, staggering down the highway, and they told us that everyone from Tela was either dead or dying from a highly communicable form of hemorrhagic fever. Within twelve hours, we started losing people. By ten days, thirty of our original thirty-one were dead. I believe that this part of the story is well known, and unfortunately it became the sole focus of everyone's attention and concern.

What was lost in the chaos was the truth of how most of our people died. The virus itself only killed seven of our thirty; the rest died violently. I'm guessing that shortly after exposure the infection spreads to the brain, causing hallucinations, paranoia and, in many, uncontrolled rage. After I became infected, I experienced each of these symptoms, and I can't overstate their intensity. It is quite possible that, given the appropriate treatment, some of our people might have been saved, which brings us back to the situation in Colorado Springs.

As of last Thursday, there have been no cases of hemorrhagic fever reported in Colorado, and the only reasonable explanation is that no one is looking for it. The Colorado Health Department is reporting an unusually high number of deaths from a particularly virulent form of the flu, and I believe that many of those cases are, in fact, related to the Honduran Virus.

There has also been an unprecedented spike in the rate of violent crime in Colorado Springs. In the past six weeks, there have been forty-two murders and suicides—that's twenty-five times their average. This is not a simple statistical anomaly.

If you check, you will find that the Colorado Health Department and Colorado Bureau of Investigation have already started investigations and, not surprisingly, neither one has found anything. You need to help them make the connection; you need to tell them what happened seven years ago!

I can imagine how an unsolicited e-mail asking for an investigation into an obscure virus will be received, but as I see it, you are in my debt. I also want you to consider the source; no one else knows what really happened in Honduras. I'm not asking a lot. Do your job, and let the Colorado Health Department do theirs. I'm certain that the results will confirm what I'm telling you.

I've reviewed your biography on the Internet and, despite what you've done to me, I believe you can be motivated into doing the right thing. Otherwise, I'll be forced to deal with this in my own way.

Amanda Flynn

***

Response: v.induction@cdc.org
Sent: March 7, 2015, 0654 EST
To: a.flynn@home.com

Ms. Flynn, I'm not sure how you got my personal e-mail address, but it has long been suspected that you were more than what you appeared. As far as remembering you, rest assured there are many who remember you well, myself included.

I'm not in any way apologizing for what we did for you, and please note, I didn't say "to" you. When you were flown out of the jungle, you were in severe shock from blood loss and exposure. Neither the U.S. government nor I had anything to do with your quarantine. When we learned of your plight, we evacuated you to the best facility in the world for such problems.

As far as what you think you witnessed before you were rescued, you must realize that your impressions were heavily influenced by the infection that very nearly killed you. There was no evidence that anyone died from anything other than the EDH1 virus.

As far as being indebted is concerned, I think I've shown that it is you who are indebted to us. So, I will rely upon your honor and ask that you allow us to re-examine you so that we can find out how you survived this universally fatal infection. I am sure you know that a number of people have been trying to find you for seven years.

Finally, I have contacted the Colorado Department of Health, and they have noted an unexplained rise in acts of violence. However, there is no evidence to suggest that an infectious agent is the cause. They assured me that they have specifical-ly looked for one and have carefully reviewed all the autopsy results. I trust what they told me, and I don't do that lightly. If it makes you feel any better, I will admit to having a deep institutional bias and a basic distrust of everyone outside of my little world, but in this situation, the CDH did their job. I'm sure there is an explanation for this worrisome cluster of vio-lence, but it's not EDH1.

I have hesitated to contact the FBI. By all rights I should, since they want to see you very badly. From my perspective, at best, you are key to answering some critical medical questions, and at worst, you could pose an overwhelming public health risk. Seven years ago we were unable to find any evidence of the EDH1 virus in your blood, yet you had all the clinical features. This makes you quite unique. We have made many technical advances in the last seven years, and there's a very real prob-ability that we can determine why you alone survived. I think you owe it to the thirty-one people who didn't.

N. Martin

***

Response: a.flynn@home.com
Sent: March 7, 2015, 0503 MST
To: v.induction@cdc.org

I appreciate that you contacted the local health authorities, but it's frankly not enough. They are not equipped to evaluate this threat. You are. Trust your institutional bias.

You were wrong about what happened down in Honduras. I was not sick when the Marines arrived. They made that assumption—an honest mistake, but one that was propagated down the line until it became viewed as fact. My memories were not affected in any way. If your records show that all the deaths occurred due to EDH1, then they are either incorrect or have been altered, for whatever reason. I am not some conspiracy nut. Things were incredibly chaotic, and for now I choose to believe that the soldiers saw what they were told to expect. Certainly, they recovered the remains of my team, didn't they?

Amanda Flynn

***

Response: v.induction@cdc.org
Sent: March 7, 2015, 0712 EST
To: a.flynn@home.com

Apparently I've caught you awake. I'm not in the habit of exchanging e-mails back and forth like some adolescent, but for you I'll make an exception.

Without something concrete, I've done all I can. I do not have the authority or inclination to demand that the Colorado Department of Health do any more. You have given me nothing but unsupported recollections and statistical anomalies. I can't commit resources based on that.

Just so you know—the bodies of your Red Cross team were destroyed on site. We did not have the ability to bring them home. For that I am sorry.

I've read your file many times, and know that you've experienced more than your share of tragedy but, as you have pointed out, I have a responsibility to the health and welfare of the citizens of this country. If you are right, and EDH1 has found its way into the population, we need to see you now more than ever, not only to identify your unique resistance, but because YOU are the only natural reservoir for this virus. If there's an outbreak, it is because you have chosen to remain at large. I regret that I have to take such a hard line, but if I can't persuade you to come in voluntarily, I will contact the FBI before the end of today.

N. Martin

***

Response: a.flynn@home.com
Sent: March 7, 2015, 0519 MST
To: v.induction@cdc.org

Call them.

Amanda Flynn

Chapter 2

Phil watched the tiny bead of sweat slowly track down Dana's cleavage as she leaned in to refill his coffee cup. He knew he should be repulsed; sweat was a bodily secretion composed of oils, sloughed skin, and bacteria, but he couldn't help but wonder what it would feel like on the tip of his tongue. For an instant, he could actually feel the heat of her breasts on his cheeks, the tiny blonde hairs tickling his skin, and the taste of salt. Then it was gone. He filled his mind with white noise to banish the invading hallucination and its attendant disgust. He was getting so bad that even eating lunch posed a risk.

Dana had paused, coffee pot suspended between them, as Phil went rigid, his knuckles whitening on the fork and his face turning a dark shade of red. Control re-established, he felt her hesitation and consciously re-laxed his grip, mechanically returning the fork to the counter. He glanced up slightly and found her studying him. She gave him a playful, disapproving smile; Phil wasn't the first man she'd caught looking down her blouse. Then she whisked away, her smile broadening with the realization that Phil was human after all.

He waited until she was a safe distance away and then quietly, slowly, exhaled. His heart hammered in his ears and he had trouble breathing. His vision began to narrow, and he broke out into a cold sweat. He had violated the rules of their relationship, and she had caught him. He fought to clear his mind, but it was a feeble effort and shame overwhelmed him. It was a familiar feeling, and one of the few he could fully appreciate.

A powerful desire to flee, to jump from his stool and run to some dark place where he could be alone in his madness, filled his mind, and his focus narrowed even further. His heart continued to thunder in his chest, and he was certain everyone at the lunch counter could hear and feel each beat.

I am in control, he whispered to himself, but both his heart and mind ignored the mantra he had learned as a child. *I am in control,* he repeated sternly, and his pulse began to slow, although the voices in his mind snickered at his naiveté.

He stared down at his plate and what was left of the Tuesday Lunch Special.

There's nothing special about this meatloaf, a voice from a dark recess whispered. Phil ignored it and began cleaning the plate. Finishing what he started was a part of The Routine, and The Routine had to be maintained; deviations were an invitation to Chaos. His mistake with Dana may have already taken him to the edge, and he could ill afford another.

It took him two minutes and thirty seconds to finish; a little fast, and he would probably pay for it later, but he was now free to leave. He carefully reached for his wallet, moving slowly so as not to disturb either of the men sitting next to him. The physical contact, while disagreeable, would be relatively harmless, as he still wore his coat, but the obligatory conversation that followed would be another impediment to his return to Sonny's Café. He extracted a new ten-dollar bill, placed it face up immediately in front of his now clean plate, and waited for Dana to retrieve it. Phil stared straight ahead, focusing on his distorted reflection in the stainless-steel panel that lined the kitchen. The warped image was both disturbing and comforting; parts of him were stretched to absurd proportions, while others were pinched together, but it still managed to remain a discrete, individual entity—at least for now.

A minute passed, and Dana hadn't collected the money. The man to Phil's right suddenly slid off his stool, tossed a number of crumpled bills onto his dirty plate, and left without a thought. Phil didn't move. He remained frozen in place, looking neither left nor right, occupying a minimum amount of space, no more animate than a department store mannequin as he waited for Dana to dismiss him just as she had done nearly every workday for the last four years. Only today, she had missed her cue. He could hear her down the counter fending off the clumsy advances of some construction worker. He listened for her approach, not daring to glance lest she misinterpret his need to leave for something else. A minute passed, and he felt it go. The clock in front of him began to accelerate. Phil glanced down at the bill and confirmed it was where it should be. Two more minutes passed, and now he couldn't even hear her. *She must be mad,* he reasoned. Three minutes passed, and the world began to collapse in on him. Heat began to build in his chest, and he started to count. He was at forty-eight when Dana blew by, snatched the bill despite an armload of dishes, and disappeared into the kitchen. Phil climbed off his stool and left as fast as the busy restaurant would allow. No change would be coming. He refused to have money in his wallet that had passed through countless hands.

Phil popped out of Sonny's door in such a rush that a couple of thirty-somethings had to jump out of the way. He ignored their sarcastic "excuse me's" and hurried into the dwindling snowstorm. Fortunately, the sidewalks were nearly deserted, the majority of the workforce heeding the National Weather Service's warning of a late winter snowstorm. Up to eighteen inches had been expected, but only a paltry three inches fell before the fast-moving storm pushed off to the east. Still feeling the aftereffects of his encounter with Dana, Phil lengthened his stride. He glanced at his watch: 12:52—eight minutes to make it to the office. The possibility of being late suddenly flashed through his mind, and his heart raced even faster.

You don't need to be ruled by fear, said a small voice in his head. It really doesn't matter if you're late. Nothing is going to happen, so just relax and enjoy the world around you. The small voice was little more than a whisper, but it seemed to magically resonant in his mind and, in a truly unexpected moment of independence, especially considering what had just happened, Phil obeyed. He shortened his steps and, for a long, wonderful second he was the master of his own mind. A thrill rushed through him as he intentionally ignored the growing panic that screamed at him to hurry. He drew a long, luxuriant breath and almost felt relaxed.

"Pardon me," a voice said gruffly as he was bumped first by one and then by another person, the human traffic streaming past him. A wave of fear drowned out the small voice. The moment of normality forgotten, he looked at his watch again: 12:54. Six minutes to do four blocks. He could just make it with a brisk walk; he wouldn't have to start running, yet. He lengthened his stride, brushing people as he passed them. *It can't be helped*, he thought. Besides, he hadn't actually made physical contact with anyone. Three blocks: 12:55:25. If he kept this pace, he'd make it. He allowed himself to anticipate the relief he'd feel after making it to the office safe and on time. No pounding in his chest, no roaring in his ears, his mind free to focus on something less trivial than getting back from lunch on time.

The small voice returned: *You live the life of a coward, afraid and small.* Phil ignored it. He especially hated this voice; it was new and dangerous. It whispered, unlike the others, which raged. He'd learned to deal with the rages, but whispers were harder to ignore.

Admit it, you don't want to live like this, and the truth is that you don't have to. Find the courage to free yourself. Phil intentionally walked faster. He'd have to find a way to silence this small, seductive voice. It came at him sideways, not like the usual monsters that preferred a more direct and violent approach. It was so much more clever than the others, playing on his deepest desires, softly speaking of things like enjoyment, spontaneity, choice—the components of a normal life. A life free of The Routine. Only Phil knew that would never be possible. He could never have a normal life, because he wasn't normal.

One block to go—ninety seconds left. Phil stepped into the last cross-walk just as the traffic lights changed. *Perfectly timed*, he told himself, and with this tiny victory, some of his anxiety began to ease.

It's sad that such a trivial thing can make you feel better. Life doesn't have to be this inconsequential, and you know it. The small voice again.

If you continue, I'll—

You'll what? Start to count? Maybe some derivatives? How about some cube roots? Let's try the cube root of 7,315,393,542, shall we? And the answer is 1941.24, give or take a few decimal points. Math isn't going to work. You're going to have to deal with what I say!

The small voice wasn't so small anymore. Phil knew it was never a good idea to respond to a voice directly; all he had done was empower it.

Seemingly out of nowhere, a man passed Phil on his left and reached the opposite curb a fraction of a second before him. Startled, Phil side-stepped to avoid contact, but the abnormally tall man continued down the sidewalk without taking notice of their near collision. Phil chastised himself. It had been a long time since an internal debate had distracted him to the point of inattention. He resumed his hurried pace, but the tall man was faster. Dressed entirely in black—hat, overcoat, slacks, shoes—he stood at least six foot five and had a stride to match. On an average day, Phil would have found him unusual, but today the clock was ticking and he still had half a block to go. The video store, the dry cleaner, the bakery, and then the office.

The door to Loeb's Bakery opened, and a well-dressed woman backed into the sidewalk. Early sixties, Phil guessed, five foot two in high heels. Obviously not a local. She carried a large, ungainly purple box and was thanking the baker as he held the door. Unaware or unconcerned about sidewalk traffic, she tarried several more seconds, chatting away. The tall man was rapidly closing the distance and in a moment would be forced into the street to avoid running into her, but she gave no sign of moving. Phil watched with interest: the woman had positioned herself directly in front of his office door, and in a matter of seconds he too would be forced into the street. The tall man slowed and at first looked as if he were going to join the conversation but, instead, he suddenly kicked her outstretched leg.

The woman's leg flew out from beneath her; she fell hard onto her back and right side. Phil was close enough to hear the heavy thud and the whoosh of escaping breath. One of her shoes slid down the sidewalk as the man stepped over her. The box she carried skidded into the slush-filled gutter, where it split open, and the flowing snowmelt washed away a large purple dinosaur cake.

Almost against his will, and completely against his nature, Phil found himself running to her aid. She was less than twenty feet ahead of him, three or four strides, and he covered the distance in a moment. The tall man sensed his approach and turned to face Phil, his black overcoat billowing in the wind. A wave of fear every bit as tangible as a gust of bitter cold struck Phil, and he pulled up short. The man's face, if one could call it that, was grotesquely deformed. The skin was a mass of twisted gray tissue, with no discernible nose, eyebrows, or ears, and his mouth, partially open to reveal pointed white teeth, was no more than a slit. But it was the eyes that froze Phil in place. Blood-red orbs with vertical pupils bulged from malformed sockets, and they bored into Phil.

"You are too late, Phillip," the slit-mouth said slowly in strangely accented English. He turned abruptly and walked up the sidewalk. Phil remained frozen in place as the dark man strode away.

Something brushed Phil's arm and the spell snapped. The prostrate woman lay at his feet. Her long fur coat had fallen open, and her sky-blue pleated skirt had worked its way up her thighs. Instead of trying to get up, she was working to regain a degree of modesty.

Embarrassed, Phil looked up and found that in a matter of seconds the assailant had managed to disappear. The sidewalk was empty, and so was the street. Puzzled, Phil jogged the hundred feet to the intersection, but found no six-foot-five-inch man dressed all in black in any direction.

The office! The realization hit Phil. *He's waiting for me in the office!* He ran back down the sidewalk and pulled the side door open so abruptly that the guard jumped to his feet.

"Dr. Rucker, are you okay?" José Ortega said, his hand over his holster.

"Did anyone just come through this door?" Phil demanded. The strain in his voice triggered a memory and he saw the face of a madman, his distorted features pressed against a thick pane of safety glass as men in white coats struggled to subdue him.

Control! Always stay in control! Phil admonished himself.

"No one," Ortega quickly answered.

Phil pushed the door closed, cutting off Ortega's questions, and turned back to the sidewalk and the fallen woman. The baker and several passersby were helping her back into the store. Phil waited for her to clear the doorway and began to follow her inside. Just as he was crossing the threshold, he hesitated.

I could just go back to work, he thought. *She doesn't need me.* The baker was helping her into a chair, while someone else was bringing up a second one for what looked like a sprained right ankle. *I don't need to do this,* he thought, but some internal force compelled him forward.

The woman was in obvious pain and, despite extensive plastic surgery, her age was evident. "Excuse me, ma'am," Phil said, "but I saw what happened and got a look at the man who kicked you."

She stared up at him blankly. "I'm sorry, sir, but I don't think I understand," she said, with a deep southern drawl.

"The man, dressed all in black. About six-five. I saw him kick your shoe." Now Phil was confused.

The woman looked at the baker, who returned her quizzical look. Then both looked back at Phil with a mixture of suspicion and confusion. "I think you are mistaken," she said. "It was my shoe. I probably shouldn't have worn it in all this snow, but I can assure you no one struck me."

"She tripped, that's all," said the baker, all his confusion gone. "I was right there. She lost her balance and fell. No one kicked her." His tone suggested that Phil should leave, now.

Phil's face flushed. He muttered an apology, clumsily left the bakery, and returned to the office.

"Anything I can do to help, Dr. Rucker?" Ortega asked with a tone that suggested he wanted to do anything other than help.

"No," Phil said darkly. He was angry with himself. He knew better than to involve himself in situations not of his making. Chasing the man up the street had been a reasonable and appropriate response, a moral obligation, and he had to meet moral obligations. But what had possibly compelled him to follow the woman into the bakery?

He walked up the short corridor to his office.

Phillip Rucker, M.D., Chief Medical Examiner, Colorado Springs, Colorado, was stenciled across the frosted glass.

I wonder for how much longer, the small voice whispered into Phil's brain, and he had to agree. No one had seen an impossibly deformed tall dark man, because he didn't exist outside of Phil's increasingly unstable mind.

Chapter 3

Nathan Martin stared at the blinking words: *Amanda has signed off.*

He could have handled that better; he should have handled that better. Amanda Flynn was important. He thought of her often and remembered the entire Honduran affair clearly. Everything about it made him anxious. There had been other cases in his nine-year tenure as Director of Special Pathogens that he and his group hadn't fully resolved, but none of them bothered him as much as the Honduran affair, as he had come to call it. So many unanswered questions.

He looked for the file on his cluttered desk. It had long ago been digitized and added to the CDC database, but Martin had kept the paper file for himself. About twice a year, he thumbed through it hoping to find something they had missed, or perhaps to trigger some new insight. He knew he had taken it out yesterday, after hearing from the long-lost Amanda, but now he couldn't find it.

"Martha, are you in yet?" he called out. His obsessive-compulsive secretary had a knack for taking the very thing he needed most and "putting it away."

"No, I'm not," Martha Hays yelled back through the open door.

"Did you take the EDH1 file?"

"No, it's on your back desk. I saw you put it there last night." She appeared in his doorway, feigning frustration.

"Right, I've got it. Don't take it again."

His secretary flipped him off, making him laugh.

"I could fire you for that!"

"Fat chance. I'm a civil servant. I could set you on fire, and the most I'd get would be a reprimand."

Martin opened the file and his handwritten notes spilled out. He picked up the nearest one. *Origin?* was written across the top. Where *did* this virus come from? It had always bothered him that nothing like EDH1 had ever been described before. He knew that the majority of viruses in the world had yet to be seen, much less described, but he had never come across one so radically different from everything else. There was no structural analogue or one that killed so efficiently; not even Ebola was this evil, and nowhere near as complex. They had been given a very limited sample to work with, barely enough to culture, but the virus mutated into unstable forms so rapidly that Martin couldn't trust his own findings.

He shuffled through the notes and found the one labeled *Bodies.* If he could have examined one of the victims, he would know so much more. But all the U.S. military had been allowed to retrieve were tissue samples. The official story was that the Honduran military had orders to sterilize the entire area, including the corpses. A U.S. colonel had tried to convince a Honduran general that with minimal precautions the bodies posed no substantial risk, but he was overruled and sent packing with samples and the single survivor. Martin supposed it was understandable, considering the situation: the general's nation had just been devastated by a hurricane. An entire town and nineteen of his soldiers had died of a mysterious illness. He could hardly fault him for not wanting to risk more lives recovering bodies for scientific reasons.

The last of Martin's notes was labeled *Survivor.* These were the most detailed. More than three hundred people had died in this outbreak, including the thirty at the Red Cross camp. Only Amanda Flynn had survived. How? Why? Even after holding her for thirteen weeks, he couldn't answer either of these questions. He had lied to her in his e-mail. When she had arrived in Oklahoma, she was dehydrated, in shock, and suffering the effects of exposure, but her life had never really been in danger. He had held her as long as the military would allow, and in the end he failed to find anything of significance. She had no signs of infection, either acute or remote. They couldn't culture the virus from her blood or even her tissues, but the tissue samples from those that had died grew the virus readily. Martin finally concluded that Amanda had some type of immunity to EDH1. He toyed with the idea of purposefully exposing her to the virus to confirm it. *Okay*, he thought, *maybe I did a little more than toy with the idea.* This inexcusable breach of medical ethics and morality had finally caused Martin to realize that he had lost all perspective. Amanda had become a personal obsession, one that time had only managed to dull.

In the solitude of his office seven years later, Martin was embarrassed by his actions and shamed by his motivations. How could a man his age, and in his position— someone who had accomplished so much—still be motivated by petty jealousies and childhood insecurities? He had convinced himself, and told others, that they needed to know what made her so special for legitimate medical/scientific reasons. It was valid, cogent argument, but it in reality it was little more than subterfuge. He was driven by darker and far more personal motivations.

Amanda and her virus had shown up shortly after Martin had been appointed the Director of the Special Pathogens unit of the CDC. His predecessor was a living legend, having literally written the book on special pathogens. Most of their colleagues were polite enough to whisper that the department was euphemistically going through a transition period, while others were less discreet. And then Amanda appeared with her frustratingly obscure immunity to the most special of all special pathogens. For three months she became the focus of Martin's entire section. They tested virtually every square inch of her, but she refused to give him the answers and the validation he needed. After spending over twenty million dollars, all he had learned was that she was a completely healthy twenty-four-year-old woman.

A beautiful twenty-four-year-old woman. He winced as he turned to her photograph. All his life he had known people like Amanda: the popular, the pretty, and the privileged. Why had God selected her above the other three hundred people? When she first arrived at Tellis he knew next to nothing about her, but her looks and the way she carried herself allowed Martin's imagination to fill in all the gaps. She was the cheerleader surrounded by friends, floating down the high school hallway on the arm of the football captain. Which made Martin the slightly built Jewish kid from the shadows who both loved and hated her. Only later, after she had disappeared and everything had gone to hell, did he find out just how wrong he had been. She wasn't the stereotype he needed her to be, far from it. Which made his offense all the more difficult to forget, or forgive.

Martin gathered the file and turned back to his computer. He scrolled up to Amanda's first message and reread it. He'd often thought that the last chapter on EDH1 had yet to be written, but there was nothing to link this virus, or any virus, with the situation in Colorado, no matter how strange it was. He closed his e-mail file and opened a pathology file. The Colorado Springs medical examiner had asked for help identifying a potential viral encephalitis case two weeks before Amanda had contacted him. It was a routine request, no different from the dozen other requests his office received weekly, but he had never believed in coincidences. He reviewed the report again, and again found nothing suspicious. Both the local pathologist and Martin's own section found all the requisite abnormalities associated with a viral infection of the brain: heavy lymphocytic infiltration of the gray matter, inflammatory cells around the blood vessels, and macrophages along the linings of the brain's ventricles. Nothing very interesting. Viral encephalitis was usually caused by an arbovirus, which was carried by mosquitoes. Probably not a lot of mosquitoes in Colorado this time of year, but the victim could have been bitten elsewhere. Electron microscopy had confirmed inclusion bodies consistent with an arbovirus, so that pretty much closed the book.

He had taken an extra step by calling the Colorado Health Service and asking them to forward their report on this unusual blip in violence south of Denver. They had done a reasonably good, if somewhat bureaucratic, job of chasing this down to its logical dead end. He also asked if there had been any cases of hemorrhagic fever that had gone unreported to the CDC. Not surprisingly, there hadn't been. An inordinate number of deaths from a particularly nasty flu, that was also giving them a little trouble in typing, he was told, but certainly nothing as exotic as hemorrhagic fever.

"Excellent, you're already here," said a voice, startling Martin. Adam Sabritas rushed into the room. Thirty-six, dark, and pudgy, Adam was constantly in motion. When he sat, one or both of his legs would bounce. When standing, he was constantly shifting his weight, giving everyone the impression of a six-year-old needing to pee. When he talked, it was in a torrent, a loud torrent. Martin had recognized the talent beneath the frenetic activity when Adam had taken three months off from his infectious disease fellowship at Johns Hopkins to intern at the CDC. That had been four years ago. Now Adam had his own research lab and a dozen journal articles to his credit, and was fast becoming the world expert on the Hanta virus.

"We finished the sequencing of the R2 serotype last night and found eleven base-pair changes."

"That's good news. So we don't expect R2 to ever become a significant player." Martin had always expected that the Hanta virus would develop less virulent subtypes, and it was Adam's job to prove it.

"Nope. Whatcha got there?" Adam seemed to vibrate.

"Oh, you wouldn't be interested in a case of encephalitis in Colorado." Nathan dangled the word "Colorado" before the bouncing Adam. Hanta was especially active in neighboring New Mexico.

"In March?" Adam's bouncing increased in frequency.

"No, February. Dick Fernung took a look at the case." Martin enjoyed winding Adam a little tighter; only Adam stopped his incessant leg bouncing. "What's wrong?"

"Dr. Martin, Dick Fernung is in Africa. He's been there since January. Uganda, I think."

"Damn, how did I forget that?" Martin said. He needed a break, or an assistant, probably both. He returned to his computer, but the report was unsigned. "Martha, can you get me file . . ." He donned bifocals to read the case number from the computer. "434-w90?"

"No," she shouted back.

Both men were surprised by her response. "And why the hell not?" asked Martin.

"Because I got you that very file yesterday, and you haven't returned it. Did you look on your desk, Oh organized one?" She didn't even bother to get out of her chair.

Nathan began rustling around his desk, and just before he was going to shout that it wasn't there, Adam found it on a chair next to him.

"Found it," he said, handing over the thin manila folder. "Dr. Fernung has a post-doc working for him. It's, ah . . . Larry Strickland," he said sheepishly. His left leg began to bounce.

Martin sneered as he thumbed through the file, looking for the signature page.

"Great! Guess who signed it out?" he said sarcastically. Larry Strickland was a post-doc who would never rise above research assistant if Martin had anything to say about it. He was as much of a mistake as Adam had been a find. "He's lazy, sloppy, and stupid." The words slipped out, and immediately both were embarrassed, especially Adam, who was just two years older than Strickland. "I'm sorry, I shouldn't have said that."

"Said what?" Adam popped to his feet. "Well, I've got some time on my hands. I'll be happy to review it."

"I don't know. How are you with arbovirus? They can be tricky," Martin said with mock concern, handing him the file.

"Well, I do know that they're not nearly as sexy as the Sin Nombre virus. If I need to know anything else about them, I can always look it up in a book." Adam was back in full motion as he thumbed through the file. "This shouldn't . . ." Adam stopped moving again.

"You were saying?" Nathan had turned back to his desk and waited for the younger man to finish his thought.

"Dr. Martin, I don't think this is an arbovirus," Adam said softly, staring at an electron micrograph. "This doesn't look like anything I've ever seen. Definitely not an arbovirus. It's too big and much too complex." Adam awkwardly bent over Martin's desk, pointing at a photograph.

"What? Just give me the file. I can't see it from way over there." Nathan was more annoyed than concerned. A six-sided wheel with what looked like arms at each corner stared back at him. It took about five seconds for his brain to process what he was seeing, but it took his stomach less than one. A wave of nausea hit him, and he dropped the file. It hit his knee and fell to the floor.

"Have you seen anything like . . . Are you okay?"

Martin was light-headed, and his mind was racing. "This has got to be a mistake," he mumbled as he felt the wheel of karma turn. He reached for the file, but Adam had already scooped it up.

"I take it you know what this is," Adam said.

"Let me see it again." Martin's heart was palpitating, but his mind was clearing.

Adam fumbled with the pages for a moment and handed his boss the electron micrograph. The picture hadn't changed. There were four more pictures of the virus, and each showed the six-sided wheel with short arms. Martin checked the file numbers and found that they all matched. It was too much to hope that a clerical error had been made.

"Hold this for me," said Martin, passing the file back to Adam. Martin retrieved the old EDH1 file, and after several minutes of rifling through its pages, he threw it back onto the desk. "No goddamn pictures," he said, turning to his computer and pounding away at the keys.

Adam cautiously walked around the desk and watched with growing concern as his boss punished the keyboard.

Finally, Martin stopped; he had found another hexagon with six arms. A fist tightened in his chest, but the angina wasn't what concerned him.

"They're close, but not the same," Adam said. Martin jumped a little, having for the moment forgotten his protégé. "Look, this Colorado virus has much smaller appendages." Adam shoved the file in Martin's face. "I'd guess that it has less nuclear material as well, but they're definitely related. This one has to be a mutation of the one on the screen." Adam made the obvious connection, but Martin had stopped listening. "We have a problem, don't we?"

Martin didn't answer. Instead, he picked up the phone. "Martha," he said, his voice uncharacteristically controlled and business-like, "I need you to get me William Branch. He's assistant director of the FBI in Washington. You should have his number. Tell him it's an emergency." Martin hung up the phone.

"She knew." Martin said to himself.

***

Amanda slid off the high-back aluminum chair and into her parka. Out of habit, she had signed off, but it probably wasn't necessary. She walked up to the counter of the Internet café and gave the night clerk a ten-dollar bill. She had worn gloves since she had come in, and the bill was clean. She had every expectation that within a very short period of time it would be confiscated as evidence, and she didn't want things to be too easy for the FBI. She had signed in using her real name. No sense in disguising that. Everything else, however, was artifice.

***

Kurt Campion, the night clerk for Missy's All-Nite Internet, could only stare. Not many coeds used the café this late, and he'd never seen one that looked like Amanda Flynn.

Amanda smiled at Kurt, and she had the attention of every atom in his body.

"You a student here?" he asked awkwardly while slowly making change.

"Yes, I am. I transferred here from Texas this semester." She used her sweetest voice and projected the image of an innocent, carefree small-town girl who had no idea just how attractive she was.

Kurt could hardly breathe. Nearly twenty-one, he was, and would always be, the quintessential geek, and beautiful women didn't give geeks the time of day. At least, none had ever given Kurt the time of day. "Um, I'm in . . . computer engineering," Kurt said. "I got this job because I can fix just about anything in here. Besides, it's quiet enough that I can write my code."

Amanda glanced over his shoulder; his laptop was paused on a fantasy role-playing game. Kurt followed her gaze. "Oh, that's the latest version of *The End of Time*—"

Before Kurt could explain all the secrets and intricacies of the game, and conveniently slip in the fact that he was the first person ever to become The Grand Executioner, Amanda cut him off. "I think games like that have led to the dissolution of American society."

Crestfallen, Kurt's eyes dropped. "Seven-fifty is your change."

***

Amanda took the money from the sad college student. She didn't like embarrassing him, but it was important that he remember the image of a twenty-year-old sociology major, five foot two, with short brown hair and stunning green eyes. In twenty, maybe thirty minutes, Kurt was going to get a visit from the FBI, and they would have a seven-year-old photograph of a five-foot-seven blonde with blue eyes who would now be thirty-one. They would try to convince Kurt that the stuck-up bitch was actually Amanda. In the end, they would conclude that Kurt was an unreliable witness or that Amanda had used a stand-in—either way, the confusion would work to her advantage.

"'Bye," she said politely, and she walked out the door, swinging a book bag over one shoulder. Outside, Boulder was cold, quiet, and asleep. Constitution Avenue, the university's main drag, was completely deserted, and Amanda's clogs echoed off the storefronts. She continued up the street as far as the main campus. Comfortable that her deception was now complete, she turned onto Peak Street. Her five-year-old Jeep Grand Cherokee was parked in front of a Starbucks, and she quickly got in.

"Damn him," she said after strapping on her seat belt. Her breath frosted the windshield. It had been a mistake to contact Martin, a mistake to believe that an ass like him could ever change. Now more than ever, she would have to cover her tracks, which meant leaving her apartment, her job, and ultimately her car behind. Aside from a few precious keepsakes from a life that ended years earlier, she would have to dispose of everything.

"The burden of a federal fugitive," she said to herself. Two narrow escapes in the last seven years had taught Amanda that even the most innocuous aspect posed a risk to her new, carefully crafted, sterile existence.

She started the car and, as it heated up, so did she. Seven years ago she had given Martin and his minions three months of her life. She had submitted to dozens of their exams and had answered thousands of pointless questions, but it never seemed to be enough. They wanted something she couldn't give them. "That's not entirely true," she whispered. She could have given them something; she could have given them the whole truth. It wouldn't have answered any of their questions, but it would have told them that they were asking all the wrong questions.

It was Martin who first suspected that she wasn't completely forthcoming. "Bastard," she said. "He's responsible for all this." That wasn't entirely true, either. But he simply wouldn't let it go; he wouldn't let her go. He refused to accept the fact that he would never have his answers. It was more than just professional responsibility. Somehow it had become a personal challenge. He would know her secret or he would destroy her life. As it turned out, it wasn't her life that had been destroyed. She had no regrets about what she had done; she was well past feeling regret. They had put her in a no-win situation, and they were the ones who had lost. For seven years, they had hunted her and, up until this morning, the trail had grown decidedly cold. She put the car in gear and pulled out into the empty street, passing a deli on the left. Above the door was a large sign with the words *Martin's Deli* painted across it.

"Can't shake you, can I," she said, turning south. There was no point in returning to her apartment; she had planned for this eventuality and had everything she needed in the backseat. Her life in Boulder was over, and with it five years of relative peace. It had taken Amanda more than two years of ceaseless wandering before she gained enough perspective and control of her condition to stop running from it. Resolution of her inner turmoil was still a long way off, but she was comfortable enough to come home to Colorado and eventually settle in Boulder. The quirky little city casily absorbed her minor eccentricities, and Amanda's life slipped imperceptibly into a dull, monotonous routine. The predator within was slowly lulled to sleep, and the restraint that anonymity demanded became almost second nature.

But all that changed a month ago. It started with an occasional slip in her usually carefully controlled behavior. A rude counter attendant suddenly develops an incapacitating headache. An oblivious driver talking on his cellphone has a blow-out moments after drifting into Amanda's lane. A series of relatively minor but escalating events, each followed by a warm rush of satisfaction, forced Amanda to recognize that something was off.

A disturbance in the force, she joked to herself. At first she thought it was just her old problem resurfacing in a different guise. The passage of time had done nothing to resolve the fact that she was at war with herself. Her life in Boulder had always be one of impermanency and expectation. At some point she knew she would reach a crossroads and would be forced to choose a life of restraint and limits, or one of glorious self-indulgence.

But despite its immediacy it wasn't that decision that had disturbed her uneasy equilibrium. Something in her world was different, and it had awoken her predator. It had begun to whisper softly and gently pull at Amanda. Her dreams became orgies of violence and wanton indulgence, and she felt the return of forbidden desires.

It finally took a hike into the mountains—away from the thousands of unguarded minds that assailed her every waking moment—for Amanda to isolate the faint but unmistakable scent of either a threat or an opportunity. A consciousness beyond her own floated through the cold mountain air. An enemy or perhaps a kindred spirit was in search of her. The something different was actually someone different. She wasn't alone anymore, or even anonymous.

When the car finally warmed, Amanda shimmied out of her parka and tossed it onto the crowded back seat. She had one stop to make, and then she would be on her way back to Colorado Springs, a place she had hoped never to see again. She wondered half-seriously if it was the karmic center of the whole universe, or just hers. She had grown up in Aspen—not the famous resort, but a small farming community east of both Boulder and Denver—but it was Colorado Springs where she had lived and been happy. She had gone to school there, met and married her husband there, had a son there, and finally buried them both there.

The car bounced over a frozen mound of snow, and the wheel jerked in Amanda's hand. Even her car was reluctant. "Easy girl," she said. "We still have to see Auntie Em before we go."

Regency Care Center was the only medical facility in Thompson County, and the only place Emily Elizabeth Larson would consider living. At 72, she was Amanda's oldest living relative; in fact, she was Amanda's only living blood relative. She had retired from her professorship, sold her home in Enid, Oklahoma, moved back to Aspen, Colorado, broken her hip, and had surgery all in the span of one very stressful month.

Amanda had made the sixty-mile drive from Boulder back to her hometown several times in the last few weeks despite the obvious risk. Normally, it took less than an hour over the new highway, but this morning she took the old route. It was a shorter distance, but took a half hour longer as most of it was over one-lane roads that wound down the Kenner Pass. She had avoided these roads for eight years; bad memories lay ahead, but she had to face them before she faced her uncertain future.

Nearly an hour later the road finally began to level off and Amanda could hear the swollen Kenner River as it flowed parallel to the gravel road. A few more bends in the road and then there it was, looming above her: the bridge. It was an old steel structure with dark rust stains at each rivet site. It hadn't received a lot of attention in the eight years since she was last at this spot, but it still appeared solid. The river had become popular with kayakers as it plunged more than a hundred feet in the last quarter mile before passing under the span. Amanda could see several cars parked in the makeshift gravel lot just to the left of the bridge. It bothered her that people were here now, and that this place, which had become a nexus for her family, had become a recreation destination for others.

She let the Jeep coast into the lot and finally come to rest in front of a tree that was perched precariously over the narrow gorge. By all rights, she should have this place to herself; she shouldn't have to listen to the sounds of yelling and laughter while she faced her past. It was not quite dawn, so no one had entered the rapids. *It wouldn't take much to make them leave,* she thought. She could feel the six people crawling through the trees down to the water's edge; they were so full of life and excitement in a place that only reminded her of death and misery. She climbed out of the car and walked out to the road and up to the bridge. She saw the kayakers carefully climbing down the path, each carrying a small boat and dressed in a thick wet suit.

Her father had died at this very spot almost thirty years ago. He had been a small, mean-spirited man whose attitude permeated their tiny house like a bad smell. One of her earliest memories was of him towering over her screaming that she was a burden he had never asked for. He died the day after her ninth birthday; the official story was that he had just finished changing a flat tire when a half-drunk lawyer plowed into the back of his car, apparently throwing him into the river below. It took them three days to find and recover his body. Amanda never believed the official story. Somehow, she knew that her father had jumped into the river long before the drunk ever showed up, and that the only time in his life he had ever been lucky was after he was dead.

Amanda noticed that the group of kayakers had stopped on the path and were staring up at her. Her first thought was to scare them back to their cars so that she could be alone in this terrible place, but after a moment of contemplation, she turned away and walked farther up the bridge. The last time she had been here, there were police crawling down that very same path. The memory teased at her, but she wasn't ready to relive that evening; still, the face of an impossibly young state trooper, and the images of flashlight beams whipping through the air, seeped through her mental walls. It had been more than a month after her husband and son's funeral, and she had resolved to join them, but a despondent farmer with his own impossibly heavy burden had gotten to the bridge before her.

The pain of their loss could only echo in her empty heart; a distant reminder of a life she had once lived. A life that now she both cherished and reviled, a life stolen by nothing more significant than a flu virus. A simple set of proteins and a strand of DNA had hollowed her out and remade her into something she had never imagined, or wanted. Something that for the last seven years she had kept hidden from the world, and herself.

She watched the water cascade off the large rocks below for another five minutes before the first kayaker entered the water with a triumphant yell. She took that as her cue to leave. This place had no memory of her, her father, her family; it was nothing more than a metal bridge and a small, inconsequential river.

Chapter 4

The blisters were back; they always came back when he was frustrated. It had been over six weeks since he had arrived in this frozen corner of hell, and he had almost nothing to show for it. Time wasn't running out anymore, it had already run out. Klaus was more than two weeks overdue, but he couldn't make himself leave.

It doesn't really matter, he thought. What are they going to do, start without me? The thought made him laugh.

They could try to kill me. That thought didn't make him laugh. They had made it quite clear that while they did need him, they didn't necessarily need him alive. But trying to kill him would be a major inconvenience, and he was balancing that against extra time. Soon, however, the balance would tip.

The professional inside told him to leave—to pack up and slip away before anyone even knew that he had been there. He had already completed his primary objective, and his remaining responsibility could be completed anywhere. He knew that the risk of discovery, capture, and failure grew with each passing moment, but still he stayed. He had to find her. He had to know who Amanda Flynn was, and what she had become.

From the moment he learned of her, the significance of Amanda's existence had reached cosmic dimensions. He tried to convince the planners that she posed an unacceptable risk to the mission, but no one listened. He was told that she would die along with everyone else, and that he should let them worry about the overall strategy. For the first time in his professional life, he seriously considered using his considerable talents against those who had engaged him. The only thing that stopped him was the undeniable and inconvenient truth that, for a while, he needed their logistical support. They were fools, but well-funded and organized fools. He turned his back to the shaded window and tried to suppress his growing anger. When all of this was over, he would pay them a visit and extract from their flesh the three weeks he had wasted trying to find Amanda.

They weren't really fools, he admitted after his frustration began to ebb. They were simply focused on the singular opportunity that had fallen into their collective laps, and they would not tolerate any distractions. He couldn't fault them for not seeing Amanda's unique potential, or threat; it required his particular, unique perspective to fully appreciate it. Maybe, for a while, he would spare them. Still, they could have helped him; they had the resources, and with just a little assistance both of their objectives would have been completed by now. The thought of their intransigence forced his anger to the surface again. Maybe a visit to their dirty, smelly homes was in order, but only after he found Amanda.

His problem was that he had no idea how to find someone who did not want to be found. He had never been an intelligence officer. His instructors had taught him a hundred different ways to kill a man, but not a single way to find this very special woman. All he had was a name, a ten-year-old address, and a vague description. The name turned out to be wrong, probably misspelled somewhere down the long line of information. Amanda Lynn was actually Amanda Flynn. It had taken him two weeks to find that simple error; somebody who knew what he was doing would probably have picked it up in a day. The address he had been given was now an office building. Her old house had become a victim of something the newspapers had called the Sunshine Project, urban renewal by any other name. The description was equally unhelpful, fitting about every third woman in Colorado Springs. The only solid lead he had managed to turn up was a dangerous one: Greg and Lisa Flynn, Amanda's in-laws.

He had watched the Flynns for weeks now and couldn't find an opening. He was certain that they knew where Amanda was, or at the very least how to contact her, but he didn't know how to enlist their cooperation, something he would need if he proved to be correct. It would have been so much easier if he could just break in and take what he needed from them, but if he did that, one, if not both of the Flynns, would have to die, and that would ruin everything. All he wanted was to spend a moment with their daughter-in-law. That's all he would need, just one moment, and then he would know.

He shivered under the thick blankets as much out of frustration as fever. It was always the same: first the blisters, then the fever, and finally the madness. He could live with the blisters and fever, but when the madness came, it enveloped him completely, obliterating any sense of purpose or urgency, and he could ill afford that now. Over the years, he had learned how to control it; delay it would be a more accurate description. The problem was that every time he denied the madness it only came back stronger. He tried to clear his head, but it resisted. Flashes of his parents assaulted his mind: his mother beating him after he had been expelled from school because he had hurt another student; his father unceremoniously dumping him on a train that would take him to the military school that would "straighten" him out. The images of his early years flowed through his mind and he smiled, wondering if that foolish man and his wife ever realized what type of creature they had brought into this world. Maybe on their deathbeds they had been graced with the knowledge that they had played a part in creating the most powerful being that had ever inhabited this planet.

Another spasm wracked his body. He had to empty his mind to control the madness, but the unbidden review of his early life was proving to be wondrously indulgent. The metal archway that lead to the Honnecker School for Military Studies flashed through his mind. It was a brutal, primitive place that changed little while the world beyond its stone walls experienced cataclysmic change, but Klaus Reisch had found himself there.

Unconsciously, he began to rub the small tattoo on his right wrist. In faded black, the words *ex chaos ordo* were etched into his skin. *Out of chaos, order.* He had done it himself, and the beating he survived because of it only increased its value. It was the school motto, and it had taken Klaus more than three years to fully appreciate its meaning.

***

It had been a true epiphany, one prompted by a public humiliation. His philosophy professor had asked him to explain the phrase's apparent contradiction in the context of the ancient Greek belief in a god of order and a god of chaos. Klaus couldn't remember his response, only that it caused his teacher to launch into a tirade that somehow ended with Klaus being removed to the disciplinary cells. Hours later, as he sat in the dark on the cold concrete bunk, his thoughts of revenge and violence slowly being consumed by a growing exhaustion, his mind began to clear and an understanding crept into the void: he was completely alone. He had no family; by mutual consent he hadn't seen his parents in years. His schoolmates feared more than respected him, and he was fairly certain that most of the faculty held the same opinion. He had no one to trust, no one to tie him to a society that he found both restricting and absurd. If he was going to survive, he would do it alone. From the chaos that threatened to stifle and control him, he would create his own order. It was in this moment of true inspiration that Klaus Reisch saw his life stretch before him.

For the next six years Reisch reworked himself. In public he fought to control the innate abilities that were viewed by others as antisocial, but in private he honed them to a fine edge. When he was sixteen, on a school trip to Berlin, Klaus killed a man simply because he felt that the experience would be beneficial. His victim wasn't important. Death was a personal and singular event for the individual involved, but Klaus was only interested in generalities. He stalked several people before he found his test subject, a middle-aged man who had the misfortune of turning, at the wrong time, into a dark alley to urinate. Klaus stabbed him in the back four times and then quickly turned the slumping body onto its back so he could watch the man's dying face. All Klaus saw was a pained look of surprise as the man bled to death. No soul left the body; no great insight was muttered with a dying breath. The man gasped, then shuddered a little and was dead. Moments earlier this decaying mass had been a living breathing human being, with thoughts, desires, a future, maybe even a family, and Klaus had taken all that away in the blink of an eye. A part of him reveled in his power. A simple act, four thrusts of his arm, had taken everything this man possessed or would ever possess. The dead man's face slacked into a mask of death and Klaus almost started to laugh. He had done this, by himself, in secret. He stared at the face and tried to memorize every detail. He was struck with a desire to know everything about his victim. Did he have an important job, or was he just some mindless drone, surviving day to day in some office cubicle? Who would do his job now? Did he have a wife, and would she miss him? Maybe children, and how would they grow up without a father? Did he drive a car to work today, and if so who would drive it home? It was as if he had tossed a stone into a still pond and the ripples reached farther and farther. Reluctantly, Klaus left the body and found his group at the hostel. No one had missed him, and life went on exactly as it had all his sixteen years.

***

A snowplow rumbled down the street below Reisch's room, its blade scraping snow and pavement and grating his nerves. He opened his eyes and cursed; the reminiscent spell broken, he was left with only the shaking chills and the imminent madness. He crawled out of bed and pulled back the curtains of the hotel room, intent on killing the driver of the plow, but the truck had already turned the corner. It had snowed again. God, how he had learned to hate snow. As a child, it was one of the few things that he had loved but, after six weeks of watching it fall unceasingly, he could die quite happy if he never saw it again.

It was still dark but close to dawn, and a handful of people filed into the large church across the street. Klaus silently watched them. He felt the smallest measure of kinship with those poor souls. They sought understanding in a world filled with chaos, and prayed for transformation, not just for themselves, but for society as well.

"Fools," he said. The order they sought was false, artificial. They denied their true selves, sacrificing in the name of a greater good. God, society, it didn't matter what they called it; all they accomplished was to contribute to the very chaos they tried to control. Human society was the greatest force of disorder ever devised, and religion was its most potent weapon. Jesus, Moses, Mohammed, Buddha were all agents of chaos. Each of them, in their own way, tried to supplant the natural, universal order that was written into every man's soul with their own perverted version. The universe had given man intelligence, cunning, and instincts so that he could further himself, but society and religion stifled thought, punished guile, and blunted the natural desires of man.

Klaus let the curtain fall; it was cold and he had to start moving. There would be no stopping the madness now that it had a hold on him; he could already feel the gnawing inside his belly. "An incomplete immunity," the virologist had told him long ago, "similar to shingles." Reisch rubbed the blisters and the usual yellow fluid ran down his hand. The image of Jaime Avanti floated through his mind; the virologist had helped to save his life seven years ago, and until recently had a pivotal role in the overall plan, at least until he tried to betray it. He would be with the Americans now, unless he was dead.

Reisch smiled again. Everyone, from Avanti to the terrorists to Reisch himself, had their own agenda, and it was the sticky yellow fluid that steadily oozed from his blistered hands that held them all together. It was the true agent of transformation. He was the first to experience its power and was convinced that Amanda was the second. A wave of desire that bordered on panic swept over him. He had to find her and, if it was appropriate, protect her from the forces that wanted to destroy her.

Another, more powerful rigor wracked him; the demons were stirring. For a moment, his desire and their needs were balanced but, as always, the equilibrium was fleeting. Amanda would have to wait, because the madness wouldn't.

Klaus took less than ten minutes getting ready, his movements becoming more frantic as the need grew. Normally, he was meticulous in his grooming and presentation, but for the time being basic hygiene was all that was required. A part of him hated the madness. The periodic and unpredictable interruption in his life to feed the demon that lived inside him was demeaning. A little like defecation, necessary but repugnant. Still, it was a small price to pay.

"*Ex chaos ordo*," he said while stepping into his shoes.

His jacket came next and, as he slipped into it, he wondered if Amanda had her own demon and, if so, what it demanded of her. The thought of Amanda quickened his pulse, but she would simply have to wait, his demon was almost overwhelming conscious thought. He never considered himself a violent man. It was true that for decades he had made an excellent living from the strategic application of violence, but it was never a random act. The planning, the anticipation of obstacles, and finally the dispassionate execution were intellectual tasks that demanded precision and clarity. The actual execution was often just an afterthought. Violence for the sake of violence was new to him, but it was the price his demon demanded of him.

And now, his demon needed release. He needed to feel a knife in his hand as it tore through human flesh. He needed to hear that sharp intake of breath as surprise and pain flooded through his victim. He needed to feel hot blood spill over his blistered hands. Klaus closed his eyes as the madness overwhelmed him. He had to find someone and quickly; a little while more and all caution and reason would be lost. He began to run down a list of potential victims. He knew the whereabouts of at least a dozen people, all related somehow to his search for Amanda.

Or someone new? It was an exciting thought but entailed more risk. It took him a few moments of consideration to reject the idea; after weeks of idleness, he wasn't up to his usual standards and needed the advantage of knowing his victim. *But who?*

"The pathologist!" Reisch said triumphantly. The dour image of Phillip Rucker filled the German's mind; it was never very far away, particularly of late. Reisch had become irritated with Rucker's newfound resistance. He could still overwhelm the American, as he had done the day before, but it was requiring more and more effort. He had found the pathologist through Greg Flynn four weeks earlier. The two had briefly met at a downtown coffee shop where they discussed the outbreak of violence; Klaus had listened in on their conversation but quickly became fascinated with Phil. Rucker had a towering intellect but was without a doubt the most unstable mind he had ever visited. He began to follow the pathologist, and within a week the man had become a passion. He researched his professional works and learned his routine, and the more he learned about Phil, the more he had to know. Rucker was special in every sense of the word. He worked out like a professional athlete for seemingly no reason at all. He didn't have any relationships, sexual or otherwise, and he rarely left his home. Yet, his brilliance was legendary. At the age of thirty-four, he had been appointed chief coroner for Colorado Springs, despite the fact that each of the other three pathologists had greater seniority. Yet no one seemed surprised or upset by his promotion. He had authored thirty professional articles in his three years as chief coroner, and not even one had a co-author. Yet he did all this with his sanity hanging by the thinnest of threads. Reisch had made a practice of fraying that thread a little more each day. *No*, he thought, *it can't be him. It would be much more fun to snip his thread.*

There was always the priest—Reisch's other obsession. But here again, there were reasons to allow him to live. He had been infected for more than a month now and, unlike all the others, showed no signs of dying, or evolving as Reisch had. He never really expected the priest to evolve, but then he never really expected to have to kill him, either.

***

Like Rucker, Father John Oliver had come to the attention of Reisch through Greg Flynn. Newly retired, Flynn began spending a fair amount of time volunteering at Sacred Heart Catholic Church and working with its associate pastor, a short, stout Chicago transplant in his early sixties. Thinking that the priest could be an easy avenue to Amanda, Reisch had introduced himself to Father Oliver as a new parishioner.

"I have come ahead of my wife and son. They are still in Brighton." Reisch had donned his proper British affectation. It was one of the few times he had directly engaged someone, but the risk was acceptable. The priest would not remember his visitor well, except possibly that he was very tall.

"So you're from England. Is your wife English as well?" The priest seemed sincerely interested, which unnerved Reisch.

"Actually, she grew up in Colorado Springs and graduated from this very high school. I was supposed to look up some of her old classmates, but I have been having a bit of trouble tracking anybody down." Reisch smiled at the cleric, hoping he would take the hint.

"Well, we are a fairly mobile society. Do you know if any of them are still members of Sacred Heart?" Oliver asked.

Reisch fumbled in his jacket for a moment and retrieved a PDA. "No, I'm afraid I do not. All I have is a list of names and old addresses. I would guess that a number of the names have changed as well. Does your parish have an online database that would be helpful?"

"We're not nearly so organized. Was there anyone in particular you were hoping to find?"

"Yes, my wife's closest friend was Amanda Larson. She married a young man named Michael Flynn. I think they have a son who should be school age by now." Reisch felt the priest's mind darken. Suspicion played around his face.

"Michael and Jacob died several years ago in a plane crash," Oliver replied. "It was before my time, so I don't have very many details." His affect and demeanor had changed almost instantly with the mention of Amanda. He looked up at Reisch with open skepticism. "Tell me why you really want to find Amanda," he said bluntly.

Reisch was surprised. The priest had seen through the subterfuge fairly quickly and, while that was somewhat remarkable, what really impressed him was the fact that Oliver addressed the deception so directly. Most people when confronted with an obvious lie are more circumspect, less confrontational. Reisch tried to search the priest's mind, but all he saw was Greg Flynn. Oliver had no idea where Amanda was; in fact, he had never even met Amanda. Reisch realized that he had wasted his time with this silly little man. He tried to cloud the priest's mind and blur his memory of their encounter, but the priest, now on guard, resisted the confusion and remained focused on the tall, dark man. Reisch backed off, his mind withdrawing from Oliver's.

"I don't mean anyone harm, Father," he lied, then quickly grabbed the priest by the neck and exhaled strongly into his startled face. Caught off guard by the sudden and strange assault, Oliver's guard fell, and Reisch seized control of his mind. Five minutes later, Oliver awoke in his office alone and confused, his encounter with Reisch now as fragmentary as a nightmare. He coughed violently, but it was much too late. Virus particles by the hundreds of millions had already penetrated his lungs and were invading all of his major organs.

***

But the priest didn't die, as Reisch had wanted, and that meant he was worthy of further study and manipulation. Maybe have him commit suicide during Sunday Mass? Reisch smiled at the thought. That would be beautiful, but it would take preparation, and his need for violence was immediate. So, whose life would satisfy both his intellect and his monster? Then the perfect solution came to him.

Chapter 5

Father John Oliver walked through his dark church collecting missals. It wasn't actually his church; it belonged to the Roman Catholic Church and the diocese of Colorado Springs. He wasn't even its pastor, just associate pastor. For five years, that had been enough. Associate pastor was all he had ever wanted or would want. It fulfilled every spiritual need without overly burdening him with the worldly responsibilities that running a church demanded. He had earned the respite. For twenty-two of his twenty-nine years as a priest, he had been a missionary. He had brought the Word of God to some of the most remote places on Earth. Like Saint Paul before him, he had laid the groundwork, sometimes literally, for churches all over the known world. His role was to get things started and then turn the fledgling parish over to someone else. Fourteen churches carved out of deserts, jungles, and swamps bore his blood, sweat, and tears. At the age of fifty-two, he had his first heart attack. By fifty-seven, he had two more and a triple bypass. God had decided that John Oliver was needed elsewhere.

His order had sent him to help the pastor of a burgeoning parish in Colorado Springs. Oliver had never even been to Colorado and had never really been a parish priest. He arrived in the dead of winter, when the ambient temperature was eight degrees below zero, and there was a foot of new snow on the ground. Father Francis Coyle had picked him up at the airport. Father Coyle, a sixty-four-year-old Dominican, had been an academic for most of his professional life. He spoke five languages, including Latin, and could read ancient Aramaic. He had taught philosophy at the University of Notre Dame for twenty years before asking his bishop to grant him the opportunity to put philosophy to work. Like Oliver, he had been sent to Sacred Heart as an associate pastor and, also like Oliver, when he had started, he had felt like a fish out of water.

By the time they reached the rectory, Oliver was starting to feel at ease with his new boss. Over the next four years, the two got along exceptionally well, despite their widely different backgrounds. They were often found embroiled in philosophical debate that to anyone else looked like a heated argument. Father Oliver approached problems from a pragmatic, reality-based point of view, while Father Coyle preferred the academic, idealist approach. They were a formidable team, and the parish prospered.

Oliver's only sister had called six months earlier and broken the terrifying news that she had been diagnosed with ovarian cancer. It was an especially cruel twist of fate as Mary's deepest desire, to have and raise children, had never been fulfilled because of a condition called primary ovarian failure. Eugene, her husband, had died nine months earlier, which meant Mary was facing her ordeal alone. Oliver took a leave of absence and flew to Chicago. He hadn't been home in almost thirty years, and his unease grew when he found a mere shadow of his beloved sister in a hospital room. She was dying, and dying badly. She looked more like a concentration camp victim than a fifty-eight-year-old social studies teacher. She didn't have the strength to lift her head and kiss Oliver, and before either could say a word, they both started to cry.

Oliver stopped collecting the missals and recalled his sister in her younger days. He remembered the glow in her face as she raced her spider bike around the block, pigtails flying, skinned knees pumping away at the pedals, and peals of laughter echoing off the neighbors' houses. He refused to believe that the person lying in that bed could at one time have been that little girl. He had seen terrible, horrible things in his work for God, but they all paled to insignificance when compared to the realization that this was his little sister. It was an obscenity beyond compare. How could God take one of his most perfect creations and distort it so? Every priest had crises of faith, and John Oliver was no exception, but he had always been able to find his way back to God. Despite all his experiences, his belief had never been truly tested until he watched cancer devour his sister, cell by cell. She was in severe, unremitting pain, and nothing the doctors or nurses did seemed to make a difference.

He stayed with her in the hospital for seven weeks and, with every tablet of Dilaudid she was forced to take, Oliver cursed his indifferent God. After the first month, he stopped eating, stopped sleeping, and stopped being a priest. He didn't doubt the existence of God; he blamed Him directly for his sister's agony.

Father Oliver sat down on the hard wooden pew and remembered a day in early December. He had been alone in the hospital's garden, and everything around him was dead. "Your son died in three hours," he yelled up to the gray sky. "Why are You being so cruel to Mary? Where is all Your mercy and love now that we need it the most?" No one answered on that cold, late fall morning. It wasn't until the next day that God answered. Mary was being taken home; the hospital could offer her no more comfort than her own bed. A hospice team would meet them and assist with the transition.

For the next three weeks, the hospice team members lived with Mary and Oliver. A group of five did tag-team shifts around the clock, attending to her every need. They anticipated all the bumps ahead and helped the brother and sister negotiate them. Oliver watched in awe. The depth of concern they showed Mary was beyond any financial reward. These people weren't doing this kind of work for a paycheck; their devotion was much too deep, too genuine. It was almost holy. Mary wasn't a case or even a patient: she was an individual, she was a widow, she was a sister, and she was going through the most difficult period any person would ever face. They didn't see an incontinent, eighty-six-pound, semi-comatose problem; they saw a girl in pigtails riding her spider bike around the block, laughing as loud as she could. They saw God in his sister, and Father Oliver began to see God in them.

Mary died December twenty-third, two days before Christmas Day, the birth of Christ. She was at peace now, and her brother slowly began to make peace with their maker. By the New Year, he had returned to Colorado Springs. He hadn't recovered, but he was close enough to be a priest again.

He never talked with Father Coyle or his bishop about his experience, even though he knew he should. At a minimum he had to confess to someone, or perhaps talk it through, but it was too soon, still too sensitive. Everyone wanted to know how he was doing, but he just smiled and told them that he was doing just fine. It took another month before he actually began to feel fine again and, by that point, there was no reason to reopen the wound. That was when things began to happen.

Oliver set the missals down and knelt on the padded kneeler. He looked up at the crucified Christ hanging over the altar, but didn't feel worthy to pray. He had never believed that God tested people. Life tested people, and Jesus had lived and died to show us how to survive those tests.

Oliver had preached this a hundred times but, over the last six months, he had ignored his own preaching. And now, God was ignoring him.

"Hell isn't a place; it is the condition that exists after a person has removed himself from the grace of God," he whispered to the darkness. It was hard to believe that less than a month earlier, his life had been returning to normal. "Your torment was pure and redemptive; mine is deserved," he whispered to Jesus. Unconsciously, he rubbed the fine scar that stretched the length of his right thumb.

***

It had begun on February eighteenth, his mother's birthday. He was just getting over a respiratory infection and, for the first day in five, he felt good enough to shave. For forty-eight years, he had used a straight razor without ever having a problem, but that morning, as he was reaching for it, he cut his right thumb. The blade sliced cleanly down to the bone. For the first instant, he marveled at the beauty of the glistening white tendons, his brain refusing to accept what had just happened. Then pain and blood forced the issue. He tried to squeeze the wound closed, but his palm quickly filled with blood. When it came to blood, Oliver had always been a "fainter" and, true to form, his head hit the floor just after the first drop of blood. He was out only an instant before consciousness began to re-form around him. His blurry eyes focused on the water-stained plaster on the ceiling, and his lethargic mind wondered idly who was going to paint it. It took a few moments for his head to completely clear and process how he had ended up on the floor. He had managed to wedge himself into the small space between the bathtub and the commode; his neck, twisted at an awkward angle, was beginning to ache. He rolled over onto his back and felt a pool of warm blood ooze into his nightshirt. He squeezed his lacerated thumb and managed to climb to his feet without looking at the bloody hand.

He was reaching for a washcloth when he suddenly felt everything around him change. The rectory had always been poorly insulated, and every morning the frigid winter air managed to seep through the porous walls, chilling the bathroom to just above freezing. This morning had been no exception, at least until now. The air abruptly became unnaturally stagnant and increasingly warm. The cold mirror began to fog over, and Oliver wiped at it with his good hand. It was hard to move through the heavy air and harder to breathe. He slowly wrapped his hand and was about to sit on the commode when it struck him that he was no longer alone.

At first, he thought it was nothing more than an after-effect from the fall, but the feeling intensified. He wheeled around but found no one. The sudden movement made him a little light-headed, but it passed quickly. He felt foolish. The bathroom was tiny, and it would have been impossible for someone to enter without him knowing. Besides, the door was locked from the inside. Still, the feeling that someone was watching him persisted. Blood began to run down his forearm and drip to the floor from his elbow, but he ignored it. He felt exposed, naked before an unseen presence that was growing stronger all around him. The hairs on the back of his neck began to stand and, despite the heat, he broke out in goose bumps. He wiped the mirror again as the room became steadily hotter, and he half expected to see a face besides his own in the reflection.

I'm in shock, he thought. *Nothing more.* He wrapped the towel tighter around his throbbing thumb and turned back to the door. He reached for the knob, and a loud click made him jump. He whirled back towards the mirror, only to find his crucifix swinging upside down from its rosary. He stared at the handmade, polished silver cross, which was his most prized possession. It had been a gift from the members of the very first church he had ever worked in. It had taken six people over a week to carefully mold each bead and to shape the crude figure. An unknown artist had long ago inscribed *Mamhda, Kenya* across the crossbar, the lettering barely legible after nearly three decades of use. It was precious to him, and it had been lost for more than a week. It clinked again as it tapped the glass of the mirror. The unseen presence had crossed the threshold that separated imagination from reality.

Believing in ghosts was of course a prerequisite for a Catholic priest, but this was Oliver's first experience with one. His heart was thundering in his chest, and he felt the first squeeze of angina.

"Be gone, unclean spirit," Oliver commanded, but the phantom ignored the order. He took his crucifix down and started to pray aloud. "Our Father who art in heaven, hallowed be thy name . . ." He closed his eyes and concentrated on his God, ignoring everything around him. Before he reached the end of the prayer, Oliver realized that he was alone. He thanked God and opened his eyes. The room had started to cool down, but not yet enough to clear the mirror. Oliver's heart then gave another squeeze. Written in the dissipating steam was a message: *MARY SAYS HELLO*.

***

Perhaps if that had been the only message, Oliver could have gotten past it. He was still kneeling, his head down, avoiding the eyes of the crucified Christ. It was funny; for the last month, his mind and soul had been repeatedly assaulted, yet his body seemed to grow stronger. For years, his doctors had told him that his arthritic knees needed replacement, yet he could now kneel and even run short distances, two things he hadn't been able to do for decades. Even his heart seemed to be working better. The last time he had felt the all-too-familiar squeeze of angina had been a morning three weeks ago when he had awakened to the vision of his sister burning in unquenchable flames. She writhed in agony at the foot of his bed, calling his name, cursing him for her torment. He had reached for her, and a tongue of flame shot from the pyre and scorched his hand, and then she was gone. The skin of his hand was burned off, and only charred muscle and bone remained. He tried to scream, but the shock had stolen his breath. The pain was, in a word, beautiful. It was all-encompassing, filling every fiber of his being. Oliver had never experienced anything so absolute; not even the love of God was as complete.

He pleaded for it to stop, and then it was gone. Oliver examined his hand and was amazed to find that it was back to normal, right down to the age spots that covered his wrist. Intellectually, he knew it had all been just a hallucination, another manifestation of his ordeal, and that there was no reason to be surprised. He dropped his arm and stared through the now-vanished apparition. Illusion, nothing more, he told himself. Mary, his hand, the pain, they were all a trick. Only this illusion had a purpose—an intent. It tore away his façade of intellect and belief and exposed him for what he really was: a hypocrite and a fraud. A real pain in his chest began to intrude upon his reflection, and he reached for his Nitrobid. It was the last time he would need it, despite five more equally horrific and revealing visits from his dead sister.

***

Oliver stood. He had to get back to work. Morning Mass was scheduled to begin in less than twenty minutes, and he still hadn't gotten everything ready. The bishop was coming at Oliver's request. Father Coyle would also be there. Oliver planned to celebrate the small weekday Mass and then confess to both of them. He should have done this weeks ago, but all his life he had dealt with personal problems in his own very private way. It had been one of his father's defining traits, and Oliver carried on the tradition. Apparently, even priests weren't immune to living the stereotype of the strong, silent type.

This would be the last Mass he would celebrate. He couldn't go on playing the part of the devout priest after his faith had been systematically deconstructed by whatever or whoever was haunting him. Francis Coyle wouldn't be surprised. He knew something was bothering his colleague. On three occasions, he had violated their unwritten code of silence and tried to pry it out of Oliver. The bishop probably was also aware that something was wrong; he had accepted Oliver's invitation without question or comment, which was quite extraordinary for the usually loquacious cleric. Oliver guessed that they both would try and talk him out of his decision, offering a vacation or some therapy as an alternative and, in the end, they would all agree on an extended leave of absence that Oliver knew would prove to be permanent. He would return to Chicago, where his sister's estate had passed to him and, instead of selling it and donating the proceeds, he would stay there for a while and collect himself. After that, he had no plans.

Oliver was distributing the last of the missals when he heard voices in the back of the church. Larry Ham, the parish's deacon, was laughing with one of the church's lay ministers. Oliver looked up, and the two men waved.

"Good morning, Father," said Greg Flynn.

"You beat us in again, Father," Larry Ham said. "You know, it would be okay for you to sleep in every once in a while. Greg and I can get things set up, and you can just come waltzing in at the last second as Father Coyle does. But then again, he's so old, and you are in the flower of youth." The two men chuckled, waiting for Oliver to take the bait so they could start the day with some good-natured ribbing of their pastor, but all Oliver could offer was a weak smile.

"I'll tell him you said that," Oliver said. Greg Flynn smiled back, and Oliver suddenly almost remembered something. A fragment teased just below his consciousness, something he was supposed to tell Greg or maybe ask him. Oliver waited for it to bob to the surface, but it disappeared.

"You okay, Father?" Greg asked. "You look preoccupied."

Greg Flynn was a good man, a very good man in Oliver's eyes. He had had his share of tragedies, but instead of becoming scarred and bitter, he seemed to have gained some perspective, some inner peace that so few people ever realize. Greg lived his faith, while Oliver only preached it. It was for the Greg Flynns of the parish that Oliver was stepping down. "Nothing serious," Oliver replied, hiding behind the smile that he had refined so well these past two months.

"I was wondering if I might have a word with you?" asked Greg.

"Can it wait until after Mass?"

"I'm afraid I can't stay for Mass. I promise that it will only take a few moments." Greg's face had darkened.

Oliver guessed that something important must be going on in Greg's life for him to miss morning Mass. "Of course, let's go to the sacristy." As the two men walked into the priest's changing room, he realized that this would probably be his last official confession. Oliver locked the door and showed his guest a seat. "What's on your mind, Greg?" he asked.

"It's my daughter, Amanda. Actually, she's my daughter-in-law, but we're . . . close."

Oliver was surprised by how nervous Greg seemed; he couldn't remember the retired policeman being so hesitant in his manner. The stirrings of a memory struck Oliver a second time; he was supposed to ask Greg something—that was it. No, that wasn't it. He was supposed to tell him something. His mind went back and forth, but couldn't come up with it. He cursed his leaky memory.

"I'd like this to remain confidential, if you don't mind. I know that this is not exactly confession, but I need to talk about something sensitive."

Oliver stiffened visibly, afraid of what he was about to hear.

"Oh my God, it's nothing like that. I know how that must have sounded, but this is not about me, it's about her. She's coming down here, and there are people looking for her, people that I'm afraid want to hurt her."

Oliver felt relief flood into him. He didn't know how he would have reacted to someone he had grown to admire confessing to an illicit love affair with his daughter-in-law. "How can I—"

He never finished his sentence. His mind suddenly exploded in pain. It was as if someone had sneaked up behind him and hit him in the back of the head with a baseball bat. For a moment, his identity was lost within the pain and, in that moment, he glimpsed the world through someone else's eyes. He was inside a moving car; in fact, he was driving the car as it slowly coasted down a snowy residential street. He was looking for something or someone. It was at once familiar and disorienting. He worked his fingers and watched as the fingers in the vision opened and closed at his bidding. He turned the steering wheel and felt the car skid along the slick road. Then, abruptly, he was back in the sacristy with Greg Flynn. His head throbbed, but the pain began to recede.

"Father, are you okay?" Greg was standing over him, his hands on Oliver's shoulders, steadying the teetering priest.

"I don't know what happened. Just a sudden, sharp headache, but it's better now." Oliver reached for Greg's hand, and the pain struck again, only this time he watched himself grimace in pain through Greg's eyes. The pain and the disorientation were not as intense as with the first attack, and they seemed to pass almost immediately. In their wake, Oliver was left with an almost euphoric, transformative sensation. Energy surged through his mind and body. He suddenly felt like he was eighteen again. His heartbeat became strong and regular, his breathing deep and unlabored, his limbs light and powerful. A door opened in his mind, and a fresh breeze blew away all his stale thoughts and self-doubts. Something had freed him and, unencumbered, he could for the first time in his life see the world as it really was. He took Greg's hand and squeezed it; he felt his own hand as well as Greg's, and the strange duality made him laugh.

"I know about Amanda, my friend," Oliver said. "She's driving down from Boulder to see if your suspicions are correct, and you're worried that the FBI will try to take her." The words exploded out of Oliver's mouth. "And if they do, you're worried that she will hurt, maybe even kill, some of them. She's been changed; she has grown into something different. I can see it all in your mind."

Greg pulled his hand away from the priest and stared at him dumbfounded. "How?" was all he managed to say.

Oliver sagged as the connection was broken. He was sixty-two again. His heart returned to its old familiar, irregular rhythm, and the heaviness found its way back into his limbs, but his mind remained invigorated, nearly completely transformed. It raced with excitement and wonder, the disillusionment and depression that had troubled him for weeks suddenly dissipating as if they were no more than a puff of smoke. It was inexplicable and amazing, like suddenly discovering that he had wings and could fly.

"I don't know, Greg, nothing like this has ever happened before," Oliver said, amazement filling his voice. "You touched me, and suddenly I could see myself through your eyes, but it went beyond just sensation. Somehow, I knew what you were going to say. I saw your thoughts. I felt them in my mind, in my chest, everywhere."

"Can you feel them now?" Greg sat back down, eyeing the priest with suspicion.

"No, I guess I'm back to normal," Oliver said.

Greg stared at him, fear and caution written across his face.

Oliver was coming down from his high and, as the exhilaration began to fade, reality crept back into his mind. "Just before you touched me, I was somewhere else. I mean . . . I saw . . . except I more than just saw . . ." Oliver struggled to put the experience into words. "I was in a car driving down a road. It was only for a moment, but I got the distinct impression that it was near here. I wonder if it was Amanda. We were talking about her just before it happened."

Oliver watched as Greg's entire appearance changed with the mention of Amanda. He suddenly became aware of just how physically threatening the police detective was, and a hint of fear crept into Oliver's mind.

"It wasn't Amanda," Greg said, barely contained anger coloring his terse words. He quickly got to his feet, and his chair skidded to the wall. "I have to go." He began to edge his way around the priest.

"Greg, I didn't mean to . . ." Oliver stood and reached for the retired detective.

"Don't touch me!" he screamed, recoiling from the small man. Greg was red-faced. "I don't know what's going on here, but you stay away from Amanda."

Oliver stepped aside and gave Greg a clear path to the door.

"I'm sorry if I've hurt you, Greg. I had no control over it. Please don't leave like this," Oliver pleaded.

As Greg opened the door, the sounds of the awakening church invaded the sanctuary. He hesitated and turned back to face the priest. His emotional energy now spent, Greg seemed to shrink back to his usual size. "I need time to work this out, Father. It was bad enough with Amanda."

"I understand, but there's something you need to know. If it was Amanda driving down that street, she urgently needs help. I can't be completely certain, but I think she's come here with the intention of killing someone. She's sick. I felt the illness inside her."

"Amanda would never intentionally hurt anyone," Greg declared defiantly. Greg was a bad liar, and the lie was all but written across his face. "I'd like to help," Oliver said simply.

Greg stared back at the priest, and Oliver could tell that Greg was appraising him from a new perspective. "I'll talk with Amanda," he said and then left quickly.

Chapter 6

Phil awoke with a start, certain someone was in his room. He clicked on the light but found no tall, dark, deformed man looming over him. His heart was in his throat and it took a full minute for it to resume its normal anatomic position. It had been a rough night after a rough day. The waitress had caught him staring down her blouse; he had hallucinated a fairy-tale monster brazenly knocking down a woman and then disappearing; and finally, he had alienated the entire office by demanding that he be left alone. Now, after a night filled with tormenting voices and dreams about invisible phantoms, he faced a day filled with menial tasks and a sullen staff. Phil couldn't relate to his staff any better than to the rest of the world, but their emotional states mattered to him, if only at a professional level. He needed order and consistency in the office, and it was his secretary and the rest of the staff who created it. He would have to make amends today. He would apologize to a few, and to others he would find an excuse to praise some trivial accomplishment, all for the sake of his own inner peace.

He rolled over and found that he still had eight minutes before his alarm sounded, officially starting his day. Eight minutes of solitude. He breathed deeply and tried to let his mind float free. It was an ability he was trying to cultivate, but with little success. It should have been a simple, natural thing, but to him, it was anything but simple or natural, and it never had been. Even as a child, perhaps especially when he was a child, he had never been able to simply sit and daydream. There were the rare occasions in which he could shut down his mind and simply exist outside of thought, but he had never been able to just let go and let his thoughts wander without direction. He had been conditioned to always remain focused, always be on guard, lest the unstable, dangerous portions of his fragmented mind seize control. For nearly forty years his mind had been racing, trying to stay ahead of the insanity that matched his every step.

Seven minutes left, he thought. He stared at the dark ceiling, willing his mind to relax. He tried closing his eyes, but all he saw was the dark man kicking a woman's shoe. He changed his mind's channel and watched a bead of sweat slowly meander down Dana's cleavage. He watched for a moment and began to feel an unfamiliar stirring. She stood before him, only now she was naked and beckoning to him; the café had dissolved into a sleazy hotel room. *I'm dreaming*, he thought, and Dana immediately disappeared. Now all he saw were the blood vessels in his eyelids. *I'm awake*, he thought, and opened his eyes. He tried relaxing all his muscles, but he still felt the passage of every second.

You're going to be late, one of his old voices said.

Phil could ignore this one; it dated back to his childhood and, instead of growing stronger with time, this one had weakened, making room for the new and more dangerous small voice, the one with the power to destroy his carefully created and insulated world.

***

As a child, Phil, along with his parents, was forced to accept the fact that he would always be different. When he was an infant, his mother noticed that he rarely cried, and by age two Phil rarely verbalized at all. When she fed or bathed him he almost never made eye contact, preferring to stare over her shoulder and track unseen objects. On occasion, however, he would stare at her intensely, following her with his eyes, even crawling and later walking after her if she left the room, and after finding her he would simply sit down and resume his quiet staring. At first she found it adorable; later she found it disturbing. When he started stacking his unused toys and the cans in the pantry, his parents sought help. The diagnosis of autism wasn't much of a surprise, but it was still devastating. Aside from institutional placement, no treatment options were offered. He was still young and required no more care than the average three year old, so the Ruckers made a promise to themselves and to Phil to keep him home for as long as they could safely manage him. Molly Rucker became a full-time stay-at-home mom and slowly coaxed Phil out of his mental prison. Within a year, he had begun to use words, quietly voicing his needs. By age five, his occasional speech was punctuated by verbal outbursts of astonishing clarity and detail. It was clear to the Ruckers and to the pediatricians who examined Phil that, while he was emotionally stunted and socially retarded, he was not in the classic sense autistic; whatever was going on was much more complex. By age seven, Phil could pass for a normal child. A strange, intense, and reserved child, but functionally independent. His intellectual development was extraordinary, which only intensified his emotional isolation, both of which intensified the fragmenting of his mind. He explained it to himself in Freudian terms as a lack of self: superego versus id, a constant battle for control. He tried to explain it to his father in terms he would understand; they were at a local swimming pool and the two watched as several boys wrestled over a beach ball in the deep end of the pool. The smallest of the group managed to grab the ball and swim away, but a moment later his bigger and stronger playmates overwhelmed him. They took turns dunking him over and over again. Finally, the lifeguard was forced to intervene. Phil took his father's hand and pointed at the near-drowned boy, and said simply, "That's me."

It doesn't have to be, the small voice said.

Phil refused to take the bait. This voice was no different from any other; they were all parasites, and if given a chance, they would destroy their host. For thirty years, a pedantic life of discipline and routine had allowed him to live independently. He forced himself to remember some of the faces locked behind tall, steel doors. Their screams still echoed in his ears. "That is what happens when control is lost," Phil said to all of the voices in his head.

The start of a motor made Phil jump, and a moment later his alarm went off. It took him a moment to realize that his neighbor had just started a snowblower. Phil climbed out of bed with unusual agility. His back didn't seem to bother him. He stood to his full height and waited for the deep, boring pain to settle into its usual place. It had been with him for eighteen years, ever since the car accident that had taken the lives of both his parents and crushed two of his lumbar vertebrae. Except, this morning, it was little more than a muted ache. He slowly arched his back until he felt and heard an audible pop. One of the large bolts that had put his bones back together had broken ten years ago, and his back had popped ever since. It needed to be replaced, but he couldn't face the ordeal a second time.

He made up his bed exactly as he had for the last thirty years. He didn't have to be at work for three hours, but two of those would be spent on a treadmill, pushing his body to the limit. Exercise was a constant in his life, serving the dual purpose of minimizing his lower back pain and anesthetizing his Monsters, who had recently developed an unnerving capacity to adapt.

An hour into his run, Phil heard his neighbor's snowblower abruptly shut down. George and Patsy Van Der had been Phil's neighbors all his life. He was as fond of them as he was able. George was a retired lawyer and, despite being in his mid-eighties, was as sharp as he had been half a lifetime ago, and could easily pass for a man in his early sixties. Patsy, on the other hand, had gone around the bend, as George had said on many occasions. She was moderately senile, but not so far gone that George couldn't care for her on his own.

Phil listened for George to restart the blower, but it remained quiet. There was no way George could be finished, and no way he would stop before he was finished. Phil ran for another five minutes, and still there was no sound from George. Concern started to grow in Phil's mind. If George needed help, no one but Phil could deliver it. He still had fifty minutes to run, but it was becoming obvious that it would have to wait. Phil's mind may have been ruled by The Routine, but his life was ruled by Moral Responsibility.

He climbed off the treadmill and pulled the curtains back. It had snowed more than anyone expected. George's driveway was cleared almost all the way to the street, but his snowblower sat idle in the middle of a drift, and George was nowhere to be seen. Phil couldn't see all the way up the driveway from his windows, so he quickly toweled off, put on warm clothes, boots, and a jacket, and opened his front door. The snow had drifted several inches in front of his door. It always did that when the wind blew in from the west, and some of it spilled into his entranceway. He poked his head out the door and saw George sprawled spread-eagled across his cleared driveway. A tall, dark figure stood over him.

"Hey," Phil yelled. Not very eloquent, but it managed to redirect the man's attention away from George. Phil started to run towards them, but immediately tripped and fell face first into foot-deep snow. He scrambled up, but the tall man was already striding across George's lawn, leaving a trail of deep footprints. "What did you do?" Phil screamed after him.

"You are too late again, Phillip," the man called back.

"Come back here," Phil demanded, but the tall man continued across the yard, seemingly unhindered by the snow. He reached a Ford Taurus parked and idling at the curb just as Phil reached George. Phil bent over his neighbor as the Taurus pulled into the unplowed street. George was dead, his eyes squeezed closed, his face contorted in a mask of pain and horror. Phil reached to check for a pulse, but the blue, livid face told him he wouldn't find one. Nothing. He started CPR with no real hope and after five minutes gave up. He sat down next to George, breathing hard from the exertion and the pressure of what would have to come next. Patsy was inside, lost in the bliss of a deteriorating brain. Someone would have to explain to her that George, her husband of sixty-four years, would not be coming back inside to make her breakfast ever again. Unfortunately, she had enough of herself remaining to understand what that meant.

Two hours later, Phil was doing his best to console Patsy Van Der while the police ran tape all around her front yard. Initially, there had been a considerable amount of resistance from the officers who responded to Phil's call. George Van Der had obviously died of a heart attack, that was plain to all who had responded, and the opening of a murder investigation based on a neighbor's report of a man standing over the body was a waste of their precious time—at least, until they found out that the neighbor was the coroner. At that point, the not-so-well-disguised grumbling focused on Phil and his eccentricities. Reluctantly, they sealed off the crime scene and began to process it. They worked slowly, waiting for the detective in charge to arrive and convince Rucker that this was a misapplication of their already strained resources. Phil was uninterested in their problems. He sat with Patsy, waiting for her son to arrive so he could finally get to work.

"I don't think I have enough eggs for all these nice people, Phil. Would you mind running down to the store and getting a dozen more?" Patsy asked. She had retreated into her mind, refusing to believe that George was gone.

"Why don't we wait for Patrick to get here," Phil answered, relieved for the moment that she had stopped asking about George. Dementia was easier to deal with than grief.

A large black man opened the front door and stomped snow off his shoes. The officer at the door immediately straightened, accepted the man's wet overcoat, and directed him to the couch. The sudden flurry of activity caught Patsy's attention, and she watched as he approached.

"Are you with the police, young man?" she asked in a soft, grandmotherly voice.

"Yes, ma'am, I am. My name is Rodney Patton. I'm here to find out what happened to your husband."

Phil stiffened, waiting for Patsy to break down again. As far as he was concerned, Patsy was in a good place—cooperative and unaware.

"I appreciate that, Detective," she said sadly. She was lucid again, and Phil desperately wished that her son Patrick would get there.

"Can I ask you if your husband had any medical conditions, heart disease, blood pressure problems, anything?" He had the well-practiced voice of a veteran cop, and directed all his attention to Patsy, but it was clear that he was also talking to Phil.

"He had a heart attack about twenty years ago, but he's been fine since. His blood sugar was a little elevated, but he didn't have to take any medications for it." She sounded like the Patsy Phil had grown up with.

"I don't mean to leave you alone, so I'm going to ask this officer to stay with you until your son arrives." Patton motioned the uniformed policeman to sit next to Patsy. "In the meantime, I need to borrow Dr. Rucker." He spoke directly to Patsy, not even acknowledging Phil.

"Oh, you mean Phillip," she exclaimed with a bright smile. Her mind had gone away again.

"Yes, I need Phillip for a moment," he stressed the name, but the insult was lost on Phil.

"Go with this nice young man, dear, and when you're finished, don't forget my eggs." She gave Phil a smile.

Phil followed the huge man into the kitchen. At six feet two, he was no taller than Phil, but he was very close to twice his weight, somewhere in excess of four hundred pounds. Two uniformed officers immediately found their way out of the kitchen as Patton approached.

"Dr. Rucker, I've been meaning to introduce myself since I arrived in Colorado Springs three months ago but, as you know, things have been somewhat busy."

The words were cordial enough, but Phil sensed his underlying frustration.

"I appreciate that, Detective, and your attempt at being friendly, but you're wasting your time. I will not be persuaded to drop this," Phil said without emphasis.

Patton stared at him, inhaling giant gulps of air. For a moment, Phil thought that Patton was trying to pressure him by sucking up all the air in the room. He almost smiled at that absurdity.

"You told the officers that you saw a tall, dark man standing over the deceased, and that he simply strolled away after you yelled at him." All attempts at being friendly were gone. "Further, you saw this same man yesterday assault a woman and then disappear down an empty street."

"That's correct," Phil said simply.

"Doctor, please try and look at this from my perspective. Mr. Van Der was eighty-six. He had a history of heart disease, and he was clearing ten inches of snow with a snowblower that was designed for no more than six. As I see it, your neighbor suffered another heart attack, and this man just happened to be driving by as Mr. Van Der collapsed. I don't see a crime here." His voice had a subtle, manipulative undercurrent.

Phil would not be moved. "That is one possibility, Detective, but it happens to be the most expedient possibility. Experience has taught me that the most expedient possibility is rarely the correct one."

"Experience has taught me that the simplest explanation is usually the correct one," Patton fired back with a touch of anger.

"But not always. Otherwise, we wouldn't need detectives," Phil said just as quickly.

"I can't authorize this. I will not pull people off of legitimate investigations to prove that Mr. Van Der died of natural causes." His voice was now adamant.

Phil hesitated. They both knew that he had the legal authority to compel Patton to do whatever he wanted. Patton's defiance was curious, and Phil was intrigued by it. Only Phil was never intrigued by the motivations of others. The realization played across his mind, but didn't change it.

A part of him registered the arrival of Patrick Van Der. "You will continue to investigate this as a crime until you are told otherwise, Detective," Phil said, without emotion. He had no desire to continue this discussion, or to share the grief of the Van Ders' only child. He retrieved his coat from the back of a kitchen chair and left through the back door.

Phil trudged through the snow to his own back door. Several of the police stopped what they were doing and stared, hoping he would fall.

Chapter 7

Regency Care Center was half acute-care hospital and half rehabilitation center. Emily Larson didn't feel she needed either, and Amanda found her aunt outside walking in the cool morning air, a heavy coat covering a hospital gown. Amanda quickly parked her car and hurried over to her aunt.

"What are you doing out here?" Amanda asked, coming up behind her.

"What are you doing here?" Emily answered back, emphasizing her last word.

"You know you're not supposed to be out here, and why aren't you using the cane?"

"The only way they'll let me out of here is if I can walk, so I'm walking."

Amanda smiled for the first time in days. Her aunt was a true force of nature. On the surface, she was a carbon copy of her brother: rude, loud, and opinionated. But whereas he justified his behavior with some fanciful notion of inherent superiority, Emily had earned the right to be loud and opinionated. She had been a sociology professor for more than four decades, and at the center of every academic circle that she had ever found herself within. Even her critics—and she had quite a few—listened respectfully when she spoke. In the hyper-liberal world of academia, she championed the unpopular view that individuals had become too reliant upon society for their welfare, and now here she was, in sub-freezing temperatures, living her philosophy. "Aunt Em, it's cold out here; let's at least go inside."

"Might as well; no one has taken the time to properly clear the ice off of these damn sidewalks, and in front of a hospital no less," Emily said, wheeling around and heading back to the door, a four-post cane tucked firmly under her arm. The pair silently walked back to Emily's hospital room. Along the way, she didn't spare any of the nurses or aides a good long glare.

"All they do at night is laugh and talk on their cell phones . . ." Emily stopped mid-sentence and studied her niece's face. "Why are you here, Amanda?" Her voice and demeanor were suddenly serious.

"I'm going back to Colorado Springs."

"Why?" Emily asked sharply.

"Greg called me a little over a week ago." Amanda hesitated. Emily knew about her infection and some of the subsequent events, but she didn't know everything. Amanda had hidden the most important consequence of her infection because she couldn't predict her Aunt's reactions. "I'm fairly certain that a version of the virus that I contracted in Honduras has found its way to Colorado Springs." The one thing Amanda did know about Emily was that she was an excellent intellectual sounding board; she would examine Amanda's reasoning and logic and dispassionately pass judgment.

"The flu that everyone is talking about—don't we have a health department to deal with that?" Emily continued to study Amanda. "Are you planning on turning yourself in? Are you going to sacrifice your freedom to help them? Or is it that you are responsible?"

Amanda smiled. Her aunt didn't believe in subtleties; she believed in pouncing. "I'm not responsible, and I'm not really sure what I'm going to do."

"Then why are you going?" Emily's expression sharpened while she waited for an answer, but only silence filled the room. "Amanda, we've never discussed this because you've never wanted to, but the time for secrets is over. Something happened to you in Honduras. When you came back, you were a different person. I can only imagine what you went through down there, but it doesn't explain everything. It doesn't explain what you've become."

"No, it doesn't." Amanda began to fidget with the straps of her purse.

"I think I have earned the right to know," Emily said firmly.

***

Four years after her father died, Amanda's mother was diagnosed with lung cancer. She didn't put up much of a fight—it wasn't her style—and, mercifully, the end came quickly. Amanda was thirteen; her brother William was turning eighteen, on his way to college, and didn't require a guardian. Amanda was shipped off to Tulsa, Oklahoma, where she would become the burden of her only surviving relative.

Amanda met her Aunt Emily for the first time at her mother's grave site. Her world had been turned inside out. Her mother was gone; her brother was gone; the three-bedroom apartment that she had called home for three years was gone. Even her bed was gone, sold to some stranger for fifty-five dollars. All that she had in the world fit into two small suitcases, and, with the exception of her older brother, no one in the world cared. She was nothing more than a "disposition issue," as one social worker had phrased it. Aunt Emily's disposition issue, to be exact.

"They wanted to put you into foster care, and I'll admit I thought long and hard about it," Emily said as the pair left the grave site. "After all, what's the difference if you live with a family you've never met or an aunt you don't know? If there had been a reasonable chance of you being adopted, I would have left you here. At least you'd still be close to your brother and friends, but no one adopts thirteen-year-old girls, at least not for the right reasons. So, I guess we're stuck with each other." Emily made no attempt at hiding her emotions from her new charge. "I'm not your mother, God rest her soul, and I'm nothing like your father. He may have been my brother, but the man never worked a hard day in his life, and it showed in what he made of himself. I don't mean to speak ill of the dead, but you are half him, and if you think you'll skate by on good looks alone, you're in for a rude awakening. Only with an education can you hope to escape your family's legacy of unrealized potential. They don't give scholarships for being pretty."

Her aunt's ground rules clearly established, Amanda was ushered into the car by large, rough hands. Before the door closed, she waved to her brother; tears streamed down their cheeks.

"Do you think that was the most appropriate way of introducing yourself?" Amanda challenged her aunt as the car pulled away.

"I make no apologies for how I communicate," returned Emily.

"It's unworthy for an educated person to speak with complete disregard for another's emotional state. It's an abdication of personal responsibility," Amanda fired back, her grief now being focused into anger.

"Impressive. Do you actually know what you said, or are you simply mouthing someone else's words?"

"I've been able to read since I was three, and had independent thoughts before that."

"I must remember that," Emily said, breaking out into a smile of respect.

"So tell me about yourself; what should I know about you?"

"I'm an orphan," Amanda answered, managing to be both sullen and defiant at the same time.

***

"You do have a right to know. I'm just not sure you want to know," an older Amanda said to her aunt.

"I do want to know. I'm not a very emotional person . . ." Emily's eyes began to tear.

Amanda smiled again. "You told me that the first day we met."

"There's some salt on that table, if you'd care to rub it into the wound." Emily dabbed at her eyes and smiled back at Amanda. "God, I was such an ass that day. If I had bothered to spend five minutes talking to you, I would have realized that you were not the self-absorbed, lazy thirteen-year-old girl I had expected."

"You're different now. Time has mellowed you." Amanda gave her aunt a weak smile. It had been nearly eighteen years, but the memory of that day in the cemetery was still fresh. "I'm still an orphan, only a different kind," Amanda finally said. "The infection did change me, and probably not for the better."

"Greg told me what you've done. Seven people?" Emily's voice betrayed her conflicting emotions.

"It was more than that." She waited, almost hoping for a trace of guilt or shame, but those emotions had been burned from her mind long ago. "I can do things that others can't. I can feel your horror and revulsion, but also your love and understanding. I can put names on the things that you're feeling even when you can't."

Emily stared back at her niece with a bewildered expression.

"No, it's not a mental illness. And no, it's not related to the terrible things that have happened to me."

"So you can read thoughts as well?"

"Yes, and a good deal more." Amanda paused for a second to allow Emily to compose herself. "I think it started even before I got back from Honduras. I was . . . different. Changed. My thoughts, actions, everything seemed to be affected." Amanda began to nervously rub her fingers. "I shot four soldiers that were trying to kill some of us. They were all sick and out of their heads with fever and paranoia. I had to do it; they gave me no choice."

"That's understandable, Amanda," Emily patted Amanda's hand. "If somebody was trying to kill me or my own I would have shot them."

"You always did remind me of Rambo." Amanda smiled briefly. "Would you have done it without remorse, or any trace of regret?" Amanda paused and read the answer on her aunt's face. "That was the beginning. The start of my new life. A life born in blood and violence, without regret or consequence." Again, Amanda gave Emily a chance to collect her thoughts. "Things got worse when I got home. That's when the voices and . . . the other things started to appear. I became pretty unstable. The violence, the power, the blood. They're a powerful and intoxicating elixir." Amanda closed her eyes and felt Mittens, her predator, the embodiment of all her dark desires, prowl through her mind. "I still struggle with it now."

"And that explains the self-imposed isolation."

"Well, the fact that the FBI wants to either arrest or shoot me has something to do with my isolation."

Emily shook her head in argument. "You're still the same person. No matter what's happened, you still have a choice to be who or what you want to be. It may not be easy, but it's still a choice. "

"I know," Amanda said, and Emily was taken aback by her niece's sudden agreement. "And that's the problem. I'm torn down the middle. A part of me wants to go back to my old life, to love, to hurt, to feel again. But the other part wants to embrace who I've become and live beyond the restraints of society. To do what I want, when I want, and without the thought of consequences." She avoided her aunt's eyes.

"I can see why you kept this a secret. Society can't tolerate your existence." Emily stared at Amanda. "You're in a very dangerous place." Two long minutes passed before Emily spoke again. "You're hoping that by going back to Colorado Springs you will find redemption? To save the day and balance the scales so that you can move forward?" She phrased it as a question, but it was more of a statement.

"Not redemption; I need some clarity. I have no remorse about what I've done, but I don't want to live this half-life anymore. I'm not even sure I care about those who are going to die; this is about me, not them."

"That's a load of crap, Amanda. If this were entirely about you, and you truly had no concern for those who could die, there would be no debate, you would have already made a decision, and you would be lost to me and everyone who cares about you." Another minute passed. "Life isn't fair; you more than anyone should know that. You have been hurt so many times I'm surprised that you can get yourself out of bed each morning, but you do, and because you do, it is your responsibility not to turn your pain into anger." Emily began to cough, and it took her another minute before she could continue. "Anyways, how do you know that Greg is even right about this? He has been wrong before."

"He's not wrong," Amanda said quickly.

"Look at this logically, Amanda. Your virus killed hundreds of people, and that's just not happening now."

"No, they aren't dying—at least not yet. Someone has changed the virus."

"Amanda, this sounds a little fantastic and more than a little irrational. There are other more reasonable explanations. Or is this another thing that you . . . can do?"

"There are no other possibilities. Someone is purposefully spreading this new virus. He is close enough that I can almost feel his mind, and I know that he is aware of mine."

"I see." Emily began to fidget with her gown. "So you are going there to find this person."

"I'm going to get some answers," Amanda said.

"And once you have those answers, will you stop him or join him?"

"I won't help him," she said flatly.

"But will you stop him?" Emily countered.

"I've already tried. I contacted the CDC this morning and they ignored me. I'm done trying to help"

"You're done! I won't accept that from you, Amanda, and you can't accept that from yourself. Maybe you have been changed, but not to the degree that you've grown comfortable lying to yourself. If you're going to claim that you've tried to stop him, then really try to stop him. Go to Colorado Springs, get your answers and then, if you have to, kill this bastard in the most painful manner possible. Then make a decision as to how you're going to restart your life." Emily's face was bright red and spittle flew from her lips.

Amanda waited for her aunt to calm down. "Maybe you haven't changed."

"There's no reason to change when you're always right. So what are you going to do?"

"What I have to."

Chapter 8

Rodney Patton did not need this; he did not need this at all. He watched Phil Rucker walk out the Van Ders' back door, and all he could do was shake his head. Of course, he had heard all about Rucker before this morning, but even those estimations fell well short of the mark. Rucker really did live on another planet, one without the realities of this one.

A uniformed officer eased into his view and waited for Patton to compose himself.

"What is it?" Patton said gruffly.

"We're done with the scene; nothing much to report, except for some footprints that lead out to the road. We're having some trouble getting a casting . . ." He spoke slowly, hoping Patton would take the hint.

"Castings in snow," Patton said bitterly. This job was not turning out to be what he had been promised. Over a year ago, the Colorado Springs chief of police had personally recruited him out of the Baltimore Special Homicide Unit. That unit had been his life for eleven years, and he had been its chief for seven of them. He had hated to leave, but the success he had achieved, and the pride he felt, was easily overshadowed by the pain of the familiar surroundings. He saw his wife, Connie, everywhere. Each time his desk phone rang, he expected to hear her voice. Every time he reached for his car keys to go home, he remembered the thousands of nights he had taken solace in the fact that no matter how bad work got, he would sleep next to a woman he loved. He felt her presence in the grocery stores, the dry cleaners, and the gas stations. He never realized how much of their life had become routine, or how special that routine really was, until he tried to live without her.

Connie had fought breast cancer for four long, hard years, and he had balanced work with helping her through biopsies, radiation therapies, chemotherapies, and surgeries. His unit deserved more loyalty than he had shown them. They supported him through all of it but, after she died, he saw her in them, and that was just too much to take. He should have retired like he had planned, maybe written a book. Lord knows he had enough material to write about, but his chief knew the Colorado Springs chief and, before he knew it, he was moving to Colorado. A change of scenery seemed a reasonable alternative to premature, boredom-induced senility. He was only fifty-eight, and a thirty-two-year veteran of some of the meanest streets in America. He had earned a change of pace, but maybe not yet a gold retirement watch. Only the sleepy little town of Colorado Springs had chosen this moment in time to come apart at the seams.

"Don't bother with trying to cast footprints. It doesn't work, despite what the book tells you. Take photos with a ruler." He ratcheted down his frustration. It wasn't their fault that they didn't have the necessary experience. "Is there a bullet out for the Taurus the witness described?"

The uniformed cop stared blankly at Patton. "A what, sir?"

"Sorry, old habits—an APB. I doubt there are many vehicles out now. Maybe we'll catch a well-deserved break."

"Already done, but our patrols were limited by dispatch this morning. It seems that everyone is out with the flu. We've got the main streets covered, but not a lot else." He spoke in a stiff, unnaturally professional voice.

Patton guessed that the officer was in his early twenties and anxious to please. "What's your take on this, Officer . . .?" Patton searched for the young man's nametag.

"Yeager, sir." He quickly answered. "You mean the body, sir? I think Mr. Van Der died of natural causes. There are no signs of a struggle. No marks on the body. No real motive. I don't think we're going to find much here." Yaeger's expression quickly changed from border-line terror to pride. Patton watched as the young man's posture straightened and his chest puffed out. He wondered if Yaeger would be bragging back at the precinct that the new chief of detectives had asked for his opinion.

"What about the witness's account of a man standing over the body?" It was strange, but Patton was starting to see things a little from Rucker's point of view. What were the odds that someone had driven by just at the instant that Van Der fell over? Especially on a morning like this. And then, after stopping to help, why did he calmly walk away when Rucker showed up? Good Samaritans didn't do things like that. His brain began to itch, a sure sign that he was missing something.

"I'm sure it was someone stopping by to help."

"Probably," Patton said, with less conviction than a few moments earlier. The overheated kitchen was starting to close in on him, and he began to sweat under his new suit. "Thank you, Yaeger. That will be all."

Patton wanted to express his final condolences to the widow and her newly arrived son and get back outside, where he could breathe.

Ten minutes later, he was inhaling lungs full of clean, cold mountain air as he stood in the middle of a set of tire tracks that cut through the snow of the unplowed street. He considered the situation. A single set of tracks. Only one car had driven down this road since late the previous night. All the police units had been directed to park at the opposite end of the street and walk down to the Van Ders' house. The original responding unit was still parked in front of Rucker's house, just behind the idling ambulance. No one except Rucker's mystery man had come this way. *What are the odds of that?* he thought. His brain itch was really going now.

Rucker's garage door opened with a loud scraping sound, and Patton jumped. He watched the coroner's GMC Power Wagon bound over the snow effortlessly. Rucker expertly spun the four-wheel-drive vehicle in the street and drove north, towards the city's downtown, away from Patton and his solitary tire tracks. The crime scene unit or, more properly, what passed for a crime scene unit in Colorado Springs, watched Rucker drive off and, almost as if on cue, they turned as one to Patton. Their collective intent was obvious: *Okay, the bizarre man is gone. Can we stop now?* Patton turned away, feeling their disappointment on his back, and trudged up the street. Following the tracks was a little obvious, and in real life they never led anywhere. But still, someone had to do it.

He walked to the corner, and the tracks turned left. Looking up the street, he saw that the parallel tracks were once again the only ones in the snow. "This is too easy," he said to himself. He reached for his cell phone and called the detective on the scene. "Mayer? It's Patton. I'm following this set of tire tracks, and they head east. Have someone who knows how to drive in this shit follow me, and tell them to stay away from the tracks."

After a moment of silence on the other end, Mayer responded, "No problem, Chief."

"I'm not the chief anymore," he mumbled to himself. He was a cross between a baby-sitter and a tutor. The ringing of his cell phone brought him back to the moment. "Hello," he said gruffly.

"Hey, Dad," a voice said and Rodney's mood immediately lifted.

"Hi sweetheart; how's life in the big city?" His daughter Laura had from the day she was born the unique ability to make Rodney feel good about the world.

"Oh, you know, exciting, glamorous, thrilling, same thing every day."

"I realize what a heavy burden you bear just being you. How's Glen; how's my favorite grandchild?"

"Glen is wonderful, as always, and your favorite grandchild is right on schedule to appear May first. How's life in the mountains?"

"Turning out to be a little more challenging than promised. Is that why you're calling?" One of the networks had just done an investigative piece that compared the violence in Colorado Springs to Detroit.

"So what's going on up there?"

"Is this my daughter asking, or the Assistant to the Special Prosecutor?"

"Just me. Your high crimes and misdemeanors have not reached the ears of anyone important, yet."

"To tell you the truth, Laura, I don't have a clue as to what's happening here. Whatever it is, it's affecting the very fabric of society. Even in the bad old days, I never saw such an outbreak of wanton violence." Rodney's voice had become painfully serious.

"Drugs?" Laura asked.

"Not like any I've ever seen before. I suppose it could be a new designer drug, but the problem cuts across all social strata and age groups. Besides, the health department says no. We've looked for contaminants in the air, water, food—you name it, and we've checked it twice."

"How are you holding up? You sound more tense than usual."

"I'm all right. Things here really aren't set up to deal with a problem of this magnitude." He always tried to stay positive with his daughter.

"You're not in Baltimore anymore, Daddy."

"I know that. Everyone looks to me for direction. I'm not used to that; the people I worked with back home were professionals—they had experience and instincts of their own. No one here can make a decision without first running it by me." He was afraid that he was starting to pull her down and wanted to change the subject.

"Two comments," Laura said in her characteristic pattern.

"Yes, counselor," Rodney answered sarcastically.

"First, this is a grossly unfair comparison. The men and women . . ."

"Woman," he corrected her.

"You are such a sexist SOB. Now as I was saying, the people in your unit were seasoned veterans handpicked by you for those very characteristics. Secondly, and this is the most important point, are you letting people follow their instincts and make their own decisions, or are you, in true form, overwhelming everyone with your charming personality?"

"You're asking me if I'm being an asshole?"

"I would never be so crass, but you do have an understanding of the question," Laura teased.

"I always told your mother we should never have encouraged you to talk. You were so much better when all we had to do to shut you up was to put a pacifier in your mouth." Rodney loved being teased by his daughter. "It may not matter much longer, because if I don't figure out what's happening here, and soon, I may just show up on your doorstep applying for the nanny position."

"I'm sure it's not that bad."

"Actually it is. The mayor has been dropping some not-so-subtle hints that he may have made a mistake hiring outside of the department." So much for staying positive with his daughter. "Hey, you're not going to believe what I'm doing at this very minute."

"I'm guessing it's not scuba diving."

"No, but you're surprisingly close. I am walking through the snow following a set of tire tracks left by a potential murder suspect."

"My father the bloodhound; I am so proud," she pretended to choke up with tears. "Daddy, I do have to go. I'll call you this weekend."

"All right, honey. If anything changes call me sooner." He closed his phone and the usual wave of emptiness filled his heart. She was so far away and he missed her so much, but she had her own life now, and the days of holding her hand as he walked her to school were gone.

Yaeger and his partner came up behind Patton in a police cruiser. They drove slowly, careful not to obscure the tracks or run over their new boss. Patton glanced back and thought that they looked like a couple of teenage boys out for a joy ride in the old man's car. "This is my backup," he said to himself. He kept walking, choosing the cold over their obligatory nervous banter. Despite his size, he could move quickly if the need or desire arose, and this morning he wanted to cover some ground. After thirty minutes, he had followed the tracks two and a half miles. They crossed two major streets but, as luck would have it, each time the tracks continued straight across the intersection. *This is absolutely incredible*, he told himself. Things like this just never happen.

After ten more minutes, the tracks turned into a parking lot shared by a Sheraton and two restaurants. A pickup truck was busy plowing away Patton's tracks. He turned back to the car and noted that Yaeger and his partner had that resigned, that's-the-end-of-the-road expression plastered across their faces. He ignored them, opened the driver's side door, told Yaeger to get in the back, and then drove them around the large parking lot. Most of the cars were still covered in blankets of snow, but there were about thirty that had been cleared and obviously driven. Of the thirty, three were Tauruses. Unfortunately, all three were brown. Patton had Yaeger get out and clear the snow from the three license plates, and then he ran the tags. As he waited for the computer to slowly work its way through the DMV files, he wished that Rucker had seen the plates. Even a partial would have been useful. The screen stopped flashing and displayed the details about the three cars. The first was owned by a fifty-two-year-old Asian woman, and the other two were Hertz and Alamo rental cars with Florida registrations. A hunch told Patton that the person they were looking for probably wasn't the fifty-two-year-old Asian woman.

"Yaeger, stay with the car and position yourself so that you can watch both of those vehicles. Try to be as unobtrusive as possible, and stay alert." Patton had turned his bulk to stare directly at Yaeger, and the inexperienced officer nodded his understanding so eagerly that Patton was reminded of a bobble-head doll. He stifled a biting remark and turned to the other policeman. "What's your name?"

"Johnson, sir." His voice was very nearly a squeak, and his eyes widened in fear.

"It's okay, Johnson, I'm not going to eat you. I had a detective for breakfast, so you're good for another hour or so." Patton wondered if Johnson was his first or last name and decided that he didn't care. "You come with me. We're going into that Sheraton to see if we can sweet-talk someone into giving us the names of the drivers of those two cars." He turned back to Yaeger. "Don't be a hero. If you see someone approach those cars call me, or call for backup. Am I clear?"

"Crystal, sir."

Within ten minutes, Patton had the names and room numbers of both drivers. He couldn't decide whether he appreciated the trust the desk clerk had shown him and his gold detective's badge, or whether it was just another sign of how far away from home he really was. *What a cynic you've become*, he admonished himself, *confusing good faith with naïveté*. Still, he had always enjoyed the give-and-take with the more worldly and skeptical big city dwellers.

Johnson appeared by Patton's side and craned his neck to read the two names scribbled on the notepad. "Two middle-aged males: a Texan and a Bulgarian. What do you suppose a Bulgarian is doing in Colorado Springs in the dead of winter?" Patton asked himself.

"The academy," Johnson offered. "We get a lot of foreign visitors. Most of them are affiliated with the Air Force. Either theirs or ours."

Patton looked up from his notepad at the slight policeman. He was five feet eleven and couldn't have weighed more than a hundred and thirty pounds; the name "Barney Fife" flashed through Patton's mind. "Well done, Johnson. Maybe I should have you follow me around and introduce me to all the local customs and peculiarities." He tried to sound sincere, but by the young man's expression Patton was certain that his comment only added to his insecurity. "The Texan makes more sense. I doubt someone would fly half way around the world just to kill Mr. Van Der." Patton paused. He was investigating a murder now; something along his three-mile trek had changed his mind. He dwelled on that thought, but his subconscious hadn't finished sorting through the situation. "Room 341," he said simply and took off for the elevators.

It took Patton about half a second to rule out Edwin Reese as Rucker's witness/assailant/murderer. Reese was not the middle-aged male that the desk clerk had promised. He was older than God, and, with the arthritic bend in his back, wasn't even five feet tall.

"Yes, that's the car we rented," the octogenarian said in a very loud voice. "My daughter is meeting us in Denver." He was in no mood to be disturbed or, apparently, to put in his teeth, or put something on other than undershorts. A frail, white-haired woman appeared at Edwin's side.

"Please excuse Edwin. He is mostly deaf and completely deaf when he doesn't wear his hearing aids. I'm his wife, Clara Reese." Her voice was calming after the gruff Edwin. "Is there a problem with the car?"

"Probably not, Mrs. Reese, but can I ask if anyone drove the car this morning?" Patton turned on the charm.

"Yes, I moved it to this side of the building so Edwin wouldn't have to walk so far." She had a friendly voice with a prominent North Texas accent that made her draw out every last syllable.

"Did you sweep off all that snow?" Patton cocked his head to the side and clicked on his two-hundred-watt smile, playfully patronizing her.

"Goodness, no. I paid the man who carried our bags to warm up the car. I think he cleaned it off for me."

"Is it possible he drove it, maybe to heat it up a bit?"

"I don't think so. He was terribly busy . . . Well, I suppose it's possible." Confusion added to the lines in her face.

"And you said that he works here, downstairs?"

"Yes, the hotel manager arranged for him to bring our bags down to the car." She was trying her best to be helpful.

"Were you planning on going on to Denver today?" Patton asked.

"Yes, we are. Our daughter has a house in Grange."

"I doubt you'll get out of here today. The interstate is closed, and I don't think it'll open before tomorrow." Patton felt sorry for the woman; she was barely able to function herself, and appeared to be the primary caregiver for her irascible husband. "Why don't you give us your daughter's name and number, and we'll let her know that you'll be spending the night here and that everything is all right." A little of the small-town attitude was seeping into Patton.

Clara carefully and shakily wrote out the information about her daughter and gave it to the detective, who immediately handed it to Johnson. Patton thanked them and left for the lobby, Johnson in tow.

"Do you think it might be the bellhop?" Johnson asked breathlessly, jogging down the hall, trying to keep up with Patton.

"I don't know, but it sure wasn't Edwin or Clara. I don't want you to forget to make that call to their daughter. Do it while I'm talking to the manager and our helpful bellhop." Patton emphasized the term. He couldn't remember the last time he had heard anyone referred to as a bellhop.

They reached the stairwell, and Patton began to pound down the metal stairs. Johnson hesitated as the entire structure rocked and clattered with each of Patton's footfalls. "Move your ass!" Patton's voice echoed up from below, and Johnson forced himself onto the landing. He paused only for a moment and then made a headlong dash down the swaying stairs. Patton was already through the door and in the lobby before Johnson reached safety. He ran for his boss, all dignity lost.

"Afraid you were going to fall?" Patton laughed as his junior caught up.

"Things were mov—"

A pop, and then two more in rapid succession, interrupted Johnson. Patton's hand didn't wait for instructions from his brain; he had his weapon out even before he consciously recognized that the shots were fired from a standard-issue police thirty-eight.

Chapter 9

The snow had slowed Amanda's progress, but it would equally slow any pursuit. She had passed a few police cars along the way, but none of them seemed to notice or care about her.

It had been almost an hour since she left her aunt, but her words still rang in Amanda's ears. She would find whoever was spreading this new virus, tear open his mind, and perhaps kill whatever was left. The prospect excited her, and she had to consciously ease her foot off the accelerator. Almost as if on cue, her cell phone went off.

"Good morning, Greg." Amanda tried to project a confident and playful tone.

"You're on your way here aren't you," he said without preamble.

"I gather there's a reception party waiting for me. They sure don't waste any time."

"Honey, this is serious. There are two agents up by the Harrisons, and they're not exactly being covert, which means there are probably a lot more sneaking around. Somebody with real pull wants to see you bad. What did you do?"

"I e-mailed Martin."

"That son of a bitch from the CDC? Why would you do that? He's the last person in the world you should be talking to."

Amanda smiled. She loved Greg's paternal tone. She knew that he would protect her, even with his dying breath, from anybody or anything that could harm her, and that included herself. "I had to give it a try. He's the one person best positioned to help. Besides, he's going to find out very soon and come after me anyway."

"Then there is no point in you coming here. Just turn around and disappear," Greg pleaded.

"I can't," she said.

"I'm sorry for calling you. I never meant for you to get involved."

Amanda could hear the anguish in her father-in-law's voice. "Greg, I already knew something was going on; you just helped to bring it into focus. Someone is spreading a virus, and that same someone is looking for me. I would rather meet him on my own terms."

"Why haven't you told me about this before?" Greg asked. Amanda saw something in his mind. For most of the last seven years, she had restrained her ability around family members, but this particular thought was so powerful that Amanda couldn't avoid it.

"You've seen him," she said.

"I've seen someone, and Lisa has seen the same person several times as well. It's probably just Internal Affairs making sure that my retirement is not too comfortable."

"You don't believe that and neither do I," she answered. "I'll know more as soon as I see you."

"Amanda, don't be a fool. If you come anywhere near here, the FBI will be all over you."

"O ye of little faith, with a wave of my hand, they will all disappear."

"Amanda this isn't funny," Greg rebuked her.

"What's wrong with you, Greg?"

He waited a moment before answering her. "There is a priest in our parish. I've known him for a few years. He's a good man—at least, I thought he was a good man."

"Greg, you're babbling."

"It seems he has abilities similar to yours and has managed to conceal them for I don't know how long." Greg paused, but Amanda remained quiet. "He said he saw you early this morning, and that you were looking for someone to kill."

"He's wrong," Amanda said rather unconvincingly.

"Honey, we can't do this again. The last time . . ."

Amanda cut him off. "I gave you my word, and I've kept it," she said sharply. "I am coming home to find the man who is purposely spreading this infection. I will tell you now that I will do whatever is necessary to stop him. You can't ask me to do anything less."

"Even if you do it for the right reasons, it's still murder."

Amanda didn't respond. She didn't want to argue with Greg, especially over a cell phone. "I should go, Greg. It's starting to snow, and traffic is picking up. I'll call you once I get in, and please don't worry about me."

"I will always worry about you, Amanda. Please be careful."

Over the next half hour, the snow worsened. Travel was being discouraged, but no one seemed to have listened. There had been three multi-car accidents within a twenty-mile stretch along I-25 before the road was closed. Amanda had been lucky; she had been able to follow three huge snowplows into Colorado Springs a little after nine. The Highway Patrol finally directed her off onto a downtown exit. The surface streets had been plowed and sanded, so the going became a little easier. Her first order of business was to find a place to stay. For more than six years, she had successfully evaded the FBI by assuming the identities of others. She was surprised how easy it was. Even with the additional scrutiny over the last few years, Amanda could effortlessly become half a dozen different people. She had credit cards, driver's licenses, and bank accounts—everything a normal person would need to move through society without arousing suspicion, including getting a hotel room.

"Good morning, and welcome to the Hilton," the desk clerk greeted Amanda with a tired smile. Normally, she would have preferred a place with a lower profile, but all the low- to medium-range hotels were filled with stranded travelers.

"Morning!" Amanda returned the smile and read his nametag and his mind in the same instant. David Ruiz was twenty-seven, married with three children, all boys. He and Sophie, his wife of six years, had just moved into a new house, and David was working two jobs to manage the mortgage. Sophie was a legal clerk, and David's greatest fear was that he would lose her to a better provider. Normally, he was home by this time, but the rest of the hotel staff was having trouble getting in, so David had volunteered to stay for a while. He needed the extra hours almost as much as he needed the gratitude of his boss. He was a good, decent man, which made it all the harder to accept that he was infected.

"How long have you been sick?" Amanda asked. She could have pulled the answer directly from his mind, but that would have required an active search, and she didn't know how he would react.

"About a week. It's just this flu that's been going around. I think I picked it up from one of my kids." He seemed somewhat embarrassed by his haggard look. "I'm pretty much over it now, but last week was pretty rough."

"So you're getting better?" she asked, her voice too high for casual conversation.

David paused and looked at Amanda. She realized that she had slipped out of character and he had picked up on it. "I can assure you that I'm not infectious."

She stared at him with a blank face. His embarrassment changed to curiosity, and then just as fast to the special, viral-induced brand of anger that Amanda was all too familiar with. He stared back at Amanda, his rage building. He tried to fight the rising fury, but the more she stared at him the harder it became for him to control himself.

She regretted having to do it but, just before he exploded, her mind reached for his and enveloped it. David responded by screaming and grabbing his head. She tried to be as gentle as possible while sifting through his mind. It took seven seconds before Amanda retreated back into herself. By that point, David was on the floor, howling in agony.

"Are you okay?" Amanda leaned over the counter, back in character. It took him a full minute to register that someone was talking to him.

"Huh? What?" He looked back up at her, wondering who she was and why he was on the floor.

"I asked if you were okay. You slipped on something, and I think you hit your head."

He climbed back up to the counter, dazed, and still confused. "I'm fine, I'm fine," he repeated. He looked at Amanda as if he had never seen her before. "Are you checking in?"

"You were about to give me the room key." Amanda's comment was more instruction than answer.

He looked down and found a room card and a sleeve with the number 456 scrolled across the top. "Oh yes, I'm sorry. Please excuse me. I'm just getting over a cold, and I'm moving a little slower than usual." He handed her the card. "It's room 456. Go through the lobby and take the elevators to your left. Do you need help with your luggage?"

"No, thank you," Amanda answered. She walked away, leaving David Ruiz with a headache and a five-minute memory gap. She reached her room, dropped into the chair by the window, and called Greg.

"Hello," Greg answered on the first ring.

"I'm here," she said quickly. "It's not the same virus, but it's close. The clerk downstairs has been sick for a week. If it was my virus, he would be dead by now. I'm fairly certain that this is a mutation, and that's why peo-ple aren't dying by the thousands."

"What about the violence? Is it related?"

"Absolutely."

"Do you know who's doing this?" Greg's voice was rising in excitement.

"Not yet. I can feel him, he's close, but for some reason I can't break through."

"So how do you find him?"

"I don't know, but I'm worried that we may be too late. What do you know about viral infections?" Seven years and the internet had turned Amanda into an expert on viruses and special pathogens. In particular she followed the work of Nathan Martin and his department closely for any word on EDH1.

"Nothing more than not to shake someone's hand after they've sneezed into it."

"Aggressive viruses kill so quickly that any outbreak generally burns itself out. A slower-acting virus has greater infectivity. Moderately sick people still walk around; they go to work and the mall. And some shake a lot of hands. Thousands could already be affected." Amanda wondered how many travelers Ruiz had infected in the last week, and how many those people had infected once they left. "We need help, and it's not going to come from Atlanta." Amanda quickly summarized her exchange with Martin.

"Our Chief Medical Examiner is brilliant but somewhat unusual. I can start with him."

"It might be more effective if I talk with him."

Greg laughed loudly. "I think if you met with Phillip Rucker, we wouldn't be able to get him out from under his desk for a week. You better let me handle this."

"All right," Amanda said. "Greg, I really do need to see you and Lisa." Aside from Emily, they were her last real contacts with humanity. "Let me find someplace safe, and I'll call you back with a location. 'Bye."

Amanda put her phone away and let her mind drift. The killer was frustratingly close, but he remained shrouded. If she could find him, she could extract every thought from his mind and quite easily take what was left of his life without ever getting up from her chair—except, she couldn't find him. His presence was all around her, but trying to snare him was like trying to grab a handful of smoke.

Her mind came back around to the early morning conversation with Greg. His parish priest had abilities similar to her own? It wasn't possible; she would have been aware of him long before now. Could he be the one that was spreading the virus? The man who was seeking her? The killer?

There was no way of knowing without seeing him, but first she needed some sleep. It had been over forty-eight hours since she had last slept, and while her need for sleep wasn't great, her body did need to recharge every once in a while. *Two hours, I can afford two hours.* She turned back the sheets, stripped down to a T-shirt and panties, and fell into the bed. She was asleep before her head hit the pillow.

***

It was the same dream; it was always the same dream. She was walking along some sugar-white beach in the early evening twilight. She was alone—not by herself, but alone. There wasn't another human being left on the planet, or perhaps the universe. Either way, she didn't care. Nothing else had changed. Everywhere she looked, the world was the same; the birds sang as she kicked up the sand, waves lapped at her feet, and the wind blew through her hair. Off in the distance she heard her dog bark. Mittens, her mottled and often mangy mongrel dog from childhood, now a sleek golden retriever in the prime of life, ran towards her with a smile on her face. She had a look of sheer contentment, and Amanda realized that she too was completely content. She bent down to greet Mittens, who lapped at Amanda's face relentlessly. She was naked, but it didn't seem to bother Mittens, and as they were the only sentient beings in this entire universe Amanda ignored her nakedness. Besides, Mittens was naked, too. Amanda felt liberated, free from more than just clothes. The worries, the responsibilities that had crushed her all her life were gone. She ran, jumped, and wrestled with Mittens for hours, and the sun never set. She was both child and adult, fused in some strange synergy that only dreams can produce.

Mittens leapt from her grasp and streaked down the beach, running for the absolute joy of it. She crested a dune and jumped far into the sky, snapping at the seagulls as they took to flight. She landed in a heap, rolled over, and came up shaking, sending sand flying in all directions. Amanda laughed, and Mittens's smile broadened. For the moment, Mittens existed only to make her happy.

A sudden loud drumming noise broke their reverie, and Amanda instinctively covered herself. This wasn't part of the dream. Mittens stood alert, searching for the source of their interruption. Her fur began to stand on end, and Amanda could hear a low, menacing growl over the surf. Mittens stared up the dune that she had just run down. Something was over there. More specifically, someone was over there, unseen, but watching. Amanda could feel the curious eyes exploring her, and she felt more naked than she ever had felt in the waking world. Mittens jogged back to her, waiting for the command to destroy the interloper.

"Easy, big girl," she said, patting Mittens, who seemed to have grown to an unnatural size. Amanda stood, fully clothed, no longer the fragile flower of her youth, but a force of nature, more than capable of defending herself. "Let's see who it is." Her mind reached for the intruder, but it slipped her grasp. She chased it, but it kept scurrying away; it was like trying to pin a mouse with a tennis racket. Mittens barked and shot across the sand and over the dune with dreamlike speed. Through her dog's eyes Amanda first saw him, the intruder, and he saw her.

"Let me kill him," Mittens whispered, and Amanda was suddenly by her old dog's side, standing at the crest of the dune, staring at a man dressed all in black. She looked down to see a ferocious wolf where Mittens used to be, her eyes burning with a murderous light. "He's the killer, and he means to destroy us. Evil runs through his veins. I can smell it." Mittens the wolf was drooling and licking her chops.

"No, he has answers that I need. Besides, I promised," she said weakly to her dog. But a part of her, a part beyond Mittens, toyed with the idea. Did she really need answers? Were they as important as stopping him, killing him? It would be so easy. There was no possibility of escape. She could see him, and that was all that was necessary. She felt the old cruel smile cross her face, and the blood lust rose in her chest. Mittens tensed, waiting for release, but Amanda hesitated. She had promised Lisa and Greg, and for seven years she had lived by that promise.

"Aunt Emily said to kill him," Mittens countered. Amanda looked down at her enormous wolf, but still she hesitated.

The Dark Man started to speak, but Amanda couldn't hear him. His mouth moved, but she couldn't understand him. They were closer now, and the sound of the surf had receded, but she just couldn't make out what he was trying to say. She strained to listen, but all she could hear was an annoying buzzing sound.

"I can't understand you," she said over the buzzing. Mittens's tail brushed her leg, her threatening growl vibrating the sand around them.

The Dark Man started waving his arms, and Mittens jumped to her feet. "No," Amanda commanded, and Mittens obediently sat. She didn't feel threatened. It was her dream, her mind, and her turf.

The intruder became more agitated with her lack of response, and he took a step closer, his face registering anger now. Mittens had risen to a crouch, ready to launch at the strange man and tear off one of the waving arms. One more step and Amanda would release her, but the man stopped. He put down his arms and just stared at her, frustration and anger radiating from him.

"Who are you?" she demanded. "What are you?" Authority filled her voice. He didn't respond, and Amanda wondered if he was having the same difficulty with hearing as she had. "Can you hear me?" she screamed, although she was not really sure why she screamed the words. Dream or not, she was in the realm of thought where screaming only communicated emotion.

Apparently, he had heard something. He took a step back out of surprise, then suddenly screamed and lunged at her. Mittens, now the size of a bear, exploded from her crouch. Amanda was struck by the thought that the Dark Man hadn't seen Mittens the Bear. She sidestepped their collision as the two tumbled into the sand. Mittens was up first, and she bit deep into the Dark Man's right shoulder. At that instant, an explosion of blue light blinded Amanda.

***

She awoke in agony, her face and chest burning from the flash. Her skin was searing, almost as if she had been splashed with a powerful acid. Blindly, she rolled out of bed and stumbled over to the sink, but before she reached it, the pain was gone. She stood over the sink, her chest heaving, and her heart hammering against her ribs. She blinked several times, but all she could see were blue dots. Slowly, her vision returned to normal. She studied her reflection in the mirror, but her skin appeared to be unharmed.

She rubbed her face and chest, and they both felt normal. She looked back at the bed and, instead of finding a pile of smoking, charred linen, there were only rumpled sheets. She had managed to knock over the bedside clock, and its upside-down numbers told her that she had been asleep for less than sixteen minutes.

Chapter 10

It hadn't gone as planned, but it had turned out better than he could have hoped. He had met the old man briefly two months earlier when he had first started following Rucker, but he had long forgotten George Van Der; he just didn't seem relevant at the time. Reisch had originally intended another of Phil's neighbors, Brandi Dees, a pretty mother of two that lived directly across the street from Rucker. She had caught his eye on several occasions, and each time he had found himself aroused, which made her unusual, and therefore interesting. He had grown beyond desires of the flesh—the very thought of sex nauseated him. Rutting was something animals did. Still, she was capable of eliciting a physical reaction from him, which at some level was disturbing and enticing. On several dark nights he pondered this weakness, finally concluding that he was changing, but not yet changed. His evolution was a process and not an event, and parts of him had taken a step backwards in anticipation of a leap forward. This theory also nicely explained the presence of the madness, and the irrational need for violence. At some point his ordered mind and ordered life would return. *Ex chaos ordo.*

Until then, he had to deal with the reality of the situation and, presently, that required a sacrifice on her part. Years ago, when the madness first began, a blood sacrifice had been sufficient, but as time went on, more was required. A simple violent death would no longer appease the demon; it demanded body, mind, and soul.

On the drive to her house, he had barely been able to contain his excitement. One of Reisch's earliest sacrifices had been a mother of four. She had survived hours of Reisch's torment before her body and mind finally broke, and at the end she willingly offered Reisch her very being. It had been one of the most satisfying and memorable experiences of his life. Reisch had been certain that Brandi Dees would exceed even that. He had seen her run in the early morning cold, her long legs wrapped in skin-tight Lycra. She was fit, vital and young, and so were her children. She had so much more fight in her, and so much more to fight for. So much more to lose. He would touch her, stroke her, have her, and when the moment was right, when the horror had reached unimaginable heights, when every coherent thought and shred of will had dissolved away, he would destroy her.

But Reisch had found that she wasn't home. Her house was dark, and her carport was empty.

The madness within him had raged, demanding an act of extreme violence and bloodshed. He imagined driving his car through the front of her house, crashing through her picture window, and destroying everything she owned. He saw himself searching for a pet—a dog or a cat—and then tearing it apart with his teeth, its hot blood smeared over his face, the thick coppery taste filling his mouth. But he knew that his imagination would not feed his need, which was immediate. He had already decided that at some point in the future he would return and visit Brandi, and on that occasion he would include her two small children, their lives the price for having delayed his gratification, but that wondrous thought didn't stop the madness from overwhelming his sense of reason and purpose.

He had slipped his car into gear deciding to kill the first person he found no matter who it was or where they were when the sound of a motor disturbed his tortured thoughts. He found George Van Der attacking a snowdrift with his blower. Plumes of snow shot high into the air, and Reisch had accepted the gentle guidance of Fate.

His murder of the old man hadn't been nearly as gratifying as he had imagined the hours spent with Brandi Dees would have been, but it had been better than he had initially expected. The old man's mind had been stronger than his failing body. At first, he resisted Reisch mightily, which only made the inevitable collapse more satisfying. He died slowly, horrific images filling his mind, while Reisch watched and fed off the old man's terror as a vampire feeds off its victim.

The bonus, which nearly made up for his missed opportunity with the pretty mother, was having Rucker discover him. It was almost as if everything had come full circle. Phil had become somewhat of a problem of late. His mind had become more difficult to access, and Reisch didn't have a satisfactory explanation as to why. No one had ever been able to resist him as well; of course, Reisch had never given so much attention to one individual before. It was possible that the frequent forays into Phil's mind had led to a type of resistance. In the end it didn't matter. Phil had watched Reisch kill George Van Der in broad daylight, and there wasn't a single thing he could have done. It was another step closer to the precipice and that endless fall into insanity.

After killing Van Der, Reisch drove slowly back to the hotel, basking in the ecstasy of another life absorbed into his being. The only thing left of George Van Der was now a part of him. He had quieted the madness and, anytime he wanted, he could reach back into his memory and feel George struggling for life. It had been a good morning, and he had turned his mind back to Amanda. As he stripped off his jacket, he imagined that he could almost reach out and touch her. The certainty that today was the day he would find her filled his racing heart. He had restored the balance that had always guided him, and now it directed him to the Flynns. They knew where their daughter-in-law was hiding, and before the day was out they would tell him. He had enough of circumspection; the direct approach had always served him well, and he knew that it would not fail him this day.

He stood, suddenly determined to ride his wave of good luck through the Flynns all the way to Amanda. He looked for his jacket but a wave of fatigue rolled over him instead. It wasn't uncommon after a kill and, despite the fact that he had already slept nearly four hours, he reasoned that a nap was probably in order. After a moment's thought he crawled beneath the covers and fell deeply asleep, feeling like a lion that had eaten its full.

***

Every dream he had ever had as an adult started out in exactly the same way. A six-year-old Klaus sits at a small kitchen table watching his mother make breakfast on a rainy Saturday morning. She is droning on about something utterly mindless, and Klaus finally stops pretending to listen. He stares out the kitchen window wondering how he could have sprung from this utterly inconsequential person.

This particular moment in time was not the first time he had had that thought—in fact it was one of his earliest memories—so why his mind kept coming back to this point he couldn't explain. It had no particular importance as far as he knew, but it always had to play out before the good stuff started.

He loved watching himself kill women. Their fear was so real he could actually taste it. He didn't hate women, at least no more than he hated men; they were just better fear factories. In his dream, he had just finished cutting off the clothes of a screaming blonde when a powerful consciousness outside the reality of his dream interrupted him. It wasn't human, and it came from a plane of existence far beyond human thought. It was his plane, his special world, and something had invaded it. He left the blonde behind. She would wait; she had no choice. He had sacrificed her to his demon three years earlier. His mind floated upward—at least, it felt upward—but it could have been downward or sideways as far as he knew. It was a familiar trek, and he didn't need to worry about directions. He reached the Barrier, which marked the limit of human thought and existence. Past this point was a world that until now had been his and his alone, a place beyond the feeble consciousness of man. A realm of Gods, free of lesser beings. He had been the only one to ever breach this barrier, the only one to sever the bonds that confined consciousness to a physical reality. The key was to relax, and the barrier would open. Try to force it, and it would forever remain closed. It had taken him months to learn this simple trick. His mind became a void, free of thoughts, emotions, memories, and finally existence, only to re-form an instant later in his new, special world. Except now, it was someone else's world.

He was on a beach, and he hated the beach. The sun, the heat, the bugs, the salt, the sand, the wind—he loathed everything about the beach. He tried to change it with a thought, but nothing happened. It should have changed, but it didn't. She had control. *Amanda.* So his question was answered. She had evolved just as he had. He wasn't alone anymore. He had thought and prepared for this moment from the instant he learned of Amanda's existence more than six months earlier.

A blast of hot wind suddenly knocked him down. He rolled down a small hill, but the wind seemed to follow. Four more times he was brushed by it, and each gust seemed hotter than the last. Reisch didn't know the rules of this new reality, but it was becoming obvious that Amanda did. A lone figure appeared at the crest of a dune and, for a long moment, they stared at each other. At first, he couldn't see her clearly, and he suspected that was her intent. She was caught off guard by his arrival and was naturally cautious. He reached for her mind, but she blocked him. He could feel her suspicion and a good deal more. Hostility and anger, tempered by curiosity. He sifted through her emotions, and a part of him was disappointed that there was no fear. He wasn't ready to reveal his true form or intent, and instead projected his usual dark and sinister guise, which had up until this point reliably provoked some degree of terror. She moved closer, and he could see that she now felt comfortable enough to reveal her true self. She was older than he had expected, but still very lovely.

"I know who and what you are," Reisch said, his tone slightly threatening. He wanted to regain the upper hand. Amanda simply stared back at him with a questioning look. He repeated himself, only louder, and she still didn't understand. She mouthed some words at him, and now it was Reisch who didn't understand. Out of nowhere, a wave of hostility struck him, the heat of animosity prickling his skin. He looked back at Amanda, but her questioning expression hadn't changed.

"Why did you do that?" he demanded, but her only answer was an even stronger wave. His face actually felt singed. This was getting out of hand. He took a step toward her, but she didn't back away. She looked more than frustrated and started to speak again, but all he could hear was a screeching sound. The screeching only got worse as a third wave of hate hit him. He stumbled backward from the intensity of it. Somehow, she could cause him pain, a great deal of pain. A blinding rage overwhelmed him, and he lunged for her.

***

That was the last thing he remembered before waking up in his hotel room, blind, unable to move his right arm, and screaming. He was certain that somehow his arm had been torn off and that his upper body had been set on fire. He rolled to his left and continued rolling until he found himself on the floor entangled in the sheets, his maimed arm beneath him. He tried to move, but it only made the agony worse. He was going to die on the floor of a cheap hotel room, wrapped tight in bed linen, screaming in pain, and there was nothing he could do about it. He felt the blackness starting to envelop him. He struggled with all his remaining strength, but the pain and the darkness engulfed him.

Chapter 11

There was no doubt in Nathan Martin's mind: EDH1 had mutated into a new virus, and now it was working its way through the population of Colorado. They would do more testing, get fresh specimens, and do their own cultures, but he knew in his heart that none of it would disprove what he already knew. It had taken the FBI less than an hour to determine that Amanda Flynn's e-mails originated from an Internet café in Boulder, Colorado. There wasn't much mystery in figuring out where this new strain had come from. Agents were looking for her all over Boulder and Denver. With a snowstorm stopping all travel, they had a reasonable shot of finding her. They had to find her; he didn't even want to imagine the consequences if she remained at large.

"You're late," said his secretary, suddenly popping her head into his office and then just as suddenly disappearing. He had assembled most of his staff and all the section heads of his department for a meeting. It was the second one of the day; the first had been with his boss and the Secretary of Health by videophone. Both had listened to his hastily prepared presentation politely, but neither was overly impressed with his dire conclusions. He was told that if he wanted to mobilize his section, that was his prerogative, but until he had something more substantial, they were hesitant to provide more resources. Their response was eerily similar to the one he had given Amanda just a few hours earlier, and the irony did nothing to improve his mood.

"I know," he said, in no mood to spar with his secretary. He spent several more minutes finishing his organizational plan, then stood and gathered his notes. No one was going to be happy with this, but that didn't matter. All the pet projects, all the special interests, were about to be put on hold until he said otherwise. This new virus was most definitely a special pathogen, and it was his responsibility to deal with it. The Secretary of Health had made that abundantly clear; he was to do whatever it took to investigate and eliminate the threat from this new virus, and he was going to do it without outside help. It had been an excellent political maneuver. Martin would receive all the blame for not preventing the disaster after being given a "free hand," and the Secretary all the credit for having mobilized the Special Pathogen Section personally.

"Politicians," he scoffed. He shut down his computer and grabbed his coat, hoping that after the meeting he would get a chance to get home before dark. Looking at his watch, he was surprised to see that it was already after six. He glanced out his window and watched as the final rays of the setting sun disappeared into the dusk. "So much for that hope," he said as he left his office.

"Dr. Martin, these men are here to see you, and they are very persistent," his secretary said, scowling at two tall and very determined-looking Marines. Martin took the whole scene in at a glance and was reminded of a high-school principal being called upon to discipline two football players.

"At ease, gentlemen, and come back tomorrow; I don't have time for the boy scouts." Martin turned back to his secretary, who continued to glower at the soldiers. "Martha, I'm going home after the staff meeting. I sent all department heads an e-mail outlining their new responsibilities. I would like you to call each of their secretaries in the morning and get them to—"

"Excuse me, sir, but we need to speak with you. Now," the nearest Marine said, his last word spoken as an order. He turned to Martha and added, "Alone."

Martha jumped to her feet, rising to her full five feet two inches. "Listen to me, Corporal—"

"I am a captain, ma'am," he responded with restraint. Martin couldn't help but smile broadly. He knew what was about to happen.

"Well, I am a *colonel* in the Army Reserve, and if one of my officers addressed a civilian like that, they would be a corporal, but only after I made them a eunuch. Do you understand me, jarhead?" Her face had become scarlet, and Martin could easily imagine her on the parade grounds, scaring the hell out of new recruits.

"Yes, ma'am, I understand what you're saying, but our orders come directly from Lieutenant-General McDaniels. I apologize for any inconvenience, but I must insist that we speak with Dr. Martin alone. If you would like to hear it from the general directly, I can get him on the phone." The captain was more than a foot taller than Martha and stared down the long distance, not giving an inch.

"Here, use mine." She stepped away from the desk, pushing the phone towards him.

"Martha, I don't have time for this," Martin said. "Go home. I can handle it." She glared back at him.

"Go, now."

Very slowly, she gathered her purse and coat and stomped out of the office, but only after shooting a dirty look at the pair of Marines and then her boss.

"Dr. Martin, I am Colonel Scott Simpson." The second Marine spoke for the first time. "Captain Winston and I have been ordered by Lieutenant-General McDaniels to invite you to accompany us to a meeting called by him."

"And by invite, do you mean I have a choice?"

"No, sir. Our orders are quite clear that, with or without your permission, you will come with us. I am hoping you make this easy on all of us." Colonel Simpson was polite, but his tone made it clear that he would do whatever he had to.

"Let's just say for argument's sake that I don't wish to accompany you. What do your orders tell you then?" Martin was half a foot shorter than the colonel and probably a hundred pounds lighter. A vision of being thrown over the Marine's shoulder and carried out kicking and screaming popped into his head.

"In that case, we were to give you this," Simpson said. He extracted an envelope from his pocket and handed it to Martin.

"What's this?" He opened the envelope and scanned the heading. "Impressive. The Office of President of the United States, and down at the bottom is his actual signature."

"Perhaps you should read what's in between, sir," Simpson suggested.

Martin leaned back on Martha's desk and looked up at the two Marines. They were both staring at him, at attention. "I'm not going to like this, am I, Colonel?"

"No sir, I doubt you will," Simpson said, his expression deadpan.

"To Lieutenant-General William McDaniels," Martin began reading aloud. "Effective immediately, Captain Nathan Martin, M.D. is to be recalled to active duty, and is to be assigned responsibilities that require his unique talents and capabilities. Those exact duties are to be left to your discretion. He will continue to serve in the United States Army until all promised obligations made by Captain Martin on July 12, 1974 have been met." His mocking tone quickly changed into one of alarm, and he could almost imagine the two Marines laughing inside. "This is bullshit!" Martin spat out the words. "This can't be legal."

"I am not a lawyer, Dr. Martin, so I will reserve comment. However, legal or not, you will be coming with us." Simpson's tone had developed some arrogance.

"Not before I talk with a lawyer." Martin was back on his feet. He circled the desk and found Martha's Rolodex.

"Please feel free, Doctor, but I have to ask you to hurry. We have a plane to catch." Simpson took a step forward as Martin dropped into his secretary's chair and started furiously dialing a number on the desk phone.

"Ira? It's Nathan. Thank God, I caught you . . . No, I'm not in jail. I've been drafted, by order of the president . . . Yes, it's very funny and, no, I'm not joking. There are two Marines in my office right now . . . I served fourteen months on active duty after residency. I was supposed to be in for six years . . . Huh? It was the only way I could pay for medical school, and then they gave me a stipend during residency." His tone became defensive after listening to his friend and lawyer's response. "They let me go. I didn't ask for it. I was offered an early out; forgiveness, they called it, and I took it. I don't owe anyone anything . . ." Martin's face was turning red as his lawyer talked. "What do you mean, 'go with them'?" He jumped to his feet and shouted into the phone, "You can't possibly be serious! They can hold me for the entire six years?" He listened with bulging eyes. "Screw their fine print, and screw the 'balance of what's left.' This was over thirty years ago. There has to be a statute of limitation, or something!" Martin listened to his lawyer for another couple of minutes, and then collapsed back into the chair. "They want me to go somewhere with them and are using this as a threat." His voice was now filled with resignation, the reality of his position becoming more obvious. He glanced up at Simpson, whose face remained completely impassive. "I haven't asked." Martin started chewing a fingernail as his lawyer spoke rapidly. "Okay, Ira," he said, his voice filled with frustration. "Thanks." He hung up.

The two Marines waited while Martin took several moments to compose himself. "It seems, gentlemen, that you have me at a disadvantage," he said finally.

"Yes, sir, we do. Unfortunately, we need a decision now. Are you coming along as Dr. Martin or Captain Martin?" As if by telepathic command, two MPs appeared in the doorway.

Defeated, Martin handed the presidential order back to Simpson. "I wouldn't want you outranking me, Colonel, so keep calling me Doctor, and sir." He slowly stood, then rounded the desk. "I have to address my staff first."

"It's already been taken care of, sir," said Simpson, giving the last word a little more emphasis than necessary.

Martin looked up into the gray eyes of the Marine. "I guess you guys have thought of everything," he said sarcastically. He could face going with them to some secret meeting—that was intriguing and a little exciting—but interfering with his department was over the line.

"If we did, we wouldn't need you," Simpson said just as sarcastically, and headed out the door.

Chapter 12

Oliver sat across the table from Father Coyle and Bishop McCarthy; both men had similar looks of confusion.

"Let me guess. You don't know whether to have me exorcised or committed." He meant it as a joke, but it clearly hit embarrassingly close to home. "To be honest, up until this morning, I wouldn't have objected to either."

McCarthy and Coyle looked at each other and then back at Oliver. It was Coyle who spoke first. "That's quite a story, John. I have to admit, it's not what I expected. I knew something was wrong, you've been withdrawn and not yourself since you came home, but I assumed it was about your sister's passing."

"I had similar thoughts," the bishop said, and then noisily began searching through his briefcase. He retrieved a large manila folder, placed it on the table between them, and looked back up at Oliver.

"What's that?" Oliver asked.

"This is your life, at least your professional life, John. Your legacy. I brought it here so you could read through it before you made a decision." Oliver reached for the folder. "The church has received a hundred or so letters and commendations from various government officials and charitable organizations, all praising your work. There is probably twice that number from parishioners, some dating as far back as twenty-four years. And if that didn't convince you," Bishop McCarthy extracted a thin folder with a single sheet of parchment, "I brought along this."

Oliver knew what it was the instant he saw the cream-colored paper. It was a special note, handwritten by Pope John Paul II himself, thanking Oliver for all his work and congratulating him on the creation of his twentieth parish. "I appreciate your effort, but this is not a crisis of faith. I will admit that as I watched Mary die my faith was shaken, but this has nothing to do with that. What happened this morning with Mr. Flynn was real and verifiable. It was not a manifestation of a psychiatric or personal disturbance, nor was it demonic possession. The visions are related—I'm convinced of that."

"John, I don't want you to take offense, but you know my background is in psychiatry," the bishop started. "Everything that you've shared with us could have a psychiatric explanation, including your encounter with Mr. Flynn."

"So you think I have a dissociative disorder severe enough that my perceptions are being altered, but not so severe that it disables me." Oliver tried to keep his tone neutral, but his frustration was embarrassingly evident.

"I realize that you truly believe what you are saying, but that's the way . . ."

Bishop McCarthy didn't finish his sentence because Oliver had seized his wrist. For the third time this morning, Oliver felt his consciousness flow into and mix with another. His body felt light and his mind free; he wanted nothing more than to stay in this particular moment, but he knew he couldn't. Reluctantly, he let his bishop's wrist go and the connection was broken. He fell back into his chair exhausted, and it took several moments for him to realize that Francis was standing over the prostrate form of Bishop McCarthy.

"What did you do, John?" He was yelling, but Oliver was having a hard time coordinating his movements and processing what he was seeing.

"I'm all right," a voice said from the floor, and it took Oliver a moment to realize that it was McCarthy.

Francis helped his bishop back to his feet and then into a chair. It took several long seconds for the two men to resituate themselves. Oliver waited quietly. His breathing was still heavy, but his mind was clearing. "Still think it's a dissociative disorder?" he said. Both of the men facing him wore expressions of fear and anger.

"That was hardly necessary, John," Francis said. "You could have killed him."

"I think you're probably right. I'm sorry, Steven, are you okay?" Oliver said.

"Nasty headache, and a bump on my head, but otherwise I'm fine." The bishop rubbed the back of his head and Oliver could distantly feel the pain. "I think you have proven your point."

"What did you see, if I may be so bold?" Oliver asked, and Francis Coyle shot him an angry look.

"All of it. Flynn, your sister, a burning arm." McCarthy stopped and examined his hand. "I felt it as well." He flexed his fingers and worked his wrist. "You're right; this is no dissociative disorder, or any kind of disorder." McCarthy looked at Oliver with a quizzical expression. "Who was the tall man?"

Oliver looked confused. "What tall man?"

Now the bishop looked confused. "The one with the British accent."

Oliver searched his memory, but came up empty. "I'm not sure who you're talking about."

The three men exchanged glances. "What are we going to do with you, John?" the bishop finally asked.

"I'm sorry to say that things can't stay the way they have been. I don't think I can continue to be the associate pastor anymore. It would be somewhat unethical."

"It would make confession go a whole lot faster," Coyle said, and the mood in the room lightened.

Oliver smiled. "Probably. I would like to stay here until we figure this out, if that's okay with both of you?"

"Of course you will stay here," Father Coyle said. "We are all going to help you through this, and when you're ready, you pick up just where you left off."

"This is going to be a major hardship on you, Francis. The parish has grown beyond one priest," Oliver said.

"I'll manage." Father Coyle smiled and reached for Oliver's hand. Then he snapped his hand back, and his face flushed with embarrassment. "I'm sorry, John," he said, but didn't offer his hand again.

"Don't worry about Sacred Heart," the bishop said quickly, trying to get past the awkward moment. "You know I'm going to have to talk with the cardinal about this, John. Would you be available to go with me?"

"I'm at your disposal."

"Excellent," Bishop McCarthy said, getting up from his chair. Oliver and Francis quickly got up as well. "Do me a favor and spend a little time writing this up. I think it would be helpful for all of us."

"Of course. It's a good idea. My memory isn't what it used to be."

***

The clock on the wall ticked loudly. It had taken him almost two hours, but he was finally done. Choosing the right words proved to be more challenging than he would have imagined. He reread the report, and once he was satisfied that he hadn't forgotten any important details, he printed three copies, one for himself, one for the bishop, and one for Father Coyle. Then he saved the file to his hard drive.

He was drained, physically and emotionally. He turned off his monitor and unconsciously rubbed his crucifix. He was done—done with the report, and probably done as a priest. Sadness and exhaustion washed over him. So many thoughts, so many emotions to deal with, but so little energy to spend on them. He put his head down on the desk and closed his eyes. He prayed for guidance and, if it was appropriate, a glimpse into God's plan. Fervent prayers rolled through his mind, but it began to slow and at some point he drifted off.

He floated above his hunched and sleeping form and realized that he would pay for this position later. His back and neck would surely hurt tonight. He drifted out of his office and into the rectory offices. Phones were ringing and people were scurrying about, but no one noticed him. He tarried a while, watching each individual, feeling each individual. They all seemed to be unaware of the halo of softly pulsing light that enveloped and flowed about each of them. He moved through the halo surrounding Deacon Ham and touched his mind. He felt a rush of energy, and his body stirred in his office.

So this is how it works, he thought. He moved away from the deacon and left the rectory with no clear idea of where he was going or why. He became a balloon floating through the cold wind high above the neighborhood that surrounded Sacred Heart. He watched small clumps of school-age children enjoying the snow and the unexpected day off; he watched giant snowplows as they tried to clear the interstate and the main roads; and he watched the snow silently blanket the city, hiding all of its sins. Somehow, he had stepped out of the world, and he was content to simply watch it unfold before him. It seemed so harmonious, so interconnected, and he felt a rush of joy and hope.

Then he felt their presence. There were two of them—a man and a woman, but not together, definitely not together. The man he knew; they had spoken some time ago, but on that occasion, he had been pretending to be something he wasn't. He was the tall man that the bishop had asked about. Oliver could feel the man's pain; he was suffering, and he knew that she was the cause of his torment. The man was dying, or at least he thought he was dying. Oliver felt his own skin start to burn and found himself in a hotel room watching as a tall man wrapped in sheets and blankets flailed to the floor. Oliver's initial reaction was to help, but as he drew closer a wave of fear froze him in place.

Finally, the man stopped moving and the room was quiet. Oliver didn't know what to do next. He couldn't just leave him like this. He waited for a moment and, when nothing happened, he decided it was safe to get a little closer. He closed to within a foot of the aura of pale green light that slowly swirled around the unconscious man. Little tendrils, no more than playful puffs, began to reach for him. At first, he avoided them, but after watching for a few seconds, curiosity overwhelmed his instincts, and he let one brush over him. He heard a sharp snap and felt a slight burn across his face as images flooded into his mind—foreign and violent images. Oliver recoiled, and the images disappeared. The tendrils followed him, and he backed off even farther, well beyond their reach.

The man stirred and let out a moan, and Oliver suddenly felt exposed and vulnerable, just like he had in his own bathroom so many weeks earlier. Except, the feeling wasn't because of the man on the floor; he was still enveloped in darkness. The woman had found him, and she was watching him. Oliver was filled with panic and fled the hotel room. He streaked back to his office, feeling her presence the whole way. He awoke with a scream loud enough for the entire office to hear.

"Father, are you all right?" One of the secretaries had thrown open his door, and several others were rushing in to help.

"Um, I'm fine," Oliver said breathlessly. "Dozed off for a second and had a terrible nightmare." He looked around his office, half-expecting to see her: Amanda Flynn, Greg's daughter-in-law. She was the woman, and the man had been Klaus Reisch. Information flooded into his brain, and suddenly everything made sense. Reisch had infected him with a virus. *He tried to kill me*, Oliver thought. The realization hit him like a bucket of cold water, and he shivered involuntarily. He looked up and saw the concern on the faces of his secretaries. "I dreamt we elected a Polish pope and then a German one." They stared back at him, not knowing what to say. "It's a joke, and I'm all right, really. You can get back to work now. I have to do some penance for making fun of the pope." He gave them his artificial smile, but they hesitated. "Go! Now!" he playfully yelled and pointed at the door. They left, but each of them looked over their shoulder, and Oliver heard them wondering what had become of their rock-solid associate pastor.

The door closed with a muted click. He was alone again. He couldn't feel Reisch or Amanda, which probably meant that they couldn't feel him either. Suddenly, he understood everything. It was a virus. It wasn't the Devil, it wasn't God, and it wasn't him—just a simple little virus, no more than a bad flu. Only this flu was meant to kill him. His mind filled with anger. Priest or not, he was still very much human, and Reisch had tried to kill him, simply because he had seen the German's face. Reisch was beyond redemption. He was evil incarnate, and a part of Oliver's mind rejoiced in his torment. It was a very unchristian thought, and he would do some real penance for it later, but right now, at this moment, he couldn't find any compassion in his heart for the German. He had seen inside Reisch's mind. He had seen what Reisch had done this very morning to a helpless old man, and he had heard the plans he had for a young mother and her children. He would have seen even more if he hadn't been chased away by Amanda. And what of her? He saw her face, and his mind reflexively reached for hers. He restrained himself, but not before he had gotten close enough to feel her emotions. She was in pain as well, but it was confusion that occupied her mind. She didn't understand what was happening either.

Chapter 13

Peter Burnum watched the snow from the window of a city bus. Pueblo was getting dumped on. It was not as bad as Colorado Springs to the north, but bad enough that the bus was running late. He braced himself as the driver slowed for another stop. Damn, he had a headache. It had started a week earlier, and it was only getting worse. He felt every bump in the road, and even the driver's gentle braking was enough to send bolts of pain through his head and down his spine. His aunt was sick as well, but she'd had the good sense to call in sick. Peter really didn't have that option. If he missed work, he wasn't paid.

Two people got on the bus and they swayed down the aisle looking for a seat while the driver took off, trying to make up for the delay. Both women eyed the seat next to Peter, but chose to keep walking.

"Bitches," he said, not too quietly. "Never seen a black man before?" He hated white people. He hated Colorado. He hated being cold. He hated having to take this fucking bus to his fucking job. In L.A., he hadn't had to work or take the bus. *And it never fucking snowed there either.* Damn, his head hurt.

"Why the hell did you ever come to this place, Ten Spots?"

Peter looked over and found his friend Eddie sitting in the seat the white women didn't want.

"And why did you drag my ass here?" Eddie asked.

"I didn't drag your ass anywhere, motherfucker. You followed me." Talking hurt his head. "What are you looking at?" Peter got tired of people staring at him and, if the asshole in the seat opposite them didn't look away, he was going to get his ass kicked.

"Wow, man," said Eddie. "You got to keep it down. Low profile, remember?"

"Yeah, I remember." Peter looked over his cousin. "Does that hurt?" he asked, motioning to the gunshot wound in Eddie's chest.

"No. Isn't that a fucking trip? Nothing hurts. Maybe it's the cold." They both laughed, but Peter grabbed his pain-filled head. "Man, you got to get that checked out," Eddie said. "Maybe you got a tumor or something."

"It's not a fucking tumor; it's this fucking place, and all these fucking WHITE PEOPLE!" His scream produced another explosion of pain.

"Man, if you don't shut the fuck up, I'm gonna leave your ass here." Eddie got up, but Peter motioned him to sit down.

"Okay, okay. I can't think with this headache. Why are you going with me, anyways? You can't work like that." Peter flicked Eddie's blood-splattered shirt.

"I'm not gonna do any fucking work. I'm keepin' an eye on you, Mr. Peter Burnum." Eddie flicked the nametag on his cousin's coverall. "Who in the hell is Peter Burnum, anyway?"

"My aunt's neighbor's son. He's dead or something. It was her idea. It's a stupid fucking name." He wanted to scream again, but his head hurt too much. "Whose blood is that, yours or the other guy's?" They both looked at Eddie's shirt.

"I think most of it's mine," said Eddie, playing with the bloody tatters while Peter rubbed his throbbing forehead. They rode in silence through three more stops.

"This next one," Eddie said. The bus was slowing again, and several people got up. Peter let them get off first and then followed Eddie out into the cold. A gust of wind and sleet hit Peter as the bus drove away. "I hate this fucking place," he said, tucking his chin as low as it would go. He had two blocks to walk in this shit. The Veterans Administration hospital loomed above him, but he had to walk around to the back. "Not good enough for the front door," he told Eddie, who also was shivering from the cold.

"Fuck, this place SUCKS," Eddie called out, his voice echoing off the dirty building as he trudged up the hill in front of his cousin.

Peter rounded the side of the building and pulled up when he saw a number of police cars parked around the loading dock. "Fuck, man, do you think this is for us?" he said as Eddie ducked into the shadows.

"Why don't you fucking go ask them?" Eddie said from the cover.

Peter realized that he was standing on the path in plain view of probably twenty cops, but before he could turn away, one of them called out.

"Excuse me!" the cop yelled, and several more turned his way. They were all white. "Do you work here?"

"Yes, I fucking work here!" Peter yelled back. The pain in his head had taken over, and if he was going to hurt this bad, then goddamn it, other people were going to hurt just as bad. Peter stomped over towards the collection of cops. "You got a problem with that, you white motherfucker? Any of you assholes have a problem with a black man trying to make a living?" He was half running at them.

"Slow down there, big guy." The officer had one hand out, and the other was reaching around for his nightstick. "We had to close this entrance because of the governor's visit. You can go around to the front and enter the building there."

Peter's head was bursting, and he didn't hear a word the cop said. He just kept charging. Peter Burnum, aka Ten Spots, aka Lamarr Bost, had ceased to exist. The twenty-year-old refugee from the mean streets of Watts, who two years ago showed up at his aunt's house in Pueblo, Colorado, after a failed armed robbery that had resulted in the deaths of the liquor store owner and his cousin Eddie, was no more. All the progress he had made in two years—the schooling, the clean work record, the mentoring of troubled teens—was washed away in an ocean of pain and rage. He barreled into the nearest cop and started pummeling him, only slightly aware that the other officers were giving him the same treatment. It didn't matter. As Eddie had said, it didn't hurt because of the cold.

They struggled for several minutes, and Peter took out two cops before they brought him down. They knocked him on his back, bending him over the first cop he had knocked out. The rest piled on top of him or hit his legs with their nightsticks. He had long since been consumed by the pain in his head and was nothing more than a rabid animal, bent on destroying everything and everyone around him. They forced his arms down and tried to turn him on his stomach, but Peter found a gun instead. It was still holstered in the unconscious cop's belt, but through the cloud of pain, Peter recognized release when he felt it. He twisted the weapon free and found that it had a familiar feel. *A Glock*, he thought, then clicked off the safety and began firing.

He had to have hit some of them, because he was suddenly on his feet and running. The pain in his head hadn't eased an iota, and it drove him forward. A crowd had gathered at the loading dock, and he turned towards them. He saw Eddie behind several more cops and some other white people. Realization struck him with a force greater than the bullets that slammed into his chest and back: they were the cause of his pain, and it would continue until he destroyed them all. He opened fire and saw the blood fly from their bodies; he saw their pain, and it eased his. He kept pulling the trigger long after the gun was empty, and only stopped when his pain had stopped.

Chapter 14

Phil slammed the transmission into drive and powered over the snow. He felt the eyes of the investigative team drilling holes in his Power Wagon as he drove away, but that was unimportant. They had a job to do, just as he had a job to do, and they would do theirs, just as he would do his.

Despite the fact that the road crews had cleared most of the main roads, traffic was almost nonexistent, and Phil made good time. Even with the delay caused by the death of his neighbor, Phil was only an hour late. He was surprised to see that most of his staff had made it in to work as well. He greeted his secretary with his usual stilted "Good morning" and quickly escaped into his office. A moment later, she called his phone and ran down the day's activities. He took notes, as she detailed not only his responsibilities for the day but the department's as well. The notes really weren't necessary, since he immediately organized the information in his head, but notes were a part of The Routine, and that made them necessary.

"One last thing, Doctor," Linda Miller said. "The CDC has made an unusual request this morning. They want all our tissue samples on a case we sent them about six weeks ago, and they are to be delivered with stage four isolation precautions as soon as possible."

***

Linda had been Phillip Rucker's secretary for seven years and, while she knew his habits and special needs quite well, she still didn't know him on a personal level. She was loyal to his brilliance and need for perfection, but not to the man. She had been offered other positions in the past, some with better pay and benefits, and she had secretly considered some of them. However, it always came down to a choice between personal or professional satisfaction. Rucker's mood was always unpredictable; there were days when he was as he was now, approachable in his own unique way, and then there were days like yesterday, when he was savagely reclusive. Even at his best, he was a challenge. She wanted to like the people she worked for and with, but to like someone, you first have to know them. And long ago, she had resigned herself to the fact that she would never know Phillip Rucker. Still, she took great pride in being a part of a highly regarded group of experts, and Phillip Rucker, M.D., was the principal reason the Colorado Springs coroner's department was hands down the best in all of Colorado, and one of the best in the nation. She couldn't give that up, so she stayed with him year after year.

"I remember that we sent them a case to review over a month ago," Phil replied. "They signed off on it without comment."

"You may want to review it personally if the feds are starting to take a renewed interest. I took the liberty of loading the case files onto your computer."

"I'll do that right now," he said, while sorting through the files. "Can you please get me the original slides, Linda?"

Phil rarely used her first name, and it was an obvious peace offering after yesterday's unpleasantness. "They are already loaded in your microscope," she said flatly. *It's going to take more than that, Doctor,* she thought.

"Thank you. I would also like to apologize if I in anyway offended you yesterday. You do an exceptional job, and I want you to know that I appreciate it."

Linda paused and wondered what he meant by the word "appreciate." Did he mean that he valued her work, or that he simply was aware that she did exceptional work? After seven years, she knew that he could only mean the latter, but this was as close to being appreciated as she would ever get, so long as she worked for him. "I appreciate that you're aware of it," she said. "Good-bye."

***

Rucker turned to his microscope, glad that things had gone so well with his secretary. Now he could get to work with a clear conscience, or for what passed as one in his turbulent head. He turned the machine on and, while it warmed up, he opened the case file. Case 324-A23 was that of a thirty-nine-year-old man who in January was shot by the police during an armed confrontation with a neighbor. The report said that after shooting and seriously wounding his neighbor, the man opened up on the police, who had responded to the 911 call. Apparently, the assailant was previously healthy and mentally stable. Further, he was married, a father of three, and employed—not exactly the profile of a man who attempts to kill his neighbor in a dispute over a lawnmower in the dead of winter.

The first pictures appeared on the screen, and Phil started scanning through the twenty-seven slides. It took only a few seconds to find the unidentified viral particles that Henry Gorman had described in his original report. Gorman was correct; the particles appeared only in the brain. The heart, lungs, liver, and kidneys were all normal. Gorman had good instincts, and if it weren't for Phil, he would be the chief coroner now. Phil turned back to his desk and dialed an extension.

"Dr. Gorman, it's Phillip Rucker. I'm glad you made it in. Nasty weather we're having." Phil was learning the art of small talk.

"What can I do for you, Phil?" Gorman was in his early sixties and would retire soon, having never been the head of the department he had been a part of for nearly forty years. A week earlier, in a near-singular moment of empathy, Phil had apologized to Gorman for that oversight. The older man had been rendered speechless for several long moments and then admitted that he harbored no ill will towards Phil and actually enjoyed the intellectual stimulation Phil offered, adding that most of their work had become cut and dry and Gorman had found himself falling into complacency before Phil took over.

"About a month ago, you told me that you had a case of viral encephalitis that was sent on to the CDC. Do you remember it? I'm looking at the slides now, and I have never seen anything like this before."

"I remember the case well. I took a pretty close look at what was left of the brain, which wasn't much. He had a nine-millimeter entrance wound in his left frontal bone, and I found the bullet in the right occipital lobe. I took a lot more sections than usual because I couldn't see a young father going crazy like that without a reason. He had all these inclusion bodies in the walls of his ventricles that were definitely pre-morbid. So I figured he had an encephalitis, right, probably viral, most likely an arbovirus. I know—there are no mosquitoes around in late January, but by this point, I was grasping at straws. Did you see the electron micrographs?"

"Yes, I'm looking at them now," Phil said, not entirely comfortable with Gorman's unprofessional familiarity.

"Well, those, my friend, are not arboviruses, either in season or out of season. I sat on the case for a week while I researched it, but I couldn't find shit. Nothing ever published looks like that sucker. I thought it might be a new species, or some radical mutation of a herpes virus."

Phil was about to ask Gorman why he had not consulted him about it, but then he thought better of it. If this did turn out to be a new species, or even a new dangerous mutation, Gorman would be credited with the find and, in today's culture of instant fame, the credit could be considerable. This was one of the rare moments when Phil was happy that he was not burdened by human nature. "I see," he said. "So you sent it on for identification."

"Yeah. We got an answer pretty quick. Let me see if I can find that." Phil listened quietly as Gorman rummaged through his desk. "Oh hell, let me just look it up . . ." His voice trailed off as he began to type at his keyboard. "Got it. Arboviral encephalitis. Signed, sealed, and delivered by the gods of the CDC, Special Pathogen Division."

"They were wrong," Phil said simply, staring at an electron micrograph of a six-sided viral particle.

"You think they just rubber-stamped it?" Gorman asked, with a subtly more professional tone. "It never sat well with me. I was hoping they would have given us something more. Maybe a better explanation. But what was I going to do after they sewed it up so nicely? So eventually I let it go. But there's been this little voice in the back of my head that keeps screaming 'bullshit' whenever I roll that case around in my mind."

Phil was quite familiar with little voices in his head, but the profanity made him wince. "Have you thought of anything else that might help shed some light on this case?"

"No, I haven't. What's your initial impression?"

Phil paused for a moment. He remembered being asked by Greg Flynn a month earlier if he knew of anything that might help to explain the recent social unrest. He had mentioned that they had found an unusual case of viral encephalitis; this very case, in fact, but until now, he hadn't made the connection. Phil recalled that Greg had reacted strangely to the mention of a virus, but, as it wasn't important at the time, Phil simply filed the encounter away. He glanced down at his schedule and confirmed what he already knew: Greg Flynn had called this morning asking for an urgent meeting. "Do you remember a conversation you and I had four weeks ago about the increase in homicides and suicides since the first of the year?"

"I remember having the discussion, but none of the specifics. I gather you think that this upswing in violence may be related to our little friend here."

"This virus is unprecedented. Your initial instincts were correct. It is either a mutation of an old pathogen, or a new pathogen altogether. This escalation in violent death is also unprecedented. I cannot look past the possibility that they are related."

Gorman took a moment to respond. "I think you're probably right. We'd better start broadening our search for this virus."

"Yes, we should. Please let everyone know. Also, remind them to adhere closely to the rules of universal precautions. We don't know how this virus is transmitted, so everyone coming in contact with tissue is potentially at risk. Thank you, Dr. Gorman. We will speak again later." Phil ended the conversation no more abruptly than usual. He picked up his ancient Dictaphone and started to dictate a letter to the department when his phone rang. "Yes, Mrs. Miller?"

"Dr. Rucker, something terrible has happened." There was a slight break in her voice, and Phil waited for the bad news. Linda Miller was never emotional. "The governor has been shot. He's dead." She paused, presumably waiting for a reaction, but Phil was waiting for her to tell him how this news affected the department.

"Was he here in Colorado Springs?" he finally asked.

"No, goddamn it, he was in Pueblo," she screamed. "For God's sake, he was your father's best friend. You do remember that, don't you?"

Grief! Phil admonished himself for missing the social cue. "I know who he was, and it's a terrible loss. I don't know what else to say." He was going to add something about being sad, but thought it would sound a little over the top.

"Dr. Rucker, I know you don't understand situations like this, but very soon there are going to be a lot of people focusing on you, evaluating you and your reaction to this 'terrible loss,'" she said, mocking his words. "I am going to write out some quotes for you to use when you're asked for a comment. I sincerely hope that your utter lack of emotion is mistaken for a feeling of overwhelming loss. After that, I am going home. I don't think I should be around you any more today."

Chapter 15

Crystal Hempner wheeled her Suburban into a snowy parking spot that normally was reserved for compacts. Today, however, a Suburban was as compact as anyone was going to get. Besides, the parking lot was less than a quarter full. She opened the door and a gust of wind almost blew it off. Her daughter laughed from the back seat as her mother struggled with the heavy door.

"That's enough out of you, young lady—" A wave of nausea cut her off, and she swayed in the wind. It took a moment for her to regain control of her stomach. "Okay, let's get you inside before we both freeze to death." Crystal unbuckled her fragile little snow bunny and carried her into the clinic. It was a miracle that they were open today, but Crystal couldn't imagine waiting another day for the test results. They were greeted at the door by Samantha Wood, one of the clinic's nurses.

"Get in here, Miss Karen, and bring your mom, too, before you both catch pneumonia." Samantha had that infectious smile that all good pediatric nurses should have.

"Hi, Sam," Karen said, with a distinct lack of enthusiasm. The vestibule opened onto three hallways, each colored a bright, happy color, and four-year-old Karen Hempner headed down the purple hallway without being told.

"Good morning, Sam," Crystal said, apologizing for her daughter.

"It's okay, honey, we're old friends, Karen and I." Sam smiled, and her eyes seemed to twinkle, unaware how sad it was for a four-year-old to be old friends with a pediatric oncology nurse. "Dr. Ryan is running a little late, so just follow your little angel."

Crystal found Karen slumped in a plastic purple chair, her arms folded across her chest, her mittens and hat discarded on the floor in front of her, and her face screwed up into a scowl. They were surrounded by that damnable color. Everything around them was purple—the carpet, the walls, the toys. Karen hated purple because purple meant pain.

"Honey, do you want to take off your jacket?" Crystal asked. Karen got up, stripped off her coat and dropped it to the floor, then slumped back into that horrible plastic purple chair with palpable resignation. "I brought your coloring books," said Crystal, trying to entice her daughter out of her sullen mood. Karen brightened and reached for the crayons and books and then stretched out on the floor.

As Crystal watched her daughter silently color mermaids and giants, she cursed God and prayed to him at the same time. Karen was dying of acute lymphocytic leukemia, or ALL, as it was known. She had been diagnosed more than half her life ago and all she had ever known were hospitals, blood draws, and bone marrow exams. She had already survived two crises, but the odds were very long that she would survive a third. Crystal began to pray again, the words running through her mind with all the emotional energy she could muster, which wasn't much. She had long ago lost any hope that God would personally intervene and save her little girl, but still she prayed, because if she stopped, there was only one thing left to do: accept the inevitable.

She was pregnant again, but she hadn't yet told her husband, Ron. At very best, she was six weeks along and, if they did an early C-section at thirty-four weeks, they may be able to get some cord blood, with its life-saving potential—if the baby and Karen were a match, if she carried this baby to term, and if Karen could last the twenty-eight weeks. Crystal was overwhelmed by the "ifs," and her eyes swelled with tears. It all seemed so hopeless, so futile. She turned away from her daughter, pretending to look out the window.

"Look, Mommy, I drew Aladdin and I stayed inside the lines," said Karen, tugging at Crystal's sleeve.

Crystal dried her eyes and gushed over her daughter's latest masterpiece.

Karen scratched at the feeding tube that was taped to her nose. For weeks, it had been the only way they could get nutrition and fluid into her, except lately she had done an about-face. She had been eating reasonably normally for the last several days and had actually begun to complain about being hungry. Her energy level seemed to be better as well. On most clinic visits, Karen had been too weak to walk down the hall, forcing Crystal or her dad to carry her. Today, however, there had been no question about her walking from the car or stomping down the long purple hallway by herself.

"Mrs. Hempner, Dr. Ryan is ready for Karen now." Crystal and Karen both looked up at an unfamiliar nurse. Karen's face dropped, and Crystal's heart raced. He was going to give them the latest blood counts today. Her cell phone suddenly started to cluck, and Karen stopped mid-stride to cluck along with it.

"It's Daddy," she sang out.

"Yes, honey, it is. Now go sit down for a moment." Crystal made the nurse wait; she had earned the indulgence. "Hi. We're about to go in now. I guess he was running late. I'll call you as soon as I know something." She listened to her husband's response and then said, "I'm trying to be. Love you." She closed the flip phone and fought back another set of tears. "Okay, babe, let's go." She reached for her daughter's tiny hand and followed the nurse down another ridiculously purple hallway.

The nurse walked them past the three exam rooms that Dr. Patrick Ryan normally used and led them to his private office.

"There has to be a mistake. We always see Dr. Ryan in an exam room," Crystal said, panic filling her voice.

"He wants to see you in his office today. Is your husband with you?"

It was happening too fast, and suddenly Crystal couldn't breathe. The corridor began to narrow, and the nurse took her arm. "Please just have a seat in there. Dr. Ryan will be here in just a moment."

Crystal lowered herself into one of the sofa chairs. Everyone knew the routine. Good news was given in the exam rooms, bad news in the office. She couldn't stop the tears now, and she turned away from her fidgeting daughter. She stared at a wall filled with pictures of smiling children, most of whom had lost their hair from various treatments and, to her horror, she recognized that many of the children whose pictures hung on the wall had already died. She wanted to throw up, and it had nothing to do with pregnancy.

Patrick Ryan walked in through his side door. Rail-thin and six feet four inches tall, he looked more like a beardless Abe Lincoln than a pediatric oncologist. His lab coat was rumpled, and his tie was crooked and stained. Dark black circles under his eyes told the world that he needed a good night's sleep. He sat in his chair flipping through the pages of a chart, barely acknowledging their presence. Crystal waited, dreading but needing to hear what he had to say. He rustled through the chart one last time, and then finally closed the file. The name *Karen Hempner* was stamped across the bottom tab. Dr. Ryan looked up at Crystal .

"Crystal, are you all right?" he asked with genuine concern.

"No, I'm not all right. Why are we in here instead of one of the exam rooms?" She began to cry uncontrollably, but didn't break the lock with Ryan's eyes.

"We'll be going to an exam room in a few minutes, but before that I need to talk with you. How are things at home?"

"At home?" Crystal practically screamed. "How are things here?" She reached over and grabbed her daughter's chart.

"I think you have the wrong idea, Crystal. You're not here because I have bad news. I brought you in here so I could understand how Karen's blood counts have normalized."

"Normalized? What does that mean? Is that your way of saying she's having another crisis?" Crystal's eyes grew as big as saucers as confusion and fear entangled in her mind.

"Absolutely not. In fact, and I find this hard to believe, I can't find any sign of leukemia in Karen's blood smear." He leaned forward. "I want you to understand what I'm saying. I don't see any evidence of any abnormality." He spoke slowly and emphasized each individual word. "Either past or present. It is inconceivable, unbelievable. I had the lab repeat the tests, but we got exactly the same results. I checked the blood myself, and the machines were correct. Karen doesn't have a single malignant cell in her blood smear. It goes beyond even that. Her liver and kidney functions have both normalized, and her nutritional state is exactly what we would want for a four-year-old. By every objective measure, Karen is a healthy little girl."

Crystal listened to Dr. Ryan, but the words made no sense. "How?" was all she could manage.

"I don't know, but Karen is not the only one. She's had the most miraculous turn-around, but there are two other children who seemingly out of the blue have erased their cancer. Have you or Ron had the flu this year?"

Crystal was having a hard time processing information. "The flu? Maybe—I don't know. I think I may be pregnant, and I assumed a lot of my symptoms were related to that. Ron was sick about two weeks ago. He had to take some time off from work because of it. Why? Do you think that has something to do with it?"

"Did Karen get sick?" His question was pointed. He had warned her several times that she had to do everything necessary to keep Karen from being exposed to contagions, especially the flu.

"Maybe. It wasn't bad. She had a fever for a day and coughed a lot, but then she got over it," Crystal answered defensively.

"The parents of the other two children both got sick, and their children had a very mild case, just like Karen. There has to be a connection. The changes are too amazing, and the coincidence too great. I'd like you to do a pregnancy test while we check out Karen. Is that all right with you?"

Realization finally crashed in on her, and Crystal broke down. "Are you saying that Karen is cured?" she asked through choking sobs.

"I wish I could, but I just don't know." Ryan was visibly struggling with his emotions. "This is uncharted territory, especially in pediatric oncology. Occasionally we get to talk about remissions . . ." His voice trailed off for a second and Crystal waited breathlessly. "Except these aren't remissions, they're eradications. Only things like this never happen. Miracles happen to other people; we . . ." His arm sweep included Crystal and Karen and ended with him patting his chest. "Have to deal with reality, no matter how difficult . . ." he paused again, but Crystal didn't give him the chance to find the right words.

"But we have a chance. Tell me, Doctor, that my daughter has a chance," she pleaded.

"Mrs. Hempner, Crystal, your daughter has a chance to grow up." He would have finished, but she flew across the desk and pulled him out of the chair by his neck, covering his cheeks with kisses and tears.

Chapter 16

Amanda was beginning to calm. Her heart was still racing, but it was starting to slow. She turned away from the mirror and began to pace the length of the hotel room. She was a little off balance and swayed into the bedside table, nearly knocking it over.

"Damn it," she cursed, and slowly cruised back to the bed, where she carefully sat down. For a moment, the room spun around her; she closed her eyes and waited for the vertigo to pass.

She could still feel Him. "Klaus Reisch," she said unexpectedly. The name reverberated in her head. He was the one, and he was just like her. She wasn't alone anymore, and in fact, had never really been alone.

That thought should have made her happy, but it didn't. There were times over the past seven years when she had thought that she felt *Another*—a consciousness beyond her own that always seemed to be just beyond her mind's reach. Someone who had survived and then Changed, just as she had survived and Changed. Someone who could answer all her questions and finally set her on the right path; someone whose very existence would confirm that her survival had not been some random event that only served the laws of probability; someone who would finally prove to Amanda that her survival, and everything that had come before it, served a purpose—that it all had meaning, even the loss of her family. Except Reisch wasn't Another, he was just an Other.

She tried to close her mind to the experience, but his name continued to echo in her head. She replaced the clock on the nightstand, hoping that the insistent need to explore what she had just learned would begin to abate. It didn't.

She turned her mind to the priest. *John Oliver*, she thought, but there was little more. *How does he fit into this?* He hadn't been on the beach, and he hadn't been with Reisch, but he had been somewhere, because a trace of him gently floated through her mind. Greg had mentioned that his priest had abilities similar to her own, and she had doubted him. It was clear that she'd been wrong; they were a group of three.

She looked up at the mirror and tried to focus on Oliver, but Reisch would not be denied. He was many times more powerful than Oliver, and the small remnant of his mind that she retained after they were so suddenly ripped apart clawed at her.

He was German and purposely infecting the people of Colorado Springs while he searched for her. It was all part of something bigger, but the details were lost in a fog of half-formed thoughts and violent memories.

A need to move overwhelmed her. She suddenly had to get away from this hotel room. She looked around and was repulsed by its shabbiness. It reminded her of rooms that she had shared with her mother and brother when she was young. A powerful wave of claustrophobia washed over her. She jumped off the bedspread, certain that something was crawling up her leg, but there was only the sheet. It was Reisch. The part of him lodged in her head was spilling out and infecting her. This wasn't the first time something like this had happened. Years earlier, when she had first started invading the minds of others, she found that if she wasn't careful she would take something from them, a remnant of their psyche that would quietly insinuate itself into her own. The remnant of Reisch wasn't quiet though, and it was more powerful than anything she had ever felt before. It began to crawl through her mind like some subterranean rodent as it struggled to incorporate itself. She tried to force it from her mind, but it resisted. It took several moments, but she finally trapped it and squeezed it out of existence. The effort forced her to sit back on the disheveled bed. *Klaus Reisch is a monster*, she thought breathlessly.

She felt nauseous. He had been inside her mind, and they had just been more intimate than she had ever been with her husband. That thought nearly made her vomit.

"*Why?*" she asked after her stomach had quieted down. Why was she reacting so strongly to Reisch? She had more in common with Reisch than any other living thing. The same thoughts, questions, and desires occupied both of their minds. They both had survived the same lethal infection, and then miraculously Changed into something beyond a human being. So, how were they so different? *Maybe that's why he disgusts me*, she thought. "Because we aren't so different," she said out loud.

Had the virus turned her into the female version of Klaus Reisch? Was his depravity her destiny? She tried to reject that thought, but she knew objectively that they weren't that different. They had both knowingly taken lives, joyfully taken lives for their own selfish pleasures, and the willful taking of a human life represented the ultimate disconnect from humanity.

What they had become and what they had done had made them outsiders, forever looking in but always excluded from humanity. Reisch had made peace with that fact, he reveled in it, but Amanda still struggled with it. A part of her longed to be free—to embrace who she had become, and happily live outside the restraints of society, as Reisch had done. But another part of her longed to recover what she had lost—to love, to be loved, to hurt, to cry, to experience the joys and pain of a life truly lived. She wanted to be a part of a family again; she wanted to be a part of *anything* again.

Amanda felt Mittens stir deep in her mind as she closed herself to the endless and futile debate. *He's not human, and you know what that means? He doesn't count.* Her old dog whispered to cheer her up.

"He has answers we could use," Amanda answered.

Imagine how it will feel tearing him open and feeding on his soul! Mittens was lost in images so powerful that even Amanda began to pulse with the old familiar lust for blood and violence. *It will be just like the old days. We get to play and do something good at the same time.* Mittens purred like the Cheshire cat, and for a moment Amanda and her predator were of a same mind.

"Maybe just once more," Amanda whispered to herself. For seven years a promise she had made to Greg and Lisa Flynn had suppressed Mittens and her violent desires. *But Reisch doesn't count. He's not human!* She smiled but suddenly felt a bitter taste in her mouth. Without a doubt Klaus Reisch was in a class by himself, but she had used similar justifications before. A woman who killed a baby, or a street corner drug-dealer; the list went on and on. In the end they were just excuses for indulging her dark desires. She had sworn an oath to the Flynns that reached past them to her late husband and son and stretched all the way back to Amanda's soul.

"Does it matter why I kill someone, or only that I have killed someone?" she asked the universe, not expecting an answer.

It is the why that defines you or separates you from Reisch, said her long-ne-glected conscience. It used the voice of her dead husband, and Amanda still clung to the distant hope that it was truly Michael communicating to her. *Are you doing it for your benefit or for the benefit of others?*

After more than a moment's thought Amanda answered herself. "Both, in equal measures."

***

Confusion was his first clear thought. Where was he and why was he on the floor wrapped in a blanket? He tried to move, but had managed to mummify himself quite securely, and it took a minute before he finally fig-ured out how to extricate himself. He rolled onto his back, trying to catch his breath. The room was dark—so dark he couldn't see a thing. *How did it get to be night?* he thought. His mind was thick and sluggish, and he slow-ly began to piece together what had happened. "Amanda," he whispered. The name caused his heart to race with hopeful anticipation, but then he remembered their meeting. She was what he had hoped, but not who he had hoped. She wasn't Eve to his Adam; she was like everyone else, unwor-thy. Except, unlike anyone else, she could hurt him. He blinked and saw blue dots. It dawned on him that the room was too dark even for night. He painfully turned his head and could only dimly make out the bedpost and tousled bed sheets. He blinked several more times, and each time the blue dots became fainter. He turned his head the other way and looked up at the curtained window. Muted sunlight was streaming in through the cheap drapes.

"At least I'm not blind," he said, his voice sounding normal enough. He took an inventory and found that the skin on his chest and arms was as pink and as healthy as ever, but that his right arm was lifeless. His right leg was also weak, but at least it would move. He clawed his way up to the bed and just lay there breathing heavily from the exertion. He couldn't begin to understand what had happened to him, or how she had managed to do it, or even why. What he did know was that he would not give her a second chance. He had come all this way to protect her from the others, and now he was going to kill her.

He fell asleep again but didn't dream. His mind simply shut off and began to repair itself. He lay there for an hour until the awkward position forced him to move. His right arm still refused to respond and, once again, ended up beneath him. The pain in his shoulder woke him. When his eyes opened, he found that his vision was back to normal but that his right side remained weak. His fingers still wouldn't move, but he could weakly flex the elbow. His right leg moved, and he thought it had enough strength to bear his weight. Sliding off the bed into a semi-standing position, he braced himself with his left arm. He started to walk around the bed, but his lame right foot caught on the fallen bed linen. He clumsily worked his numb leg and nearly tripped himself. He managed to make it into the bathroom without causing himself any more harm and began to collect his things. He would have to leave Colorado Springs—no, he could finally leave Colorado Springs. He hobbled around, picking up any evidence that might betray the fact that he had been there. Since he had only been at the Sheraton for two days, not much cleaning was needed. He thought for a moment. What did it matter if the authorities searched his room? They would never find him. He would be long gone before anyone even knew he had been there. His confidence bolstered and his leg growing more reliable, he finished packing.

Ten minutes later, a bag hanging from his left shoulder, Reisch limped out into the snow. A pickup truck with a plow attached to its front end was clearing the parking lot, and he had to wait for it to pass. As he stood there, while the wind and snow found ways under his long wool overcoat, he felt the mind of the police officer. He was being watched with more than just idle curiosity. He surveyed the parking lot and found the cruiser. Reisch focused the mental connection a little tighter and, with a shock almost as great as finding Amanda, realized that the police were specifically looking for him. He saw a long line of parallel tire tracks in the snow, and a large black man trudging through them.

He was stunned by his colossal stupidity. Without a thought, he had driven from the Van Ders' house directly back to his hotel, leaving a yellow-brick road in the snow for the police to follow. He had avoided capture and even positive identification for almost thirty years; every major intelligence agency in the world had at one time or another searched for him, never really knowing if he existed or not. He was the best at what he did—his longevity had proven it—and now he was going to be undone by some small-town cops because of tracks in the snow. The absurdity of the situation overwhelmed him, and he laughed out loud.

The plow passed, leaving him in a cloud of snow and exhaust. The cop was waiting anxiously, hoping Reisch would get into his rental car. He felt the excitement pulse through the young officer. He was eager to impress someone. Reisch waited, and the cop's mind focused in on the face of a large black man, the same man who had followed the tracks to Reisch's hotel. Rodney Patton was the name that played off the officer's mind. Patton had told him to stay put, just observe and not to be a hero. Good advice, but Reisch wasn't going to let the cop follow it.

He hobbled across the parking lot to a snow-covered sedan three cars away from the waiting officer. Painfully, he took the overnight bag off his shoulder and made a show out of laying it down next to the car. He stood for a moment, pretending to survey how much work he had ahead of him, and then with his good arm he slowly began to push the snow off the roof. His attempts were deliberately feeble, and he stopped frequently to catch his breath, his right arm hanging limp at his side. The cop watched every move, and when it became obvious that the tall, dark man needed help, he got out of his car.

The officer walked over to Reisch with a long ice scraper. "Excuse me, sir, can I help you?"

"Yes, that would be nice," Reisch said, with a New York accent. "I had a stroke a few years ago, and this damn arm ain't good for much now." Reisch moved to the back of the car, but the young cop skirted him and walked to the front, sweeping the long scraper through the eighteen inches of snow in long arcs. The cop was just about the same height as Reisch, but he was easily fifty pounds heavier, and in much better physical condition. Even if he had use of both of his arms, Reisch couldn't ensure a quick and quiet kill.

The officer had cleared most of the windshield and hood, and Klaus was pleased to find a BMW beneath the snow. The god of fate had allocated a reliable German car for him to use. But first, he would have to dispose of this young and eager cop. There were two more officers inside the hotel, and he could just start to feel their minds, so he had to act quickly. He finished clearing off the back window and maneuvered around to the passenger side as the officer was beginning to work on the top of the car.

"I don't think you and your family are going to get very far today," the cop said. "Most of the roads are closed. But at least your car is going to be clean."

"Family?" The question was out of Reisch's mouth before he was even aware of it. The word sounded unfamiliar, and for a moment his confusion was obvious.

"I saw the car seat. My wife and I have the same kind." The cop motioned at the carrier strapped to the back seat, confusion now playing across his face.

"Oh, that's for my nephew. I'm up here visiting my brother and his family. We drove up to Denver yesterday and got back so late that I decided just to leave it for the morning." Reisch sounded convincing, but he knew that the cop had picked up a trace of the lie. Reisch moved closer, pretending to help clear the roof. They bumped elbows, and the young cop smiled, but Klaus felt his mind darken. He was closing himself off as instinct and training began to raise the alarm that this dark man was more than what he seemed.

It was always easier taking control of an unsuspecting mind, but Reisch thought he would have no trouble with this one. He extended his mind into Brian Yaeger's a moment before the cop asked him for some ID. He struggled briefly, but Reisch overwhelmed him. He wasn't interested in playing. He needed to dispose of Yaeger as quickly and as quietly as possible and then get out of this city. He needed time to recover his strength. Reisch began to squeeze the life out of the young man. Yaeger responded by grabbing his head and dropping to his knees. He howled in pain as Reisch focused harder and harder, but he wouldn't die. Reisch began to sweat despite the cold. Never before had he had so much difficulty. His head began to hurt, and his heart was pounding in his chest. He imagined his hand closing around the cop's brain, turning it into a bloody mess, but even that didn't work.   Yaeger finally passed out, and the screaming died away. Reisch slumped against the car, panting from the mental exertion. He couldn't do it. A few hours earlier, he had luxuriated in the murder of George Van Der, taking his time, prolonging the old man's agony and his own ecstasy. But now, making this simple man pass out was the best he could do. He watched the cop's breath turn to steam in the cold, wondering what this meant. He felt exposed and vulnerable. *She has done this to me*, he thought. A blind rage started to build in his mind as the image of Amanda flashed before him. He fought to redirect its energy; he couldn't afford to lose control now. There were still two more cops looking for him.

He managed to clear his mind and found that the two cops inside the hotel were busy interviewing an elderly couple, asking them about a vehicle. Relieved that he had a few minutes, Reisch returned to the task at hand. He looked down at Yaeger, sprawled out in the snow between the BMW and the pickup next to it. At the moment he was partially concealed but would be completely visible after Reisch took the BMW. He bent down to the cop and slowly rolled him beneath the wheels of the Ford. It took longer than it should have, and a sense of urgency began to grow in him. Finished, he kicked snow over the unconscious cop and returned to the BMW. It was a long shot, but he tried the doors anyway. Fate was still on his side, and he smiled when he found the rear passenger door unlocked. He pushed aside the car seat and reached up to unlock the driver's door. Yaeger had rolled further beneath the pickup, and Reisch could feel his mind begin to stir.

He walked quickly around the car and got in again. Time was running out. He found the ignition wires and started the car as expertly as a professional car thief. The radio sprang to life, and it took him a moment to turn it off. He felt the other cops on the move and Yaeger regaining consciousness. The car slipped into gear as the young cop began to struggle beneath the Ford, throwing off his cover of snow and rapping his knuckles against the truck's exhaust pipes. Reisch backed away, but the car was cold and stalled. He started it again, but only after a few more precious seconds had elapsed. He gunned the engine, and the motor began to purr smoothly.

Yaeger struggled to his feet, grabbing at the sedan doors. His eyes were wide with confusion, surprise, and fear as he struggled to free his weapon. Reisch struggled in turn with his lame right arm; he had slid the gear selector past reverse and into neutral and was having trouble pushing it back into the correct gear.

Yaeger raised his weapon and started yelling for Reisch to get out. His hands were shaking visibly.

Reisch found reverse and flew past the officer. Yaeger fired into the passenger-side window, shards of safety glass showering over him and Reisch. Twice more he fired at the fleeing car. The last bullet ricocheted across Reisch's upper right arm. He barely registered the pain as he quickly shifted into drive. Yaeger tried to block the way, his weapon pointed through the windshield directly at Reisch's head in a perfect police academy tripod stance. Reisch barely registered driving over the young man as he spun his way out of the parking lot.

Chapter 17

They sure know how to travel, thought Nathan Martin. He was the only passenger aboard the Gulfstream G550; the two Marines who sat together in the back of the jet didn't count. He quietly played with all the buttons in the console next to him. He knew he should still be angry. They had threatened him and then interfered with the workings of his department. It was this violation that still made him fume, but damn, this was exciting. Never once, in all his years of travel, had he ever flown first class, and now he was flying to a secret meeting in a multimillion-dollar jet.

"Hey, Colonel, how much do you suppose this plane cost us taxpayers?" Martin loved to play the liberal card. It was part of his image, but image was all it was now. Nearly four decades of work in the real world had erased any semblance of idealism. Human society would never fully mature so long as humans were involved. There were long spells in his life when he had more respect for the special pathogens he tried to eradicate than for the people he tried to cure.

"I really wouldn't know, Doctor, but it is my understanding that your taxes are specifically earmarked for the purchasing of army latrines. So, on behalf of a grateful nation, I thank you," Colonel Simpson said, with a deadpan expression.

Martin laughed out loud. "Never let it be said that I didn't give my all for my country." Simpson was beginning to grow on him. He wasn't the stereotypical army automaton. He actually had a personality, and there was an outside chance that he could even think on his own.

Martin watched the clouds go by. Occasionally they opened enough for him to see the Earth far below them, revealing all the tiny ant-people in their tiny ant-cars living in their tiny ant-cities. "So. can you tell me now where we're going?"

Simpson responded by getting up and retrieving his briefcase. Martin watched as the Marine officer walked up the aisle and sat in the seat opposite him. "What I'm about to tell you is beyond classified. As such, you are required to sign a non-disclosure agreement. If you violate this agreement, we will know, and we will arrest you. Do you understand this?" Simpson's voice conveyed no emotion but still managed to be threatening.

"I do, and I assume that if I decide not to sign this, you will execute your presidential order, or perhaps just toss me out the door?" Martin smiled, trying to get Simpson to lighten up.

"I have not been given that option, Doctor." The colonel handed Martin a single sheet of paper.

Martin took the letter. "You have to learn to relax, Colonel," Martin said absently while reading through the page. "Have you got a pen? Security took mine back at the airport."

Simpson's only response was to hand Martin a ballpoint pen.

Martin scribbled his signature and returned the pen and paper back to the colonel. "Okay, I'm listening," Martin said, becoming serious.

"A little more than seven years ago, the United States attacked and destroyed a terrorist compound in Libya. We had reliable intelligence—"

"Reliable intelligence? For God's sake, not that excuse again," Martin said, with contempt.

"Doctor, neither of us is here to have a geopolitical debate. Your views on past events are a matter of public record and have no bearing whatsoever on the here and now. I need you to focus on what I am saying and keep your personal opinions to yourself." Simpson's eyes bore into Martin.

Martin accepted the rebuke; he knew he had made an ill-timed and inappropriate comment. "I'm sorry, Colonel. Please continue."

"Roughly nine years ago a network of Arab extremists rather blatantly built a camp in the southern desert and began to train in full view of our satellites, which was somewhat unusual. They are usually more circumspect about their activities. It was a small camp, much smaller than others throughout the region, and seemingly of little concern. At first, we thought that this represented a shift in the Libyan government, back towards state sponsorship of such activities. Later we found that that was not the case.

"No one seemed all that eager to deal with them, so for a time they went about their business, and we simply watched them. In an ideal world, we would have demanded that the Libyans handle the problem, or conversely, allow us to deal with it. However, neither side had enough political will, so the camp remained.

"Just about eight years ago, we began to hear rumors that this camp was more than it seemed. Eventually, someone took an interest, and a disturbing pattern of activity was found—unusual purchases, deliveries of electrical and mining equipment, but most importantly, medical equipment." Simpson paused and reached into his briefcase. He retrieved a folder and passed it over to Martin. "These are some photographs taken inside the camp seventeen days before it was destroyed."

Martin shuffled through a dozen black and white eight-by-twelves, most of which showed only sand and dirty boots.

"Nothing much to get excited about with those, but these are a good deal more interesting."

He handed Martin six more photos, and Martin stared at each one closely. The quality was much better, and it was clear that they had been taken inside. Incubators, autoclaves, and isolation stations were readily identifiable. The last photograph clearly showed the arm and paw of a small ape.

"It's too much to hope for that they were just doing some cosmetic testing," he said, returning the pictures to Simpson.

"No, they weren't," the colonel said, and he passed over a final photograph to Martin. "Do you recognize anyone in this picture?"

Two men stood side by side, almost as if they were posing for the picture. A tall, thin, dark man dressed in desert fatigues was listening to a much smaller man with a riot of black hair, bushy eyebrows, and a cleft lip. "The tall figure I've never seen, but the other man is Dr. Jaime Avanti. I've met him many times, but I don't think I've seen him for a few years. A Russian, if I remember correctly. A microbiologist who grew up in the Soviet system, but defected to West Germany years before the collapse of the USSR."

"Actually, he was Ukrainian, and it's probably a good thing you haven't seen him in years, because back in the nineties he began working for Al-Qaeda, long before they were fashionable. In 1998, he tried to buy some anthrax using his old university credentials. Security wasn't what it should have been, and he came very close to taking delivery of seven vials of weapons-grade anthrax. The FBI managed to intercept the shipment and apprehend several of the individuals involved. Unfortunately, Avanti wasn't one of them. He was convicted in absentia, and for a number of years, he stayed underground—I'm guessing part of that time was spent in this very secret lab that he and a few other disenfranchised researchers developed.

"The other gentleman is an intelligence officer, formerly with the Russians. We think that he was brought in for security purposes. When we entered the camp, neither this fellow nor Avanti could be found. Everyone else was already dead. The interesting thing is that we didn't kill them, and neither did the Libyans. Apparently, they did it to themselves. We think that they had a rupture in one of their isolation rooms and something ran through the entire camp over a two-day period. Probably some form of Ebola."

"What do you mean, some form of Ebola? Either it was Ebola or it wasn't." Martin was sitting high in his seat, anxiety beginning to grow in his chest.

"It was definitely Ebola, Doctor. We recovered samples from the bodies and the lab. Unfortunately, we couldn't do any nucleotide sequencing back then. We can now, and a month ago, we traced the source of the Ebola. It came from your lab." Simpson waited for a response.

Nine years ago, someone had breached the security of the CDC. They had gone straight to Martin's lab and vandalized it. Nothing had been taken, at least at a macroscopic level, but anyone with the expertise to reach his lab undetected could very easily have taken enough samples to stock a number of bioterrorism labs. There hadn't been any public comment about it, but Martin and his staff had come under intense scrutiny. Everyone, including Martin, assumed it had been an inside job, and over the next few months, his research team was pulled apart by external pressures and internal suspicions. "So, this is what it sounds like when the other shoe drops."

"That's not why you're here," Simpson continued. "We know how the Ebola got from Atlanta to Libya. It's what happened after the virus was stolen that's interesting." Simpson produced another photograph and passed it to Martin. It was a very good electron micrograph of a hexagon with six appendages at each corner. "This is why you are here. You recognize it, don't you?"

"Of course I do. You got this from Libya?" Martin's voice was artificially controlled, but inside he was shaking badly. He was finally getting answers to questions that had been haunting him for years, and they were only confirming his worst nightmares.

"Yes, and you got yours from Honduras. Any idea how it went from the deserts of North Africa to the jungles of Central America?"

"Carrion birds," Martin said after a moment's thought. "You said that you didn't kill the terrorists or the researchers. They were dead before you got there. I'm guessing that the vultures got to the bodies before you did. Hurricanes form off the African coast, and I'm betting that some infected birds probably got a free ride to the New World—which means that birds can carry the virus and disseminate it."

"You see our problem then," Simpson said.

Martin looked at the colonel. "No, I don't. These pictures are seven years old. What does this have to do with anything now?" It was a transparent bluff, and Simpson looked disappointed.

"Don't try and play me, Dr. Martin. You contacted the FBI this morning after Amanda Flynn contacted you. We have the file from Colorado Springs and pictures of the new mutation. We have the report from your department wrongly identifying this new pathogen as a benign arbovirus. I have been honest with you, and I request the same in return."

"All right, so you know everything that I know. What's the reason for the plane ride?" Martin asked defensively.

"Look at the picture again, Doctor."

"I don't have to look at it again, Colonel. I've got it burned into my memory." Martin tossed the pile of photographs back at the Marine officer. "I see it in my sleep. What I want to know is if you people knew what this was seven years ago, why didn't you share it with us? Why did you let us release Subject Zero back into the population?"

"Look at the picture again, Doctor," Simpson ordered, tossing the micrograph of the virus back at Martin. "Now ask yourself, is this an Ebola virus?"

The disconnect in his thinking finally became apparent, and Martin looked again at both of the photos. "No, it's not," he said, looking up at Simpson, recognition painted across his face. "You found Ebola in this? That's not possible. Ebola doesn't have DNA; it has RNA, the next step in the formation of proteins. This is a DNA virus; there's no question about it. What else did you find with the sequencing?"

"The original virus contains both DNA and RNA. The RNA is the Ebola stolen from your lab. The DNA is from the common herpes simplex virus. This is an entirely new form of life. It is not viral or bacterial. We are in the process of collecting some of the mutation for sequencing, but our best guess is that it has reverted back to a classic viral form. We think that somehow it has managed to drop some of the Ebola RNA along the way, which would explain why people aren't dying by the thousands."

Martin's head was swimming with questions. How did they get DNA and RNA to coexist in the same virus? Did it have replicate proteins, stabilizing proteins, ribosomes? How did they splice herpes DNA with RNA back then? Dozens of other scientific questions swirled in his mind, but the most important question remained unanswered by Simpson. "If you knew about this virus, why did you let us release Amanda Flynn? She is the only carrier of this virus. Not only that, but she is also the only survivor of the infection. She is both the problem and the solution."

"Amanda Flynn is not the originator of the Colorado Springs Virus. She is also not the only survivor of the original EDH1 virus."

"There is another survivor?" Martin asked, wide-eyed, not knowing if he should feel relief or fear.

"This is what we need you to find out from Jaime Avanti. Five days ago, he walked through the front doors of the Pentagon and turned himself in. He gave us just enough information to prove credible, most of which I've shared with you. However, he won't say any more until he talks with you." Simpson closed his briefcase. "Buckle your seatbelt. We'll be landing in just a couple of minutes."

Chapter 18

Rodney Patton started for the door the instant he heard the shots. It always amazed him that every time he faced potentially lethal situations he had the most unusual thoughts. Instead of worrying about his own safety, or the safety of his men, he was struck by how gunshots sounded more like firecrackers than the sharp, echoing reports Hollywood was so fond of. *The .44, now that sounds like a real gunshot, no mistaking that baby,* he thought, yanking on the handle of the glass doors. It rattled on its hinges, but didn't open. He pulled and pushed, but the door remained locked. Johnson was already outside, having gone through the revolving door. Patton watched him streak across the parking lot to the crumpled form that could only be Yaeger. Patton squeezed himself around the rotating door and followed the younger man to the fallen cop.

Yaeger looked bad. His right leg was broken high up in the thigh, and it lay twisted at an unnatural angle. His face was as pale as the snow he lay in, which meant that his pelvis was probably also fractured and that he was bleeding internally.

"I didn't see it coming, Chief," he babbled. "I was helping this guy who had a stroke, and the next thing I know he's trying to kill me." His voice was strong and his eyes were clear. Johnson was standing over the two of them, screaming at dispatch to tell the ambulance to hurry.

"Was that him in the BMW that just drove outta here?" Patton tried to immobilize Yaeger's twisted leg.

"Yeah, that was him. Six feet six inches. Black overcoat, black pants. Medium to light build. Walked with a limp, and couldn't use his right arm. I'm pretty sure I hit him with one of the shots." He began to rush his words.

"So you fired before he hit you? How was a guy who couldn't walk well or use his arm trying to kill you? Was he armed?" Patton's questions became somewhat accusatory.

"No, he wasn't armed. It's hard to explain, but he sort of reached into my head and started to squeeze my brain. I could tell he was trying to kill me, because I could hear him . . . in . . . inside," Yaeger stammered. "It doesn't make sense, I know, but that's what happened. I woke up under that truck, and he was trying to get away. I fired into the glass, and then he ran me down. I know I hit him. I felt it in his arm."

"Yaeger, you're not making sense—" Patton said, with a good deal of frustration, but Yaeger interrupted him.

"I know it doesn't make sense," the young man said, grabbing Patton's arm. "His name is Reisch, Klaus Reisch. He's German, and he killed Mr. Van Der this morning, just as he tried to kill me, only he couldn't because someone named Amanda stopped him. She hurt him; that's why he couldn't move his arm." The words rushed from Yaeger's mouth, and his eyes pleaded with Patton to believe him. An ambulance siren began to screech nearby.

"All right, Yaeger," Patton said, trying to pry the young man's grip off his arm. "The ambulance is right around the corner, and we're gonna get you to the hospital."

"Chief, you've got to believe me. I'm trying to be as clear as I can. He's different from everyone else. I'm not even sure he's human." Yaeger began to cry. The ambulance pulled up and the motor almost obscured the last thing he said, "Don't let him get her, Chief."

The EMTs pushed Patton aside, and he watched only for a moment longer before turning to find his other charge. Johnson was standing in front of a gathering crowd, openly crying as his friend was loaded into the ambulance. "Pull yourself together, or take off the uniform," Patton whispered in his ear. Johnson wiped his face and followed his new boss inside the hotel lobby. "Did you see the vehicle that drove outta here as we were running outside?"

"Black BMW. Windshield was starred, and one of the passenger windows was shot out," Johnson said, with growing vigor. "A Taurus was also parked nine cars from where Officer Yaeger was injured. I've already called in for an APB and a forensic team."

Patton stopped and regarded Johnson. "Good work, Johnson. Did you get a look at the driver?"

"All I saw was a blur of black, sorry."

"Don't be. You saw more than I did, and you handled yourself well. Don't be ashamed of crying; just don't do it in public," Patton said gently. These men had potential and, for better or worse, he had accepted the responsibility to shepherd them and develop that potential. Even Yaeger had kept enough of his head to give a reasonable description of his assailant. Patton still didn't understand what had happened, but it was clear that Yaeger had fired his weapon before he had been run down. The question was, why? He stopped for a moment and focused on what Yaeger had told him: he had been helping a man who had had a stroke, and then that man had tried to kill Yaeger by reaching into his head and squeezing his brain. At face value, it was ridiculous, but it wasn't unusual for someone with a head injury to come up with a distorted, but nearly accurate, account of events. Patton guessed that the dark man had spotted Yaeger watching the Taurus, and then feigned a disability to lure the cop out of his car, where he had hit him over the head. Yaeger must have come to just as the man was driving away, which was why he shot into the car. It was a believable story, and probably enough to keep Internal Affairs happy. The last thing he needed right now was an officer-involved shooting investigation. Johnson shifted nervously as Patton thought about the situation. Then Patton said, "Okay, we need to find out who owns that Taurus, and the BMW. I'm fairly certain at least one of them is missing."

Johnson's lapel microphone squeaked into life. "Johnson, are you still with the chief?" The young policeman winced at the lack of radio protocol. "This is Officer Johnson; please identify yourself."

"This is Detective Mayer. Please inform the chief that we have a gentleman here who claims his car was just stolen. He says it was a dark green BMW. He says that he saw the guy who stole it and what happened to Yaeger."

Patton bent down to Johnson's mike. "Hold him there. I'll be right out." Patton straightened back up and looked at Johnson, shaking his head. "This shit just doesn't happen in real life. Come on, Johnson. Let's go talk with our witness. Is Johnson your first name or last?" he asked as he went through the revolving door.

"Last, sir. I'm Henry Jackson Johnson," he said, with more pride than Patton thought he should have for such a name.

"Did your parents hate you, son?" He chuckled while walking over to a group of plainclothes detectives.

"Chief, this is James Michener," Mayer said as Patton got close.

"No shit," he answered.

"I'm only a nephew," the balding, middle-aged man said. "I saw the man who stole my car, and what he did to the other police officer. I was getting ready about fifteen minutes ago when I happened to glance outside at my car. A very tall man, dressed all in black, was sweeping the snow off the roof when your cop came over and began to help him. I thought that they had just made a mistake and, once they figured it out, they would move over to the right car. Only the cop suddenly grabs his head and starts screaming, and this tall guy just stands over him, watching. His eyes were bugging out—"

"Whose eyes?" Patton asked.

Johnson was busy writing everything down.

"The tall dark guy. I don't know what he was doing, but it was definitely something."

"So, when did the officer start shooting?" Patton asked.

"Well, this tall guy rolls your cop under that truck over there and starts kicking snow over him. That's when I tried to run outside, but I got lost in the hallway. I should have gone out through the lobby, but it seemed too far out of the way. I ended up in the pool area, and by the time I got outside, you and the other officer were already there."

"Could you tell what this tall guy was doing to Officer Yaeger?"

"He never touched him. He just stared at him, very closely, and after the cop goes down, this tall guy stands back up, panting like a racehorse. To tell you the truth, I don't know what he did to the cop."

"Did you get a good look at the tall man?" Mayer interjected.

"Yes, I did. He turned towards my window several times. Very tall—taller than you." He pointed to Patton. "But, not nearly as wide. He was thin, but not skinny. Pockmarked face, that's for sure, and very light eyes. I think he had black hair, but I can't be completely sure because of the hat. He had a limp, and one of his arms was just hanging there." He stopped and thought for a moment. "The right arm. His right arm didn't move. His right leg, too. He tried to kick snow with it and nearly fell. That's about the last thing I saw."

"Good enough, Mr. Michener. You've been very helpful."

Patton walked away, now more confused than ever. Johnson tagged alongside, but Patton needed some alone time to sort this out. "Henry, go interview the hotel clerks, see if anyone remembers this dark man. Also, have someone run a check on this Michener guy. I'm not looking a gift horse in the mouth, but I always get a little uneasy when I get so lucky."

"Right, Chief. Are you going to work the scene?"

"No. I'm going back to the office. Call me if anything turns up." Patton was already deep in thought and didn't realize until after Johnson had left that his car was three and a half miles away. He had a uniform officer run him over to the Van Ders. Only a few people remained, and the ambulance had already left. Patton found his car and drove slowly back to the station, the names Reisch and Amanda echoing in his mind.

Chapter 19

Amanda left the Hilton through the back door. She didn't feel comfortable staying any longer. Although Reisch had never actually been in her room, she felt his presence everywhere. She was skipping out on the hotel bill, and it should have bothered her, but it didn't. She slid into her Jeep and felt sad about not feeling guilty, but was pretty sure that the Hiltons could afford it.

The car was still warm, and she pulled out of the parking lot without a clear destination in mind. She drove aimlessly for more than an hour, when she suddenly realized that Reisch was close. Their connection was weak, but good enough to steer by, and she let her subconscious guide her. He would come after her now. She had hurt him during their unexpected encounter, and that was something he would not let go unpunished. She hadn't meant to, and even in retrospect had no idea how she had done it. Initially, all he had wanted was answers, which is all she had wanted as well.

An image of him driving out of a parking lot suddenly filled her mind. He was on the move, and he was scared and in pain. She tried to reach out to snare his mind, but their encounter had taken something out of her; despite his proximity, she couldn't reach him. She tried again and her reach was even shorter. A wave of exhaustion overwhelmed her, and she was just able to pull the Jeep to the curb before nearly blacking out. Panting from the effort, she knew that she was in no shape for a confrontation. Their connection became weaker, then sporadic, and finally, it was gone. He was going to get away, and there was nothing she could do about it.

It was ten minutes before she was safe to drive again, and a distant siren spurred her into action. She steered south for no conscious reason and fifteen minutes later was driving through what was left of her old neighborhood. A six-story office complex now stood where her house had once been and, for no good reason, she drove through its virtually empty lot and finally parked. She turned off the engine and felt the car cool. The silence enveloped her, and she waited.

This was the spot where she and her husband had bought a house and conceived a perfect son. But now, only the dirt was left, and even that was buried beneath a thick slab of concrete. It should have called to her. Even beneath the parking lot, it should have been proclaiming to all those who could hear that here, on this very spot, ideal happiness once existed. But the soil was as quiet as her emotions.

***

She had met Michael Flynn the first week of college. They were both freshmen at Colorado State University; Amanda was eighteen and Michael was twenty-two. He had spent four years in the army, most of it in Iraq, and was getting a late start. When he introduced himself during orientation and learned that she was on full scholarship, he insisted that she pay for all of their future dates. She found him mildly amusing but had no interest in any romantic pursuits. Her brother had been killed in a car accident three months earlier and, for the third time in her young life, she found herself grieving. He had been the one constant in her life, and suddenly, senselessly, he was gone. It had taken every ounce of strength to leave her aunt's house and start a new life; she simply didn't have the energy for Michael or anyone else. Except, he was not to be denied. At least twice a week he would "casually" bump into her and list the reasons why she should go out with him. After two months, she finally relented; a year and a half later, they were married. The next three years of her life were idyllic. It ended when the plane that carried Michael and their son plowed into a Wyoming wheat field. A mechanic had improperly secured the door before takeoff. A senseless error.

***

That life was gone and she had to accept it. A hundred people had told her that, but no one told her how. And now this Change, this God damn virus, had taken a magnifying glass and blown up that sense of loss to unbearable dimensions. Coming to Colorado Springs had been a mistake.

Reisch was gone, and all she had accomplished was to stir up what little emotions she had left and make herself completely miserable.

Why are you here? Her conscience had switched to Aunt Emily's voice.

Amanda couldn't answer that simple question. She had carefully crafted a life beyond Colorado Springs—a rather sterile life, but a safe one. And she threw it all away in less than a second after Greg called. "So why am I here?"

She closed her eyes for a moment and then her cell phone rang. "Hello, Lisa," Amanda said. She no longer needed caller ID.

"Hi honey, are you all right?"

"Honestly, no. I am anything but all right. Where are you?" Lisa was the one person Amanda could confide in fully and, right now, she needed her mother-in-law's advice.

"The Walters'. They're away for the winter, and I've been taking care of their plants."

"You're okay; no one is tapping this line." Amanda spent the next five minutes explaining all that had happened since she arrived.

"Is he gone?" Lisa asked.

"For a while, but I think he's already done the real damage."

"Can he hurt you?" Lisa asked, and Amanda smiled at her math. In Lisa's mind, a threat to Amanda was on a par with the possible deaths of thousands of strangers.

"I don't think so," Amanda answered. If anyone else had asked her that question, the answer would have been a categorical no. "I was hoping to get some answers from him. Now I've lost that chance."

"What answers, Amanda?"

"What am I, and where do I fit in?"

"He wouldn't have those answers," Lisa said.

"He seems to have answered those questions for himself."

"Do you want to follow in those footsteps?"

"I don't know," Amanda whispered. "This should never have happened to me; it should have happened to Michael." It was a thought that she had carried in secret for years. Amanda knew that Michael had witnessed, and possibly even done, terrible things in the military, things that haunted him. He never once spoke of them; he locked them away in his memory, and they only managed to escape when he was deeply asleep. But they never had the power to change him. "He was the strong one," she said.

"I know, honey," Lisa answered.

"I'm sorry for dumping on you. I'll be all right. . ."

Lisa cut Amanda off in mid-sentence. "Don't do that to me, Amanda. Don't push me away by apologizing or saying things are all right. You haven't been all right for years."

"Okay, I'm not all right." Amanda tried to derail the conversation with humor.

"And don't do that. I can hear the pain in your voice."

Amanda took a moment to respond. It was pointless to try and lie to or distract Lisa. Amanda learned long ago that the telepathic connection was reciprocal, and Lisa had learned to use it effectively. "Nothing has changed in the last seven years. There is a side of me that is just as violent now as it was then, and it pulls at me relentlessly. I am constantly at war with myself, and there are times when I just want to surrender and lose myself."

Lisa was quiet for a long time, and Amanda could feel her pain and fear radiating through the cell phone. "I am so sorry, sweetheart." Lisa had begun to cry. "I don't know how to help you."

Amanda smiled as a bright ray of sunlight lit up the dark room that housed her disorganized emotions. For the first time in many years she actually felt loved and in her own stunted way was able to return it. "Lisa, listen to me," Amanda said as a solitary tear rolled down her cheek. Her first thought was to somehow save it as proof that she wasn't lost. "You and Greg are the only reason I haven't become Reisch."

Lisa took another long moment and managed to compose herself. "Don't let your aunt hear that."

"Okay, her too, but the point is you've done enough. This is a problem I have to solve." She paused as the mind of John Oliver brushed against hers. His efforts were clumsy but insistent. Quietly, she followed the connection back to the priest and was flooded with his anxiety and excitement. He was new to this and not the equal of Reisch or herself. "Greg mentioned your local priest . . ."

Lisa seized on the idea. "That's a wonderful thought. I love the man!"

"I think I can be a bigger help to him than he can be to me," Amanda said, and was so distracted by Oliver's renewed attempts that she nearly missed Lisa's confused silence. "Greg didn't tell you about this morning?"

"No, he did not." Lisa's confusion darkened to irritation with her husband.

"He thinks that something has happened to your priest. Greg thinks he's like me."

"Nice of him to share that with me."

"Sorry." Amanda knew first hand that sometimes Greg didn't communicate with his wife as well as she thought he should. "Listen, you better go. The FBI has been watching the both of you since this morning, and I'm sure they're beginning to wonder why the Walters's plants need so much time."

***

Oliver stared at the door for a long time, listening to the muted exchanges of his office staff. They spoke softly, sharing their observations and theories, all of them hoping and praying that the old Father Oliver would return soon. Slowly, their activity and voices returned to their normal levels, and life became routine again. *At least for them,* he thought.

Oliver's head was hurting again. It was strange that everything about him seemed to be undergoing a sort of rejuvenation, except his head. He had never been one to get headaches, but they were now an everyday event, and today's was shaping up to be a real doozy. He reached for his aspirin bottle, which had become his constant companion this past month, and washed down three tablets with a gulp of coffee. That was one consolation. For the last ten years, his doctors had told him to avoid caffeine in any form, including coffee. The problem was that he was a coffee addict. It had taken two more episodes of cardiac irregularities to convince him that the doctors were right, at least until now. "Thank you, Mr. Reisch," he said, finishing the cup.

He cleared his mind and focused on the throbbing in his head. It was a technique that worked well for his arthritic joints and back, but it wasn't very effective on these new headaches. What he really needed was a good night's sleep, but there was no way he was going to risk that again. He closed his eyes and visualized a knot untying, but the ache continued. Finally, he gave up and found his headphones. He had a large collection of African tribal music, almost all of which he had recorded himself. Long ago, he'd had the idea to record the vibrant and pulsing rhythms of the local tribes and bring the recording home to America. He sent tape after tape to large and eventually even small studios, but no one seemed to be interested. This music wasn't commercially viable. He turned the volume up as high as his head would allow, and he drifted back to pitch-black nights in front of a large fire watching those incredible people celebrate life. He had almost finished the first tape when a hand shook his arm. He jumped and let out a small yell, which startled his secretary in return.

"I'm sorry, Father, but we have been ringing your phone for ten minutes. We thought there was something wrong with you," Lucy Cummings said, worry lines creasing her face.

"No, I haven't completely lost it, Lucy. Just trying to hide from a headache." He was pleased to find that the headache had receded into the background. "What's up?"

"There's someone here to see you. She says it's urgent and can't wait. It's Greg Flynn's daughter-in-law."

Lucy had taken two steps away from the desk, but she may as well have been two miles away, because Oliver had stopped listening.

She was here. He could feel her presence through the door. It was as if a very strong heat lamp had suddenly been turned on, inches from his face. He looked up and was surprised to see his secretary standing in front of him, waiting for a reply. "Would you mind asking her to come in, Lucy?" His voice became tentative, and Lucy hesitated for just a moment, presumably thinking that he might change his mind. "It's okay. Show her in," he said, with a little more confidence.

Lucy turned and left the office, leaving his door ajar. Through the crack, Oliver saw Amanda Flynn for the first time, at least in the flesh. She was a beautiful young woman: short blond hair, light blue eyes, and a magnetic smile, which she had turned on for the ladies in the office. She wore a simple gray wool coat that broke just below her knees.

Lucy led her back to Oliver's office, chatting briefly about Amanda's father-in-law. As she entered the office, Amanda looked up at Oliver.

"I'll hold your calls if that's all right with you, Father," Lucy said, closing the door. Oliver and Amanda thanked her simultaneously.

Oliver found himself standing, not remembering when he had gotten up. His headphones dangled around his neck. Amanda stared in return, and neither of them knew what to say.

"Well, this is a little awkward," Amanda finally said.

"Yes, it is. Should we pretend that we don't know each other and start with introductions? I'm John Oliver, or Father Oliver, or just plain John—take your pick. Oh, I'm sorry, please, can I take your coat?" He quickly took off the headphones, walked around the desk, and reached for her coat. She handed it to him, and he hung it on a hook behind the door. They stood facing each other in the middle of the room.

"I'm Amanda Flynn," she said and offered her hand.

John reached to shake it, but just before he made contact, there was a loud snap, and both of them were thrown to the floor. Oliver's hand was badly burned, and the sleeve of his cassock melted halfway up to his elbow. His first thought was that this was just another hallucination. Then the pain set in, which, for a time, blotted out any other thoughts. He managed a glance at his hand and forearm, which were red and blistered but not charred, and after a moment, the pain began to recede. He looked up and found Amanda working her hand as well. It too was red, but not blistered, and by the look on her face, she was more shocked than hurt.

"What the hell was that?" Oliver said breathlessly.

"I have no idea, but I dreamed something very similar earlier this morning. This is real, though. Look at your sleeve," she said, motioning with her head. "It's still smoldering."

"I know. So much for one hundred percent polyester." He worked his hand more vigorously. "The pain is going away. Isn't that interesting?"

"Mine, too. So is the redness." Amanda got to her feet, and Oliver followed. "Maybe we should just keep our distance."

"Fair enough. You sit there." He motioned to one of the chairs that faced his desk. "And I'll sit way over there." He indicated his desk chair. He rounded his desk and sat down, all the while opening and closing his hand. He still had some blisters, and his sleeve was ruined, but otherwise he was back to normal.

"So, we've learned something already," Amanda said, her tone upbeat. She stared at him, and he stared back.

"Small talk, anyone?" Oliver said.

"I suppose I should begin." She waited until he had nodded his assent. "As far as I can tell, there are only three of us. I know a little about Reisch and almost nothing about you, so I'll start off by telling you my story."

"Fair enough," Oliver said, suddenly feeling very uneasy. Her existence was a real objective fact. No theory, no doctrine, or dogma. This petite young woman could in the span of a few minutes dismantle sixty-two years of religious beliefs.

"Seven years ago, I went to Honduras with the Red Cross to assist the local population after a hurricane. We were sent to a small town to set up a relief center, but many of the people we were supposed to help had already died. Most of them either killed themselves or were killed by someone else, but several had died from some form of hemorrhagic fever. We came in unprotected, and everyone I was with ultimately became infected and eventually died. I was the lone survivor. The U.S. military finally flew me home, at least back to the States. They held me for several weeks while researchers from the CDC tried to find out why I didn't die like everyone else. That's when the Change started." She twirled her short blond hair, and Oliver was surprised by how nervous she appeared.

"At first, I thought that they were drugging me," she continued, "so I stopped eating and drinking, but the voices in my head only became stronger. So I thought that maybe they were putting something in the air. But after they moved me out of isolation and into a regular room with unfiltered air, I only got worse. Finally, I came to the conclusion that it wasn't them, it was me. I was losing my mind. They didn't seem to notice, and I doubt many of them would have cared. I was an oddity, a mystery that had to be solved before they could move on to other mysteries. Only I wasn't giving them what they needed. I could feel their frustrations even through the locked doors, and in time, it grew into resentment, and then finally, anger.

"I remember a morning sitting on my bed, listening to a disembodied voice run through my head as some technician drew my blood. It was so clear and so disturbing. He was struggling with the vein, and each time he missed, the voice became louder and more irate. After several attempts, I finally told him to stop. He ignored me, so I grabbed his arm. I could see the anger in his face, and the voice in my mind became furious. It screamed that all it wanted was to go back home, but I was keeping it here. The technician pushed my face into a pillow and brutally stabbed me with the needle. It was then, when I was trying to breathe through a pillow, that I realized that I had changed. I was thinking his thoughts, not mine. When he finished, and finally let me up, I told him I knew why his wife had left him the year before. He managed to hit me several times before someone pulled him off me."

"Amanda, I'm so sorry," Oliver said.

"I survived," she said simply. "Towards the end, they needed to figure out what to do with me. No one wanted to release a potentially infectious person back into society, but they had run out of tests to do, at least humane tests. Some of them wanted to push me, to find out how I survived, no matter what the cost. A few wanted to do even more. I listened as their thoughts turned into possibilities, and then into plans. I was mostly alone in the world, and it wouldn't take much to make me disappear, just another casualty of an unnamed illness that had claimed the lives of an entire Red Cross relief team. They began to see me as less of a mystery and more of an opportunity."

"That's incredible," Oliver said, but he knew it wasn't impossible. Nearly three decades as a priest had driven home the point that man was inherently flawed and easily corrupted. In the hearts and minds of most people, the river of needs and desires ran much deeper than the river of morals and ethics.

"At the time it seemed incredible, but now, seven years later, it seems predictable. I was finally released. I think the CDC plans were leaked to someone in the military, because one day the doctors and nurses were removed by a squad of soldiers and replaced by the Army Medical Corps.

"I came back to Colorado Springs and the Flynns a very different person from the one that had left. I was fairly unstable, and did things I could never have imagined doing." Amanda's voice trailed off.

"Can I ask you a personal question?" Oliver finally said as the moment stretched. "Do you believe in God?" Amanda looked up and smiled. "Sorry, but it's an occupational hazard."

"Yes, but He's been strangely absent for the last couple decades of my life. I think you can relate." Oliver gave her a confused look. "Your sister and how she died."

An uncharacteristic flash of anger ripped through Oliver and he nearly jumped to his feet. He allowed it to pass, and composed himself. He stared back at Amanda, who had begun to nod her head very slowly. "That is private and personal," he instructed her.

"John, you have to realize that nothing is private or personal any more. There is nothing you can hide from Reisch or from me."

A second pulse of anger tore through Oliver, but once again he let it burn brightly and then fade. His headache had started to return, and he unconsciously rubbed his forehead.

"It's the virus, Father," Amanda said, and John looked back at her. "The headaches, the emotionalism."

"I've always had headaches," he flicked his wrist to dismiss them, but watched as Amanda's smile broadened. "All right, you caught me. I never realized how easily I can stretch the truth."

"It's human nature, but your intentions are good. The headaches will pass. Unfortunately, the emotional lability is considerably more enduring, but you seem to be handling it better than I did."

"Why don't we get out of my head and back to your story for a while?"

"Okay." Amanda sat back into her chair and crossed her arms. "This part gets a little uncomfortable. In the beginning, the infection seems to bring to the surface everything that we spend a lifetime trying to sublimate. And then it amplifies it. Anger, hostility, suspicion, lust, all of it. They're all . . ." Amanda started waving a hand in front of her. "In your face. They're right here, driving and pulling at you. They make you do horrible things." Amanda's head dropped and she broke eye contact with Oliver. "I had developed a desire to control and dominate others—aggressive tendencies that I had never felt before, and they were completely intoxicating. In time, the desire became an addiction, a need. I actively sought confrontations and then began to create them, just to hurt people. Several times, I went beyond hurting them." Her chin rose and she faced him. "I'm sorry that I've disappointed you, Father, but you should know from the beginning that I'm not a sweet, innocent little thing."

"I don't know what to say. You seem so unrepentant."

"I'm not sorry for what I did, and maybe not even for what I've become." Amanda stared at Oliver with a face lovely enough to grace a magazine cover. "The truth is that I never harmed an innocent person, and when I started, I never intended to kill anyone. Hurt them, punish them, maybe, but not kill them. Later, as I evolved, my intentions changed."

"That doesn't absolve you. You hurt people; you killed people," Oliver started to whisper. "To satisfy a need." He couldn't keep the judgmental tone from his voice.

Amanda closed her eyes, and Oliver could sense her anger and frustration. "I hope for your sake that when you are faced with your darkest desires and have the ability to indulge then without fear of consequence or retribution you do better than I did."

Oliver suddenly felt like a heel. "I'm sorry, Amanda. Let's talk about something a little safer. Why don't you tell me why so many people are looking for you?"

Amanda gave a rueful chuckle and looked down. "Oh, you must mean the FBI, the CDC, and the Colorado State Police."

"Let's start with them," Oliver said, glad that the name Klaus Reisch wasn't added to the list.

"About three months after I came home, I met a man named Ted Alam. He was an FBI agent who had worked with Greg on a couple of cases, and they were friends. I was staying with the Flynns at the time, and Ted came by quite a bit. A week or so before he died we were at a barbecue together, but Ted seemed out of sorts. Greg pressed him, and he passed it off as simple fatigue, but I knew that he was lying. For a few months, he had been passing information to a Chinese official. He had never given them anything of real importance, until now. He was about to pass them the security plan for the Port of Los Angeles, and he kept rehearsing the exchange in his mind. A week later, I followed him to Washington and the National Mall. It turns out that his contact was not actually a member of the Chinese government, or any government; he wasn't even Chinese. He worked for himself and was selling the information to any interested party.

"I was so comfortable with myself that I never really thought through what I was about to do. Ted was a trained FBI agent, and the other man was, for all I knew, a trained killer, but I just walked right up to them with every intention of subduing them as painfully as possible. Before I could do or say anything, Ted saw me, grabbed his briefcase, and began to run. The other guy shot him in the back, and then he shot me in the chest." Amanda touched a spot just below her right shoulder. "For some reason, I didn't feel any pain. He was about to shoot me again when something inside me reached into his consciousness and tore through it. I ripped his mind apart." Her whole affect changed, and a subtle smiled crossed her face. "I enjoyed it more than anything I had ever done before. He died as slowly and as painfully as I could manage. It was horrible and beautiful at the same time, and I loved it."

Oliver stared at Amanda with wide eyes and a slack jaw.

Chapter 20

The phone was ringing again, and Phil counted seven rings. Finally, the digital answering machine played his secretary's greeting, and the office fell silent again. It would be another reporter asking for a comment. The governor, his father's closest friend, was dead, and so was his murderer. The governor's body was being flown back to Denver, but his murderer's body was coming here, and everyone wanted to know how Phil felt supervising the examination of a man who had killed a close family friend. Apparently, not many people knew that Phil wasn't capable of feeling much of anything.

After two dozen phone calls and interview requests, Phil understood why the Pueblo medical examiner had deferred to the Colorado Springs office. The media circus was in full swing long before Peter Burnum's body had arrived. His secretary, Linda Miller, stayed long enough to release a one-page comment describing Phil's grief and commitment to the memory of the late governor, and then she went home, leaving Phil to face the onslaught alone.

Each of the other three pathologists in the department had called Phil and volunteered their services, trying to spare him the obvious emotional trauma, but he declined. It was his turn in the rotation, and he would not violate The Routine. He listened to the purring of his computer's fan and wondered why everyone was making such a big deal out of this. It was true that the governor and his father had been close friends, dating back to the time they were both Marines in Vietnam, but that had been before Phil was even born. It was also true that the late governor had been a partner in the small but successful law firm John Rucker had started shortly after the two had finished law school. It was even true that the governor had been Phil's godfather, but he had had no say in that decision. The emotional math of this situation just didn't make sense.

His cell phone vibrated, and he checked the caller ID: Gregory Flynn. He wasn't surprised. Even with Flynn's old police connections, he was probably having trouble getting through the added security. "Phillip Rucker."

"Dr. Rucker, it's Greg Flynn. We were supposed to have a meeting today. With all that's going on, are you still available?"

"I have only about ten minutes for you, Detective, but I think it is important that we speak. I will clear you through security." Phil abruptly closed the cell phone and used the office phone to clear the retired police detective through the front desk. Five minutes later, Greg Flynn was stomping snow off his boots in Phil's outer office. Another minute passed as Phil waited for the knock at his door, and Greg looked around for Linda Miller to announce him.

"Come in, Detective," Phil finally called from behind his desk, and his door opened tentatively.

"I see that Linda didn't make it in today," said Greg.

"She needed to leave early," Phil said flatly.

Greg Flynn was six feet, but well over two hundred pounds. He was a powerfully built man, and even in his mid-sixties hadn't yet developed a middle-age spread. As much as he was capable, Phil admired the detective. "Is it still snowing?" Phil asked as Greg stripped off his wet parka.

Greg smiled. "Small talk just doesn't come naturally to you, Dr. Rucker, but no, it stopped a couple of hours ago." Greg smiled and settled into the uncomfortable straight-backed chair that faced Phil's unnaturally clean and organized desk. "At our last meeting, I mentioned that we had found a new virus in the brain of a man who shot his neighbor," Phil began, and Greg nodded his understanding. "I think it may be related to the epidemic of violent behavior you spoke of." Phil's tone conveyed no emotion, no fear, and no concern.

Greg didn't react. "Actually, I already knew that. I wanted to see you today so I could share with you what I know about this virus."

"I suspected you knew more than you indicated. It is somewhat unusual for a police detective to query a pathologist about general autopsy findings without some specific concerns."

"My daughter-in-law, Amanda, was infected with a virus seven years ago in Honduras. Everyone except Amanda died, but only a handful actually died from the virus. She said that the majority of the deaths were from suicide or murder. The federal government knows about this. They held

Amanda for weeks after she was returned to the States, and they've been covering it up ever since."

"When you say the federal government, do you mean the Centers for Disease Control?"

Greg nodded. "I have a name: Nathan Martin. He's one of the department heads at the CDC. He tried to have Amanda killed."

"That's a strange reaction to a patient. Why would Dr. Martin try to have Amanda killed?" Phil watched as Greg's expression quickly changed to one of suspicion.

"Do you know Martin?" Greg asked.

"I know of him, but I have never met him. His office contacted us this morning, asking for more information on this patient." Phil tapped the notes on his desk. "We had sent them samples a month ago, and apparently they want to do some follow-up tests. It is somewhat of an unusual request."

"So he knew already," Greg said, with obvious disappointment. "Amanda exposed herself for nothing," he added to himself.

"You still haven't explained why Martin would want your daughter-in-law killed."

"Perhaps I wasn't being completely accurate or fair. The truth of the matter is that I don't think he ever wanted her dead, but he did initiate a series of actions that spun out of control. Now she is wanted for the deaths of two people." Greg's voice communicated both regret and anger.

"So, did Dr. Martin believe that her violent behavior was a result of her infection?" Phil asked.

For a moment Greg looked back at Phil with confusion written across his face. "No, you've got it all wrong. Amanda has never been violent, or even sick."

"So she survived the infection without any ill effects. That would make her very interesting to Dr. Martin. If there's a connection between her infection and this case, she's even more interesting today. Do you know where she is?"

Greg Flynn's expression changed again, and Phil recognized that Greg was hiding something. The moment stretched and Phil continued to study his guest. Greg's gaze had shifted five degrees to the left—subtle, but telling. His right hand, which had been lightly tapping the arm of the chair, was now in his lap. The pupils of both of his eyes had dilated a fraction of a millimeter. Phil continued to catalogue all of Greg's physiologic and autonomic reactions to deception until he realized that he was experiencing an emotional reaction himself: fun. He was having fun discerning Greg's thoughts and emotional state through simple observation.

"I can assure you, Detective, that you can trust me."

"That may be the problem. I do trust you to do the very thing that you're supposed to do, which would mean calling the FBI and the CDC. So, for now, let's just say that I haven't seen her in over a year."

"At some point, it may be necessary to see her."

"Perhaps under the right circumstances," Greg said.

Neither said a word for a moment, both comfortable that all that needed to be said had been said.

"Was there anything else, Detective?" Phil asked.

"Actually, I was hoping you had a theory as to how this virus caused so many people to go mad."

"I don't have enough information yet to make any definitive statements, but it is possible. There are a number of infections, viral, bacterial, even parasitic, that are characterized by personality changes. The most obvious is tertiary syphilis, but even the ubiquitous herpes simplex virus has the ability to destroy the medial temporal lobes of the brain, causing any number of bizarre behaviors." Phil felt a little uncomfortable discussing bizarre behavior, but the small voice inside his own mind stayed quiet and didn't offer any rebuttal statements.

"I see." Greg shifted uncomfortably in the state-issued straight-backed chair . "So the virus destroys a part of the brain, and the person suddenly becomes unstable. That makes sense." Greg shifted again. "How about the opposite? Are there places in the brain that if destroyed, or even damaged, would make the person more stable, or perhaps smarter?" he asked casually.

"There are certain neurologic conditions that respond to extremely well-placed lesions in the brain, but these are only used to control abnormal symptoms, not to improve a normal person beyond their baseline." Once again Phil detected a shift in Greg's demeanor, and a feeling even less familiar than fun crept into Phil's mind: curiosity. "That's a very unusual question, Detective, and somewhat leading."

"I know a man, a priest, actually, who I think got sick, I'm guessing with this virus, and then he got better. I don't mean he recovered from the infection—he actually got physically better. His heart became stronger, his body became stronger, and so did his mind. Do you think there might be a connection?"

Before Rucker could answer, his pager began to beep loudly. Greg jumped, but Phil didn't react. "No," Phil said simply, and he studied Greg's reaction to the simple answer. He could elaborate, and normally he would, but he remained curious how far the detective would take this line of questioning.

"So nothing you know of would improve, enhance, the mind or body?"

"I know of nothing." Phil answered, and even to his ears he sounded artificially formal. Greg took the answer in stride and once again betrayed his inner thoughts with subtle behavioral changes. *What are you hiding, Greg? What are you afraid to tell me?*

Greg abruptly stood, and Phil followed suit. "Thank you, Dr. Rucker. I know you are very busy, especially with all that's happened. I'm sorry for your loss." Greg didn't offer his hand. Phillip Rucker didn't shake anyone's hand.

"Thank you," Phil said awkwardly, not entirely certain of the appropriate response. "If your daughter-in-law does contact you, I would like to have the opportunity to meet with her."

"I would have to ask her," Greg said, almost defensively.

Phil met Greg's gaze and held it; in and of itself this was almost a singular event, as his curiosity grew into an imperative. "May I ask you a question, Detective?"

Greg's face darkened. "Go on," he finally said.

"Did she do it?"

"She was responsible," Greg said returning the stare.

"That left you with a conflict of interest, didn't it?" Phil had no clear idea where this curiosity had come from or why he was indulging it. Thoughts and actions that extended beyond the very restricted mental reservation of Phillip Rucker were universally prohibited. Straying beyond the walls that had kept him safe all his life threatened his survival. But the fact that Amanda was a murderer and Greg a police detective fascinated him.

"You don't know the whole story," Greg said definitively just as Rucker's pager beeped a second time. "Thank you again, Doctor, but we both must be going."

Phil watched as Greg Flynn left, wondering more about his own sudden burst of inquisitiveness than Greg's obvious discomfort. He finally checked his pager and wasn't surprised to find that Peter Burnum's body had at long last arrived.

Chapter 21

They shot me! The realization kept spinning through Reisch's mind. The indignity of being treated like a common criminal fueled his impotent rage. He paced the floor trying to stay within himself, restraining the desire to reach into the ether and punish the inconsequential creature that had the impudence to shoot him.

"Punish him?" Vladimir Pushkin scoffed. "You barely escaped with your life. If his aim had been any better, that bullet would have been in your head instead of your arm."

Reisch glared at his mentor. "It's not in my arm," he said sullenly. The bullet had passed through his bicep and then disappeared into the upholstery of the driver's seat. Unconsciously, he rubbed the wound, which had already sealed itself. It stung, but he used the pain to focus his thoughts. No matter how much he wanted, Reisch was simply unable to punish the cop who shot him, or anyone else for that matter. Amanda had stripped him of something vital, and if he tried to use what little he had left she would know and would come looking to finish the job she had started. Their interaction had forged a connection, and very distantly he could sense her and was certain that she could sense him in return. His only option was to pull back into himself until he recovered what she had stolen.

"You certainly are doing your very best to completely fuck up this job," Pushkin said as he watched his protégé pace in front of him.

"The one thing I know I do not need is a lecture," Reisch said through clenched teeth. Pushkin had a penchant for profanity and rubbing salt in wounds, but Reisch was forced to admit that his old boss was probably right. The only good that had come from the last two hours was a clarity of thought. Reisch tried never to lie to himself, and a critical appraisal of his behavior the last few weeks was not flattering. Up until now there had only been rumors of his existence. Not a single bit of hard evidence existed in any file or database, but now they had a witness, a police officer no less, who could positively identify him. And once they were done searching his hotel room, they would likely have his DNA; and after they found the car he had stolen, they would have a sample of his very special blood. On top of all of that, he was two weeks late for his extraction and still hadn't completed his assignment.

"All because of a girl," Vladimir Pushkin mocked.

The garage had been the only stroke of luck he had had all afternoon. He drove the BMW south, trying to get out of the city, but then thought better of using a stolen car on nearly empty streets, especially after attacking a police officer. It took him five minutes to find the closed auto repair shop and, even with his damaged mind and body, he was able to break into the empty office with ease. The garage door proved to be a bit trickier. The release mechanism was designed to be used by the uneducated, but all he saw were the constituent parts, not the mechanism as a whole. He randomly pulled and pushed at the fasteners and handles and, after ten frustrating minutes, he finally hit upon the correct combination. The door was weighted well, it rolled up easily, and the stolen BMW disappeared from the street.

"You know better than that." Reisch shot Pushkin an angry glare.

"Why are you even here?" Pushkin asked.

Reisch finally looked up at his mentor. The Russian rarely asked banal questions, and he never asked metaphysical questions; his mind was stuck somewhere in between. "There's no sense in having this discussion."

"I think there is. I think it has a direct bearing on what you should do next. For reasons that you have failed to fully realize, you accepted a mission you were never meant to perform. In fact, you didn't just accept it, you demanded it as the price for your cooperation. It's clear why; it was clear to the others—that's why they refused to help you find her. They couldn't have you distracted, and that is exactly what happened."

Reisch knew that Pushkin was right; he had been distracted when he should have been focused on the simple task at hand. He just didn't have the energy to admit it. Still, the conviction that he had to be the one to find Amanda remained strong, even after the debacle of the day. "I accepted the mission and have completed the most important part. The virus has been released."

"In one small city. You were to spread it across the entire state, simultaneously; instead you created a single hot spot. A place for them to concentrate their resources and cover it up. You were warned about this very thing and, more importantly, I trained you better than this." A faint shade of red colored Pushkin's nearly translucent face. He had died ten years earlier, twenty-five years after first saving Reisch's life. He was an inconstant visitor now, a product of Reisch's evolution.

"It will achieve the same result."

"So you still trust what Avanti told you, despite the fact that you know that at this very minute he is betraying you to the Americans?"

"We all have our own agendas," Reisch answered.

"Which leads us back to the question of why you are here. What is your agenda?"

Instead of answering, Reisch wondered, as he had so many times before, if Pushkin was simply an extension of his own consciousness, or something more. The Russian refused to discuss it, and if pushed would disappear for weeks. "I am compelled to be here," Reisch finally said.

"Who or what compels you?"

"Do you really think that this is the time or the place for this discussion?"

Pushkin began to float just above the sofa. "I think that this is precisely the time, although I would prefer a more sanitary place."

"You've never agreed or understood before. What makes you think now would be any different?"

"Because now this irrational need has put you at risk. I'm hoping that it is you who will understand."

"It is only irrational to you," Reisch answered angrily.

"Because the voices don't talk to me?" Pushkin mocked.

If this had been anyone else, Reisch would have responded differently. Instead, he controlled the rage. "There is an underlying natural order to the universe, something in your current state you should be aware of. I am simply trying to live in harmony with it."

"I never took you for a religious man."

Pushkin kept pushing Reisch to the edge. "Religion is a human construct, and one of the very things I am trying to destroy," he said, with what little control remained. "In time we will establish a civilization that has eliminated the need for religion."

"I liked you better when you were a common sociopath."

Reisch's response was cut off by the sound of car wheels crunching through snow and ice. He sensed two minds, as well as two vehicles. A minute passed, and a pair of keys along with a note were pushed through a slot in the door. Reisch waited for the couple to leave and then collected the keys to a Mercedes SUV that needed an oil change and tire rotation. "This is what I was talking about," Reisch said triumphantly to Pushkin. "This is the natural order," he said, holding up the keys.

"This is what I call luck," the Russian answered, fading into the wallpaper.

***

Twenty minutes later, Reisch was driving west on Highway 24. The GPS told him he was sixteen miles away from a small town called Manitou Springs, where he would turn south. He still had one more task to perform, and then he would drop off everyone's radar, including the men who had hired him. He would disappear into the jungles of Costa Rica while the mighty United States of America imploded, but hopefully not explosively. The virus he had spread these past six weeks was just a taste of things to come. Just enough to get the world's attention and have them close their collective doors to the U.S. before the real attack began.

No collateral damage, Reisch thought. *At least not yet.* He smiled, and then with a start quickly searched for the small black satchel that he had kept close for the last two months. It was still in the passenger seat where he had placed it earlier; inside was all he needed to restore balance. Over the course of the seven years that Pushkin had started appearing, Reisch had tried to explain the concept of universal balance to the Russian, but all he saw was religion in another guise. Even in his corporeal life he had had limited vision, interested only in his comfort and the pursuit of pleasure. At the beginning, Reisch could relate to and revel in such an existence, but over time, as Pushkin became more extreme in his pursuits, Reisch became more repulsed by them. Neither of them chose to live within the constraints of society, but to Reisch's thinking, that didn't require you to deconstruct your personal identity. To be true to yourself, to follow the path that had been written in your soul, was the only way order could be derived from chaos, the only way to peace and contentment. Reisch had tried to follow that path from the moment his eyes were opened in Honecker's dark dungeon. Along the way he had occasionally strayed, as he had while sampling Pushkin's life of excess, or the time of instability after his infection, but in the end he found his way back to the straight path that led to the universal constant of balance.

"Universal constant of balance," said Pushkin playing with the black satchel. "How grandiose."

"So now you're reading minds," Reisch answered. It was rare for Pushkin to appear twice in one day.

"It works for you." He smiled at his protégé. "So, up is balanced by down, a positron is balanced by an electron, which would make you balanced by . . . Amanda? I can see that."

Reisch was momentarily confused and hazarded a glance at the specter. "No patronizing tone? No obvious flaws in logic? I'm disappointed."

"I can see your logic, but I didn't say that there weren't flaws in it." Pushkin waited for a response, but Reisch continued driving. "All right, since you asked, I'll tell you. There will be survivors of this pandemic who, like the two of you, will evolve, correct?"

"Go on," Reisch said.

"From these survivors you will create a society that is the embodiment of balance. Everyone will have the same abilities; there will be no lies, nothing hidden, no agendas, no jealousy, no hatred, etc., etc., etc. A veritable communist utopia. I understand that, but what you fail to realize is that it can never work. Right now, your ideal society is composed of two, you and Amanda, and you both are vying for control or planning to kill the other. This isn't balance, it's chaos."

Chapter 22

The plane landed with a bone-jarring bounce. Nathan Martin wondered if that had been planned for his benefit, or if it was just another training exercise for the two Marines in the back. All his earlier excitement had faded with the realization that a genetically engineered virus was right now infecting untold numbers of Americans, and the military-style touchdown only served to darken his mood even further. He had tried to remember everything he could about Jaime Avanti, but it wasn't much.

Martin stared at the picture of Avanti as the plane taxied. He remembered the hair. Avanti was probably the hairiest man he had ever met. A shock of gray and black hair that would put Albert Einstein to shame was only the beginning. He had a beard that crept up as far as his eyes and hung as low as his large abdomen. A mat of black fur escaped from below each of his sleeves and completely enveloped the back of Avanti's hands. Nathan remembered thinking that Avanti was more of a health risk than the viruses he studied. They had met several times over the years, but their last meeting had been many years before Martin was named Director of Special Pathogens at the CDC. *When we were both young*, he thought. A lifetime ago they had both been rising stars in the small world of public health, and now Avanti threatened that health.

The only constant in life is change. Someone famous once said that. Now he couldn't remember who.

The plane came to an abrupt halt, and Martin was thrown forward against his seat belt. A groan, followed by a curse, escaped his lips before he could suppress either of them. Simpson was already up and heading to the door, and Captain Winston was right behind, both demonstrating that U.S. Marines were not subject to the laws of gravity or momentum. Martin followed them out of the plane and down the flight of stairs, disappointed that he didn't get to thank, or hit, the pilot. Two black Suburbans waited at the bottom of the steps, and a large, powerfully built man in full dress uniform was returning the salutes of Simpson and Winston. The three of them talked while Martin cautiously descended the steps.

"Welcome to Bolling Air Force Base, Doctor," the large man said as Martin drew closer to the three.

"Where the hell are we?" he asked, his head swiveling to find something familiar.

"Washington." Above his impressive array of ribbons and colorful insignias, the big man wore a nametag with *McDaniels* stamped across it.

"I take it you are the famous Lieutenant-General McDaniels that Colonel Simpson spoke so highly about." As Martin was framing his next sarcastic remark, it dawned on him that he had seen McDaniels before, not in person, but on television, and recently. His tone changed markedly. "Aren't you the General McDaniels that's . . . what?" Martin couldn't remember the exact context of his familiarity.

"I have just been confirmed as the new chairman of the Joint Chiefs of Staff."

"I'm honored," said Martin, and he half meant it. "I'm glad to see that someone in this government is finally taking this threat a little more seriously. This morning, I spent an hour with the Secretary of Health trying to convince him that this was an urgent problem, and all I got for my trouble was 'it's your problem.'" He did a poor imitation of the small and somewhat effeminate Secretary.

"The Secretary is not involved with this, Doctor. In fact, less than half a dozen people know that you are here, and even fewer know why. It is important that we keep it that way." He said this in a friendly tone, but his true meaning was clear. "Please come with me; we have a madman to see." McDaniels turned back to the trailing vehicle and opened the door for Martin. Simpson and Winston climbed into the lead car.

They sped out through a series of gates without once pausing, and within minutes they were rocketing down the Beltway expressway.

"If all this is for my benefit, General, you can order the driver to slow down now, because I am suitably impressed with his driving abilities."

"Relax, Doctor. You are perfectly safe."

"I think that's what the captain of the *Titanic* was saying just before he rammed an iceberg." Martin had a death grip on the handhold mounted over his head as the two Suburbans weaved through traffic.

"Actually, I know for a fact that it was 'Oh, shit!'" Both men laughed. "You don't remember me, do you?" McDaniels asked. His tone shifted to serious, with a touch of menace.

Martin glanced up at the officer but, aside from the recent press coverage, he would have sworn that he had never seen him before. "We've met?"

"It was a long time ago, and we were both very different people then. At least, I hope we are different people now." McDaniels let the clue dangle between them a little longer.

"No, I still don't recall us ever meeting before today."

"January eighth, nineteen sixty-eight."

Martin froze as a sea of bad memories flooded back into his head. "That was you?"

"I was the one in the wheelchair. You and your merry band didn't expect a wounded Marine, did you?"

"No, we didn't, and we didn't expect the reporter, either." Martin's voice was down to a whisper. He had been seventeen and a freshman in college, with all the answers to all the questions anyone would ever need to ask. He and his friends were intellectuals, blessed with an intelligence that others could only dream about; at least that's what they had been told. They had a responsibility to educate and lead all those less fortunate than themselves. A duty to undo the mistakes made by those that had come before, the worst of which was the Viet Nam war. It had been Martin's idea to meet the returning soldiers at the airport gate wrapped in body bags with the words *Baby Killer* painted across the front. It had been someone else's idea to bring along a gallon of pig's blood. "We were so stupid, so immature," he said.

"You deserved everything that you got. If I'd been capable, I would have joined in." McDaniels's voice was flat and even, which made Martin's shame all the more sharp.

"I have never regretted anything more than that . . . day, in my life," he said, his voice a little louder. "I don't think I ever got to apologize, at least publicly." Martin had been a minor at the time and, despite having been one of the instigators, he was never prosecuted. He was expelled from college, though. The dean visited him in his hospital room and delivered the official notification personally, along with his scathing opinion of Nathan and his fine friends.

They rode in silence for a while. "I still have the *Time* magazine cover," McDaniels said, and Martin wanted to crawl away. "I framed it. It was the first time I had ever been in a national magazine. I don't remember if you were in it, though."

"They couldn't print pictures of me or give my name because I was a minor at the time." Martin was starting to think that maybe they weren't driving fast enough.

"That's right; I remember now. They wouldn't even let you testify. Whatever happened to the other ones, the ones who were old enough to be held responsible for their actions?"

"Why don't we talk about Jaime Avanti instead?" Martin was having one of the worst days of his life. First, Amanda had resurfaced and dredged up all his shortcomings as a physician; the virus that he had hoped had disappeared turned up in the brain of a dead man; and now McDaniels appeared to remind him of how thoroughly irresponsible and reckless he had been when he was younger. All that was missing was for an old girl-friend to appear on the nightly news, describing in detail every one of his physical inadequacies.

"Life certainly takes some strange twists, doesn't it, Nathan? Can I call you Nathan? For almost forty-six years I have wanted to confront you, and now here you are, a captive audience, and suddenly I no longer have the desire to tell you what I think of you or your well-bred, well-educated friends. I want to thank you for that."

McDaniels paused, but Martin didn't have a response. The silence between them grew, and then the moment passed.

McDaniels continued, "Jaime Avanti walked into the Pentagon thirty-seven days ago. Before that, he was the subject of a worldwide search. He is, or as he would have us believe, was a member of Al-Qaeda. We know that at one time, he was a close confident of bin Laden, but now he insists that he is no longer in contact with anyone within the Al-Qaeda network. Our intelligence believes him to be a founding member of a group that calls itself Jeser. It's Arabic for "bridge." It is our belief that Avanti and a few other non-Arabs parted ways with bin Laden before 9/11 and that they have been exploring other means to inflict harm upon the U.S. and its interests, beyond the use of airliners.

"I have had two conversations with Avanti, and I will tell you this—he scares the hell out of me. He is cold, calculating, and very, very smart. He is not the type of man to simply turn himself in, or to sacrifice himself for the cause. I am certain that he is executing a well-thought-out plan. He gives me the impression that he is holding four aces, and I need you to tell me if he's bluffing."

"I really don't know him well enough to tell if he is bluffing you or not. What I can tell you now is that if he is responsible for the virus in Colorado, he may very well be holding five aces."

"If that's the case, then why is he here?" McDaniels asked rhetorically.

"Obviously, he wants something, and he thinks I can either give it to him or get it for him." Martin couldn't think of a single thing Avanti could want from him. Even illegal viral pathogens were seemingly available to him.

The two Suburbans took an exit into an enclave of large, gated homes and continued their breakneck pace down the two-lane roads. Puzzled, Martin looked around at the surroundings. "You've got him out here?"

"It's safer, more secure, and private," McDaniels said. "Besides, he insisted."

***

Patton stormed through the detectives' bullpen enveloped in a cloud of confusion and frustration that discouraged any of the half-dozen detectives from asking questions. He closed the door to his office and lowered the blinds. He needed time to think.

He took a pen and legal pad and drew a line down the middle of the page. On the left side, he wrote in block letters *Van Der*, and on the right, *Yaeger*. For the next few minutes, he wrote short notes about each case. Both columns started with *Tall, Dark Man*, but the Yaeger column had *Klaus Reisch* written next to it. Witnesses came next: Phil Rucker on the left and James Michener on the right. Then, *murder?* under Van Der, and *attempted murder?* under Yaeger. *No wounds* for the Van Der column, and *no contact* for the Yaeger column. Finally, *Taurus—Rental* on the left, and *BMW—Stolen*, on the right. He wrote two more entries under the Yaeger column: *Amanda* and *injured*. He drew a box around the last two entries, and then after a moment added another question mark.

He surveyed his work and waited for inspiration to make some sense out of it, but all he felt was hunger. He turned his chair towards the window and purposely cleared his mind. More snow was starting to fall across his adopted city. The wind was picking up as well, and clouds of snow swirled around the downtown buildings. Patton could barely make out the interstate, even though it was less than a half mile away. Nothing on it moved. He could see a few abandoned cars on the elevated section; otherwise, it was deserted. He sat and stared, trying not to think of anything. A patrol car approached the Third Avenue overpass, and he wondered if it would have more success with the slippery hill than had the drivers of the abandoned vehicles. Patton watched, but at the last minute, the state trooper slowed and came to a stop, his vehicle blocking the traffic lanes and officially closing the overpass. Patton was disappointed and was suddenly filled with annoyance at the state police's inability to find Reisch.

The spell broken, he admonished himself for thinking of the tall, dark man. Maybe he should just start thinking of him as the German. Either way, the rules of the game dictated that he turn away from the pieces of the puzzle and think about something else. It was a trick some shrink had tried to teach him years ago, but it only worked if he could completely clear his mind of the problem. Then his subconscious could work on all the pieces and magically reassemble them into a coherent picture. The problem was that he could never completely clear his mind.

"Magic," he said to his frosty window. That was the missing piece. He smiled. "That's it; I've solved the case." He spun his chair back and faced his desk. "Klaus Reisch, you are a magician, and now you've vanished into thin air." He returned to the legal pad and had to restrain himself from writing four-letter words all over it. After tossing the legal pad in the garbage can, he turned to his computer. He keyed in the name Klaus Reisch, but every databank he tried came up empty—nothing local, statewide, or even federal. This was the kind of luck he was used to, not the Johnny-on-the-spot witness, or the tracks in the snow leading right to the perp's parked car. He did have a couple off-the-books sources he could tap, one in Homeland Security and another in the CIA, of all places.

He stared at the phone, wondering if he should call one of them. It was late in Washington, after business hours, which narrowed the choices down to his brother-in-law at the agency. A stab of pain and longing struck him when he remembered his beloved Connie talking about her brother, the spy. He really wasn't a spy, but he was a senior analyst. Patton hated treading on family ties, but his gut told him to make the call. If he ended up looking like a fool, it wouldn't be the first time. He opened his cell phone, hit the number four, and held it long enough for the phone to beep and make the connection.

"Michael, did I catch you at work?" Patton kept his voice light. He had always been on good terms with his brother-in-law, but their relationship had subtly and understandably changed after Connie's death.

"Rodney! How the hell are you? Man, I haven't heard from you in a couple of months. So what's new?" Michael Weigel sounded genuinely happy to hear from Patton. "Is the baby here?"

"No, we are all still waiting." The thought of his new grandson buoyed Patton for an instant. "You may have heard that we're having a bit of a problem up here, and I was wondering if I could bounce a name off you?" He just didn't have the heart for any more small talk.

"Sure. Is this an official request, or more of a discreet inquiry?"

"Let me tell you what I know, and you tell me what would be best for you." Patton described the events at the Van Ders' and then later at the hotel. "In both cases, this tall, dark man is somehow central. Now, this is where things get a little strange. Both witnesses say that this tall guy never actually touched either victim, and my officer, the one who survived, insists that this guy—now don't laugh—reached into his head and tried to kill him by squeezing his brain." Patton paused to let the absurdity sink in.

"Okay, that is strange. Sounds like your officer had some head trauma that the witness missed." Michael's tone was all business.

"That's what I thought as well, but I checked with the hospital before I got back here, and there is no sign of one. Yaeger, that's my officer, said he heard a name in his head, Klaus Reisch, and he was fairly certain that this guy was a German. He was also ranting about some woman named Amanda hurting Reisch. I know that this is probably a wild-goose chase, but I'll be honest with you, Michael . . . Things are not going well here, and chasing wild geese is about all I've got left."

Michael didn't respond for several seconds. "Klaus Reisch, did I hear you correctly?" he finally said, but all familiarity and ease was gone from his voice.

"Yes, that's what he said. Klaus Reisch." Patton had picked up on the change in his brother-in-law's manner.

"This is strange, Rodney, very, very strange. There are probably fewer than twenty people in the whole agency who know that name, and that he is a German. What are the odds that your brother-in-law just happened to be one of them?" His voice was low and thoughtful.

"So this guy really does exist?" Patton said, with surprise. With the way this day had been going, the only thing that should have surprised him was that he could still be surprised.

"Some of us, most of us, think so. He's sort of the Carlos the Jackal of our generation. He's so good, no one is really sure that he exists. We stopped hearing about him a few years back, and some of us thought that he had retired."

"This can't be the same guy. Our man was sloppy and amateurish," Patton said, feeling better that he wasn't chasing some international criminal legend. "Maybe he's just using your guy's name as an alias."

"Maybe, but I doubt it." Michael paused. "Rodney, I would like you to make a formal inquiry about these events, and I think it would be appropriate to include Mr. Reisch by name. I'm not at liberty to discuss this matter any further, but I can tell you that very recently that name has come up in conversations with people far above my pay grade."

"This doesn't sound too good," Patton said, the weight of this recent development adding to the burden he was already carrying.

"Let me give you some advice. Stay away from this one. About fifteen years ago, we put together a task force to track this son of a bitch. He grew up working for the Soviets, and even those ruthless bastards had to keep him on the shortest possible leash. But after the wall fell, he began to freelance. Rumor has it that he even went after a couple of his Russian handlers. They're scared shitless of this guy. One of the old KGB boys told me that he goes to bed every night worried that he's going to wake up with Reisch standing over him."

"Any physical description?" Patton knew what was coming: tall, thin, and dark.

"Tall, really tall. Six and a half feet, maybe, but apparently he's rail thin, maybe a hundred eighty pounds. Don't hold me to that—this guy is like a ghost. Even with the Russians' help, we could never find anyone who actually had seen him in the flesh."

Chapter 23

Amanda realized that she had shocked Oliver to the core, but for the moment she ignored his distress while the memory of the Korean spy's slow, exquisite death played through her mind in vivid detail.

Oh those were the days, Mittens whispered from the shadows.

"You speak of a man's death with such utter disregard," Oliver finally said.

Reluctantly, Amanda left the dying man and returned to the priest that faced her. "That's not true; I regard his death very highly," she said, with an evil grin.

"That's not what I mean and you know it. I believe in the sanctity of human life. All human life." Oliver's round Irish face was turning red and Amanda felt the anger rise within him. For a third time he momentarily allowed it to color his thinking and then the anger dissipated without having a lasting impact.

"How do you do that?" Amanda leaned closer to Oliver and she felt an uncomfortable tingling in her skin. "I felt you get mad, and then it just faded away."

"My emotions don't rule me," he answered with resolution. "I would like to get back to the man you murdered. How did you survive?" His voice was a bit terse, and for a moment Amanda wasn't certain she liked his tone, but then she too let it pass.

Amanda looked down, unbuttoned the top three buttons of her blouse, and then slipped the sleeve over her shoulder. The skin was smooth. "I shouldn't have, and I should also have a scar." She pulled her sleeve back into place and rebuttoned her blouse. "I was less than ten feet away when he shot me. Ted was probably twenty feet away, and the bullet passed right through him. He had an exit wound as big as a grapefruit. I ended up with a bruise and a sore shoulder."

"How is that possible?"

"It took me a couple years to figure it out." She reached down and found her purse. After rummaging through it for a moment, she extracted a photograph and passed it to Oliver. "This was taken a couple of months after I came home, just before I went to Washington."

Oliver studied the photo while Amanda returned to her purse and found a second picture. Greg Flynn in a bathing suit, and standing behind an elaborate sand castle were two other figures, but their faces were obscured by a starburst of color. "All right, I see Greg, and I think that's Lisa standing next to him, but the third person—"

"Is me."

"Did this get wet?" Oliver asked.

"No." She pushed the second photo towards him. "What do you see in this one?"

"You," Oliver said. "You wore your hair longer then." He returned the photo. "I don't get it."

"The first photo is on regular film—the old fashioned kind. The second is a digital picture that responds only to specific wavelengths of light." She gathered the two pictures and looked back up at him. "All living beings emit a tiny electrical field that some photographic films can detect. Remember back in high school science class when you put your hand on a cathode ray tube and sparks seemed to fly from your fingers? This is the same thing. Somehow the infection increases the strength of that field."

"To the point where it can deflect bullets?" Oliver was openly skeptical.

"It sounds ridiculous, I know, but I was shot. He didn't miss. I remember throwing my hands up just before he fired, so I did have an instant to react."

Oliver took another full minute to respond. "So, in that instant this electrical field slowed down the bullet," he said in a controlled voice that betrayed the difficulty he was having in grasping the concept.

Amanda wasn't surprised by his attitude. "I know it's hard to believe, but there's no other explanation for how I survived—or for this." She tossed a small object on his desk, and it came down with a muted thud.

Oliver examined the flattened metal object. It was about the size of a half dollar, gray, and dense. One side was completely smooth, and the other was pitted and irregular.

"I had Greg check that. It once was a bullet. I found it at the feet of the man I killed."

Oliver rubbed his thumb down a well-worn groove. "It's like my crucifix," he said softly. "What happened after you came home—from Washington, I mean?"

"It took the FBI only a few months to piece it all together. Apparently, there were enough witnesses to get a fairly accurate description of me, and then I guess it was just a matter of cross-checking airline records and hotel records. Don't ever underestimate the FBI when they really want something. After they finally had my name, all the pieces seemed to come together. They linked what happened to me in Honduras and Ted's association with the Chinese, and a conspiracy was born.

"When they came to arrest me, I was living in a small apartment not very far from here. They brought along a SWAT team, just for little old me." She flashed her evil grin again. "They surrounded the complex and took a couple of shots at me. Both went awry. I was forced to disable several of them."

Again, Oliver had a distressed look on his face.

"I have been on the move ever since," she added.

"Did you kill any of them?"

"No. By that point I had regained some control over my emotions, but more importantly, I had promised Greg and Lisa that I would stop. I have kept that promise ever since."

"So, Greg has known about this all along. That would explain his reaction this morning. Aren't you afraid that they'll find you?"

"They won't find me unless I let them."

"How can you be so sure?"

"Because I've done this for a long time, and I can always tell when they're near."

"How?"

"It's not so different from what you've already been doing." Amanda leaned forward in her chair. "Can you feel the people in the next room?"

At first, Oliver didn't understand the question, but after a moment he switched his attention from Amanda to the people in the front office. "Yes, I can."

"How many are there?"

Oliver hesitated a moment. "Six. Five, the Deacon just left. "

"How do you know that?"

Oliver hesitated even longer. "I honestly don't know."

"Is your right knee bent or straight?"

"What?" He said trying to follow her sudden change in conversation. "Bent."

"How do you know?"

"I've got nerves in my knee which send electrical signals to my brain." Oliver's expression was openly skeptical.

"This is no different. It's not magic, it is purely physiologic. A portion of your brain senses the presence of others and responds with the same electrical signals the nerves use in your knee." Amanda watched Oliver's face and quietly listened to his thoughts. "Everyone has this ability; in some it's very latent, in others it's a little more accessible." Oliver slowly shook his head in a sign of reluctant acceptance. "In time it will become second nature; you will be much more aware of your environment. Of course, you can also take it a step further."

Oliver suddenly grabbed his head.

"I'm sorry, but at least one time you should experience what happens when you turn your mind into a laser pointer," Amanda said. "You can quite literally rip through someone's mind, exposing their deepest thoughts, emotions, and memories. It will tell you everything you ever needed to know about someone in an instant. It will also disable them. One last thing—it's a two-way street. You will be just as exposed as your . . ." She hesitated for an instant, because she was about to finish her sentence with the word *victim*. "Subject," she finally said.

"So that's how you do it. I mean, did it." Oliver stumbled over the words. "That's how you used to kill people."

"That's one way. This is another." The letter opener on Oliver's desk suddenly flew across the room and embedded itself deep in the plaster wall. "The infection not only strengthens the bioelectric field around us, it allows us to direct it."

"Scary," he said. "This whole thing is scary. That laser pointer, I've felt that before. I don't have a clear memory, but Klaus Reisch used it on me."

"That doesn't surprise me. He's been looking for me for a while. He probably hoped that I had maintained contact with someone at the church. Before this morning I wasn't completely certain he existed. Over the years I've occasionally caught a trace of someone, but until recently I was never sure whether it was real or simply imagined."

"He tried to kill me only because I had seen him." Oliver's face started to turn red again, and anger clipped off his words. "He's got to be caught and brought to justice."

Amanda suddenly laughed. She knew how rude she was being, but the absurdity of what Oliver had just said overwhelmed her manners. "Father, do you really believe that there can be justice for someone like Klaus Reisch?" Amanda shook her head, surprised by Oliver's naïveté. "You don't arrest people like him; you kill them."

As painfully as possible, Mittens quietly added.

"I don't appreciate being patronized, Amanda, and you can't possibly believe that I would be a party to cold, calculated murder, even if it is a monster like Reisch."

His irritation wiped the smile from her face. "I'm sorry for laughing, Father, but there are some things you just don't understand." She hesitated, wondering if she should tell Oliver what Reisch had planned. *He'll overreact and go off half-cocked*, she thought. *Already, he's wondering if he should turn me in for killing a few criminals. What would he do if he knew Reisch was planning on killing millions of innocents?*

Something that would probably get him killed, or worse, she answered herself. Despite his willful naiveté, she liked Oliver. He was a good man who had spent his life trying to live his beliefs, and she didn't want to see him hurt.

"He's going to keep killing and infecting people until he's caught," Oliver said, filling the void in the conversation.

"Probably, but who do you think can catch him, our government? Maybe you didn't know, but he's a trained assassin, and governments around the world have been trying to catch him for decades. Let's also not forget the small fact that he has the same abilities that I have. Besides, once they know what he's capable of, their desire to stop him will be overshadowed by their desire to use him."

Oliver looked at her strangely. The animosity she had for the authorities shone brightly.

"Use him or not," Oliver said, "he has to be stopped; that's first and foremost. Besides, I don't believe 'they' exist, Amanda. Once people know what he is and what he has done, he'll spend the rest of his life in jail." Oliver's face was turning a deeper shade of red as his energized emotions were finally having an impact. "I know you don't trust the government and, after what happened to you, I can't really blame you. But you have to know that yours was an isolated incident, nothing more. Every institution has a few individuals who will take advantage of their position, and our government is no exception, but like it or not, they are the only ones with the resources to stop Reisch."

No, they aren't, she almost said. Finding Reisch would be easy; catching him might be a little tricky. *Killing him would be a pleasure,* Mittens added. "Listen, Oliver," she said, dropping his title, "forget the government. If Reisch is stopped, it will be because I have stopped him." Her face hardened, and her eyes took on a cruel light.

This is the face others saw before they died. Oliver's thought hit Amanda hard, but it didn't stop her.

"He is hurt, but he will recover, and when he does, he will not hesitate to kill anyone in his path. Including you . . . especially you." Amanda bore into Oliver. "This is the grown-ups' table, Father, and we all play by the same rules. You deal with Reisch as cruelly and as violently as he would deal with you. Notions of due process and justice don't belong here. They will only get more people killed." Amanda was starting to get seriously aggravated. *Why did it have to be a priest?* she thought.

"This argument is giving me an old-fashioned headache," Oliver said as he began to rub his temples again. "For almost thirty years, I have witnessed some of the most vile, dehumanizing behavior you or anyone else could possibly imagine. In Rwanda, I set up an orphanage for twenty-two small children whose parents had been tortured and then burned alive just because they were in the wrong clan. As a warning to neighboring tribes, each one of those children had had their right arm severed above the elbow. The stumps were cauterized with branding irons. I don't need a lesson on what people are capable of doing. I believe that given the right set of circumstances, any person, including you, me, and even Reisch, is capable of any act, no matter how heinous or holy. I have accepted that as part of the human condition. Now, that doesn't mean that I condone the behavior. What it means is that I don't condemn the individual."

He stared at her, and she stared back, her face remaining hard.

Oliver continued, "We voluntarily constrain our behavior through the rule of law so that a society can exist, and we live by that rule, even at the grown-ups' table especially at the grown-ups' table. Otherwise, we create the very conditions that will turn us all into Reisch."

But what if we don't want to constrain our behavior? Mittens quietly asked Amanda.

Then we all turn into Reisch, Amanda answered her violent alter ego.

"The rule of law is for normal people, and we are not normal people," Mittens said using Amanda's voice. Oliver rocked back in his chair as if he had been pushed by the words, and it was clear that they needed a moment for the air to clear. "There is no point to this argument; neither one of us will convince the other," Amanda said after a suitable pause.

"So what do we do about Reisch?"

Amanda wondered how she and Oliver had suddenly become a *we*. "I haven't decided yet," she said.

"Greg could help." Oliver said with a tone Amanda knew was meant to be conciliatory.

Amanda nodded. "I will talk with him later, but you worry me. I want you to promise me that you won't do anything or expose yourself to anyone unnecessarily."

Oliver smiled. "I'm going to ignore the double meaning, and I promise not to do anything, including exposing myself unnecessarily."

Her comment had been unintentional, but well timed. "I'm sorry, Father, how politically incorrect of me to mention a priest exposing himself." She smiled as she got up.

"Be nice," he said as he too stood. He almost offered his hand, but instead put both his hands in his pockets.

Amanda noticed. "How about if I just wave good-bye." She gave him a small wave and turned to retrieve her coat. "I will call you after Greg and I speak," she said, slipping into her coat.

"I'm glad you came," he said.

Amanda stopped and turned back to Oliver. "Are you really, or are you just being polite?"

Chapter 24

"Cause of death: exsanguination. End dictation." Phil replaced the microphone and began to strip off his cloth gown and mask. He wasn't surprised that Mr. Peter Burnum had bled to death; he had been shot eleven times. Phil had recovered all the bullets, one from the left arm, three from the legs, two from the back, three from the chest, one from the abdomen, and one from the neck. There hadn't been much left of poor Peter after Phil had finished with him. He checked the clock on the wall and was surprised to find that forty-five minutes had passed since he had sent out the tissue samples, which meant that the slides should be ready for viewing. He had a fairly good idea what they would show. Burnum's brain had been swollen, red, and grossly abnormal; he was infected with this new virus. Phil had taken samples from every available organ and tissue.

It took him another two hours to sort through the slides. "Addendum to previous report. Contributing cause of death: viral encephalitis, type unknown. End dictation." They would have to give this infection a name, but that would come later. Right now, he had a different responsibility: to report this to the CDC. If they cared to give it one of their usual catchy names, then so be it. *Actually, that honor belongs to Henry Gorman*, Phil thought, surprised that it had slipped his mind. He picked up the phone and dialed the main number for the Centers for Disease Control and Prevention in Atlanta. It was after hours and, as expected, the operator routed him to the voicemail of Nathan Martin's Special Pathogens Division. Phil left a brief voicemail and hung up. His next call was to the Colorado Department of Health, and he was annoyed to find that they, too, were closed. He left his second voicemail, which was considerably more terse than the first, and then returned to the slides. He reviewed the nine that showed the clearest signs of infection; all nine came from the brain. The virus was too small to be seen with a light microscope, so he would have to wait for the electron micrographs to confirm that it was Gorman's virus that was causing the profound inflammatory reaction at the base of the brain. It was curious that the worst parts of Peter Burnum's brain were the ones most associated with memory and emotions. His thalamus, hypothalamus, and amygdaloid nuclei, along with both hippocampi, were almost liquefied.

Phil began to wonder how Burnum had survived so long. He changed objective lenses to his highest power and began to review the morphology of the individual nerve cell bodies. He started with those closest to the ventricles, but the architecture was so disturbed that he began to scan outward. The further he moved away from the fluid-filled cavities, the closer the anatomy conformed to normal.

Melissa Shay, the department's senior lab tech, quietly walked into the reading room and placed a tray of slides next to Phil. He felt her presence and looked up.

"I did a KL-124 stain on some of these," she said. The KL-124 stain was a good multipurpose stain that made inflammatory cells appear blue. "He's got loads of inflammation, but there's something strange going on here. You should look at these six slides."

Phil took the first of the six slides and held it up to the ceiling light. It was almost entirely blue. "Curious," he said. He replaced the slide that he had been scanning with the new one.

Melissa waited, and for an instant they made eye contact. He gave her a moment to say something and then went back to the slides.

Phil made a preliminary inspection and confirmed that Melissa hadn't made a mistake during the staining process, and then he focused down to the cells. As expected, the brain tissue was rife with the small blue lymphocytes indicative of a viral infection, but there was something else, something that shouldn't be there. A thick band of large, blue-stained neurons lined the walls of Peter Burnum's ventricles. Phil looked up from the microscope.

"It doesn't make any sense, but I think that's germinal matrix," Melissa said.

Normally, the brain develops from a thin layer of cells called the germinal matrix. Never more than a few cell layers thick, all the neurons a person will ever have derives from these stem cells. The problem was that the germinal matrix all but disappears in infancy, and yet Peter Burnum had a thick layer of these very special cells lining the walls of his adult ventricles.

Phil returned to the scope. The stem cells were so densely packed around the ventricles that nothing normal remained, but two to three millimeters away, the inflammation predominated. It was two sides of the same coin. A destructive inflammatory process initiated by an unknown virus, and a regenerative process that had no business being there.

"These are stained as well?" He pointed to the remaining slides in the tray.

"Most of them, but only these six are from the brain." Melissa said, with a touch of excitement.

"Right now I'm more interested in the rest of the samples." He made eye contact with her again, and this time she blushed.

"I'll have them out in fifteen minutes," she said, hurrying off.

Phil spent the next fifteen minutes looking more closely at all the remaining slides, but found nothing of interest. Melissa brought twenty newly stained slides and discreetly took a chair while Phil reviewed them. For reasons he didn't bother to explore, her presence wasn't prompting his typical xenophobic reaction; in fact, he was almost comforted by her quiet, professional interest.

An hour passed, and finally he pushed back away from the microscope. "With the exception of a small segment of bone marrow, everything else is normal," he said.

"The marrow is supposed to have some stem cells?" she asked.

"Not like these, and not clustered so tightly. The virus seems to involve the bone marrow as well as the brain."

It was a curious puzzle, and Phil didn't see any obvious connection. It was true that both the bone marrow—which was responsible for the production of the red and white blood cells—and the germinal matrix derived from the same embryonic layer but, beyond that, the brain and bone marrow had little in common. Plus, there were other tissues that also arose from the same embryonic layer, and all of them were normal.

"Is it neoplastic, maybe some kind of lymphoma of stem cells?" Melissa offered.

"No, it's not a tumor. The organization is too complex." Phil rubbed his eyes. "This is something that I've never seen before."

"We have slides from two other cases that came in today, both presumed suicides. Dr. Faraday was going to review them in the morning, but I'm sure he wouldn't mind if you looked at them tonight."

"It's after seven," Phil said.

Melissa glanced up at the clock. "This is important," she said. "Besides, I've got no one waiting on me at home, except for a very lazy border collie." She left to get the other slides.

Phil wondered why she had no one at home. Maybe she was married and her husband was out of town, or working late. Maybe she was a widow. Maybe she had never married at all. Melissa had worked for the coroner's office for eleven years, longer than he had been there, and he was surprised by how little he knew about her. He should have picked up more about her personal life just through overheard casual conversations. So why didn't he know even the most basic information about her? He waited for an answer, but none of his Monsters, not even the smart, small voice, responded. He knew the answer, of course, but he shrank from it. Melissa wasn't important to him; she wasn't a part of the small and carefully maintained Phillip Rucker universe. She was a functionary, no more critical to him than this microscope. At an abstract level, he knew that she was more important than a microscope, but he didn't—he couldn't—live in an abstract world. His behavior and thoughts were ruled by the concrete codes of Personal Responsibility and The Routine.

Phil stood and stretched his sore, stiff back; at least that hadn't changed. It dawned on him that this was the second time that day that he had found himself exploring beyond the borders of the Phillip Rucker universe, and he was surprised by how far he could venture beyond the usual narrow range of safe-thought without reprisal.

Melissa returned and placed a rack of slides next to his microscope. "Here is the first set," she said. Phil noticed a small stripe of lighter skin on her left fourth finger.

Two possibilities, he thought. She's married and has taken off her wedding ring, probably for safekeeping while she works, or she once wore a ring, but doesn't now.

"The second rack needs to be restained. I didn't like the way it came out," she said, and even Phil picked up on the fact that she was covering for the shoddy work of one of her junior technicians.

"Thank you," Phil said stiffly, trying to reestablish their normal boundaries. He reached for the first slide in the rack as Melissa left to restain the second set of slides. Phil quickly scanned the twenty-eight slides from the two patients and again found exactly what he had found in Peter

Burnum's brain: large cells lining both victims' ventricles. *Stem cells*, he thought. Somehow, the virus had reactivated the long-dormant process of cellular differentiation. The implications were incredible. If the lethal aspects of the virus could be eliminated, this virus would be a medical miracle. Strokes, brain injuries, spinal cord injuries, leukemia—almost every degenerative process could be reversed. Phil's powerful mind began to reel with possibilities.

Melissa had returned with the second rack, and as she was retrieving the original set of slides, her hand accidentally brushed his.

Phil's next conscious thought was: *Where am I?* He was on his back with several faces staring down at him. The ground seemed to be moving, and so was the ceiling. *A stretcher*, he thought. His arms were tied down, and an oxygen mask covered his face. People were talking to him, but a pain in his head prevented him from hearing them. "My head," he said through the mask, and his head lolled to the right. He spotted Melissa among the various legs and torsos. She had her own facemask, and some stranger was pushing down on her chest. "What happened?" he asked her, his words slurred. His vision began to blur as well, and then she was gone, along with everything else.

Chapter 25

"Someone will always need to rule," Pushkin said.

"Then it will be the most capable, the most powerful mind. We will create a society in perfect harmony with the natural laws." Reisch answered.

"And if that turns out to be Amanda, or someone like her, how will you respond?" The car stayed very quiet for a very long time as Reisch ignored his mentor's question. "Are you leaving, or are you going to stay around for the fireworks?" Pushkin wisely changed subjects.

"I'm leaving," Reisch finally responded. "The signal is not due for another fifty-five hours, and it can be sent from anywhere."

"Wake me when we get there," Pushkin said as he dissolved into the passenger seat.

Reisch checked the satchel again; it was back where he had put it before the Russian returned. He was glad for the silence and solitude. Pushkin had always been able to twist Klaus's ideas back on to themselves. It had started out as a lesson in logic, but over the decades it had turned into a game, a game Reisch rarely won.

As he negotiated the turn south, Reisch questioned whether Pushkin was worth the trouble. *Probably not*, he concluded, but he did owe the Russian his life.

***

Thirty years earlier, a newly graduated Klaus went to Amsterdam for a weeklong vacation, and then decided to stay permanently. The permissive society was ideal for his sociopathic tendencies, and he frequently exercised them. He was finally content and for two years enjoyed his intellectual, physical, and moral freedom. Then, as he later concluded, fate intervened and dramatically altered his young life. Finding himself low on funds, he attempted a simple transaction with an elderly woman and her purse. As it turned out, she was quite fond of her purse, and when Klaus tried to run with it, he found that she was still attached. He dragged the screaming woman a full block before being tackled by an American tourist, who beat him into unconsciousness. The entire affair was caught on tape by the American's wife, and a sanitized version aired repeatedly on CNN for the next week. When Klaus faced the magistrate, he was arguably the most hated man in all the Netherlands. His bandaged face and broken ribs did nothing to lessen the sentence of three years.

A month later, Reisch was back before the same magistrate after killing another inmate. The man, twice the size of Klaus, had been terrorizing the young German since his arrival, seemingly with the tacit approval of the guards. His assailant had every physical advantage, but Reisch had patience and endured the torment, waiting for an opportunity. It came one afternoon when the brute lunged for Klaus's lunch tray. He stepped away from his attacker, swept the thug's legs from beneath him, and then crushed the man's throat with his boot. He stood over the dying man as he suffocated. In fairness, the guards also watched the man die before intervening and subduing Reisch. His sentence was changed to thirty years in a maximum-security prison. After attempting to kill the magistrate in the courtroom, he once again was subdued and later hospitalized.

Pushkin found the broken and bandaged Reisch in an Amsterdam hospital a month later. "I see nothing in you to justify my eight-hour flight," he said after appraising the young man. "You are nothing more than a common criminal. A thug unworthy of my time or assistance."

"Then why are you bothering me? Can't you see I have things to do?" Reisch waved a shackled and casted arm.

Pushkin laughed only for an instant and then became deadly serious. "I am here to take you away, which will fulfill a promise I made a long time ago. Before that happens, however, you must understand one thing: you mean nothing to me. Your life is mine, and if I, for whatever reason, decide to take it, I will. If you attempt to escape I will find you and kill you. Slowly. If you do not do as I say, you will be punished. Severely. If you listen to what I say and do what I tell you to do, you may survive. Although your present circumstance does not fill me with confidence."

In all the years that followed Reisch never learned the name of his true benefactor.

***

Twenty minutes later, Colorado's unbroken fields of snow began to give way to tracts of homes as he approached a small town. Streetlights and sidewalks appeared next, and then a red light forced him to stop for the first time in two hours. Three of the four street corners had houses on them, but at the fourth corner there was a convenience store with gas pumps. A police cruiser sat empty just in front of the doors. For an instant, Reisch wondered if Colorado had enough resources to stake out every gas station in the state. It was a ridiculous thought, but the unaccustomed fear rising in his chest somehow made it sound reasonable.

The light changed, and he slowly drove through the intersection. He brushed up against the mind of the officer inside the store, but the contact was so brief that he couldn't be sure they weren't looking for him.

The residential area gradually became industrial. Silos and railway cars lined the highway. He drove two more miles and suddenly realized that he was outside the town limits. The streetlights and sidewalks had disappeared, and vacant wheat fields once again stretched before him. He slowed the SUV and then turned back towards town.

He made the first left he came to, and the industrial landscape quickly changed to commercial. A large supermarket appeared to his left and a Walmart to his right. The usual complement of fast-food restaurants and video stores came next, and among them he found a busy gas station. He swung the Mercedes in and coasted in front of one of the sixteen pumps. As he climbed out of the truck, he was happy to see that his right leg was almost back to normal. His right hand was still clumsy, and he fumbled with his wallet but managed to pass the attendant two twenty-dollar bills without calling too much attention to himself. It took him several minutes to fill the tank, and not a soul noticed him. He began to relax slightly. He was just another mindless American filling up his oversized foreign car with overpriced foreign gas.

Just before climbing back in, he allowed his mind to unreel for a quick peek around. Dozens of dull, undisciplined minds assailed him. He sifted through them quickly, but none of them had any interest in finding him. His mental search area was only a couple of square blocks, at best, but it was good enough to convince him to stay the night. He climbed back into the Mercedes and drove farther up the street. A Motel 6 beckoned, and he drove into the large, crowded parking lot. There were a few dark and secluded parking spots in the back, and he nosed the Mercedes into the darkest one and turned off the engine. He waited, listening with both his ears and his mind. Nothing. He climbed out and quickly walked away from the vehicle. It was unlikely that the SUV would have been reported missing this early, but of late, luck had been working against him.

The office was locked, and a small, hand-written sign taped to the glass door told him to ring the bell. He brushed off the small accumulation of snow and pressed the buzzer. He felt a mind stir and a mumbled curse. A moment later, the handle buzzed, and Reisch pulled open the door.

"Evening," said the portly, balding man in a blue T-shirt, with about as much interest as someone scheduling a dental appointment. He collected some papers and pushed them towards Reisch as he stepped up to the desk. "One night?" He had a large anchor tattooed across his left bicep. It covered a once well-muscled arm, which now sagged as much as his belly.

"Yes," answered Reisch. Brevity served his purpose as well. He quietly filled out the reservation form. His right hand had recovered enough to use the pen that was chained to the desk, but the going was slow. The fat man watched impatiently with bored eyes. Reisch almost laughed out loud when his mind saw the TV dinner and the game show that waited for the surly clerk in the next room.

"Sixty-two fifty," the man said hurriedly after quickly retrieving the forms from Reisch. He accepted the money from the German and dropped a key onto the cracked counter. "Room 127. Out the door, turn right, half-way down." He stacked and filed the papers, and then as an afterthought said, "Checkout is at eleven." Before Reisch could turn, the man had disappeared behind the office door.

Room 127 was exactly what he had expected. Threadbare carpet, cheap furniture, a smell of industrial-strength disinfectant, and an overly hard mattress. The television worked, and he turned it to the network news. Most of it centered on the assassination of the governor. Reisch stripped the bed linen and lay fully dressed on the mattress while waiting for the local news. Twenty minutes later, the local news from Denver began. Again, it was almost all about the dead governor, but near the end of the allotted thirty minutes, the beautiful brunette newscaster switched to something more of interest to Reisch.

"There was other news today. An elderly man was found dead outside of his Colorado Springs home early this morning. Eighty-two-year-old George Van Der was discovered by neighbors just before seven. The police have described the circumstances surrounding his death as suspicious."

Reisch was impressed with the woman's ability to look both serious and seductive while describing murder, and wondered what she would look like stripped naked, tied to a bed.

"Since the first of the year, there have been thirty-one murders in and around Colorado Springs. In a related story, a man is being sought for questioning in the assault on a Colorado Springs patrolman. A spokesperson for the CSPD states that the two cases may be related . . ."

Two black and white sketches filled the screen, and Reisch was shocked to recognize his own face. The image on the right showed him in a hat with dark glasses, but the one on the left was a dead-on likeness.

" . . . stable condition with undisclosed injuries. The assailant is described as being six feet five inches, two hundred pounds, and wearing a black overcoat and pants. He was last seen driving a stolen black late-model BMW. The police ask that if anyone has seen this individual, they contact the Colorado Springs Police Department, or the Colorado State Police." The brunette had reappeared, and two phone numbers floated beneath her. "This individual is considered armed and extremely dangerous and should not be approached."

"Mandy, do the police have any comment on this unprecedented outbreak of violence?" The venerable, white-haired anchor set up his sexy co-anchor.

"Well, John, as you know, the local, state, and federal authorities have been looking into this problem for a while now, and they admit to being stumped. Usually, this type of violence indicates a gang or drug problem, but that's simply not the case here. What we are seeing are previously normal citizens suddenly becoming irrationally, and in some cases extremely, violent. The Colorado Health Department has also investigated these strange events, but they haven't been able to provide an explanation either. At this current rate, Colorado Springs will log more murders this year than Chicago, New York, Philadelphia, and of course, Denver." She managed to maintain both her grave look and the sparkle in her eyes.

"Pueblo is not that far from Colorado Springs, Mandy. Any speculation that the governor's assassination may be related?"

"We do know that Peter Burnum had spent time in Colorado Springs as late as three weeks ago, but no one is commenting on a connection."

Reisch began flipping through the channels, but the coverage was virtually identical and he finally turned off the television. The death of the governor was completely inconsequential. The man was fated to die along with the rest of his constituency in a matter of days, and his assassination simply saved him from a protracted and painful death. The spreading violence and the inability of the Americans to determine its source eased some of Reisch's anxiety over the sketches. Under normal conditions, they would be nothing more than an irritant, an object lesson of carelessness. But these weren't normal conditions; Amanda Flynn had seen to that. She was still out there, waiting for him to reveal himself, and he was in no condition to renew their struggle.

"Sleep, that's all I need," he said. "Then I will disappear, and you will die along with everyone else, Amanda." A vision of her blistered face, wracked with pain and anguish, filled his sleepy mind, and Klaus drifted into a pleasant, dreamless sleep.

Chapter 26

It was late, and Martin was surprised to see so many people out walking the neat sidewalks. The two SUVs flashed down the streets at three times the legal speed limit, but no one seemed to be bothered by it. In fact, no one seemed to even notice. The Suburban braked suddenly, and Martin strained against the shoulder harness. The big vehicle turned sharply to the right, and he was squeezed against the door. McDaniels sat comfortably, convincing Martin that Marines really were immune to the laws of physics. The driver accelerated for a moment and then once again braked sharply. Martin lurched forward as the lead vehicle stopped in front of a large, well-lit brick wall, where they waited only long enough for an oversized wrought-iron gate to swing open, and then both trucks were off again. They raced down a lane lined with tall, well-tended ivy hedges, and even if there had been enough light, Martin doubted he would have seen anything more than just a blur of green.

A half mile later, the driver finally pried his foot off the accelerator and expertly coasted to a stop in front of a large Tudor manor. *Old money*, Martin thought as he scanned the front of the mansion. At least three stories, the façade was as tall and as long as the Suburban allowed Martin to see. Etched leaded glass windows with brass inlays framed a two-story portico. Marble steps lit by a sparkling silver chandelier led to massive oak doors. This wasn't one of the McMansions that were springing up all over the greater Atlanta area; this was wealth with a capital W.

"This is the place," McDaniels said.

For once, Martin was at a loss for words. He tried to think of something clever to say, but the ride, the anticipation of seeing Avanti, and the fact that he had no idea what he was doing here tied his usually glib tongue. "Okay," was the best he could manage.

"All we need from you is a threat assessment. Let him lead the discussion. Don't try to be clever; just listen." McDaniels tried to sound encouraging, but to Martin's ear, he sounded more like a baseball coach who was forced to put his weakest player into a close game

Martin had to stop himself from saying, "Okay, coach." Instead, he said, "I understand. I guess I'm doing this alone."

McDaniels nodded.

"Do I wear a wire, or something?"

"No, I don't want you to be a secret agent. I just want you to listen, and tell me how badly we're screwed."

The driver of the Suburban suddenly opened Martin's door, and he jumped. "You're not even coming in?" The pitch of his voice was rising.

"No. It's just you and Avanti. You'll be fine. He can't hurt you."

"How do you know?" The words were out of his mouth before he even registered the thought. "I'm sorry. I'm just a little out of my element."

McDaniels gave an almost imperceptible nod to the enlisted man, who reached in and helped Martin out of the car. "I know. Just listen to the man. You can do that."

The sergeant led Martin up the marble staircase. *They're too grand to be steps*, Martin thought, trying to distract himself with the opulence as the young Marine quietly opened one of the twelve-foot doors.

"He will be waiting for you in the library, sir. Across the foyer, first door on your right."

Martin stepped into the dark entranceway, wondering how a Marine sergeant came by the word "foyer." The door closed behind him with a small but resounding click. It was dark, and if it hadn't been for the lights of the two SUVs shining through the thick glass, it would have been completely black. "Hello," he called out tentatively. His voice echoed as if he were on a sound stage.

"In here, Dr. Martin," returned a thickly accented and gruff voice.

Martin immediately recalled the distinctive voice and followed it into a dark room. His eyes had started to adjust, and he could make out several wing-backed chairs arranged around a large table. One of the chairs was occupied. The thick smell of books filled the air, and he was suddenly reminded of his medical school's library.

"Excuse the darkness. I no longer have need of light, but if you feel it is necessary, there is a lamp on the table."

Martin found it and clicked it on. The harsh light momentarily blinded him, but he could see that the man in the chair didn't react.

"It is somewhat ironic that I prefer this room, don't you think, Dr. Martin? It's the smell, I think."

Martin remained standing, taking stock of what was left of Jaime Avanti. He was blind—that much was obvious. His pupils were completely dilated even in the harsh lamplight, the whites of his eyes had taken on a sickly yellow hue, and what was left of Avanti was barely recognizable. Martin remembered a thick and robust man, the prototypical Russian. *Ukrainian*, Martin corrected himself, but time had not been kind. Gone were the large belly and the powerful arms and shoulders; what remained was a skeleton, a shadow of his former self. Even his trademark hirsuteness was gone. Patches of white hair covered a wrinkled skull, and a thin beard reached down to his sunken chest.

"I am told that my appearance has changed over the past twenty years. I'm guessing that yours has as well, but hopefully not as much as mine."

"No, it hasn't," Martin said in a voice full of surprise and disgust. He hadn't given any thought as to how he would react seeing Avanti, a man he once knew who had chosen to become a terrorist. "You look like shit, Jaime," he said, with undisguised loathing.

"That's what I like about you Jews: no beating around the bush. Yes, I probably do look like shit, but that's not why you are here. What have your military people told you?"

"That you broke into my lab and stole samples of Ebola, among other things." Martin moved to a chair opposite Avanti and sat down, completely comfortable that what was left of Jaime Avanti posed no physical threat.

"'Among other things?' You are exactly as I remembered, Nathan, pompous and self-absorbed." Avanti's voice was tired. "A slow-acting virus has been released into the population of Colorado. It is a mutated and less virulent form of the virus you know as EDH1. I believe that this may have been one of the 'other things' General McDaniels shared with you."

"We have reviewed a case of viral encephalitis from Colorado, and electron microscopy does confirm an unknown virus that looks very much like EDH1. However, it is a single case, and hardly worth all this drama." Martin tried to keep his voice relaxed and casual.

"I estimate that over the next three months, more than twenty-three thousand citizens of Colorado will die as a direct result of the infection, and a much larger number will be affected by, shall we say, the consequences of the infection." He turned his face towards Martin and smiled wide enough to expose his yellow teeth. "Perhaps that's worth a little drama."

Martin was glad that Avanti couldn't watch the color drain from his face.

"Now that I have your attention," Avanti continued, "I need to impress upon you the seriousness of this situation. I asked you here so that we may discuss this as colleagues."

"You stopped being my colleague the moment you threatened innocent lives."

"Innocent. So self-righteous . . ." Avanti's voice trailed off . . . "You're not here so we could argue banalities; there are more pressing issues."

"So why am I here?"

"To hear what I have to say, and ultimately to make a decision." Avanti reached for a small briefcase on the table next to him. "Do you remember the last time we met?"

"Not clearly," Martin watched as Avanti fumbled with the latch, and had to suppress the instinct to help the blind man.

"It was the 1992 UN conference on population sustainability. You had just started working for the CDC and I was an invited guest." Avanti retrieved a glossy program guide from the briefcase and tossed it to Martin.

A collage of smiling children spelled out the word "United Nations," and beneath it in bold black script: *Social Carrying Capacity and the Population Bomb.* "I remember." Martin said softly while leafing through the distantly familiar pages. "What does any of this have to do with what you and your people have done in Colorado?"

"I need to correct a few of your misconceptions. First, they are not my people—"

Martin scoffed loudly. "Bullshit! At least give me the courtesy of the truth."

"I understand that you are under a good deal of stress, but if you could control yourself for just a little longer, perhaps we can get through this." Avanti paused for a moment and took Martin's silence as a sign that he could continue. "Now, as I was saying, they are not my people. Undoubtedly, you have been told that for a time I lived and worked with a group of 'Islamic extremists,' and it was under their umbrella that we originally created the Hybrid virus. However, I was never counted among their numbers, and I do not now wish to be remembered as one of them. They simply paid the bills and supplied the raw materials."

"I was told that you were a Muslim."

"Surely, you are not implying that all Muslims are terrorists?" Avanti chuckled.

"You seem to be both," Martin countered.

"Superficially, perhaps," Avanti smiled knowingly. "At least that's what they believe."

"Who, the Americans, or the extremists?" Martin noted that Avanti's flair for the dramatic had not dimmed with time.

"Both, of course, but in time the truth will be known." The sagging face that a moment earlier was pulled into a smile was now fixed with determination. "If you haven't guessed by now, I am quite close to death, and it is because of this that I have been sent to deliver their message. I am believed to be a good and faithful Muslim and have been given this great honor because of my service to Allah." Avanti paused and expertly reached for a glass of water on the table that separated them. "Excuse me, but my mouth gets dry so quickly these days," he said. He noisily drained the glass. "Where was I?" he said to himself.

"Delivering a message," Martin answered.

"Demands, really, and in different times I would view them as quite reasonable, but these are extraordinary times, and I have little concern for states and territories, or even for religions."

"You have me thoroughly confused," Martin said.

"The message I bring to your government is pure subterfuge. No matter what you do, the original Hybrid virus will be released, and there is nothing you or anyone can do to stop it."

"Then why bother with demands; if you intend to kill us, why not just get on with it?" A single thought kept recycling through Nathan's mind: *this is not really happening; it's just an academic exercise of a worst-case scenario.*

"From the point of view of the Islamists, it is quite reasonable. You see, they are convinced that they, along with the rest of the world, will survive this attack. That this weapon can be controlled. Their computer models, which I must say are quite sophisticated, have convinced them that the outbreak can be confined to the United States." Avanti's smile had returned.

"That's preposterous! Even the mutation that you've already released poses a worldwide threat. There is no possible way a second attack could be contained." Martin began to sweat. "How could you let them . . . ?" He cut himself off as realization exploded in his mind. "You let them believe that."

"No, I didn't let them; I had to lead them to that conclusion, and it wasn't easy. They are not madmen, much as you Americans would like to believe. They are quite sane and some are very well educated. They have no desire to destroy the world; they simply want to remake it in their own image." Avanti leaned back into the cushions of the chair, his face once again shrouded in shadow. "Dying is remarkably liberating; it allows one to think all the unthinkable thoughts," he said, his voice barely a whisper. "They may not wish to destroy the world, but I do, and they have provided me with a convenient vehicle to do just that."

"I don't understand. Most of your life has been dedicated to the eradication of disease and suffering, and now you suddenly decide to create it on a global scale!"

"Futility, utter and complete futility. What do we have to show for decades of hard work? Nothing—less than nothing. Things are far worse now than when we last met. You know the science, but you along with the rest of our 'best minds' choose to ignore it, and now we are long since past the point of no return. We had a small window back then." Avanti motioned to the conference program in Martin's hand. "But once again, we proved to be selfish, myopic people, poorly organized politically, socially, and economically, incapable of setting aside petty concerns and dealing with the obvious problems that are now out of control."

Martin reopened the program. "The 'population bomb.' That hasn't been taken seriously in more than fifty years."

"Neither was global warming until the Arctic began to melt," Avanti fired back, and Martin saw a glimpse of the old Jaime Avanti. "Twenty years ago, you yourself said that we were in retreat across every socioeconomic and environmental front. You even said it out loud: humans are the problem."

"When I said that my intent was only to stimulate discussion and, ultimately, action. Besides, what I really meant was that human nature was the problem."

"Bullshit! At least give me the courtesy of the truth," Avanti said. "I was there, I remember what you said, and we both know exactly what you meant, at least before you became a stooge for your government. I stood by what I said that day and I was stripped of everything."

Martin stared at the ruined face of the Ukrainian. He had heard of his dismissal, but really never gave it much thought. "So your plan is to eradicate the human species," he said softly.

"Not all of it. Call it a culling of the herd. Just enough to restore a social and ecological balance. A world without borders, religions, or nationalities will emerge from the ashes of the old world. "

"You're back to the problem of containing something that can't be contained."

"Now we've come to why you are here." Avanti reached for the small satchel. "Take this; open it."

Martin stood and crossed the floor that separated the two men. "What's in here?" he asked, tentatively taking the bag from Avanti.

"A choice."

Martin pulled out a small sealed canister, biohazard stickers wrapped around the length of it.

"It is all I could gather in secret. My coworkers watched that very closely. Please don't break the seal; inside is a dehydrated form of the Hybrid virus. This should help you in your work."

"What's this smaller vial?" Martin held up a glass ampule that held fifty milliliters of an amber fluid.

"Roughly one thousand doses of a vaccine that must be reformulated and administered within the next 48 hours. You see, Nathan, you are going to live, along with 999 other people of your choosing. I want you to reproduce this vaccine as rapidly as you can and distribute it worldwide. It is quite effective and should ultimately halt the spread of the infection."

"But not until after billions have died," Martin said bitterly.

"Approximately four point two billion; the computer estimates are accurate only if you begin work tomorrow."

Chapter 27

Patton watched the pretty brunette from his office television. *Great, now they want to pin the governor's assassination on us.* As if on cue, his phone began to ring. He stared at it for a moment, wondering if he had the energy to deal with the mayor. The chief was out sick, and they were the only two who would call him directly.

"Good evening, Your Honor," he said, but didn't mean it.

"Rodney, I know you've had a tough day, but I'm afraid I'm about to make it a little tougher. I just took a call from the lieutenant-governor. He's had a tough day as well, but he graciously made room in his busy schedule to rip me a new one. He's got some asshole telling him that the governor's murder is somehow connected to what's been happening here."

Publicly, the mayor was a jovial, well-spoken man. Privately, he was something very different.

"I just saw something about that on the television," Patton answered, massaging his forehead with one hand and wondering how he could have ended up so far from home, so far from where things made sense. It was one of the few times in his life that he felt completely out of step with everything around him. "I hate to say it, Billy, but it's possible." A pregnant pause followed. "I haven't got a clue as to what's happening here. There's no rational explanation, and if this Burnum character was up here like they say, hell, I'm starting to believe that anything is possible."

"Anything may be possible, except this. I'm releasing a statement tonight that in effect says that there is no connection between Peter Burnum and Colorado Springs, and I expect you to back that up. Ken Small died about an hour ago, and you just became interim chief of police." The mayor spoke so rapidly that Patton wasn't exactly sure that he had heard him correctly.

"Ken's dead? What happened?"

"It's not clear. He was at home with the flu and then he started having convulsions. He died at St. Mary's. Sorry you had to hear about it this way, but life goes on, and we have a crisis to deal with."

Patton put the shock of a colleague's sudden death aside for a moment and focused on the mayor's other bombshell. "You skipped over three more senior officers, Billy," he said, and he understood why. Each of them would be in the running to fill Ken Small's post permanently, and the mayor wouldn't want any of them tainted by this crisis.

"My prerogative," the mayor said. "Now, you have exactly thirty-six hours to come up with something I can take to the press that explains the violence. Don't let me down, Rodney." The line went dead.

Patton replaced the receiver and began to massage his head with two hands when a soft knock on the door disturbed him. "What is it?"

"I'm sorry, sir." It was one of the front desk officers. Patton tried to remember the man's name but couldn't, and the young man was so intimidated that he only poked his head around the door, hiding his nametag. "Ah, the old . . . ah, detective is here and wants a word with you."

How about scram, he thought. "Who is the old . . . ah detective you are referring to, Officer?" he said instead.

"Greg Flynn."

It took Patton half a second to recognize the name of his predecessor. "Now that is someone I want to talk to. Send him in." The officer disappeared behind the doorjamb, and Patton spotted Greg Flynn surrounded by an excited, smiling crowd of detectives and office staff. Rodney watched Flynn's easy demeanor and was struck by a pang of homesickness with just a touch of jealousy. That used to be him, walking through the precinct back in Baltimore, shooting the shit with his detectives. But now he was an outsider and a very long way from home.

"Knock, knock," Flynn said a moment later, walking in and looking around his old office. "Nothing's changed."

Patton was struck by the aura that seemed to surround Flynn. He had a way of making everyone around him feel at ease, and even Patton felt his melancholy mood lift as the retired detective rounded his old desk and pumped Rodney's hand.

"How's it going?" Flynn asked, with genuine sincerity.

"Not well." Patton felt like kicking himself for not consulting Flynn a month earlier, when things started going south. Greg wrapped himself in a cloak of conviviality and had mastered the balancing act of friend, mentor, and boss, which inspired deep loyalty in Colorado Springs's detective division. It was a leadership style very different from Patton's top-down approach. Beyond that, however, Patton saw in Flynn a kindred spirit. They were both cops down to the core. "Please sit. What can I do for you?" Rodney offered Greg a seat and then leaned on the edge of his desk.

"I think I have some information that may help," Greg answered.

"Well halleluiah," said Patton.

"Seven years ago, my daughter-in-law, Amanda, was infected by a virus," Greg began. He gave Patton the abbreviated and sanitized version of the story, but it still took several minutes. After Greg finished, Rodney walked slowly, thoughtfully, back to his chair.

"Is this an indication you don't believe me?" Greg motioned to the distance Patton had just put between them.

Patton answered, "The Colorado Health Department is sure that there is no infectious cause for this. Two weeks ago, I asked them to look again. They checked the air, the water, even the food, and they still didn't find anything. "

"They're wrong," Greg said definitively. "They've been looking in the wrong places. This virus is passed by human contact. Someone is deliberately infecting the population."

Patton's expression remained neutral, but his mind was filled with doubt. He respected Flynn, but the idea of a madman spreading a virus that turned ordinary people into violent psychopaths seemed a little farfetched, even for this situation.

"Phil Rucker," Greg pressed on, "the coroner, told me that about a month ago a previously healthy man suddenly killed his neighbor over a dispute involving a lawnmower, and then shot it out with the responding units."

"I remember the case," Rodney nodded. Internal Affairs investigated all officer-involved shootings and they were waiting for his report. It was one of the twelve thousand things he still had to do before this day came to an end.

"At autopsy they found that this guy's brain was filled with an unidentified virus, and Rucker thinks that this infection was the proximate cause for this man's bizarre behavior."

Patton winced at the mention of the coroner's name and slowly lowered himself into his desk chair. "One case, Greg?" He tried to sound dubious, but his mind was starting to turn a corner. Maybe it was Rucker's tall dark man. "Does the name Klaus Reisch mean anything to you?" he finally asked.

After a moment Greg said: "No, I don't think I've ever heard that name before."

It was now Patton's turn to tell his story, and Greg listened with an expression that questioned the relevance. "Yaeger told me that Reisch had tried to kill him, but he couldn't because someone named Amanda had hurt him. He said that Reisch reached into his head and squeezed his brain. Now, ordinarily, I'm not really a believer in this *X-Files* shit, but I got a witness who saw the whole thing, and this guy says Reisch never touched my officer; he just stared at Yaeger, and then Yaeger went down. Phillip Rucker was a witness to a similar situation this morning. Supposedly, this Reisch guy killed Rucker's next door neighbor."

Patton stared at Flynn, who remained impassive to the obvious connection between a possible murderer and his daughter-in-law.

"I have never heard of Klaus Reisch," Greg said stiffly, after a subtle shift in his bearing.

Patton slowly nodded while maintaining eye contact. He believed Greg, but the older man was obviously holding something back. "Is it possible," Patton began in a soft and practiced voice, "that Amanda knows this Reisch fella. He used to live in Russia, and they were into some really weird shit in the seventies and eighties. She could have met this guy in Honduras—"

"No!" Greg's shout stopped Patton dead in his tracks. "I'm sorry," he said after the echo died away. "You've got it all wrong. I've never heard about this Reisch before, and if Amanda ever had contact with him, she would have told me."

"I'm sure you know how that sounds, Greg, and how this all appears. The government held her against her will, you said that yourself, and then a few months later she kills a couple of guys, one of whom happens to be an FBI agent. Now, years later, in her hometown, some strange virus that she survived resurfaces."

"She's not a terrorist, and she would never knowingly infect anyone, and it's not the same virus."

"Do you know where she is, Greg?" Patton's voice had taken on a hard, formal tone.

"I'm not going to lie to you. I have been in contact with her, and I know for a fact that she hasn't been in Colorado Springs," Greg said.

Greg's gaze was steady, and Patton accepted his half-answer. "All right," he said, and then added, "for now. My brother-in-law is a senior analyst for the CIA. I called him earlier today, and he says that this Reisch character was born in Germany and is a freelance killer. He supposedly worked for the Soviets for a while, so I'm guessing they're somehow involved."

Patton continued to watch Greg until a knock on his door interrupted his scrutiny.

"Somebody better be dead!" Patton screamed out of habit. Normally, it was a funny joke for a homicide detective, but at this particular instant, he realized to his horror that it was more than a little inappropriate. "God, that was stupid," he whispered to himself. "I'm sorry, Greg, but Ken Small passed away this evening."

Greg's face dropped. "What? I've known Ken for nearly thirty years." He slumped into his chair.

"Somebody has," said a voice, and the door swung open. Patton never really appreciated federal agents all that much, and Don Heller reminded him why. Tall, well-dressed, and armed with a swagger that could only have been perfected through countless hours of practice in front of a mirror, Heller walked in and immediately made himself at home in Patton's office. "The governor and your chief of police. Congratulations on the promotion, Rodney."

"You're a living, breathing stereotype, Heller, do you know that?" Patton growled, angry that Greg had now heard that he was taking over Ken Small's job. "It's only temporary," he said to both of them. "What do you want, Special Agent?" Patton added a little extra emphasis on the man's title.

"Two things, actually. The first is to inform you that by executive order the entire state of Colorado has now been quarantined. Nothing comes in and nothing goes out. The National Guard and U.S. Army will be working together, but overall control will be federal. All local and state law enforcement agencies have come under the command of Homeland Security. That means you." Heller pointed at Patton and then paused.

It was Greg who reacted first. "They know what's going on," he said to Patton. "There must be a different source of information."

"It couldn't have been my brother-in-law. He didn't know anything about the virus," Patton answered while Heller watched the exchange.

"There are people in the government, at least in the CDC, who know about the virus. I wonder if someone has put two and two together."

They continued their private conversation while Heller listened, slack-jawed.

"No way they could act this fast," said Patton. "I think you're right; they've got another source. Michael said that people far above his pay grade had started asking about Reisch." He stood, nervous energy coursing through him.

"Who the fuck is Reisch?" Heller practically screamed.

"Sorry, Don," Greg said.

Patton started to pace, amazed that Greg had the patience to tolerate fools like Heller. *Maybe that's the reason for his success—people skills*, he thought.

"Klaus Reich is a German," said Flynn. He turned towards Patton to confirm that he had pronounced the last name correctly. Rodney nodded. "We think that Reisch is purposely infecting people with a virus that damages the brain and causes people to become violent. It seems likely that this is a terrorist attack, and that someone in the government knows something about it. That's why they ordered a quarantine."

"Okay," Heller said, regaining some of his swagger. "Fill me in. How do you know this?"

"That's not important," Rodney said brusquely. "You need to tell your people in Washington that Reisch is here, or at least was this afternoon, and that he's on the run. One of my officers may have wounded him, so I doubt he's gotten far."

Patton had positioned himself directly in front of Heller and was using his more-than-three hundred-pound frame to intimidate the much smaller man into action.

"Is this related to the officer-involved shooting at the hotel?" Heller asked, staring up at Patton.

"Yes, and we have a pretty good eyewitness description. We've passed it on to the media."

"Excellent, excellent," the FBI agent said. "I'll pass this on. There is one more thing, and it involves you, Greg."

"Me?" Greg's face betrayed the reality that there was only one reason the FBI would have an interest in him.

"I need you to come with me and convince Amanda to turn herself in." Heller's tone had become almost sympathetic. "Don't misunderstand me. I'm not using this situation as an excuse to close an open case. Privately, we all know what happened seven years ago. That's not what this is about."

"Amanda is not spreading this virus," Greg said, his anger rising to the surface.

"Honestly, I didn't know anything about a virus until I walked in here. What I do know is that more than a hundred agents have been flown into a quarantine area to find her. We know she's here, and we will find her. I don't want anyone hurt, and that includes Amanda."

"Why the sudden concern for her welfare?" Greg asked.

"Because I have been ordered by the President of the United States to bring her in alive and, if possible, unharmed. We will find her, even if it takes a hundred more agents, or even a thousand more. We both know what happened the last time someone tried to bring her in, and I don't want a repeat of that." Patton saw a new side of Heller; the man genuinely did not want Amanda hurt.

"You said that Amanda was the only person to survive the original virus, Greg," Patton said, unexpectedly aligning himself with Heller. "It stands to reason that if there is an outbreak of one of this virus's babies, she could be very helpful."

"I know that, and I don't want to see anyone hurt either, but this is my daughter-in-law, my son's wife, and the mother of my grandson." He stared into Patton's dark eyes and the pair jumped when Heller's cell phone went off.

"Jesus Christ, turn that thing down," Patton said.

The call lasted less than ten seconds. "I see. Keep me posted," said Heller, and hung up. "Amanda is driving a Jeep Cherokee, Colorado license GNM 529. It is currently parked at an office complex about three miles from here. There is a white female inside that fits the description of Amanda Flynn." He spoke without emotion. "What do I do, Greg?"

Patton watched as Greg struggled with himself. It wasn't a question of right or wrong. That was easy. Amanda could save countless lives, and because of that, he knew that in the end Greg would do what was right. It was a question of betrayal, and he wondered what he would do if it was his daughter sitting in that Jeep.

"Tell your people to stand down, now," Greg said.

"You know I can't do that, Greg," Heller said gently.

"If you don't, she will kill them all," Greg said, his voice rising. "Every one of them."

"That's not possible, Greg, we—"

"Tell them to back off now! If they can see her, then she knows where they are. If you back her into a corner, people are going to die." Greg's face was turning red.

Patton finally connected the dots between Reisch and Amanda. "Do it, Heller. Do it now! We already have one man down, we don't need others."

"Not until someone tells me what's really going on here. How can she kill people she can't see?"

"With a single goddamn thought, you arrogant son of a bitch!" Greg screamed and yanked the cell phone from the FBI agent's hand. He punched a few buttons while Patton blocked Heller's attempts to retrieve his phone. "This is Detective Greg Flynn. I'm with Special Agent Heller. Do not under any circumstances approach that Jeep. Terminate all surveillance now!" He repeated the message, but no one responded.

Chapter 28

The on-again, off-again flurries were back on again, but it wasn't snowing hard enough to obscure their view of her, even with dusk approaching. There were five of them now, and more on the way. She had sensed the lone FBI agent as soon as she left Oliver and the church. He followed her Jeep discreetly while calling for backup, and Amanda drove aimlessly through a residential neighborhood just to make his job a little more difficult. He was reasonably competent, and only twice did she glimpse his gray Ford. She led him to a small office complex just outside of downtown and then parked. He pulled into an adjacent supermarket and watched her, waiting for backup. He had enough experience to put his ego in check and do things correctly, which disappointed Amanda. She had half hoped that he would see her as an unaware 130-pound woman who would offer no resistance to his sudden appearance with badge and weapon drawn. But no, he wasn't going to confront her until everyone was in place. Five minutes after he parked, four more agents arrived and quickly fanned out to cover any possible escape routes. Then, everyone just sat and waited for orders.

She searched the mind of the nearest agent and found nothing of interest. He had no idea who or what Amanda was beyond being a fugitive. She hopped from mind to mind until one of their cell phones rang, and Greg's face suddenly filled her mind. He was irate and full of fear, his emotions pulling her across dozens of city blocks. "With a single goddamn thought—" she heard him say, and understanding blossomed in the minds of the two men that stood next to her father-in-law. Greg had finally told someone what she had become. Her secret was out. She was surprised that it didn't much matter to her; maybe it was because there were others now. Reisch and Oliver would certainly be less circumspect with their abilities, and there were probably going to be many more soon. There really was no secret left to protect.

The agents were becoming antsy, worried that she would leave the trap they were ready to spring. Escaping them would be child's play. With only five minds to control, she could quite easily walk over to the supermarket, find a car she liked, and simply drive away as they continued to watch her empty Jeep. Or, with even less effort, she could kill them all, right where they sat. Mittens got a small thrill from that thought, but it was short-lived. She wasn't going to kill anyone today, except maybe Reisch, and Mittens knew it. She felt for the German, but he was still lost in the mist of a hundred thousand other minds.

The agents were ordered to move in closer, giving Amanda only a few minutes before they swarmed her Jeep. She needed to disable them, not kill them, and make it absolutely clear that she was beyond their reach. A tiny thrill made her heart beat a little faster. Cruelty had never been part of her before the Change, but it certainly was afterwards. It was a powerful and wonderfully self-indulgent emotion, and like all the other baser instincts it pulled at her relentlessly.

The sedan behind her was feeding live images to a Command Center in Denver. She tried to follow the feed back to the other end but couldn't quite reach without a discrete human consciousness directing her. It didn't matter; whoever was at the other end would be suitably shocked as she calmly went to each of the fallen agents and relieved them of their weapons and identification. It would be a clear message to leave her alone.

Amanda heard and felt someone give the command to take her. Three agents sprang from their hiding positions and started sprinting towards her. Two more gunned their cars to block her Jeep. She hesitated only a moment and then hit them all with a concentrated blast of mental energy. It was only a tiny fraction of what she was capable of, but it was more than enough to knock them unconscious. She left the video feed running. She had an agent to her left, one to her right, and one behind her; all three had landed where she hit them. Both of the drivers had managed to slam their sedans into parked cars, and aside from being unconscious were otherwise okay. Amanda turned to gather her things and then said good-bye to her loyal and reliable Jeep. She slowly and deliberately climbed out into the snow. She turned towards the camera so that they could plainly see her and then walked to each of the three agents and took their handguns and IDs. Unclipping the radio from the last man's belt, she hit the transmit button.

"They're not dead," she said. "But they very well could have been." She waited for a reply.

It took half a minute for a voice to answer. "What do you want, Amanda?" the voice asked without introduction.

"First, don't put me in a position where I have to hurt people again." Her mind searched for the voice and found its owner in a Denver highrise. It was quite a stretch, but she could just see him as well as a dozen other agents listening and watching her image on a monitor. "You're an assistant director, aren't you, Mr. Benedict?"

"Would you like to tell me how you know that, Amanda?" His voice was calm, but all around him people were scrambling, trying to coordinate the movements of other agents.

"No, I don't think I will. But I will tell you that if I feel another FBI agent within five miles of me, you may not get them back in one piece." Mittens was on her feet and pacing through Amanda's mind. She watched as Benedict waved his arms, stopping the efforts to trap her. "Thank you, Ron. Now, I want you to leave the Flynns alone as well. They have nothing to do with this and my patience has worn thin. If I sense anyone following me, Greg, or Lisa, I will punish them, and I will hold you responsible. Am I clear?"

"I'm not in a position to do that," Benedict said. This was true. The order to take Amanda into custody had come directly from the White House.

"Mr. Benedict, I suggest you put yourself in that position. Tell the director, so he can tell the president what happened here tonight. Let them know what could have happened here as well, because next time it will."

The agent beneath her began to stir, and she restrained him. She wondered for a moment if a more dramatic demonstration of her ability was in order. She decided against it, for the time being. "I have no desire to hurt anyone, or to be taken into custody."

"This has nothing to do with what happened seven years ago. We need your help." Benedict alone knew why they had to take Amanda, and he had been ordered to keep that secret.

"You don't need my help." Amanda had to restrain the minds of two more agents. It was time to be going.

"People are dying, Amanda," Benedict said gently.

"I'm not responsible for that." Amanda could tell that he knew that; the name Klaus Reisch floated through his consciousness.

"You're too late; everyone here either is or will soon be infected. I can't help them anymore. Pass that on to Martin." The realization that all these people were going to die suddenly struck her, and for the first time in seven years, she felt a stab of guilt. "Back off, and I will take care of this. After it's done, we can talk about what I can do for Nathan Martin."

"We can take care of the German. Come in and help us now."

She shook her head. "You have no idea what he's capable of. He will kill you all if it suits his need or his fancy, and you have a better chance of stopping me than him."

The video camera exploded as Amanda dropped the radio receiver and walked away.

Chapter 29

"So all this is about a book written by a discredited author more than half a century ago. Excuse my sarcasm, Doctor, but I find that a little hard to believe," General McDaniels said as their Suburban screamed down the dark streets of Washington.

"It's not about *The Population Bomb* per se. It's the theory behind the book. Paul Ehrlich theorized that the Earth can sustain a finite number of human beings before a series of events, plagues, famines, and wars was initiated that would ultimately lead to our extinction. He made a number of dire predictions if worldwide conditions weren't changed. All of them proved to be inaccurate, but that didn't stop his ideas from entering the consciousness of scientific thought. People were influenced by his theories."

"So Avanti was a disciple."

"Disciple is too strong a word. Ehrlich believed something and shaped facts to fit that belief. Jaime would never accept that intellectual dishonesty," Martin said.

"So you are saying that there are facts to back this outlandish theory?" McDaniels was finally surrendering to the laws of momentum by bracing himself within the careening vehicle.

"I don't think you fully understand Avanti, General. He's not insane, or some nut with an idea. He is a true believer, and not because he blindly accepts what he has been told or has read." The car suddenly swerved around a corner, throwing Martin against the window. "To tell you the truth, I'm not entirely convinced that he's wrong. In many ways, our species is in as much danger as you and I are right now."

"Sergeant, I told you to get us there quickly, but I did mean alive," McDaniels yelled to the driver.

"Sorry sir, but we are being followed. Fairly sophisticated but not aggressive." The sergeant answered without taking his eyes off of the road.

Martin wheeled around to look out the rear window but was blinded by the headlights of the trailing Suburban. "Who would be following us?"

"Any number of people, some good, some not so good. It will be handled." McDaniels didn't turn around. "So you are a believer in this pseudoscience as well?"

"I wouldn't label it as a pseudoscience," Martin said nervously as he slid back into his seat.

"It's become one. When I hear the same facts quoted by radical environmentalists and gun-toting isolationists, I have a tendency to discount them."

"Wow, with a philosophy like that, how did you ever get through your confirmation hearings?" Martin scoffed. "People basically suck, excuse my French. They will use any tool at their disposal to advance their own personal agenda. Facts don't lie, people do, and when you pull all those facts together, the future becomes a very scary place. I'm not just talking about global warming; I'm talking about the loss of species diversity, deforestation, the depletion of natural resources—the list is as long as your arm, and each one of those inconvenient facts has an impact on human survival, whether we believe them or not."

"I believe in our ability to survive; it is the thing that we do best," McDaniels answered simply.

"Then you must stink at what you do, because your job is to make sure our enemies don't survive." Martin laughed again.

"My job is not to kill; my job is to protect the United States."

"Then how are you going to protect it from the seven billion incubators that inhabit this planet, and the tendency of pathogens to mutate?"

"That's your job."

"Well, I'll be the first to admit that I stink at my job. We have almost no natural defenses, and what little science can do will be too little too late. HIV, Bird-flu, SARS, NIM, and all the others that came before them matured within human tissue. The greater the mass of human tissue, the greater the probability that something really nasty will develop. There are some very serious-minded people who believe that we are on the verge of a massive natural pandemic, the results of which would be death tolls in the billions. And with the way societies and economies have become so interdependent, such a disruption would lead to famines and wars severe enough to finish the rest of us off."

"Which brings us back to Avanti. He told you that he was working outside the wishes and desires of Jeser. Do you believe him?"

"I do. I doubt he'd lie to me—that's not his style. In some ways, he's a lot like he was twenty years ago. He wants me to know that he was the one who engineered this virus and is personally responsible for its dissemination. He wants to be remembered as someone who had the courage to do what others were afraid to do. It's so insane," Nathan said softly. "He twisted the knife by telling me that he used my computer models to convince Jeser that the outbreak could be controlled. He stole them, which means that someone in my department is working for him, or them." Martin said sadly. "The outbreak in Colorado is supposed to get the world's attention so everyone will close their borders to the United States. That's supposed to limit the spread of the infection." Martin shook his head. "They're going to issue some demands so that they appear reasonable and then release the original virus no matter what we do."

A moment of thoughtful silence followed. "Avanti wants you to reproduce that vaccine to slow or stop the outbreak"—McDaniels motioned towards the small vial in Martin's hand—"to save just enough so that humanity survives, but society doesn't."

"One thousand doses, if he's correct." He gripped the bottle tighter. "I know what you're wondering: is there time to mass-produce this? The answer is no. It would take several months to maybe a year before we could produce any reasonable quantity, and I'm guessing that if things go as Avanti thinks they will, we have two, maybe three months before worldwide dissemination. At that point, there's no stopping it."

Chapter 30

Reisch slept with the television on and a commercial full of screaming children awakened him. He suffered through thirty seconds of it before finally finding the remote control and turning the TV off. The sounds of the screaming and squealing children still rattled inside his painful head. American television was reason enough to condemn humanity.

The bedside clock said that it was exactly six o'clock, and to Klaus's great relief, he found that his hand had recovered most of its function. His thinking was still a little thick, but it had improved enough that he could defend himself, at least against humans.

He began to stretch, but then stiffened. A hint of something foreign drifted across his mind. He tried to seize the trace of mental energy, but it was gone, or perhaps it had never been there at all. He was still on guard after his encounter with Amanda, and his control over his emotions was erratic. She had planted a seed of doubt in his mind, and for the first time in years he felt vulnerable. Suddenly, he took the remote control and threw it against the wall. It shattered into a hundred pieces, and after an instant of delight, he rebuked himself. He needed to stay in control; he couldn't afford any more self-indulgent displays.

He swung his legs off the side of the bed, anxious to be up and moving, but as soon as his feet touched the floor, he knew something was wrong. There was activity all around him. Dozens and dozens of minds were awake and active.

"Military," he said, with a raspy voice. They were setting up roadblocks on all of the main roads. His mind drifted through the throng of bored and cold soldiers, but none of them knew why they were here, or why they had been issued live ammunition. He would have to find an officer or someone else of importance to find out just how much danger they posed. The problem was that taking over a mind was like shooting off a flare for Amanda; in an instant, she would know exactly where to find him, and he wasn't quite ready for their next meeting. He waited a moment, giving destiny the opportunity to provide him with the information that he needed, but after several minutes of silence, he decided to shower instead.

Fifteen minutes later, clean and refreshed, he dropped his key on the unmade bed and left for his car. He made it twenty feet before the night manager called to him. The man was wearing a parka that was open enough for Reisch to see the same torn and dirty T-shirt that had graced his portly form the night before. He slogged through the snow in unlaced army boots, and Reisch thought he should kill the man on general principle alone.

"Excuse me," he called, and Reisch found his mind open enough to read. *Quarantine?* The word was unfamiliar, but the fat man provided enough of a definition to make the meaning clear. "The state police told me to tell all our guests that they were to stay put." Apparently, he had been going from room to room telling everyone about the ban on travel.

"I'm just getting some supplies. I'm going to be right back." Reisch smiled as he lied. The night manager said something else, but Reisch had already turned for the Mercedes. The small SUV sprung into life immediately despite the cold, and he let the engine warm. No one was watching or looking for him as far as his mind's eye could see. This was all about the virus, not about him. The Americans were finally reacting to the outbreak. After seven long years, it was finally starting.

Reisch's smile broadened. He knew that it was wrong to take credit for this, but he allowed himself a moment of satisfaction. All his actions had been scripted by a power far beyond even his understanding, but he had played his role faithfully. His reward for success would be survival; had he failed, he would rightly perish along with the rest of the unworthy.

Reisch turned on the radio and listened as the announcer read the manifesto of Jeser. It had been written by fools. He corrected his disparaging thought; he could afford to be magnanimous in victory. They weren't fools, just irredeemably misguided, and their time was just about up. In due course, after they had their moment in the sun, he would bring about their destruction as dispassionately as he had brought about the Americans. In the end he doubted that he would celebrate or mourn their passing.

The radio reporter had been replaced by an epidemiology expert. His conclusions were a little more optimistic than the planners', but that was understandable; it would take the Americans some time to come to terms with their imminent demise.

Within a month, American society would be in disarray. By six months, the great country would be little more than a graveyard, with a few thousand survivors wandering through the waste, struggling with their newfound abilities and searching for a purpose. Reisch would return to collect and direct them. He would help them discover the natural order of existence. It wouldn't be difficult; most of them would have begun to sense it, and perhaps live by it. They would forge a new civilization, purged of corrupting concepts such as equality and democracy; the strong would thrive, and as time passed, the new species would become their own gods. Later, Reisch would repeat the process in Europe, then in Asia, and continue until humanity had been completely replaced by the Select. The key to success was to make the process gradual, with the first step being the trickiest. The United States had a lot of bombs and was the least predictable in its death-throes; it didn't take much effort to push a button and ruin everything.

He dropped the car into gear and drove out of the snowy parking lot. The fat man was still waking people up and barely registered the Mercedes.

"Where are we going?" A tired-looking Pushkin asked from the backseat.

"I need to eat before we go," Reisch said simply, basking in the glow of all the frenetic activity around him. He drove under an overpass and weaved his way through town, finally stopping at a McDonald's. He bought some scalding but weak coffee along with a Mc-something that passed for food. He slowly ate, thinking about the thousands of survivors. The number was only a guess; it might be just a few hundred, or perhaps as many as a million.

"So we are finally off to Costa Rica," Pushkin said, drifting to the front seat. "Are you going to complete the mission now, or wait? There may not be a better opportunity."

"You know that it is not due for another forty-four hours."

"There are a lot of people out here, and some of them are bound to be looking for you. Anticipate complications, Klaus."

Reisch paused at the mention of his given name. "Sending it now will effect containment."

"In the end, your little bag here," Pushkin playfully spun the black satchel, "makes containment rather moot."

"We have to get to the end first, before we can talk about what is moot." Reisch scored a rare debate point.

"You're a little selective in your trust of Professor Avanti. You trust his estimates for spread of the first virus but not his estimates for containment of the second. You do remember that everything he told Jeser was a lie."

Reisch still hadn't made up his mind about Avanti. He first met the Ukrainian in Libya in the early nineties. Klaus had been without steady work since the collapse of the Soviets, and Pushkin arranged for the two to meet. At first they were rather leery of one another. Reisch was uncomfortable with the Ukrainian's reputation for radical Islamic beliefs and, for his part, Avanti was unnerved by Reisch's reputation of violent instability. To complicate matters, Avanti was part of a nascent organization that was forming around Osama bin Laden, the Saudi hero of the Afghan resistance.

"When you introduced us, did you know that Avanti worked with bin Laden?" Reisch asked his former boss, temporarily changing the subject.

"I knew that you had been assigned to kill bin Laden and failed."

"The failure was not mine. Your glorious Red Army packed it in before I could even make it to Pakistan."

Despite the irony, both Reisch and Avanti came to accept the fact that a former Soviet operative would provide security for a Jihadist camp that had ties with bin Laden. Years later, when Avanti split from Al-Qaeda, all conflicts of interest had been resolved, and the two men developed a mutual respect. With a free hand, and an endless stream of money supplied by the Saudis, Avanti expanded the hidden laboratory beneath the camp, assembled a world-class team of virologists and microbiologists, and Jeser was born. Much smaller, and more secretive than Al-Qaeda, they shared similar goals; at least that's what their financiers believed. Reisch knew that Avanti was no more an Islamist than he was. The Ukrainian was hardly a Muslim at all; he drank daily and frequented brothels at every opportunity. He often joked with Reisch about how the good and pious Saudi money was paying for his life of decadence. His goal was not the dissemination of the Islamic faith or the global institution of Islamic law. His goal was not nearly so noble; he simply wanted to ensure the survival of humanity by destroying the majority of humans.

"I think Avanti is correct. I don't see the Hybrid virus being contained." It was a rare declarative statement from Pushkin.

"In many ways you two were very similar," Reisch said, with a reminiscent undertone. "You both lived a life of excess, but never allowed it to interfere with your responsibilities. You both were well educated and at times quite profound, but chose to be profane as often as the situation allowed it. Both of you also managed to save my life."

***

The Hybrid virus was born an accidental death. Even Avanti was never exactly certain how the disparate components combined to create the most lethal pathogen ever seen. It was a perfect weapon with only one flaw: it mutated as fast as any virus before it. To maintain full potency, the vials had to be kept in tissue cultures or freeze-dried, procedures that demanded expertise. Somehow, containment had been breached and within three days everyone in the remote camp was dead, except Reisch. Avanti had been in Rome debauching his way through Jeser's funding when the sick and confused German managed to reach him by cell phone. Two days later, the German was in a Saudi isolation unit.

Months later, after Reisch had begun to Evolve, he learned from Avanti exactly how containment had been breached, and the depths of Jaime Avanti's duplicity. For a time Reisch had planned to kill the Ukrainian in retaliation, but then reasoned that Avanti's survival, like his own, served the natural order.

***

"Great minds—tragically, there are so few of us," Pushkin said and then was gone again.

Klaus pulled onto the nearly deserted highway. The GPS told him that the only way to reach New Mexico without using the interstate or state highways was to turn back east towards Colorado Springs. He followed the circuitous route of farm roads for almost an hour before he came to the small town of Mescali. He drove past the obligatory Walmart and noted that there was not a single car in the large parking lot when one of Mescali's four traffic lights changed in front of him. He stood on the brakes and the Mercedes skidded along the slick pavement, ending up only inches from a large military truck that had started to rumble through the intersection. His momentum lost, the driver glared at Reisch as he downshifted, rocking the squad of National Guardsmen in the back. In a cloud of black diesel smoke, they drove past him. After another moment, the light changed.

Reisch drove a little more slowly and carefully. The road twisted left, and he found a second group of National Guardsmen busy erecting concrete barricades directly in his path. Behind them were two armored personnel carriers, their cannons pointed directly at Reisch. He had only an instant to react, and he wasted it by staring into one of the barrels. Three armed men started waving their arms from behind the nearest barricade, signaling him to stop. It was cold, and they were wearing their winter gear, which disguised their insignias, but Reisch knew that the middle one was the man in charge. He was the youngest, most fit, and most dangerous. His mind darkened the instant he saw Reisch; it was nothing specific, more instinct. Reisch stopped twenty feet short of the barricade and glanced at his rearview mirror as the large green truck, with the sneering driver and twenty National Guardsmen, pulled up behind him.

Lieutenant John Fessner tapped on the driver's side window as Reisch assessed the situation. His mind was uncharacteristically slow and ponderous, and with a burst of anger, he realized that he had Amanda to thank for that. He turned and found the soldier's face just inches from him. *Concentrate*, he told himself. There were thirty-one minds focusing on him right now, and he was having trouble prioritizing them. Fessner tapped again, despite the fact that Reisch was staring at him in the eye.

Reisch realized that Fessner was not a man to be trifled with. A combat veteran with two tours in Iraq under his belt before the age of thirty, the lieutenant was capable of recognizing danger when he saw it. "Can you lower your window, sir?" he shouted, his breath fogging the window, with the last word added only out of habit.

Reisch searched for the switch, but it wasn't where he thought it should be. The armrest on the door had two switches, and neither lowered the window. Instead, he accidentally hit the switch that locked the doors, and Fessner jumped back and half raised his weapon. The sudden movement of the lieutenant alerted the platoon sergeant, who eased himself and three other soldiers around the vehicle. The sergeant didn't know what was happening, but he trusted Fessner.

Reisch found the window switches on the center console and finally lowered the window. "I'm sorry, officer, but you guys surprised me. I didn't expect the army to be . . . Hey, what are you guys doing here, anyways?" Reisch spoke like a native Midwesterner; he feigned embarrassment, and then curiosity, to keep Fessner off balance.

"The road is closed, sir." Fessner wasn't off balance. "Can I see some ID?" He was polite, but his weapon was still poised.

"Certainly." Reisch reached for his overcoat and retrieved his wallet and current identity. He was disappointed that Fessner hadn't relaxed an iota in the face of his cooperative-Coloradoan act. "There you go, young man," he continued in character.

"What's your destination, Mr. Lyon?" Fessner's voice was a little more confrontational.

"Denver," Reisch answered. "I have a flight to catch."

"Can you tell me where you are coming from?" Fessner studied the phony driver's license as if it might have the correct answer written across Reisch's picture.

"Manitou Springs. What's all this about, soldier?" Courtesy wasn't getting him anywhere, so he tried indignation.

"The state of Colorado is under martial law. There is a ban on traveling, and you are in violation of that ban." He pocketed the driver's license. "Please step out of the car, sir." It was an order delivered by a man who was used to having his orders followed immediately.

Reisch hesitated. Thirty-one minds were focused on him. They clouded out anything beyond his immediate vicinity, and he wondered if it was enough cover to avoid alerting Amanda. He motioned to get out, and Fessner stepped back, his automatic weapon lowered for the moment. Reisch seized Fessner's mind, and for a moment he felt the usual but always strange intermixing of their thoughts. It was over in less than an instant. John Fessner dropped to his knees, grabbing his head with a howl of pain. Reisch could feel the man's agony, but he could also feel his own resurgence. The power to kill had returned. He resisted the urge to tear Fessner's mind apart; he needed a diversion, not a complication.

"Lieutenant, are you all right?" the sergeant screamed. Something had just happened, and he had missed it. All he saw was Fessner drop to the ground. He raised his weapon and pointed it at Reisch. The remaining twenty-nine guardsmen did the same. "Chavez, check out the LT. You!" he screamed at Reisch. "On the ground, face down, hands behind your back, now!"

"Hold up there, Sergeant. I didn't even touch him," Reisch said, stepping out of and away from the Mercedes, his hands held high. He started to gather all their minds, and when he had them perfectly positioned, he felt the energy pulse leave his body. Just for a moment, he became almost weightless as the air around him suddenly compressed and then exploded outward towards each of the guardsmen. He watched as they flew through the air like little toy soldiers, all of them dead or dying—except for one. Reisch did a double take. Behind him stood a completely unharmed and shocked twenty-two-year-old corporal. For a long second, they stared at each other, both with the same thought: *What happened?*

Reisch was the first to recover. He grabbed the mind of the corporal and started to squeeze, but not before the guardsman squeezed the trigger of his fully automatic M16.

Chapter 31

Catherine Lee quietly pulled the curtain back and found that her patient was still asleep and still in the emergency room. *Sixteen hours on a hospital gurney waiting for a bed*, she thought. Unfortunately, the man's plight was not unique. The twelve-bed ER of St. Luke's was treating, or in this case, babysitting, more than thirty. Patients were stacked everywhere. She had seen and treated more patients in the last twelve hours than in the last twelve shifts. Gunshot wounds, stabbings, and blunt trauma were supposed to be in her past. Seventeen years as an Emergency Room Attending at Grady Memorial in Atlanta had earned her the respite in sleepy Colorado Springs, but now the violence had found its way back to her doorstep. Most of the surgical patients were ultimately "turfed" to other hospitals, but only after Dr. Lee and her ER staff had stabilized them. The medical patients had to stay; no one was accepting medical transfers. Every other hospital within a fifty-mile radius was as full as St. Luke's. It was this year's flu bug, and it had hit Colorado hard and late in the season. She had seen her first case of it ten days earlier, and it had been a nonstop parade of sick people ever since. Then, just to make matters worse, the federal government announced a ban on travel, a medical quarantine to contain a virulent strain of TB.

The head nurse reached around her waist and spun her around. "Hey sexy, how about you give me a complete physical?" Tom Lee asked.

"Not until I get a shower and eight hours of sleep," she replied, giving her husband a quick peck on the cheek. "Any hope of clearing out some of these patients? This guy over here has been down here for nearly two days."

His tone changed. "Same story as yesterday—no beds anywhere. Have you talked with Dr. Branson lately?"

"Not for a week or so." She had been so busy that she had missed all of the hospital meetings. "Why, what have you heard?"

"First, that this quarantine has nothing to do with TB."

"Oh, there's a big surprise," she said, and pulled out of his embrace to let a staff nurse squeeze by. The weak excuse of a virulent form of TB was an insult to anyone who knew better, which was pretty much everybody.

"Well, Doctor Smarty-Pants, do you know why there's a quarantine?" He pressed himself into the wall as a patient on a gurney was wheeled down the corridor.

"No, but I'm sure our omnipotent chief of staff, who knows all, revealed the deep dark secret while you both were peeing on a wall somewhere."

She started to walk back to the nurse's station, and he followed close behind, his voice falling to a whisper.

"Seriously, Cat, he says that it's because of this flu bug. Apparently, a lot of people who get it are dying."

She stopped and waited for him to catch up. "Dying? How many?" Spending all her time in the ER, she had little opportunity to keep tabs on the patients admitted through the emergency room. She would have to attend the staff meetings to get that kind of follow-up.

"About half, and it's not just the old people." They were back in public view, and he maintained a professional distance.

"Half! That can't be right. We'd be up to our elbows in Health Department lookie-lous."

"The morgue is full, and the military has been making regular trips to our loading docks, and I don't think they're delivering anything."

"Damn, this is serious. I better give Dr. Branson a call. I'll see you later." Absently, she gave him another kiss. Ten minutes later, she was still waiting for Bob Branson to return her page. *He probably won't answer because he thinks I want him to shake some beds loose,* she thought, leafing through the Health Department's notification forms. Influenza was a reportable disease, and every case they saw generated a report.

"Seventy-nine," Cary Tees said, and Cat looked up. "Seventy-nine cases in the last . . ." She checked her watch. ". . . nineteen hours. Episcopal and General are both over a hundred. TB, my ass. This quarantine is about this flu, or whatever the hell it is." Cary was from New York, and Cat occasionally enjoyed her in-your-face style, but this wasn't one of those occasions.

"Do you have something for me, Cary?" Cat passed the stack of reports to the unit assistant.

"The patient in five, Dr. Rucker, is awake and wants to talk with you. Did you know he's the coroner?"

"Thanks," Cat said. She weaved her way through the circus that her emergency room had become and hoped that maybe Dr. Rucker could clue her in on what was happening down here in the trenches. She pulled the curtain back with a flourish and found him sitting on the edge of the gurney, trying to keep his balance. "Dr. Rucker, you should not be trying to get up on your own."

She reached for his shoulders and steadied him. When she touched his skin, he went rigid, almost as if she had given him a powerful shock. "Are you all right?" she asked. She stood on tiptoe to look him in the eyes.

"Yes," he said through tight jaws. She let go, and he slumped perceptibly.

***

"What happened to Melissa?" As soon as Phil said her name, he knew. Some strange sense told him that she had died.

"She arrested, and we couldn't bring her back," Cat said softly.

Phil saw Dr. Lee running the code that would end with an official time of death for Melissa Shay. He watched her cursing the implanted pacemaker and defibrillator that kept discharging. Every five seconds, the device jolted Melissa's heart, and finally, the muscle stopped responding. In the end, a surgical resident was called to remove the device, but it was much too late. Her myocardium had been shocked to death.

The vision ended, and Dr. Lee was staring at him intently. "Are you all right?" she asked him again.

"I didn't even know she had a pacemaker," Phil said, more to himself than to her. An unfamiliar feeling of loss stole over him.

"I'm sorry," Catherine Lee said, and touched his bare arm.

A whirlwind of images invaded Phil's mind. Unbidden and unwelcome, he saw Dr. Lee with other patients, and then with her husband. Phil was paralyzed with horror as he watched them make love in the shower. He felt like a degenerate as they enjoyed each other's bodies in the privacy of their own home, and when he realized that parts of him were responding to the vision, he vomited.

Cat jumped back, but not in time, and the connection between them was broken.

Nurses arrived, and orders were given. He felt the IV in his arm sting as they injected him with Zofran. The powerful antiemetic agent began to cloud his thinking, but a part of him clung to the realization that he had been infected. His consciousness began to fragment, and he saw the tall, dark man staring into the eyes of a scared young man dressed in a uniform and holding a gun.

"Shoot him," Phil said to the young man. "He's going to kill you."

Dr. Lee and the nurses stopped what they were doing and stared at the now unconscious Phil.

"What did he just say?" Dr. Lee asked.

***

"Seventeen dead and fourteen wounded, all from some sort of explosion. The strange thing is that there was no fire, and none of them had any burns."

Rodney Patton was relaying what he knew about the situation in Mescali to the mayor. "The FBI is fairly sure it was our guy Reisch. He's using the name Lyon now."

No one was certain what had happened or how Reisch had escaped. The single survivor who could speak said that he had been unconscious before the other guardsmen were attacked. He told the FBI that Reisch had reached into his mind and squashed it, an account uncomfortably similar to Yaeger's. Rodney kept that part to himself. "They're also fairly sure that he was shot. There was a whole lot of blood at the scene that can't be accounted for. The state forensics team is working on it now."

"Good, at least the bastard is hurt. That ought to slow him down some." The mayor coughed loudly into the phone, and Patton winced. "Both the feds and the local Mescali police asked if they could borrow you for the day. Apparently, what happened yesterday at the Sheraton was as close as this guy has ever come to being caught. I guess they think that some of that luck will rub off on them." He laughed and then started into another coughing fit.

Rodney pulled the phone away from his ear until it was over. "They called me earlier. I'm leaving as soon as we are done." Patton hoped that the mayor would take the hint.

"So let me get this straight. This Reisch is a German who worked for the Russians and then for himself."

"Correct."

"Then he finds his way here and starts to infect people with a virus that only two people have ever survived—him and Amanda Flynn. I remember meeting her several years ago. She had the most amazing eyes; she was also very pregnant at the time."

Patton waited for the mayor to voice the obvious connection, but a long silence followed.

"So this virus is what's been causing all the violence," the mayor finally said. "Then why aren't people dying by the hundreds, the thousands?"

"I'm just a cop, Mayor," Patton said, trying to hide his frustration. This was the third time the mayor had asked that question.

"Yes," the mayor said. "And you did a good job. I gave you a deadline, and you beat it. I won't forget this, Rodney." He hung up.

"Finally," Patton said to himself. He had already decided that, chief or not, he would not be giving the daily briefing to His Honor for several more days. He returned the phone to its receiver, and it immediately rang. "What?" he demanded. He needed to get over to Mescali as soon as possible, and the morning was being eaten away by phone calls.

"Chief, I have a man on the line who says he's with the CIA. He claims to be your brother," the desk sergeant replied quickly.

Rodney remembered the man's name this time. "He's my brother-in-law, Sergeant Thompson. Put him through." He had to go a little easier with these men and women. They were starting to doubt themselves because of his overbearing nature, and timidity got people killed.

He listened as the connection was made. "Michael, how has your morning started?" he said after he heard background noise and his brother-in-law breathing impatiently.

"Busy." It wasn't impatience; it was excitement in Michael Weigel's voice. "I'm sure you heard about Mescali. Our German friend was busy this morning."

"I'm on my way down there in a couple of minutes. It was a Colorado Springs unit that he hit."

"Sorry. Boy, you guys can't catch a break. Okay, let me get right to it. I'm calling in the spirit of interagency cooperation, which means I'm authorized to talk to you. There are a lot of things happening that you don't know about, and need to. Reisch is not working alone. He's hooked himself up with some pretty bad people—Islamic terrorists. They somehow created a couple of different viruses and, with the help of Reisch, they've released one of them in Colorado Springs as a calling card. They have a list of demands that the president is reviewing. "

"Michael, you know that most of that is on the news and we figured the rest of it out ourselves. Now, how are you federal boys going to help us?"

A pause that stretched too far followed. "We have no plans to intervene besides the quarantine."

"So you're just going to lock us in, and when the last of us keels over you'll come in and bury us?" Patton said bitterly, and then regretted lashing out at his brother-in-law. Rodney knew that this decision could not have sat well with Michael. "What are they estimating as far as a death toll?" he asked.

"More than twenty thousand, but only if we can keep people at home."

Rodney was embarrassed that his initial feelings were of relief. Twenty thousand dead; that was manageable, wasn't it? Reflexively, a tiny fragment of his mind began to calculate the odds that he wasn't going to be one of the unlucky twenty thousand, and his embarrassment intensified.

"There's more," Michael said. "We need Reisch alive."

"Then come and get him," Rodney said savagely and then, again, regretted his misplaced hostility. "I'm sorry, Michael. I know it's not your fault."

"No need to apologize," Michael said quickly. "When you get over there, you need to let everyone know that this asshole has to be taken alive. I don't care how alive, just so long as his heart is beating."

"No one is going to listen. If they find Reisch, they're going to go after him with tanks, and I can't blame them. This guy wiped out an entire platoon . . . with a single goddamn thought." He was remembering Greg Flynn's words and Amanda.

"Nonlethal force," Michael Weigel said slowly. "Catch him any way you can, then sedate him. We'll take it from there. I've got to let you go,

Rodney. I'll call you if anything changes here, and you can call me if anything changes at your end."

"Bye," Patton said, but the line was already dead.

There was another way, one that didn't put people at risk. Amanda was immune to the same virus that Reisch was spreading. She had the same unique abilities as the German, and supposedly she was a lot better to look at. Patton smiled, remembering how she had effortlessly disabled the FBI team sent to take her. He had listened along with Greg Flynn to Don Heller's radio, and secretly applauded when she warned them off with a not-so-veiled threat. He had never met her, but had taken an instant liking to her. She had an indomitable spirit that reminded of his wife. Of late, it seemed that anyone with positive attributes reminded him of Connie.

The problem was that no one was looking for her; the FBI had specifically ordered him to leave her alone. He was told that at this time apprehending her posed too great a risk, and that they should concentrate their efforts on capturing Reisch, who at first seemed to be less of a threat. He wondered if that assessment had changed.

He pulled himself out of his chair and hurriedly put his coat on, hoping to get out before the damn phone rang again. He was anxious to see for himself what had happened, and hopefully, along the way, bump into Amanda.

Chapter 32

It had been a long, sleepless night. Martin hadn't made it home until three-thirty in the morning and was at his desk before seven with a dozen administrative tasks that demanded his attention. He slowly started working through them, avoiding the more important task: finding the spy in their midst.

"Where to start?" he asked himself after all his diversionary tasks had been completed, but no one answered. He had personally hired the vast majority of these people, and it sickened him to think that one of them was secretly helping those bastards. No, it was probably worse than that. One of his people was actually one of those bastards.

He was forced into doing a terrible thing. It was almost a violation of trust, a violation of his heritage, but he had to do it. He assembled the confidential personnel file of every person who worked in his section and would review each file. His one and only screening criterion was religion. He opened the first folder.

An hour and a half later, he pushed back from his desk and sighed loudly. Eighty-six files on one side of his desk, and six files on the opposite side. Six people who admitted to being Muslim, and he had hired each one of them. He stacked the six files into a neat pile and wondered if some low-level government clerk had done the same thing for Nazi Germany in 1938. "Twenty-three thousand dead," he said, loud enough for his secretary to hear him.

She appeared at his door a moment later, her usual banter restrained. "Do you need anything?" she asked. She had sensed that something was wrong the moment he had walked in. He hadn't explained the appearance of the army officers the night before, or his sudden need for personnel records that he had no right to see.

He looked up. "What?"

"You mumbled something, and I asked if you needed anything." Her personality could not be entirely suppressed.

He stared at her for a moment. "Actually, yes. Come in and close the door."

She moved a little tentatively. Never before had Martin closed his door.

"We have a problem," he began after she had taken a seat. If he couldn't confide in her, there was no one he could trust. "Actually, two problems." He rapidly told her what had happened after she had left. He told her everything, despite the warnings of General McDaniels. "So we have a spy among us."

Martha accepted the news calmly. "I would guess we have several spies among us. Most of what we do leaks out long before anything is published, but this—this is a betrayal of everything we stand for."

"I've gone through these," he said, motioning towards the tall stack of personnel files. "And I found six people who might fit the profile." The last word gnawed at him.

"Muslims. You've been looking for anyone who is a Muslim." She said it as an accusation. "The ethics of what you're doing aside, it has no chance of finding the mole." She straightened up. "Do you remember what happened nine years ago, when the FBI tore this department apart after the Ebola isolates were stolen? Do you remember the suspicion? The atmosphere was poisoned and the environment of cooperation was lost forever. In six months, we turned over almost the entire staff. It's taken more than five years to reestablish a coherent and dedicated group of individuals with enough skill and experience to make a difference. Those ninety-two files sitting on your desk are the start of something that will tear us apart again."

"If you have a better idea, I'm all ears," Martin said. He wasn't trying to bandy words with her; he simply had no other ideas. McDaniels had told him to quietly review his staff, and this seemed the least intrusive way of doing it.

"You could have asked me. Nothing happens in this department that I don't know about." She abruptly stood and went to her desk.

For a moment, Martin thought that he had offended her greatly, but then she returned with a pile of computer readouts. She closed the door behind her.

"This came through yesterday afternoon," she said, and pushed a pile of readouts towards him. Six lines were highlighted in yellow. "Someone tried to access your computer six times yesterday. On the sixth try, they got in."

Martin stared at the page of seemingly random numbers and words. It may as well have been Martian for all he could make out. "I take it this is unusual?"

"You are supposed to have a secure connection. No one, anywhere, should have access to it." She dropped another pile of readouts on to his desk. "Back in February they did the same thing." Three more highlighted lines.

"Martha, I'm sure this would all be very interesting, if only I had a clue as to what you're showing me." He pushed the two piles of readouts back towards Martha.

"What it means is that we have found our spy, or at least the computer he's using." She gathered the readouts and unceremoniously dropped them to the floor, then sat back down. "Yesterday, when you were on the phone with the director, I heard your computer beep. It does that when it's being accessed remotely."

"I don't remember any beep." Martin managed to look both dubious and confused at once.

"You were shouting at the time. Besides, it's a very small beep—a beep that shouldn't have happened with you in the room, so I tracked it down. That was the first set of files I showed you. I found the computer's address and looked for anything else out of the ordinary, and up popped the February readout, only that time they did more than just browse some files. I haven't finished sorting out what they did exactly, but I'm willing to bet my paycheck against yours that someone tried to change the original Colorado Springs report. I think that they tried to wipe out the original file and replace it with one of their own."

"Why wouldn't they just delete the file, or at least the micrographs?"

"First, you can never delete a file. The programs won't let you. You also can't delete the micrographs, at least entirely. Every report will have links to the corresponding images. It's that program we bought a few years ago that allows you to write a report, include a case number, and all the images are automatically retrieved from the mainframe and included in the final draft."

Martin vaguely remembered authorizing the purchase of something that sounded like that. "So why wouldn't they change the case number— hide the whole file somewhere in the computer?"

"I don't know. As I said, I'm still working on this. Don't give me that face. I printed this stuff five minutes before you called me in here."

"All right. Whose computer is it?"

"Sabritas," she said, without emphasis or emotion. "But it's probably not him. This spy is not the brightest bulb in the GE factory; these prove that." She pointed at the scattered readouts on the floor. "On the other hand, he, or she, got through a fairly rigorous vetting process and has fooled us for a while. I can't imagine them making such an amateurish mistake as using their own computer."

"So we talk to Adam," he said, letting her take the lead.

"We talk with Adam," Martha said.

Chapter 33

Amanda finally had a reasonable night's sleep, almost five hours in the bed that her husband had used when he was a boy. His presence lingered in all the things a teenage Michael Flynn collected.

"Breakfast," Amanda said as she walked into the kitchen just after Lisa flipped a pancake.

"Good morning, sleepy head." Lisa was unnaturally cheerful. Greg was distinctly glum despite the short stack of pancakes on his plate. Amanda gave each one a quick kiss on the cheek and then sat across from Greg. For fifteen minutes the three managed a comfortable silence as they devoured Lisa's pancakes.

"Worried?" she asked her father-in-law after every scrap of food was gone.

Greg nodded. "What are you going to do about Reisch?"

"Find him," she said simply, leaving the rest unsaid. "The problem is that I think we are too late. I'm guessing that a large number of people have already been exposed to the virus and that this is now more of a medical issue."

"What will you do about that?" It was Lisa's turn. "Will you help?"

"Not if it means going back to Martin or the CDC. They may be best equipped to deal with this, but I doubt that I could control myself. I probably would make things worse. What about the medical examiner you mentioned, Greg?"

"Phillip Rucker—smart guy, but very strange. I think he's probably the next best choice after Martin."

"You two should think about staying inside until this has been resolved. The virus is transmitted through human contact, and neither of you is immune." Amanda got up and rinsed her cup. "I'm going to take a long hot bath before I do anything."

An hour later, Amanda walked back into the kitchen wrapped in a thick warm robe, her hair wrapped in a towel. She could tell without reading anyone's mind that something had happened. "What's going on?"

"Reisch attacked a platoon of soldiers in Mescali. He killed seventeen of them." Pain was written all over Greg's face. "Phil Rucker is in the hospital, and the federal government has imposed a curfew on travel and quarantined the state."

"Maybe I should have just taken a shower," Amanda said.

"Can you find him?" Greg asked.

Amanda opened her mind and felt for the German, but like yesterday, all she could sense was a presence. "He's close; that's all I can say." Greg's face registered his disappointment. "You have to remember, he can do pretty much whatever I can, and it is fairly simple to fade into the background noise of a hundred thousand people. I can tell you that he's injured and mad as hell."

"They think that he may have been shot," Greg added. "Can he be killed?"

Amanda reviewed her own situation. She had been shot at very close range years ago and it barely registered with her. She was an order of magnitude stronger now, and she had every reason to believe that Reisch was also very nearly bulletproof. "Probably not like that."

"So how do we stop him?" Greg stared at his daughter-in-law.

"You don't. I do." Amanda could feel the fear in Greg and Lisa's minds. "Why is Dr. Rucker in the hospital?" She had decided to put herself in his hands in hopes of identifying her immunity and then duplicating it. She accepted that in all probability Martin would be involved at some point, but at least it would be on her terms. Now, without Rucker, it would be more difficult.

"He had a seizure or something," Greg said.

An image of Phillip Rucker suddenly invaded Amanda's consciousness. "For some reason, I think we should go see him." She was filled with a compulsion to talk with the pathologist. Greg stared at her with a look that questioned her strange statement. "I'm not sure why," she answered his look. "But I think it's important."

***

Reisch was breathing hard, but at least the bleeding had stopped. That was twice in less than a day that he had been shot, and the drive back to the outskirts of Colorado Springs had been the most painful hour of his life. He sat on the commode awkwardly and peeled off his blood-soaked shirt. A line of bullet wounds stitched across his abdomen and into his chest—seven shots, not counting the one in his arm from the baby-cop yesterday. This was definitely pushing the envelope, but most of the wounds, both inside and out, had started to seal themselves off. The blood loss, however, was a different issue. He had lost far more than the lethal limit and, although he could will himself to heal, he could not will the needed blood out of thin air. The last place in the world he had wanted to be was Colorado Springs, but he literally had no choice. He was dying, and needed a hospital. Without a transfusion, no amount of healing or willpower would save him.

He slowly changed into the surgical scrubs that he had stolen from the laundry, and gingerly left the staff bathroom. A white lab coat completed the disguise, and now he could conserve his energy and allow the tired and disinterested staff to glance up at him. He found the blood bank and was pleased that the door was unlocked. Less than five minutes later, he had four units of type AB negative blood tucked in the pockets of his gown and scrubs. Now, he just needed a nurse.

He scanned the immediate area and located the on-call physician just up the hall, but to his surprise, he also found the sedated mind of Phillip Rucker. Intrigued almost to the point of distraction, he tried to search the mind of his favorite hobby, but could only see the images of a dying woman.

Two hours later, he had almost a gallon of new blood and fluid running through his veins. All his wounds had sealed shut, and he was starting to feel normal again; a tingling sensation, almost like low-voltage electricity danced across his skin, but otherwise, he was a hundred percent. A close call, but the tragedy had been averted, lessons had been learned, and now he was off to see the surprising Dr. Rucker before disappearing for a very long time.

***

Amanda could feel his presence. He still remained shrouded, but an invisible cloud of malevolence that she could only assume was Reisch grew thicker the more they drove west. She carefully retracted her own mind and switched to a listening mode. "He's close," she told Greg as they parked at St. Luke's. "He could be here, but I can't be certain."

"Can you handle this?" Lisa asked. "You were so exhausted last night."

"I'm fine," Amanda said quietly as Greg called Patton for assistance. "He is definitely here." Her expression changed rapidly to confusion and then anger. "Don't park here, Greg. Drive around to the main entrance."

It took them only a minute to skirt the ER and the loading dock, and it became clear what the problem was. Father John Oliver was climbing out of an old Dodge Neon. "Damn," Greg said at the sight of the priest. He honked his horn and Oliver looked over at them.

Amanda was burning with anger, and was out of Greg's car before it stopped. "Get back in that car and get as far from here as possible," she demanded. She would have done more, but Reisch was far too close.

"He's here, Amanda," Oliver said, his mind filled with excitement.

"I told you to stay put. You have no conception of what you're doing and you're going to get yourself and others killed."

Oliver opened his mouth to argue, but before he could utter a syllable Amanda wound up and hit him with a closed fist across the jaw. His head snapped back and all three of them could hear the bone break. Oliver fell to the floor unconscious. "Lisa, drive him home. Better yet, drive him as far away from here as you can get." Amanda's eyes were filled with rage, and Lisa backed away from her beloved daughter-in-law.

Greg reacted first. "No, he has to get medical attention."

Amanda turned her gaze upon Greg, and he too took a step back. "He will be fine; he's like me now."

"Why did you do that?" Lisa asked through tears as she and Greg lifted the priest back into his car.

"Reisch was in his mind; he almost saw me."

***

Reisch began laughing as he walked down the hall. *So the priest has evolved; isn't that interesting,* he thought. The mutated virus could also induce the Change. The new civilization was going to be bigger than his wildest expectations. But for now, that wasn't important. Phillip Rucker was important now.

Even injured, Phil had managed to stretch his mind across dozens of miles to encourage the soldier to shoot, something Reisch found both impressive and intriguing. Of course, Phil had to be punished for impudence, but perhaps he didn't have to die. He would make an excellent ally against Amanda, and if Phil ever became a threat it wouldn't take much to snip his last thread of sanity.

Reisch walked straight through the intensive care unit and into the isolation room without challenge. Phil was sound asleep, and Reisch sat down at the foot of the bed and searched Rucker's mind. He watched as Phil gave mouth-to-mouth resuscitation to his neighbor, and Klaus suddenly understood. He had killed Van Der at the height of a breakout, when he was most infectious. He had touched the man's face, cradled his neck, and finally closed the dead man's eyes, spreading not just the Colorado Springs virus with his breath, but also the original deadly Hybrid virus with his touch. It was a hardy virus and could easily survive the near-zero temperatures of a cooling body until someone came along and tried to revive the body. Phil was doubly infected.

Reisch gave Phil's brain a jolt. "Wake up, Phil."

Phil's eyes opened, and a look of confusion and then terror shone back at Reisch. Phil recoiled in bed. "Who are you?"

"Oh Phil, how could you ask me that after we've spent so much time together?" Reisch smiled and for the first time allowed Phil to see his true face. "I need to leave very shortly, but before I go we have some unfinished business. You tried to kill me this morning. As you can see, it didn't quite work. You're going to die, Phil, and it's not going to be pretty." Reisch filled Phil's mind and shared the excruciating death of the surviving soldier, but Phil had retreated behind mental walls that no Monster had breached in thirty years. "Interesting and a little disappointing. For me to reach you I have to destroy you. I was hoping that I wouldn't have to do that."

"You were hoping that I would join you." Phil sneered in Reisch's face.

"I must say that was rather rude, Phillip. Did you learn how to be rude inside your little castle? Safe from all the Monsters, safe from the real world?" Reisch smiled. "I have just one more thing to say before we get down to business. Do you remember that pretty little lab assistant, Melissa Shay?" His voice dropped and he leaned in close to Phil's ear. "You killed her. That's right. Your infection reached out and activated her pacemaker and it shocked her to death." Reisch began to laugh as the truth sailed over Phil's defenses.

For a moment, Reisch felt Phil's torment, and he breathed it in like a favorite smell, but then it began to fade. Phil began to fight Reisch's mental intrusion. "Oh, Phil," he said and playfully shook his head. "Everybody fights, but nobody . . ."

A deafening snap filled the room, and Reisch was blinded by a bright blue light. Phil's hand had shot up and grabbed Klaus by the throat; Phil's hand and Reisch's neck began to blacken and burn, but Phil refused to let go. The grip was crushing Reisch's windpipe and a searing pain filled his mind. With almost his last conscious thought, Reisch ripped through Phil's brain like a chainsaw and he finally let go.

Reisch was thrown to the floor as soon as the connection was broken. Phil was unconscious, not dead, which greatly irritated Reisch. He slowly climbed to his feet and gathered himself. Killing an unconscious man, especially one who deserved torment, was no fun, but it seemed to be his only option at this point. Rucker was severely injured, and the possibility that he could be roused now was very low.

Reisch stood over Phil but then began to sway, and would have fallen except for the bedside table. He hobbled over to a chair and literally dropped into it. He needed a moment to recover his strength. The tingling was back in his skin and with each passing moment it only intensified. The hair on his arm began to stand on end, and the monitor over Phil's bed began to smoke and then finally exploded with a shower of sparks. The lights began to flicker and then dim. Reisch looked up to find Amanda at the door.

"Do you want to help? I'm a little tired," he said. "Your pictures don't do you justice, Amanda." Her sudden appearance revived him; energy began to flow back to his fatigued mind, and he slowly rose to his six-foot-five-inch height.

The tempered glass wall exploded next to Amanda, but she didn't move. Screams of panic filled the ICU as computers, phones, and overhead lights exploded. The air crackled with static, and small fires spontaneously erupted everywhere. A few heroic nurses tried to put them out but then switched to clearing the ward of patients as the sprinklers suddenly filled the air with water.

"Is this all your doing?" Reisch had to raise his voice above the din.

"I thought it was yours," she countered. "Now what, do we duel it out like a couple of superheroes?"

"I was hoping that perhaps you'd like to join me. After all, taking life is something you've done, and enjoyed." He took a step closer to her, but the air literally began to sizzle and steam.

"You truly believe that you have been chosen to, what . . . to be our shepherd? Rather egotistical, I'd say."

"Listen to your own words, Amanda. You're not a part of this failed experiment any more than I am. You have no place in society because you are above society. The reason you've been so unhappy is that you've tried to fit into a place that can't accept you. Listen to your aunt."

"She told me to kill you in the most painful manner possible, or can't you see that?"

"I can see the doubt in your mind. Scared of me, are you? I had thought that perhaps it was my duty to destroy you, but now I'm having doubts."

"Pushkin," Amanda snorted. "Am I pronouncing your hallucination's name correctly?"

"I don't see us as enemies, Amanda. I believe all you need to do is accept the possibility of a new world. You could even save those you want—Greg, Lisa, Aunt Emily. It is inevitable and preordained. Even now, people are evolving, just like your priest. It can't be stopped, so why don't you help us?"

"You mean your terrorist buddies?" She scoffed.

"You can see farther than that. They are simply a means to an end, and in time, they too will be gone. No one can stop this, Amanda. I know you can see that even without me the virus will be released."

"Then why do you need that?" Amanda pointed at the small bag attached to his belt.

"Call it insurance." He felt her mind darken as the energy that enveloped her focused into a single point. Reluctantly, but savagely, he threw her against the far wall of the unit. The air about him immediately calmed. "I don't want to hurt you, but I can't let you interfere. If you can't see reason, then I have no choice . . ." He wondered why he hadn't finished his thought the moment before he struck the window in Phil's room. The glass cracked but didn't shatter, and he fell across an unconscious Phil. There was another snap, another blue light, and Reisch was flying against a side wall, his forearm burned to the bone. For a moment, his white lab coat caught fire, but he quickly extinguished it. "This is getting very tiresome, Amanda," he said, picking himself up from the floor. She stared back defiantly, and he struck at her with every ounce of energy he had remaining. Amanda deflected it with a wave of her hand.

More glass exploded, and the air began to snap as she walked towards him. His face began to burn, but still she closed the distance. When she was within ten feet, she was forced to stop.

Reisch slumped against a wall, as his arm was already sealing itself. "An impasse," he said, looking into the anger that filled her eyes. "I can see the killer in you, Amanda. Why don't we take this life together, and start out our new lives right?" He motioned to Phil.

"You reach for him and I will have you," she said, fatigue filling her voice.

"And if you try and protect him, I will have you," he answered, knowing that neither could sustain this mental wrestling match much longer, but that the first to let go would die.

"Tired, Herr Reisch?" She mocked.

"No more than you," he shot back.

Amanda took a step towards him and the air audibly cracked. Reisch backed away, but she kept coming.

"You'll kill him as well," Reisch said, his back now against the window.

"Small price to pay," she said, taking a step into the thickening air. The sheet on Phil's bed began to smoke, the floor began to vibrate, and an unbearably loud, high-frequency sound shattered all the remaining glass in the ICU.

He watched and listened as she struggled with herself. A part of her embraced death, almost welcomed it as a redemptive sacrifice, but a different part stopped her from taking that last step. A shadow of doubt, buried for years under a mountain of conditioning, guilt, and responsibility had struggled free, and she hesitated. *Maybe he's right,* it whispered.

A small red dot appeared on Reisch's forehead, and then three more on his chest. A moment later, he was flying through the air and his only clear thought was *Not again.*

Chapter 34

"We've checked three times; both of them are worthless," Martin said. "The biohazard vial had nothing but wood shavings, and the bottle that was supposed to hold the vaccine was tea." They had wasted eight precious hours sifting through powdered balsa wood before realizing that they had been duped.

"Avanti insists that you're wrong," General McDaniels said.

"We're not," Martin said sadly. "So we're back to square one. Look on the bright side, maybe all Jeser has is wood shavings and tea."

"It makes no sense—why would he go to so much trouble for an utterly transparent ruse?"

"For what it's worth, I don't think he knew. I think that he believed that he had the original virus and vaccine. I'm guessing they found him out and switched the vials."

"That doesn't track well. If they knew that he was going to betray them, they would have killed him, or at a very minimum, sent someone else." McDaniels's voice betrayed his anxiety. "Do you have anything for me, any good news?"

Martin tried to think of anything positive. "We've started to culture the Colorado Springs virus. In a week, we should have enough to work with."

"A week. I doubt that's going to make the president's day."

"There are certain physical realities that limit us and wishing won't change those. What about Amanda Flynn? She would be a tremendous help."

"Yes, she would be, and we may be close to resolving that issue." McDaniels's voice was circumspect.

"You know where she is?" Martin said, with surprise and accusation.

"It's complicated. You don't know all that's going on. I don't even know everything. All I know is that right now she is not an option. That may change soon."

"It better be soon, because for the next week all we can do is sit on our asses. At this point, I'd buy a beer for the devil himself if he could help."

"The devil, huh?" McDaniels asked.

"Anyone, in fact. I am now extending a blanket offer to anyone who can extricate our posteriors from this mess."

"I will pass that on. In the meantime, I have something for you. We finished the background checks on Dr. Sabritas and his officemate Larry Strickland. Both of them are clear, but Strickland had a girlfriend . . ."

"Rachel Hill," they both said at once. The dark-haired beauty was one of the secretaries who had filled in for Martha during her yearly two-week reserve deployment in early January. She had physical access to Martin's computer and wouldn't need much time to work out his passwords. The rumors of the tall and hunched Larry Strickland dating the exotically beautiful Rachel had even reached Martin's ears.

"She's your spy," said McDaniels. "The real Rachel Hill disappeared when she was a junior at Georgetown four years ago, only to reappear in Tampa six months later. They probably killed her. The poor girl had no close family ties and, after several weeks, she was essentially forgotten. Your Rachel Hill has been quietly living someone else's life ever since. Very clever, very discreet, only she wasn't aware that the real Rachel Hill had at one point volunteered to be a bone marrow donor. She had type O positive blood. Your Rachel Hill is B negative—reasonably rare, except in certain ethnicities."

"So now what do we do with her?"

"We will handle it, but I would like you to secure her for us," McDaniels said, without emotion or further explanation. "Please thank your secretary, Colonel Hays, for me. She pointed my people in the right direction; probably saved us a few days."

The line went dead, and Martin wondered if all of McDaniels's phone calls ended so abruptly.

The general had given Martha free rein to find the spy, and she had. There would be no living with her now. "Colonel, can I borrow a moment of your time?" Martin yelled loud enough for Martha to hear.

She appeared at his doorway, freshly showered and wearing surgical scrubs. Her hair was pulled back, and she looked ten years younger.

"Mrs. Hays, you clean up well," he said. "Why . . .?"

"Sixteen straight hours of work in the same clothes," she answered. "Come on, what do you want? I have a photo shoot in five minutes."

"That was the famous General McDaniels. He sent his greetings and thanks. Rachel Hill is not who she says she is."

Martin quickly summarized their conversation.

"So she is the leak," Martha said, without surprise. "She always seemed off to me."

"You're taking this well. Did I fail to mention that, whoever she is, she had every intention of watching all of us die?" Martin was surprised by her utter lack of emotion.

"You want me to get her so we can beat her brains in?" Martha feigned to leave her favorite spot just inside his office door.

"Why don't you ask her up here, but try and leave her brains where they're at." Martin forced a smile.

Ten minutes later, the tall and dark woman everyone had known as Rachel Hill walked into Martin's office and sat in the only clear chair; behind her came Martha. Two armed security guards discreetly entered the outer office and took up station on either side of Martin's door.

"Who are you?" Nathan asked without preamble.

She stared back at him with eyes as big as saucers, beautiful saucers. "Dr. Martin, you know who I am," she said in a sweet, innocent voice that conveyed complete confusion. She looked up at Martha.

Martha finally displayed some emotion. "Drop the act. Rachel Hill disappeared four years ago in Washington. For all we know, you killed her." The colonel of the army reserves had repositioned herself between Martin and the girl.

"I have no idea what you're talking about. I am Rachel Hill." Her voice cracked, and she began to shake. Her eyes welled up, and without warning, Martha slapped her face so hard that the guards jumped. She followed the slap with a left hook. Blood from the girl's nose sprinkled across Martin's desk, and Martha threw herself at the reeling young woman. Martin jumped to his feet, not sure how to respond to his secretary's unprovoked violence. Thoughts of army "enhanced-interrogation techniques" raced through his mind.

"Grab her arms!" Martha yelled to one of the guards, and they both launched themselves at the pair of struggling women. They pinned the arms of pseudo-Rachel Hill behind the chair and quickly handcuffed her, which only made her start kicking and bucking in the chair. It took a couple more minutes to completely subdue her, and then Martha stood back up and tucked her scrubs back in. Everyone in the room was breathing hard.

"You want to explain to me what all that was about?" Martin's voice was so high, he wondered if he was squeaking.

Martha was still out of breath and simply dropped a small handgun onto his desk. "I'm fairly sure that was meant for us."

Everyone looked at the woman in the chair. Her long hair was strewn across her bloody face, and her scrub top was torn down the center, exposing her deep cleavage.

No one spoke, and Martin slowly returned to his chair and stared at her. She was older now, the façade of innocence slapped off her face. "Who are you?" he repeated.

She threw her hair back and glared at him, saying nothing.

They sat staring at each other for a long moment. "I think I am going to make a very powerful man angry," Martin said, standing abruptly. He turned to Martha. "I'll be back in a moment."

It took him ten minutes to find everything he needed, and a handful of curious lab personnel followed him back to his office. "Here we are," he said to Rachel Hill in a whimsical voice. "Now, technically, I am a federal employee, and I probably shouldn't be doing this, but what the hell. We're all friends here, and you tried to kill us, twice." He jabbed a needle into her arm.

Chapter 35

"Where is he?" Patton asked himself, looking out the broken third-story window. An entire battalion of Army National Guard had spent two hours searching every inch of the hospital and its grounds, and Klaus Reisch seemed to have vanished. "I'm telling you, he's a magician," he answered himself, and then pulled his hulking form back into the destroyed room.

"We're certain that he was hit, Chief," the SWAT team leader said. "No one could have survived three to the chest and a backwards fall out of a third story window."

"So you're telling me that a dead man got up and walked away . . ." Patton bit off the rest of his sarcastic remark. He was starting to lose control of himself more and more frequently. "I'm sorry, Captain. I believe you, but Reisch isn't just anyone."

Patton turned away and shuffled through the broken glass out to what was left of the nursing station. Greg and Amanda Flynn were sitting in the middle of a semicircle of heavily armed soldiers. He knew it had to be done—no one wanted to risk losing Amanda—but it was almost comical. If she wanted to go, there was absolutely no way of stopping her. He veered around the group and headed for the man in charge.

"Chief," the career military officer nodded as Patton approached.

"Can I have a moment with you, Captain?" Patton led the army officer into a deserted patient room. "I know you have orders, and you are just following them, but do you have any idea how dangerous that is?" He pointed to the ring of soldiers around the Flynns. "If that young lady decides to leave, we're going to have a whole lot more dead soldiers on our hands."

"I have been ordered to hold her," the captain said.

"You are provoking her at a very dangerous time. Who is your CO?" Patton had taken out his cell phone.

"We are taking our orders from federal authorities."

"Please give me a moment, Captain." Patton turned away and after a moment had Don Heller. "It's Patton. I'm here at the hospital." He paused. "No, we haven't found him, but that's not what I'm calling about. A ring of armed soldiers is surrounding Amanda Flynn." Patton paused again. "I understand, but you know very well that we can't hold her against her will. Remember what happened yesterday outside the mall, and this morning in Mescali?" He waited a moment and then handed the phone to the captain.

"I understand, sir," the captain answered after listening to the FBI agent and then closed the phone. "She is now officially your problem," he said. A few minutes later, Patton was alone with Greg and Amanda.

"You have become my problem," he said to Amanda. "Is he dead?"

"No. I doubt he's even hurt. He was focused on defending himself. Look for the bullets somewhere in the room. Their force probably shattered the glass, but I doubt any even hit him. The fall wouldn't have done much to him, either."

"I know you're tired, but do you know where he is?" Patton tried to sit on the counter in front of her, but it immediately cracked.

"No idea. It wouldn't take much for him to conceal himself, and he will after this morning." Amanda took a deep breath and looked up at the big black man. "He has to be found. Can you get Ron Benedict down here as soon as possible?" Patton suddenly looked puzzled.

"Never heard of him."

"He's the assistant director for the FBI; he was in Denver last night. You have a much bigger problem than Reisch." She looked over at Greg to include him in the conversation. "There are eleven terrorists spread out across the country, and each of them has a vial of the original virus. The bad one. My virus.

"There used to be sixteen. Reisch didn't know what happened to the other five. In less than two days, he is supposed to send a message that will coordinate the release. He doesn't know who they are, how they got here, or where they are. No one does. They were ordered to disappear, and communicate only through the Internet. They've been using a web site called In Time."

"So, he hasn't sent the message yet. If we can get to him before he can send it—" Greg said, but Amanda cut him off.

"They have contingency plans in place. They're trying to time this exactly so that only the U.S. is affected, and if the moles don't hear from

Reisch within four days, they will release the virus themselves. That doesn't really matter because I'm pretty sure he's sending the message now."

"So Reisch is out of this, aside from general mayhem." Patton said thoughtfully, but Amanda shook her head. "There's more?"

"I'm afraid so. He has a small satchel or fanny pack—I don't know what they're called—but inside are two vials. One is a large dose of concentrated virus, and he plans to gradually release it until everyone, not just Americans, has been infected. He sees himself as a new Moses leading the chosen people." Amanda pointed a finger at her own chest.

"What's in the other vial?" Greg asked.

"A vaccine. Reisch stole both vials from a man named Jaime Avanti. He created the virus and the vaccine and he was sneaking it to . . ." Amanda smiled weakly. " . . . to Nathan Martin." She looked at Greg and her smile broadened.

"So he's a part of this?" Greg said darkly, while Patton looked on confused.

"I'm starting to need a score card for this. Who is Nathan Martin?"

Amanda turned to the new chief of police. "He's one of the heads of the CDC; we have a history." She turned back to Greg. "No, he's not involved. Avanti wanted to limit the full effect of the virus and was going to give Martin the means to do it."

"So if we catch this Reisch, we're back in business. We'll have the vaccine." Amanda shook her head again and Patton wanted to scream. "There's more?"

"A vaccine has to be administered before a person is infected. If the eleven release the virus as planned, the vaccine will be worthless, at least to us."

Patton got up and began to pace through the wrecked ICU, cursing colorfully.

"I guess he needs a moment," Greg said. "Are you alright, honey?"

Amanda turned to Greg. "Reisch was correct about two things: a lot of people are going to die, and no matter what happens, there's going to be a whole new group of people like me. And some of them are going to be just like him."

Patton returned, his face red but his voice under control. "You're the only person who can catch Reisch, Amanda, but you are also the only hope anyone has for curing this thing."

"I know what you need. I'm sure I can spare a pint or two."

Chapter 36

"Don't worry, Rachel, or whatever your name is. It's just a harmless little cocktail we give to the animals when they get too excited. Just a little Fentanyl, a little Pentobarb, and a few other mild sedatives. It shouldn't hurt you too bad. How do you feel?"

Despite his even tone, Martin was in a controlled rage. He couldn't get at Jeser, but he certainly could take care of their spy. The military and FBI would treat her with kid gloves, and she would tell them nothing, safe in the knowledge that American law would prevent them from doing anything more uncomfortable than talking to her sternly.

Rachel's head dropped, and she stopped straining against the handcuffs. For a moment, everyone thought that Martin had killed her. Then she gasped loudly, and her head came up. "My nose itches," she mumbled.

"A common side effect of the narcotic," Martin said. He looked up to find that Adam Sabritas had joined the crowd of onlookers.

Adam's hair was a mess, and he obviously hadn't showered in days. He started to wave a sheet of paper at Martin, but then stopped when he saw Rachel.

Nathan turned to Martha as Rachel's head lolled again. "See if you can find a cardiac monitor. I don't want her to die on us."

"I'm not sure you should be doing this," Martha whispered.

"I'm not going to let millions of people die when she has answers in her head. Her civil rights are not more important than their lives. You know no one else will do this; no one else can do this." It was a singular moment of opportunity, and he would not look back on this moment with regret for not having done all he could.

Martha nodded and weaved her way through the growing crowd. Adam took the opportunity to move in closer.

"Dr. Martin," he whispered, despite the fact that everyone could hear him. "I want to show you something." But it was obviously not the right time. "I suppose it can wait."

Rachel looked up and then around the room. A pale Larry Strickland had worked his way forward, and Rachel's hypnotic eyes fell upon him.

"Do you want to tell him what we did on his desk?" Rachel spoke slowly and softly, each word understandable, but slurred.

Larry looked up at Martin, his face burning with humiliation and embarrassment.

"It was just—"

Martin waved him off and lifted Rachel's chin. "I don't care how many people you seduced, or where you seduced them. I want to know your name."

"Maria. I am Maria Belsky." She tried to lift her head proudly, but the wobble ruined the effect. "I am from Bosnia. You remember Bosnia." She could barely form the words.

"Who sent you here?" Martin shook her arm to rouse her. "Somebody get me some Narcan and Romazicon." He needed to reverse some of the sedative effect. A syringe was passed up the crowd to him, and he injected a quarter of the clear fluid into her shoulder. Cardiac and respiratory monitors were wheeled in, and Martha attached the leads to the young woman's chest.

It took a couple of minutes; then her eyes opened widely, and for a second, she looked frightened and confused. "You can't do this to me." She was more awake but still drugged.

"Who sent you, Maria?" Martin's voice was softer, more inviting.

It took her half a minute to respond. "Doesn't matter if you know." The words were still slow, but her eyes were open. "Dr. Avanti sent me. It was all his idea. He made the virus," she slurred.

"Who did Dr. Avanti work for?" Martin continued with his soothing tone. Her eyelids began to flutter again; the short-acting Narcan was beginning to wear off, and she was about to sink back into the depths of unconsciousness.

"He never really knew, but I did," she smiled crookedly. "It took me five years to work it out." Her head dropped again.

Nathan looked up confused, but Martha elbowed her way to the front. "Maria, honey," she said in a sweet southern drawl, "can you tell me who you work for?"

Maria tried to smile again, but the muscles in her face weren't working well. "Lots of people. Dr. Martin is one of them."

"And then there's Dr. Avanti," Martha said, and Maria nodded. "Do you work for anyone else?" Maria's head stopped swaying, but her eyelids began to flutter. "It's all right, Maria. You can tell me your secret. It's fun to tell secrets, especially ones that show how clever you are."

Maria managed to smile. "The First Directorate."

Everyone in the room blinked except Martha. "*Mokete bol nonfat mehr?*" she said, and everyone in the room blinked again.

"*Da, bol robopute ha pycckom rebike xopowo.*" Maria seemed to be more comfortable with Russian.

"Caenante bol pabotaete ara Sluzhba Vnoshney Razvedki?" Martha seemed just as comfortable.

"Da, b teyehne debrtn net."

"Okay, Martha, what's she saying?" Martin whispered in her ear.

"She's a spy, a Russian spy."

Chapter 37

"Why are you here? You should be miles from here," Amanda asked the approaching Oliver. She looked accusingly at Lisa. They had moved to the relative calm of the ICU waiting room. Amanda had repeated her story to the FBI, and they had started the process of shutting down the web site. She still had a needle in her arm as the second of two bags filled with her blood.

"We heard what happened on the radio," Oliver said sheepishly. Amanda looked at Lisa, waiting for an explanation. "It's not her fault; I made her do it." Oliver's meaning was clear.

"Sorry about the jaw," Amanda said to the priest after a second. "I'm too tired to look. Can you tell where he's gone?"

"Not exactly. I know he's pretty far from here. He started out going south, but then he stopped. I thought he was trying to get out of the state, but now I'm not so sure. Are you all right?"

"I will be; just a little down after our encounter." An idea had been forming in her mind, and she tried to appraise the priest's inner strength. "Father, do you remember yesterday's lesson, the laser pointer? Do you think you can do that?"

Oliver slowly nodded.

"Do you think you can do it well enough to isolate a single mind?"

Lisa piped in. "He certainly focused in on my mind."

"But you were sitting right next to him." She turned to her mother-in-law. "Can you do it on a stranger, in a crowd? I don't mean someone like Reisch; can you do it to someone who is unaware, if you got reasonably close to them?"

"I can see where you're going with this, Amanda," Patton said.

"I think so. How is that going to help us find Reisch?" Oliver asked.

Amanda quickly explained what she had learned from Reisch. "There are eleven people out there, and each one is as dangerous as Reisch. I'm guessing that they have to be in or near major population centers—certainly New York, L.A., and Chicago."

Oliver looked dubious. "There are millions of people in those places. How do I find just one mind?"

"It's not as farfetched as it seems. Just sniff around; open your mind as wide as it will go and I'm guessing this guy's mind will find you because you're looking for it. There will be a natural attraction. Even if that doesn't work his mind will have some unique characteristics—excitement, fear, a sense of purpose and finality. It will be a singular pattern. You should be able to sense it and then home in."

"A psychic bloodhound," Greg said.

"Well, I can try," Oliver said, and Amanda felt a singular pattern of fear and excitement pouring out of him.

"At least it will keep you out of my way," Amanda said, smiling.

"Pick a place," Patton said getting to his feet.

"New York?" Oliver said. "I've never been there and I'm sure it would be a target they would want to hit." He looked around the room for consensus.

"As good a place as any," Patton said. He practically lifted the priest to his feet. "At least we'll be doing something." Patton's gaze fell on Amanda. "I'm still responsible for you. Are you going to behave?"

"As soon as I recover, I'm going after him. I will do what I have to do." Amanda was getting tired of saying that to people. "But I have to do it alone." She looked in turn to Lisa, Greg, and finally Oliver."

"Fair enough," Patton said, guiding Oliver to the door.

"You're taking him now?" Greg asked. "It might be helpful if I went with him." He quickly looked at his wife.

Patton looked at Oliver and then Amanda.

"I feel like a piece of meat," Oliver quipped.

"Well, we'll meet you downstairs," Patton said, and he walked out of the waiting room. After a moment's hesitation, Oliver followed.

"As soon as this is done, I was thinking about going home and taking a nap. I'm in no shape to do this again," Amanda said to her in-laws.

"I can drive her," Lisa said to Greg. "Go, do your job." He kissed them both and hurried after Oliver.

***

"What's it like, knowing what everyone around you is thinking?" Patton asked Oliver as they waited for the elevator.

"I have been doing it for exactly one day, but so far it's been rather sad," Oliver said, hitting the down button for the elevator.

Patton looked at him with a frown.

"Most people scurry around, wrapped up in selfish and superficial concerns. They're so involved with the trivial aspects of life that they never really learn what's important to them."

"Jesus Christ," Patton said, without thinking. "How depressing."

Oliver shook his head. "It's not as bad as it sounds. Once you break through that superficial layer, you realize that most people are just like you. We all are driven by the same needs, we all want the same things, and we all are plagued by the same insecurities. All the same basic programs have been written into our souls, and that's what connects us."

Oliver's voice trailed away as a young couple approached. The woman was carrying a new baby and was engrossed in his smiles and cooing. The young man shuffled behind them, enveloped in an aura of blackness. Even Patton could feel the cloud of malignancy that surrounded him.

The elevator door opened, and Patton stopped his appraisal of the young man long enough to squeeze into the car behind him. The door closed, and Oliver shifted closer to the two parents, pushing Patton's stomach up against the polished stainless steel. Patton grunted and looked down at the priest and found him staring intently at the couple. For a moment, he thought he was about to bless the baby, but then the elevator dinged and the door slid open. Patton took three large steps and waited for Oliver. The priest caught up to him and paused. "Wait here for just a moment, Rodney," he whispered as the young parents walked toward the lobby doors.

The young man stumbled a little, and then he let out a scream that filled the two-story atrium. He grabbed his head and fell to his knees, cries of pain echoing off the glass. The new mother was startled at first. She tried to bend down to her husband, but he was thrashing so wildly he threatened her baby. Then she started to scream for help, and the baby began to cry. Patton leapt forward and gently brushed her aside. He took hold of the smaller man's shoulders and eased him to the floor. His screams were reduced to intermittent yelps that were almost as bad as the blood-curdling yells. His wife and child were crying so loudly that Patton wanted to be anywhere other than between them.

A few moments later, a nurse and two orderlies arrived and took over. Patton backed away as rapidly as the growing crowd would allow and just stared as the stricken young man was attended. He found Oliver comforting the young mother. He had guided her away from the commotion and was practically whispering in her ear. The baby had quieted, but Mom continued to cry. She began to respond to what the priest was telling her, nodding her head. Patton didn't think it was wise to intrude, so he waited as more help arrived, some of which was directed to the woman.

"Go with these nice people, honey. They'll take care of everything," Oliver said quietly. The woman's eyes were wide but unfocused, almost as if she were coming out of a trance. Oliver walked towards Patton. They exchanged glances and proceeded without a word through the double doors and into the early spring sunshine.

"You did that, didn't you?" Patton said as they approached the car. "Was he going to hurt them?"

"Yes," Oliver said, without further explanation.

"Be careful how you use that," Patton said softly, but then thought, *if you can't trust a priest, who can you trust?*

"Don't put too much faith in any man, Chief, including me," Oliver responded to his thought. "But I will be careful."

Chapter 38

The MRI looked terrible. Streaks of gray and black filled the screen, and no matter how they tweaked the dials, they just couldn't image his brain. The CAT scan had been a similar failure, and James Neval was running out of options. Dr. Rucker had sustained a devastating injury on top of an unidentifiable infection, and nothing they did seemed to make a difference. They had placed a small monitor under his scalp to measure the pressure inside his brain, and the last time he had checked that number blinked 42. It should have been less than 15. He was in a deep chemical coma; it was the last reasonable thing that could be done, and it wasn't working.

"I've tried everything I know, and even some things I don't know," the neuroradiologist said. "I just can't get you an image. He's got to have metal or some strange paramagnetic effect in his head." He was frustrated. It was their second attempt, and these pictures were worse than the first.

"What do you think?" Dr. Neval asked the radiologist.

"I think he's fucked," he answered. "You can't control his ICP without meds, and the meds make him hypotensive. I think it's game over."

Neval was about to respond, but his pager suddenly beeped. "Guess who?" he said, exasperated, after checking the message.

"Rucker."

"Right the first time. You're almost smart enough to be a neurosurgeon," He left the reading room, ignoring the sarcastic response of his friend.

"We can't keep his pressure up with all this sedation, Doctor," said Sandy Fuller, confronting Neval at the doors of the emergency unit. All the ICU patients had been moved to the emergency room, doubling its burden. "I've had three nurses with him for six hours now, and we're only losing ground. I hate myself for saying this, but we're going to lose other patients who can be saved."

Neval knew this was more than just nursing exhaustion. Even before the destruction of the ICU this morning, it had been working at twice its capacity with only two-thirds the nursing staff.

"If we extubate him, can we keep him where he's at?" asked Neval. Removing Phil's breathing tube was tantamount to a death sentence. Without the respirator hyperventilating him, the pressure in Phil's brain would build to the point where blood could no longer circulate.

"It's not a question of space. I just can't have three nurses in with him every moment, and right now, that's what it takes."

"Extubate him," Neval said reluctantly. Phil Rucker was going to die, but his death would allow the nurses to save two, maybe three more lives. "Turn off the Propofol drip and let his blood pressure find its own level."

"I'm sorry, Doctor; I truly am." They stared at each other for a moment. "Goddamn them," she said and walked away.

James Neval had been born in Cadiz, Spain, and had grown up in a very non-traditional family. His mother was a devout Catholic, which accounted for his given name, and his father a rather liberal Muslim. His last name was innocuous enough so that when at the age of twelve he found himself in an upscale suburb of Philadelphia he was able to blend in. At the age of eighteen he followed his father down the path of Islam and never looked back. Three years later he watched in horror as jets flew into the World Trade Center, the Pentagon, and a field in Shanksville. For the first in his life, he was ashamed of his heritage. It was a completely natural but thoroughly irrational emotion. He knew that Islam was a religion of peace and tolerance, and in a blink of an eye a handful of madman convinced the world that it was a creed of hate and violence, and that every Muslim living in America should be viewed with suspicion. Almost fourteen years later, with the wound only partially healed, Jeser and Jaime Avanti had ripped it open again. "Allah damn them," he whispered, and watched as Sandy Fuller communicated his orders to her staff.

Chapter 39

"A spy, a Russian spy!" Martin screamed.

"Dr. Martin, you are not helping matters," Martha whispered. "I think you should take a break, walk around a little bit and clear your head. Let me handle this."

He didn't like being "handled," but he saw her logic. Without another word, he walked out of his office. The last thing he heard was Martha demanding that everyone leave the room.

Nathan gave her twenty minutes and then crept back into his office. He lifted Maria's head, and her eyes opened dreamily. Given the dark hair strewn across her face, the half-open but piercing blue eyes, and the torn blouse revealing flawless breasts, it was easy for Martin to see how this woman could have infiltrated his department. She radiated raw sexual energy, and even now, when he wanted nothing more than to strangle her, a part of his mind had reverted to teenage form and wanted nothing more than to touch her. "What did she tell you?"

"Everything," Martha said, frowning at her boss.

Nathan looked up at his secretary, and although she was striking in her own right, he couldn't help but notice how much older she looked. "Tell me," he said, letting Maria's chin drop unceremoniously back to her chest.

"She's from Bosnia, educated in Berlin. Recruited to the SVR seven years ago, and has been undercover watching Avanti for the last three. The Russians wanted him almost as much as we did." Martha had donned reading glasses and read from her notes. "I gotta hand it to her, she is good. Aside from her obvious talents, she's got other things going for her. She worked out Avanti's contacts; even he didn't know who he was really working with."

"Who?" Spies, undercover agents, and international intrigues were all very interesting, but what he really wanted to know was why she was here. What was so important that Avanti would risk putting a mole right under his nose?

"A group of eight men. In this incarnation they were funneling money and directions through a front man, a Saudi prince named Al-Rhodan, who doesn't exactly share his great uncle's Western bias. On the surface he appears credible enough; in fact eight years ago the Saudi royal family issued a death warrant for him. She didn't know what he did to deserve that, but it had to be something for the royals to want to kill one of their own."

"So this Al-Rhodan guy is Avanti's contact, but someone else is really pulling the strings," Martin clarified. "So who are they?"

"That's where things start to get a little fuzzy. She only turned up two of the eight. One lives here in the States: David Moncrief. He's a French national living in upstate New York." Martha paused. "I've never heard of him either."

"Okay, so if Avanti never knew about Moncrief and his pals, how come she knows about them? Was she sleeping with someone else?" Martin asked.

"It was nothing like that," Maria said unexpectedly. Her words were slightly slurred, but she was starting to speak on her own volition. "We knew of the Group of Eight from Igor Nachesha."

Martin looked at Martha for an explanation. "Ugo oil," she said, without elaboration. Martin was still lost.

"He used his stolen fortune to join the group. One billion American dollars was the enrollment fee. We followed a hundred million dollars from Nachesha, to Al-Rhodan, and finally to Avanti. I was sent to find out what he was doing with it." Maria said thickly. "You can release me. I am not your enemy."

"Your handgun says otherwise," Martin answered. "I thought you were supposed to be spying on Avanti for the Russians. What are you doing here?"

"A fool's errand. I broke into your computer files, but there was nothing in them that posed a threat. So he had me steal the epidemiological modeling program. After that, he just had me watch you. We used the Internet to communicate."

Martin was disappointed. He had hoped for something that would be immediately useful. "So what was your escape plan, or were you supposed to die along with the rest of us?" Martin couldn't believe a Russian agent would allow herself to die just to preserve her cover story.

She looked into Martin's eyes with a gaze as steady as the drugs in her system would allow. "I knew nothing of this. For two years, I worked as a translator for him, and later as one of his aides. Then he sent me here. It was only supposed to be for a couple of months, just long enough to gain access to the computer files.

"He used me because I was educated, and because I was a Muslim, but that does not make me a fanatic, or suicidal. If I had known about any of this, I would have reported it to my superiors and disappeared."

She may have been putting on an Emmy-deserving performance, but Martin believed her. "Why don't we let her go," Martin said to Martha, who nodded her head in agreement and then undid the cuffs. "Once you found out what was happening, why didn't you come to one of us?"

"I found out when you found out. Apparently the bastard wanted me dead as much as he wanted you dead." She looked up at Martin and adjusted her torn scrub top.

"The military is coming to get you." He was starting to lose interest in her. Twenty minutes ago he had hopes that she was the answer to everything, but now she was just another dead-end. A vial filled with wood shavings and tea.

"Why would this Group of Eight want to destroy the United States?" Martha wasn't done yet.

Martin leaned back on his desk doubting that Martha was going to get anything more from Maria. She had been blown and would soon be a prisoner of the United States, in need of a large bargaining chip. "I don't think I want to share that just yet."

"Young lady, people are dying, right here, right now, and if you think I will hesitate in using all means available to me—"

"Knowing the motivations of the Group of Eight will not stop people from dying. When the time is right, and the crisis is past, I will tell the appropriate people what they need to know." Maria glared up at Martha, and it was clear to everyone that the younger woman was a well-trained professional and knew how to play the game better than Martha.

Martin watched his secretary's face turn scarlet and then her eyes narrow. "Fine, but I want you to remember that in a short while, you are going to be taken out of this sealed environment and brought to a place where the likelihood of infection is high. If we can't stop this virus, you die along with the rest of us." Martha had bent down, and the two women were now face to face.

"I am well aware of that," Maria said, her voice taking on the slightest trace of an Eastern European accent. "As I told you a moment ago, I have no desire to die, or to see any of you die."

"What happened to the real Rachel Hill?" Martin rejoined the conversation.

"That is a very good question." She turned to face Martin. "When I first came here, I met a man named Kameel Neser. He gave me all of Rachel Hill's papers and accompanied me to Tampa. We spent four days together setting up her new identity in Florida. Just before he left, I asked him about the real Rachel Hill. He said that he had taken care of her, and that there was no possibility of her reappearing. He left no doubt in my mind that he had killed her. I passed on his name and photograph to my control officer, and I forgot about Neser. Two months ago, my control officer contacted me; Neser had been arrested. I was told that he was in possession of a firearm that had been used in a double homicide, and that I was exposed. I was supposed to come in, but I had invested years of my life getting close to Avanti, and I wasn't willing to throw that away."

"Kameel Neser. Was that his real name?" Martha was writing again.

"That is his real name. He introduced himself to me as Alexander Stone, and that is the name he is using in the federal prison in Cumberland, Maryland. I am guessing that Neser took care of more than just Rachel Hill."

"You should have told us this earlier, Maria," Martin said as his phone began to ring.

Chapter 40

Phil was awake, wide awake. In fact, he was more awake than he had ever been. He tried to move, but the restraints were still holding his wrists tightly. *They should have taken these off already,* he thought. He pulled and felt first the Velcro and then the fabric rip. His right arm came free first, and a moment later, his left was free as well. He undid what was left of the straps from his wrists and tried to sit up, but the monitor screwed to his scalp pulled taut. It probably wasn't wise to remove it, but that didn't stop him. He twisted the small flange, and the monitor unscrewed like a bolt from his skull. A small suture had been thoughtfully placed around the four-millimeter wound, and he expertly tied it. He finally sat up and looked around. He was in an isolation room, with negative pressure and laminar flow. Glass walls surrounded him and he watched the frenzied activity of St. Luke's emergency room in near complete silence. No phones ringing, alarms going off, people screaming, and no voices in his head. He was alone.

He had a vague recollection of being here earlier. A memory of vomiting on a woman's shoe surfaced in his strangely quiet mind. "Catherine Lee," he whispered to himself. Her name had suddenly appeared in his mind. "Dr. Lee," he added, and a series of odd, dissociated memories of Catherine and a man Phil somehow knew to be her husband slowly played out in his head. An image of a terrified soldier standing in the snow suddenly pushed Catherine and her husband aside; the young man was firing a weapon, and then he was gone. Phil sat quietly waiting for more, waiting for the return of his Monsters, but they seemed to have disappeared just like the soldier.

The straps around his ankles began to itch and he unconsciously kicked his right leg, and then his left. Each strap resisted for a fraction of a second and then ripped loudly. Phil looked at their frayed ends and then for his discarded wrist restraints. They too had been shredded. He stared at them, at a loss to explain how four separate restraints could fail, when a distant whisper in his mind distracted him.

"Dialyzed two days ago . . ." The voice seemed to be having a conversation with someone other than Phil. It became a little louder, and then a second voice began to talk over it.

"And then he started hitting her for no reason, so I . . ."

Phil began to eavesdrop on two separate conversations in his own mind. Neither voice spoke to the other, or to Phil. Then a third, and a fourth, and finally an avalanche of voices filled his mind. A radio playing every station at once had suddenly been turned on inside his brain. The noise nearly burst his head and he tried to force these new Monsters back into the dark spaces of his mind.

More than thirty years of practice had made him an expert at corralling the broken pieces of his psyche, but this was like herding cats. After several futile minutes, the pain forced Phil to retreat into himself, but the voices continued as they began to assault his outer shell.

Wrapped inside of himself, he was safe. The Monsters would eventually tire and their voices, along with the pain, would die away. He started to calculate square roots, and then cubed roots, and when that didn't calm the storm in his head he began to calculate the value of pi. Still, he could hear the cacophony of strange disembodied voices banging on the walls.

A memory of Melissa Shay popped into his head, and along with it came a stab of regret, or guilt. Phil had a hard time differentiating emotions. Then images of cells on a microscope slide replaced Melissa, and he seized on the mystery. Anything that spun his mental wheels would wear out the Monsters.

Stem cells and inflammation. Stems cells and inflammation. Stem cells and inflammation. He repeated the phrase like a mantra until the voices beyond his protective walls suddenly began to fade. The memory of the tall, dark man slipped into Phil's refuge.

"You're going to die Phil, and it's not going to be pretty," Reisch had said, and Phil tapped into a tsunami of the killer's memories that had been unintentionally deposited into Phil's mind when their connection was so abruptly interrupted.

Klaus Reisch as a boy, as a teen, as an adult. The German's memory swamped Phil, but data was something he could handle. Reisch in the desert with a man named Avanti. The Hybrid virus. Stolen Ebola and human cultured Herpes Simplex virus. Reisch's miraculous survival and Evolution. George Van Der. Amanda Flynn. Greg Flynn. Even a Catholic priest. All the pieces began to flow together in Phil's tiny little refuge.

Reisch had infected Phil through George Van Der. As the German was killing the old man he infected George with the Hybrid virus. Not the mutated, less virulent form that Reisch had been sent to spread, but the pure lethal original virus. And when Phil showed up to try and revive his neighbor, he became infected. Only, like the priest, Phil didn't die, but began to Evolve.

Phil opened his eyes and the voices assailed him, only they weren't his Monsters, they were the mental signatures of the people around him. Benign and banal.

So boring they're worthy of punishment, said the fragment of Klaus Reisch that had burrowed into Phil's mind. Anger, fury, hate, a whole host of foreign emotions seemed to radiate from the small piece of Reisch. Phil imagined a tiny piece of plutonium spewing out toxic radiation.

He had to let people know what he had seen, what Reisch and his hidden moles were planning. He slid off his bed and for a moment felt the world shift around him, but then it found its axis again. He was in a hospital gown and tied the back after disconnecting his IV and EKG leads. He needed a phone.

A voice exploded in his head and reflexively Phil looked to his left. A nurse was pointing and running at him. Her mind was filled with shock and amazement. For a second the intensity of the nurse's emotions froze Phil in place. They filled his mind and blotted every other thought and voice. The emotions were so powerful, so compelling, and for the first time Phil had a taste of what had been missing in his life. By the time Phil had recovered, the nurse was half-way gowned up with every intention of getting Phil back in bed. "You can't come in. The virus can be spread through the air, and those masks will not protect you," Phil screamed, but she ignored his warning. He tried to hobble over to the door and lock it, but his legs were much too weak. "Stop," he yelled again, but she had reached the door. She pushed the handle just as the lock engaged. "Stay there," Phil screamed.

The confused woman futilely pulled on the door and then started banging on the glass, all the while screaming for help. A part of Phil was still exploring the smooth metal feel of the lock from across the room when he looked up and saw himself through the nurse's eyes and found that he was smiling. She paused her screaming and pounding and stared back at her patient. Once again she recovered herself and began pounding on the door hard enough to threaten the seals.

"Stop!" Phil yelled, and she was suddenly flung against the opposite wall. He watched her fly through the air and then realized what he had done. "I'm sorry!" he shouted. "I didn't mean to do that."

The nurse climbed to her feet, her elbow bleeding from where it had struck the edge of a table. People were running to her aid, and she stared at Phil, confused and very angry. "What did you do?" she demanded, her voice high and indignant.

Her fellow nurses didn't understand the accusation.

"Did you see what he just did to me?" she turned and asked them.

No one answered.

"I need a phone, now!" Phil yelled through the glass. The nurses stared at him, but no one moved. Phil began banging on the glass. "Get me a phone!" he demanded again, and finally someone passed him the cordless extension through the airlock.

***

Martin's first thought was to let the phone ring, since it couldn't possibly be as important as what he was doing right now, but then someone answered it.

"Dr. Martin," some vaguely familiar lab tech called from Martha's desk, "I have a Dr. Rucker for you. He says it's important."

The name sounded familiar, but his focus was on the young girl in front of him, and he didn't want the distraction of searching his memory. "It's always important. Tell him we're closed," he said gruffly, and then thought better of it. "Don't tell him we're closed; take a number and someone will call him back." He turned back to Martha. "What do we do now?"

Before Martha could respond, they were interrupted again. "I'm sorry, Dr. Martin," said the lab tech, "but I think you need to take this phone call. He says he's infected with the Hybrid virus."

The name Rucker finally made a connection in his brain: Colorado Springs.

"This is Nathan Martin."

"Phillip Rucker. I am the coroner for Colorado Springs. I'm calling because I have information about both the Colorado Springs virus and the Hybrid virus."

"How do you know those names?" asked Martin.

"I got them from Klaus Reisch."

"That means nothing to me," Martin said. "I've already been duped once this week, and my suspicion level is running at an all-time high."

"How about Amanda Flynn?" Rucker said, with obvious annoyance. The phone line was silent and Phil went on. "The Colorado Springs virus incites a severe encephalitic process; it's as bad as herpes encephalitis," Phil said.

Martin's mind raced with the mention of herpes.

"A mixture of herpes and Ebola," Phil said suddenly.

"How do you know that?" Martin said angrily.

"That's not important. Look for a third component. Something is stimulating cell growth in the brain, and it's not the Herpes or Ebola. Each of the victims had a thick layer of stem cells lining the ventricles. It's that growth coupled with the severe inflammatory process that accounts for the alteration in behavior and personality and, in some, ultimately death."

"Germinal matrix?" Martin said skeptically. "There has to be another explanation. No one has ever found viable stem cells in an adult brain."

"That's not correct. There have been several reports dating back to 1957. There are large pluripotential cells interspersed among the ependymal cells and the subependymal layers below. Whether we call them stem cells or not is irrelevant. I believe that this virus interacts with those cells and stimulates their growth."

"Interesting theory. I haven't seen any specimens, but you have, so for the moment I'll entertain it. Any clue what this third component might be?"

"It has to be human DNA."

"Possible," Martin said thoughtfully. "The original virus was created under less than optimal conditions. They got their herpes specimen by scraping someone's mouth. It's possible that when they recovered the virus they got a little more than they had expected. Gene therapy." It had taken billions of dollars and millions of hours and experiments to trick small viruses into incorporating pieces of human chromosomes, and then delivering those genes to specific sites. Avanti had managed it without even trying.

Adam Sabritas had followed Martin to the phone and now tugged at his boss's sleeve. "I found it," he said, vibrating with nervous energy from head to toe. Martin turned towards the young man. "I finished sequencing part of the Colorado Springs virus. About half of the DNA is human."

"Did you get that?" Martin asked into the phone, watching the frequency of Sabritas's vibration increase. He looked like an elementary student who had an answer and would explode if his teacher didn't call on him quickly. "What else did you find, Adam?"

"It's the short arm of chromosome eleven." Sabritas was breathless with excitement. "It's a purine receptor locus, but it's incomplete."

"A purine receptor?" Martin questioned thoughtfully. It was possible; purine receptors were small protein complexes within the cell membrane. When the correct key was fitted into the receptor, a cascade of chemical reactions within the cell occurred, most of which were involved with cell survival.

"That would account for the various presentations," Phil said into the phone.

Sabritas had spread out his computer sheets across Martha's desk and kept stabbing parts of them with a thick, stubby finger, saying, "Look at this," over and over again.

"I'm sorry, what did you say, Dr. Rucker?"

"I said that an incomplete purine receptor gene would explain the various presentations. In most people, the virus acts in typical fashion. It invades the cell, inserts its DNA into the host's DNA, creates millions of new copies of itself, and then destroys the cell. The immune system does the rest. As other cells become infected, they begin to display bits of the virus on their MHC proteins, and the cells are destroyed by the immune system."

"That's the encephalitic process," Martin added.

"Correct. The cause of all the destructive changes and the inflammation is directly related to this pathogen's viral characteristics. The psychiatric presentation makes sense as well, because the cells most vulnerable are located primarily in the limbic system."

Martin pushed aside Sabritas's chart and turned the speakerphone on. "I've put you on speaker phone. I want some of my staff to hear this," he said, sitting in Martha's chair.

"The limbic system?" A Ph.D. candidate said after hearing the last bit of the conversation.

"Emotional centers of the brain," Sabritas answered automatically.

"I know that—" the student answered defensively, but Martin's glare cut off the rest of his thought.

A crowd had gathered around the speaker. "Go on, Dr. Rucker," he said.

"The encephalitic process is only half of the story. I'm guessing that in a few cells the purine receptor gene is incorporated into the host DNA, where it is repaired and activated. Instead of producing viable viral particles, the cell produces the actual receptors."

"This sounds a little like Borna Disease," the Ph.D. candidate said in a voice much too loud, and every head turned towards him.

"What the hell is Borna Disease?" Martin asked with irritation.

The student's face flushed with the sudden attention. "It's a viral infection in sheep and cattle. It causes unusual behaviors in the animals." He stammered a little. "Years ago people thought that it might cause depression in humans." A dozen faces stared at him, waiting for the relevance of his interruption. "It's an RNA virus that replicates in the cell nucleus, but it doesn't destroy the cell. It causes unusual proteins to be elaborated across the cell membrane."

Satisfied, people started looking at one another.

"Interesting . . ." Martin said, stammering over the grad student's name.

"Yes, it is," Phil added. "Most of the purine receptors are associated with apoptosis of neuronal cells, but some, instead of initiating programmed cell death, cause the normally inert neurons to either grow or to differentiate. It stands to reason that with the additional receptors, the cells become hypersensitive to their ligands. That's what causes the reformation of a germinal matrix, and it is this unrestrained and rapid growth at the base of the brain that kills people."

Everyone was silent for a moment, digesting Phil's theory. "I have to tell you, I've barely heard of purine receptors." Martin looked around the crowded office. "So now that we have a theory, what do we do about it?

Fighting the encephalitic process with the usual anti-inflammatory agents isn't going to help. How do we stop these cells from dividing?"

"I don't think we can," Phil said.

Most of Martin's staff nodded their heads.

Phil continued, "The key is to start treatment before the combination of inflammation and growth are fully developed."

"At least two other people have survived this infection untreated. For the moment, let's leave them out of this. How did you survive?" Martin asked Phil.

"Discounting the possibility that I shared the same resistance to these viruses Amanda and Reisch had, my survival was based on standard medical management. I was also given antiviral agents shortly after I became ill."

"So do you think it was the antiviral?" Martin asked.

"Yes, I do. The core of these viruses is still the plain herpes simplex virus. The Ebola component seems to allow the virus to survive within the cell nucleus, away from the usual cellular defenses, and improves its overall transmissibility.

"Once a cell has been infected, it will do one of three things: die, in which case it will release more of the virus; differentiate into a harmless form; or begin to divide. I'm guessing that before any cell is induced into growth, there has to be a minimal concentration of viral particles in the brain. This is where the antivirals can be effective. There's nothing we can do once a cell starts dividing, but if we keep their numbers low, their impact will be . . . modest. The key is that the antivirals have to be given as early as possible, otherwise too many of these stem cells will have been induced into growth."

"I'm not sure there are enough antivirals to go around," Martin said.

"Then a lot of people are about to die," Phil answered.

***

Lisa was leading the way and Amanda followed. "Is there something wrong, dear?" she asked when Amanda slowed.

"No, nothing wrong, but I have to do something before we leave." She turned back down the hall and headed for the emergency room. She walked through the double doors as if she belonged. Lisa, not knowing what else to do, followed.

Amanda found Phil almost immediately. His powerful mind filled the cavernous space and Amanda smiled. Phil was much further along than Oliver. She approached the glass and Phil turned towards her.

"Come in," he said, placing the phone back into the airlock. He reached over and unlocked the door.

A nurse watched as Amanda went through the anteroom and opened the isolation door; she started to scream at Amanda to stop. Lisa turned and faced the woman and reassured her that everything was under control.

"I saw you upstairs," she started. "You missed quite a show. I will bet that you have some questions about what's happening to you." Her skin tingled in response to their close proximity, and she slid the only chair in the room away from Phil. She sat down, waiting for him to formulate a question.

"Too many to be answered now."

Amanda could see that he was struggling to blot out the collective mental energies of two dozen people. "It won't hurt you, so don't try and fight it. Organize it and learn to control your mind."

"I've been trying to do that my entire life, with little success. Shouldn't you—we—be out there trying to stop him, them? You did see what I saw in his mind?"

"That and more, Phil. Do you think you're ready?"

"No, but I don't think we have any other options." His gaze was steady, and Amanda sensed that sustained eye contact was something new to him. Swirls of bright red fear filled his mind, but even as the waves of anxiety buffeted him Phil remained resolute. He knew exactly what she was asking of him, and she felt a small part of his mind track Oliver.

"I can see how you survived. Fear and terror are his favorite weapons, but they are old hat to you."

"I'm not comfortable having my personal thoughts out on display."

"You better get used to it, and not just your thoughts, but your memories, your wants and needs, all of it is now open to anyone who can read. In time, you will be able to shield some of it, but from here on out, your life is going to be very different, Phil."

"I won't know how to survive," he said. "My blueprint for survival was just thrown out the window."

"Do you know what needs to be done?"

"The same thing you sent the priest to do. Only I can't leave here; I'll infect everyone I come in contact with."

"He will take care of that," Amanda said, referring to the very tardy Ron Benedict, who was chatting politely with Lisa. "It won't be comfortable, but at least you won't be stuck in here. I need to go, and I hope we will get a chance to talk again. You're a very interesting man, Phillip Rucker."

Chapter 41

Joseph Rider tried to finish his morning newspaper, but the violently bucking subway car and the foul-smelling drunk next to him made it difficult. The train shot out of the tunnel and into the bright March sunlight so suddenly that Joseph had to look away for a moment. The sky was the impossibly vivid blue seen only in early spring, and he focused on it as the buildings of downtown Los Angeles raced by the window. He closed his eyes and tried to absorb its energy and beauty.

"Are you done with that?" the drunk asked, sticking a dirty finger into the sports pages. Rider passed over the entire newspaper without a word. He was certain that by tomorrow it would be among the millions of pieces of garbage that littered the City of Angels. It didn't really matter. America had much greater problems. People were dying by the thousands in Colorado, and then, just to make the world a more dangerous place, the Iranians had foolishly lobbed several missiles at an American aircraft carrier as it transited the Straits of Hormuz. The president's savage and immediate response had already sparked anger throughout the Arab world, even though the Iranians weren't Arabs. People were going to die by the tens of thousands over there, maybe even more. The newspaper that was now serving as a blanket and a sunshade for the citizen next to him had casually mentioned that because of the recent crisis, units of the Strategic Air Command were being reactivated. As assistant director of public safety for the County of Los Angeles, Joseph knew what units those would be. More than thirty years ago, Ronald Reagan had advanced the premise that a biological attack would be the equivalent of a nuclear attack. Across the western United States, soldiers were unwrapping and assembling special munitions.

The train stopped and Joseph got off. People pushed at him from all sides, but he continued his relaxed pace towards the Federal Building. Even though he was an employee of the County of Los Angeles, a shortage in office space had forced him to move into the gleaming new tower two years ago. As he spent most of his time conferring with federal officials, it actually worked out better for him.

He rode the elevator to the twenty-third floor, chatting casually with some other county refugees, and made it to his desk before eight. He was an hour early, as usual, and only a couple of other early birds dotted the Public Safety Center. As an assistant director, he rated his own small office and window. He dropped his briefcase on his desk and started his morning routine. Computer on, coffee maker on, answering machine checked for messages, and mail collected then sorted.

Finished, he sat down and turned towards his window. His official responsibilities didn't start for another half hour, so he thought he might tend to some unofficial responsibilities. He pulled his laptop out of its case and opened it. The small but powerful computer began to boot itself up automatically, and after a minute, a small electronic beep asked for his password. He typed in the five-letter word and his browser came up. He checked the web site, and to his surprise found an invitation to a child's birthday party. The signal had come early, which didn't surprise him. Events were moving quickly and in a somewhat unexpected direction. Five years ago, he had been selected largely because of an ability to adapt to changing circumstances and to act independently, and now he prayed that those abilities would see him through to a glorious sacrifice. The small blue vial lay dormant, wrapped in its special paper, under the foundation of his rented house; he would slip away from work at noon and start the process that would slowly bring it back to life. It would take thirty hours to fully reconstitute, and then it would have to be dispersed within twenty-four hours. The virus needed a host.

He stared down at the commuters three hundred feet below him. They scurried about like ants, living their small, godless lives. He had been told that he needed to infect at least two hundred people to achieve a proper dispersal pattern, but he thought he could do many more than that before he himself was overwhelmed by the effects of the virus. He would be able to pass the virus to more than a hundred just by riding the subway; the rest he would find in the quintessential American institution: the mall. He had found a large upscale mall only three blocks from a mosque, and it would be there that death would find him.

For three years, he had not prayed publicly. When he first arrived in Los Angeles, he tried to carry on all the Muslim traditions and prayers, but quickly found that his thoughts colored his actions, so he forced himself to stop. He had to be anonymous, the typical American: baseball, barbecues, and beer.

He looked out to sea and tried to find the exact spot where the blue of the ocean touched the blue of the sky. He had never seen the ocean until he came to Southern California. It reminded him of the mountains in his native Afghanistan. The wind, the isolation, and nature's total disregard about whether you lived or died. It was a powerful lesson and a perfect metaphor, one that he had learned as a young man in the White Mountains of Afghanistan. He was nothing before nature. No matter how strong, educated, or rich he became, he was nothing more than dust in the wind. Only his faith could save him. Only Allah.

His mind drifted back to his small village. He wished he could see it once more before he died. He wished he could see his father and tell him what he had really been doing these last five years. He knew that at some point, after he had gone to paradise, someone would. A Mercedes, or perhaps a BMW, would drive up the dusty streets where he had once played soccer. A man would get out and, because of his Western clothes, he would at first be viewed with suspicion. After introductions, he would be greeted warmly and invited in as an honored guest.

"Izhac," he would say, "your son died bravely in the service of the Almighty. He suffered much for Allah, but never once wavered. I am humbled to be in the presence of a man who raised such a perfect servant of God." The meeting would end when his father was presented with an envelope full of more money than he had ever seen in his fifty-one years.

Izhan Ahmed, also known as Joseph Rider, closed the laptop and slid it back into its case. *Something must have happened to the German,* he thought. No matter—he had well insulated himself from Reisch. He was beyond suspicion. It was a supremely ironic twist of fate that, quite legitimately, he had risen to a position in which he was now the individual most responsible for protecting the citizens of Los Angeles from people like himself.

Chapter 42

General William McDaniels wasn't paid to track down terrorists; he was paid to kill them before they reached American soil, but he had an idea that wouldn't go away. He strummed his fingers on the small file labeled *Rachel Hill*. The information was new, and therefore subject to error, but he thought he saw the outlines of a pattern. According to Amanda Flynn, as many as eleven parasites had burrowed deep into the body of the United States, and each was armed with a dose of the original virus. Avanti had called it the Hybrid for some reason. Then, there was the fact that over the past three years, databases and storage facilities of the FBI, the Army Medical Corps, and the CDC had been systematically altered and plundered. Now, a spy had turned up in one of those very places and she admitted to altering and plundering the CDC.

There had to be a connection. On the other hand, just how big of an operation could Jeser mount and still stay below the collective radar of the Western world? Did they have the resources to both infiltrate American society undetected and separately invade its secure areas, all without their existence being confirmed?

He picked up his phone and dialed the director of the FBI. It took him two minutes to get him on a secure line.

"Good morning, Bill," said Kyle Stanley.

"Well, it certainly is a morning," General McDaniels growled. "I want to run an idea by you. Yesterday, we found a spy working in the CDC, and I'm guessing she works for Jeser."

"That's fantastic! We have to interrogate her as soon as possible."

"We're on our way to pick her up now. Listen, I have this nagging thought that these eleven infiltrators may also be responsible for some of the computer chaos we've experienced over the last couple of years? This woman assumed the identity of a college coed who had gone missing a few years back and then turned up working at one of the sites that got hit. Maybe some of them are still on Uncle Sam's payroll using the identity of a missing person, just as she did. I was hoping that you had a way of cross-referencing the local police files with the federal employment files."

"It's an idea, but the federal background checks should have kicked those out from the start."

"Even if it's just a missing person report?"

"You know, I don't know that. My guess is that it would, but let me check. I'll call you back in five minutes."

Five minutes stretched to two hours, and McDaniels had moved on to the more mundane business of punishing Iran for last night's ill-fated attack on an American aircraft carrier. They had for years threatened the safety of any ship transiting the Straits of Hormuz, and after the UN imposed a new round of sanctions on the rogue nation they tried to make good on their threat. Their timing was very unfortunate, as other matters had made the president very cranky.

A discreet knock on the door disturbed the planning meeting. "Sir, the director of the FBI is returning your call."

"That will be all, gentlemen," said McDaniels, and two three-star generals and a rear admiral filed out. "Kyle, that was a very long five minutes."

"And that was a very fine idea you had. It seems that not all missing person reports are treated the same. Fact is that in my hometown of Charlotte, if an individual can provide enough documentation, the report just goes away. Want to know what constitutes enough documentation? A photo ID."

"Damn," McDaniels answered.

"It gets worse. For years, when queried, most jurisdictions have simply reported whether the applicant has a criminal record or not. That all changed a year ago."

Years ago, after 9/11, Congress had mandated that all authorities, federal and local, tie into a single master law enforcement database. In typical Washington style, it took them nearly five years to fully fund the simple project, and then almost another five years to complete it.

The director continued, "In my hand I hold a sheet of paper that has a paltry 161 names on it. These are the names of individuals who have at one time in their lives been reported missing, and then later miraculously reappeared, applied for, and were granted federal or state clearance. Technically, these 161 people are still missing, but they're not going to be missing much longer. We're rounding them up as we speak."

"Did you find Rachel Hill?"

"Number eighty-nine. Excellent work, General. Now go blow those bastards up, and we will take care of this."

Chapter 43

"We now believe that Dr. Avanti was himself being misled. Most likely to distract us at a critical moment." General McDaniels shared a couch with the secretary of defense. He tucked his feet beneath the sofa to avoid the United States of America seal that was emblazoned on the Oval Office's carpet. New to the administration he wasn't certain if this relaxed atmosphere was typical of all presidential briefings, but he was certain that he would be much more comfortable standing behind a lectern than sitting in front of his commander in chief.

"Excuse me for interrupting, General, but can anyone tell me how…?" The president searched his notes and then adjusted his bifocals. "How as many as sixteen terrorists insinuated themselves into our society without so much as raising a hair?" McDaniel watched as the president straightened in his chair, and for the first time saw the true measure of the man. The president's calm demeanor had suddenly vanished and McDaniel's was reminded more of an angry staff sergeant addressing his platoon than a president addressing his cabinet. Furtive glances were exchanged, and heads began to drop. "God damn it, this happened on my watch. These bastards slipped in while we were guarding the door." The president slammed the arm of his chair with his palm. A tense and very quiet moment followed. "I suppose that's a discussion we will have later," he finally said. "General, do you have any idea how much time we have before these eleven infiltrators release the lethal virus?"

"Less than forty-eight hours. We're working under the assumption that Reisch managed to send out his message before we were able to shut down the web site. It is possible that some of the infiltrators did not see it before the site was taken down. Unfortunately, that will only delay the release, not prevent it." McDaniels was sitting at attention.

"All of this comes from the young woman that survived this same virus," the president said. "I'm still uncomfortable with this. How do we know that she is not in league with them and that all this paranormal stuff is just to confuse us?"

"I'm convinced of it," Kyle Stanley said. "She took out five of our agents without ever moving. I've seen the video, and the evidence is compelling."

"Any casualty estimates?" The president had turned to his secretary of Health and Human Services, who was visibly uncomfortable in the spotlight.

"Based upon what happened seven years ago, I would say a little less than the entire population of the United States."

"Three hundred million people? You want me to believe that in less than six months, there will be no one left?" The president's stare pinned the secretary to the couch. "Well, I guess we don't have to worry about mid-term elections."

The six men arranged around the president chuckled nervously at his gallows humor.

"Obviously, this is unacceptable. Options?" He searched the faces of each of his advisors, but most of them looked away. "Kyle, what is the probability that we can catch these eleven terrorists in the next forty-eight hours?"

"We have two leads that we're working on. The first may be the most promising. It seems that the spy Avanti used, who by the way was actually working for the Russians, took her identity from a missing person. We're cross-referencing the list of missing persons with federal and state employees. We'd like to branch out a little and look into municipal employees, but that would take days. The other lead is the man who helped our spy establish herself. He happens to be in a federal prison right now."

"Excellent. What about this name she gave us, the financier, Moncrief?"

"The name didn't check out. We're down to basic police work, cross-referencing residents in upstate New York with French citizenry. Unless we get extremely lucky, that direction won't get us where we need to be." Stanley finished by scanning the room, but no one had questions or suggestions.

"What we need is a little more time. We need to extend the quarantine to involve the entire country, Alaska and Hawaii included. I would recommend a complete ban on travel except for emergency and military personnel, and impose an around-the-clock curfew thirty-six hours from now," McDaniels added after the moment began to stretch.

"Why wait?" the president asked.

"It will take some time for all the federal, state, county, and city emergency plans to be activated. It would take at least twenty-four hours for everyone to marshal the resources, and another twelve to get all the people in place. To do this correctly and safely, everyone is going to need a little time."

"You're exactly right. Make it happen." The president made a show of looking at his watch. "That means that the curfew begins eleven tomorrow night." All the men in the room nodded their heads. "Now, on to other business, General. How are the Iranians getting along?"

"Poorly, sir. We are proceeding on schedule," McDaniels answered his commander-in-chief.

"But you don't agree with the schedule?" The president asked pointedly. "Answer freely, General; that's an order."

"I believe that there is no direct connection between the biologic attack and the Iranian attack."

"Of course you know that that's a minority opinion. And they did attack us again this morning. Are you suggesting we ignore attacks so long as they do not inflict damage?"

"No, sir, but a complete dismantling of the Iranian military infrastructure is in no one's best interest." McDaniels turned towards the president. "It is my belief that a single base commander initiated last night's attack after your announcement in hopes of prompting his government into action."

"Are we talkin' about the movie 'Fail-Safe?'" The secretary of state asked and everyone in the room, except McDaniels, laughed.

"Slim Pickens," the president smiled and nodded his head. "Thank you, General; I will take it under advisement. That's all gentlemen." The president stood, and everyone began to file out of the room silently.

Chapter 44

Amanda spent one more night at the Flynns. Greg had flown with Oliver to New York, Lisa had made a wonderful pasta dish, and the two spent the night not talking about anything of consequence. The unspoken fear was that this was the last night they would share, and neither wanted to ruin those last hours. The presence of Reisch and the urgency of the moment began to grow in Amanda's mind, and in the early morning hours she left without saying good-bye. There really wasn't any need; both had said or left unsaid everything that was needed.

She still had her trusted Jeep, and she drove south along the interstate. Reisch was close, no more than ten miles, and despite the ban on travel, she breezed through the roadblocks without slowing. The soldiers saw only an ambulance or military vehicle. Normally, she would be more discreet, but the connection with Reisch was so strong that he had to be just as aware of her as she was of him.

At Fort Carson, Amanda turned west onto Highway115. The town itself was small, but large enough to have its own contingent of National Guard troops at its west end. Amanda waved as she rolled through the roadblock, and the soldiers waved back. Reisch was very close now, but he made no attempt at escape. A shadow of doubt appeared in her mind as she imagined the German well dug-in, waiting for her frontal assault. She consoled herself by remembering their last meeting. He was unable to seriously harm her, but she had come within moments of killing him.

The trail ended at the Sunset Canyon Motor Lodge. Amanda drove into the gravel parking lot and immediately felt Reisch's energy pouring out of room 112. There was an old Pontiac Bel Air parked immediately in front of it, and a screen door swung lazily in the early morning breeze. She parked next to the Pontiac and waited. Something was wrong; he had to know that she was here, yet he wasn't moving. The heat of his malice stung her face, but the power of his mind was directed elsewhere.

Cautiously, she climbed out of her Jeep and approached the door. Her skin began to tingle, but Reisch apparently was so distracted that their proximity hadn't charged the air like it did yesterday morning in the hospital. She touched the screen door and gently swung it open. The rusty hinges squeaked and Amanda almost jumped at the unexpected sound. The main door was slightly ajar, open enough that she wouldn't have to worry about a lock, but closed enough that she couldn't see inside.

Carefully, she pushed open the door. His presence was strong, but it still hadn't changed in any appreciable way; he was still deeply preoccupied. The door had swung half way through its arc when she realized something was very wrong. The very real coppery smell of blood rolled out of the cheap hotel room, and she could see a bare foot. It was a child's foot, and it was covered in blood. Amanda stepped into the doorway and the extent of the carnage overwhelmed her. It had once been a family of five. Three children were arranged on the bed; arms, legs, and heads all severed, but neatly replaced. The mother had been tied to the headboard with electrical cord, stripped to the waist, and disemboweled. Both her eyes were missing, and streaks of dark blood flowed from each socket, telling Amanda that they had been removed while she was still alive. The father had a single gunshot wound to the head. He sat at the desk, facing his slaughtered family. A small handgun lay on the floor inches from his dangling right hand. On the desk was a small empty satchel, the kind that would fit two small vials. A small note sat next to the satchel, and Amanda leaned over to read it.

"Come find me, Amanda."

Chapter 45

Oliver had never been to New York and was amazed at the literal crush of humanity; there were people everywhere. Chicago, even on its worst day, was never this bad. The New York sidewalks were shoulder to shoulder, and every storefront or stoop was packed full of people trying to push their way into or out of doors. The pace was dizzying, and he regretted not having the opportunity to step out of the picture and just absorb its energy, or perhaps just step out of the picture and rest. His own energy stores were just about depleted as thousands of minds assailed him every moment, and instead of blocking them, he had to let them flow over him. The negative emotions seemed to cling to him, while the positive ones seemed to roll away, and he didn't know how much longer he could manage. The consequence of failure was the only thing driving him past the point of endurance. He had been given this ability, this power, for a reason. God had not chosen him randomly, and he would not let these people, or his God, down.

"You wanna take a break?" Greg asked after seeing Oliver again close his eyes in pain.

The two FBI agents in the front seat exchanged glances. They really didn't have time for a break.

"No," he said emphatically. So, they drove on.

***

Even with the help of the assistant director of the FBI, and then later by the director himself, Phil was still in the same isolation unit he had been the day before. The intensive care unit upstairs had been repaired enough to re-accept patients, but nobody thought to move Phil, so he watched the activity of the emergency room through the walls of a glass prison, and paced the floor. Several nurses had asked him if he wanted something to help him sleep.

"No, thank you," he said each time and continued to pace. He couldn't help but think that this must be what life was like for those faces he had seen behind the tall steel doors all those years ago. He had been eight and was simply trying to get home, away from the testing and questions. He was different but not sick, and he didn't need a hospital. Certainly not a hospital that hired employees so simple-minded that they had to use the same seven-number pass code for every door.

Phil shook his head to bring him back to the moment. His memories had intensified, and he could see himself becoming lost in them. He had to remain focused. *Maybe it was a lack of sleep,* but he knew that wasn't the problem. He was rapidly changing into something unknown, and his defenses against the unknown were poor.

Pieces of minds, dozens of them, resonated through his head. In some ways, his Monsters had prepared him for this, and he was quickly learning how to tune in or out the voices. But the fact remained that he was seeing and experiencing things that were fundamentally private, and that made his skin crawl. The thought that someday others would be able to invade his private world at will very nearly sent him into a panic attack. He doubted that what little sanity he had managed to create through nearly four decades would survive long in this new reality.

Control, he told himself. The watchword brought him back to pacing. They were coming for him. Some part of his mind was busy processing the steady stream of voices and information, filtering out the unimportant. What was left formed an awareness of the world around him. This was a tool he could use, but it came with a price Phil doubted he could pay. At some point other people would be able to slip into his mind. . .

Control, he began to repeat. He continued his pacing inside the glass cage and felt the nurses watching each step. It was a perfect metaphor for Amanda's brave new world.

Chapter 46

It had been a long and busy day for Joseph Rider. The federal government was expanding the quarantine to involve the entire United States, and the county of Los Angeles now had less than twenty-eight hours before the curfew took effect. Like most large metropolitan counties, they had a detailed action plan already worked out, and Rider had worked hard all day implementing it.

Martial law had been declared, and in less than a day and a half, no one would be allowed on the streets except for emergency personnel and the military. The National Guard had been deployed; already, their Humvees and armored personnel carriers were taking up positions all across Los Angeles County. Police cars were driving up and down neighborhood streets broadcasting the same message, along with a countdown of how many more hours the citizens of Los Angeles had to prepare themselves for a week's hibernation. Sirens wailed atop telephone poles as people rushed home to turn on their televisions and learn the latest developments; even the annoying emergency broadcast system had been activated. From sea to sea, the United States was shutting down for a week.

The military and police were of course excluded, as were all emergency service providers. Firemen, water and electric workers, hospital personnel, and other essential workers would be allowed limited access to the soon-to-be deserted streets. Some county workers, like the ones in charge of emergency management, would be given unfettered access as well.

Rider smiled. The Americans thought they were so clever. Clearly, they had stumbled across some information. Probably one of his fellow moles had been caught and been made to talk. Now the government was trying to protect its citizens by locking them inside their homes. Jeser had already anticipated this possibility, and Rider effortlessly switched to the contingency plan.

In a little over twenty-four hours, he would carefully apply a fine powder to several sheets of brittle yellow paper and then soak them in water for five minutes. The sheets would transform into what looked like ordinary notebook paper, and the deadly Hybrid virus would be safe inside tiny microscopic cocoons made of high-molecular-weight plastic, so long as they weren't exposed to intense light. Rider would then simply distribute tiny bits of paper, each no bigger than a fingernail, to various places across the county, and the sun and wind would do the rest. It would take a day or two, and then the paper would begin to break down into extremely fine dust particles that were lighter than air. It was a much slower process, but in the end, the wind would carry the virus under doors, through open windows, down chimneys, and find the hiding Americans, who would then die behind their locked doors.

He wondered how the others were doing. If everything had gone to plan, there would be one more Servant of God somewhere in northern California, and a third further up the Pacific coast. He only had a general idea where the remaining martyrs settled, or even an idea as to how many had survived to this point. Three years was a long time to be perfect, and that was what was required of them. Still, there was enough redundancy built into the plan; they only needed eight for all the infected areas to converge and completely blanket the United States. He didn't fear for himself. He was sure that a man in his position would hear the enemy long before they were close. Even if he was captured, the only thing he would regret would be his failure. The Americans could do nothing to him; he was already a dead man who long ago had made his peace with God.

Still, Rider would have preferred the original plan. He preferred the more personal touch. There was a certain satisfaction in knowing that you had personally killed the man who had just rudely brushed past you—along with his family, friends, neighbors, and city. Rider wondered if his streak of cruelty offended Allah. Certainly, the Prophet in all his battles must have drawn some personal satisfaction from the destruction of the unrighteous. Comforted by that thought, he returned to his computer and the plans for shutting down Los Angeles.

Chapter 47

He was trapped by his own cleverness.

"Maybe that's not such a bad thing," Pushkin said as he floated through the wall that separated the kitchen from the living room.

Reisch watched his mentor drift a foot off the ground; a mist of silver sparkles trailed behind as he glided towards the big picture window. The late afternoon Colorado sun shone through Pushkin, and for a moment Reisch lost him in the bright light. "Are you real, or just a product of my mind?"

"If you knew the answer to that question, you would know the answer to a lot of other questions," Pushkin said smugly.

"That's true, but it would also tell me if all those people outside can see you through the window." Now it was Reisch's turn to be smug.

"They can't," the Russian said, unconcerned with the foot and automobile traffic in suburban Pueblo. He turned towards Klaus and began to condense into his usual form. "I think it's a good thing that you're now forced to rely on your skills and experience as opposed to your 'mystical powers.' They've weakened you, made you sloppy at the worst possible time."

Reisch didn't want to argue, and there really was no point in denying the truth.

In the last two days, he had been shot three times, very nearly caught twice, and forced to flee before a foe at least as powerful as him. All three were firsts for him, and all three were a direct result of poor planning and execution. He had begun to put his infallibility before decades of experience. But that was changing now; he was out of Colorado Springs, and already he could feel the mental fog begin to lift.

The theatrics in Fort Carson had thrown Amanda off his trail, but to stay below her radar he was forced to stay inside of himself. Twice he had squared off against her and the best he had achieved with this last encounter had been a draw, but only after she had soundly thrashed him in their first encounter. Both meetings had been unexpected and on her turf; he was going to change that. They would met again, but not until everything was over.

"So when are we going?" a more solid-appearing Pushkin asked.

"Later. I can't escape the military without alerting her, so I'll have to wait until they thin out."

"I find it curious that Amanda had the chance to destroy both of you , but didn't. Why is that, do you think?"

"If I was forced to guess I would say that it was nothing more than survival instinct."

"Strange that after all she has been through that she still clings to life."

Chapter 48

Twenty-eight hours left, and they finally had Rachel Hill, aka Maria Belsky, and Alexander Stone, aka Kameel Neser, in the same building. Kyle Stanley watched as Neser was shackled to the metal table. Maria was in the next room, sitting in front of a similar metal table. Stanley had decided not to have her shackled after she had positively identified Neser. The Russians confirmed Maria's identity and story, but only after the president had called the Russian president and explained his extreme displeasure with their stonewalling.

"Are you sure you want to be involved with this?" one of the assistant directors asked Stanley.

"We are well past any need for plausible deniability, Jack. I will be quite happy to explain to a judge or the American public why I did what we're about to do. Let's get started."

Stanley walked into the interview room just as the tech was finishing with the IV. "I'm Kyle Stanley, director of the FBI. You are Kameel Neser, are you not?"

Neser looked up and sneered. "Where's my lawyer? And what the hell is this shit about?" He waved his restrained arm and the IV, still in his Alexander Stone persona.

"Let me explain the ground rules to you, Mr. Neser. As of fifteen minutes ago, you have no rights. As a matter of fact, you no longer exist. I have very little time, so you will either give me what I need now, or we will extract it from you."

Neser smiled and stared at Stanley for a long minute. "It's happening, isn't it?" He started laughing. "And you think I have the answers. That's beautiful. Go ahead, ask away, because I was never told a thing." He leaned towards Stanley as far as the chains would allow and then smiled broadly.

"I don't know what you're talking about. All we want to know is who you killed and when."

Neser continued to smile. "Bullshit. The director of the FBI doesn't bother himself with trivial little matters like homicide. What's happening outside? Tell me, and I'll give you a name."

For an instant, Stanley was tempted. "What's happening outside is that the climate has changed. As soon as we found your real name, you became the property of the FBI courtesy of the United States Congress and Executive Order 1278." Stanley slowly relaxed himself into a chair opposite Neser. "We have a small project that you have just been enrolled in. I'm afraid that it's very new. In fact, you are our first test subject. That's why I'm here. Although I am curious to know what you're talking about." Stanley smiled broadly. "But in a few minutes we'll know everything, won't we?"

Neser's smile faded, and he tried to cross his arms. "I've got nothing to say."

"You have nothing to say now; that's about to change." Stanley nodded to the med tech. "Last chance."

Neser hesitated, the blood draining from his face as the tech began to swipe the IV with alcohol, preparing it for an injection. "What are you giving me?" His voice trembled very slightly.

"Sorry, we don't need informed consent here. Tell me who you killed and when."

The tech hung a second smaller bag of IV solution, only this was colored red.

"We're going to need to restrain him better before I can give it to him," the tech said to the director.

"For comfort or for effectiveness?" Stanley asked.

"This is bullshit," Neser jeered. He didn't think they would go through with it, but he was starting to have his doubts. Technically, even starting an IV was a violation of his rights, and they had done that without hesitation. Maybe this was more than just an elaborate bluff. He wasn't a fanatic; he wasn't even a believer. He was just good at what they needed.

"Effectiveness. I assumed comfort wasn't going to be an issue today." The tech answered with concern written across his face that he had misread the director's intentions.

"Definitely not," Stanley said.

Two more men wrapped Neser in leather restraints, and he started kicking and biting. It took them two minutes to fully secure every joint in his body, and only after that did they force a bite block between his teeth.

"I believe that you are a terrorist, and you have been convicted of a felony in the United States. The American people no longer have permissive views towards people such as yourself. As a result, we have developed this technique to drain you of any secrets you are reluctant to share. It derived from a compound used in Afghanistan, Iraq, and Cuba—only this is a more effective form. It does have a few side effects, however, hence the need for restraints." Stanley nodded a second time and the new IV was opened. The red solution began to flow into Neser's veins, burning them. He began to shake and scream. "I'm told it burns a little going in." When Neser's eyes and screams took on a different tone, Stanley stopped the infusion himself. "Something to say?" As if on cue, the bite block was taken out.

Fifteen minutes later, they had a list of seventeen names and dates.

"You're a little scary, do you know that?" Stanley's assistant director said to him just before they reached the elevator. "Would you really have given it to him?"

"I was a little disappointed that he broke so quickly. I wanted to see if it really worked."

"It may have killed him."

"It may have," he said. They rode in silence to the top floor, and Stanley could see that a small crowd of people was waiting for him.

"Six matches," a tall silver-haired man said. "We have them all in custody." Six of the names Neser had just "volunteered" were among the 161 names on the "missing" list. "We've sent additional teams to search their homes."

"If all six are correct, and we subtract Maria Belsky, that leaves us with at least ten unaccounted for." Stanley's words burst the bubble of excitement that was floating through his office. It was the first break in the case, but they still had a long way to go. "How many of the 161 do we have?"

"That number is down by two. Rachel Hill and Peter Burnum are accounted for," the silver-haired man said. Stanley met him with a questioning gaze. "The man who assassinated the governor of Colorado. Of the remaining 159, we have 121 in custody. Most check out. Some were covering up felony convictions, and then we have eight who remain uncategorized. All six matches came from the uncategorized group."

"So potentially we hold two more?" Stanley clarified.

"Yes. The search teams should have something soon."

"Call me when you get something. Now let's all get back to work."

Chapter 49

We've covered less than half of New York City, and there's only twenty-five hours left, Oliver thought as he walked up Eighth Avenue, just north of Greenwich Village. Greg and the two FBI agents were getting a few hours of sleep after eighteen hours of fruitless searching. Oliver couldn't sleep. The stress, the consequences of failure, and the thousands of voices that assaulted him from every direction prevented even a moment's rest. At least he could get a decent cup of coffee here.

"Thank you, Mr. Reisch, wherever you are," said Oliver, toasting the sky and sipping the hot coffee as New Yorkers by the hundreds hurried past him. He pushed his way through the crowd like a local and had made it almost all the way back to the hotel when he felt a hand slip into his overcoat and pluck out his wallet. He knew what was happening even before it happened, and as the hand cleared his lapel, Oliver grabbed the wrist and twisted. His wallet fell to the sidewalk with a plop, and so did the well-dressed man in his thirties, but with a scream.

"You've got to be kidding. How old are you?" Oliver asked the struggling man. He was probably thirty years his junior, but Oliver held his wrist with a grip that would bend steel. The flowing stream of humanity parted, and a crowd began to form. Even to jaded New Yorkers, the sight of a sixty-two-year-old priest maintaining a wristlock on a prone man half his age was worth a moment.

The pickpocket let out a string of profanity aimed at Oliver, and several people yelled to get a cop. Oliver finally let go of the man's wrist, but kept a foot on his back. It took less than a minute for a patrol car to pull up, and two of New York's finest began to wade through the crowd—except only one of them was from New York.

"A *cop?*" Oliver screamed three times, and the crowd began to back away from the suddenly irrational priest. "You disguised yourself as a cop? You son of a bitch!" Oliver launched himself at the smaller of the two patrolmen. Several of the onlookers grabbed Oliver before he could reach the man's neck. He was screaming obscenities that would make the pickpocket blush. "He's not a cop!" Oliver finally clarified, and now the ersatz cop began to back away. "His real name is Essen Mohammed. He's one of the terrorists."

Oliver never knew how he got free. One minute he was being held by four men, and the next minute there were over a dozen people sprawled out across the sidewalk. Mohammed had been thrown against a lamppost and had slid down onto the back of a parked car. He was alive, and Oliver was filled with a blind fury. Everything around him except Mohammed had disappeared, and righteous anger filled his heart. For a moment his mind was filled with glorious images of this man in the throes of a violent death, his agony feeding a hunger Oliver never knew existed. He stared at the wounded man and smiled. *I'm going to enjoy this,* he thought cruelly, and out of habit reached for his crucifix for strength. The feel of the well-worn metal broke the spell, and Oliver shrank back into his weary sixty-two-year-old body. A vision of Amanda and understanding blossomed in his mind.

Oliver's face softened and he approached Mohammed. The terrorist saw Oliver advancing and freed his weapon. Without warning or hesitation, he fired. Bullets tore into Oliver's chest and shoulders; it was like being hit by a sledgehammer covered in velvet. People were frantically crawling and diving for shelter as the cop shot the priest over and over again.

Mohammed's partner watched the man he had known as John Curry fire his weapon into the unarmed priest. He drew his .45 for the first time in his career, and after a moment of indecision, aimed it at his partner. "Put it down, John!"

Mohammed saw the gun and calmly resighted his aim at a real New York City cop. They both fired at the same time, and both had aimed well. The two cops hit the ground a moment after Oliver.

***

"So we're down one terrorist, and light one priest," the president said to Kyle Stanley. "Are they going to make it?"

"The patrolman's fine. Bullet hit him smack in the forehead and ricocheted off. He's going to have a hard time living that one down. The priest was shot several times at point-blank range. It's a miracle they got him to the hospital alive." Stanley didn't want to add that the ER doc had already told him that Oliver's wounds were far beyond repair and that it was simply a matter of time. He had already been given the last rites. Stanley wanted to give him a medal.

"If he survives, he's going to be one helluva security risk. That is, if we survive." The president's voice was deadly serious.

"We have approximately twenty-four hours left and four more terrorists still out there." Stanley had already told the president that four of Neser's matches had indeed been part of the eleven, and that the rest had been found using the "missing" list. "But we are out of leads."

"What kind of damage can four of these bastards do?"

The secretary of Health and Human Services was better prepared than he had been that morning. "We've made a number of assumptions, but worst-case scenario is 128 million dead. Best case scenario is seventy-seven million."

"That doesn't make sense. You told me we could treat this thing!" The president was shocked and angry. "You told me two hours ago that one man has already survived with standard medical treatment."

"We have medical resources for only about two million people. They will survive, but once the supplies are gone, people are going to die."

"Stop saying that. I've heard it for the last two days," the president snapped. "What about this paper thing? Have we looked at it from that angle?" They had recovered six of the vials, all in various stages of reformulation, along with some unusual parchment.

Stanley said, "It's not really paper. We think that after it has been complexed with the virus, it becomes stable. Light and heat then release the virus."

All of them had visions of an army of sanitation workers dressed in isolation suits picking up every tiny piece of paper from coast to coast. "Anything else?" the president asked.

"The survivor, the one the secretary talked about earlier, is being sent to Los Angeles to try and do the same thing that Father Oliver did in New York," said Stanley.

"Good, maybe we'll get lucky a second time. What about the bastard who started all of this—Klaus Reisch?"

"He seems to have disappeared. We believe that he has a vial of virus, and a vial of vaccine. He stole them from Jaime Avanti," Stanley answered.

"So, even if by some miracle, we manage to find these other four, we're still not out of this?"

Chapter 50

Oliver heard someone say he was dying. Through the mass of tubes and bodies Oliver had found Greg, and the look on his face confirmed the dire prognosis. Except Oliver didn't feel like he was dying, although, as he had never been dying before, he wasn't sure what to expect. It hurt—it hurt like hell—but he could breathe. He could feel his heart beating. It was a little fast, but it was strong and regular. He moved his feet and hands, which seemed to work just fine. So, how was he dying? He was strapped to a board, and his head was taped to something, so all he could see was the bright light shining down on him. He tried to reach up with his hand and move it out of the way, but his arms were tied as well.

Okay, he thought, *just a little nudge*. He extended his mind towards the theatre light, and it swung on its rotating arm so violently that it snapped off at the joint. The aluminum and glass dome sailed across the room and exploded against the back wall. Everyone in the ER jumped, except Oliver. He was laughing through the oxygen mask. "Boy, I stink at this," he said to himself.

Faces appeared over him. "Let me up. I'm fine." Hands began to restrain him, and somehow his arm restraints were off him. He pushed people away and then brushed off the mask covering his face.

"I need to speak to Greg Flynn," he repeated enough times until someone listened. Greg's face appeared. "Please tell them to let me up. I really don't want to hurt anyone."

Greg began to undo the remaining restraints. "You should be dead," he whispered.

"I should be, but I'm not. Listen carefully. Mohammed met with two other terrorists a year ago. One of them is here in New York and the other is in Boston. The local one is Michael Moore."

"The movie guy?" Greg had his pen and pad out and began scribbling down the name.

Oliver didn't make the connection. "No, he's a clerk in the county welfare office. I know where he lives; it's about ten miles from here."

"Give me an address."

"No, get me closer and I can take care of him. I should have been smarter with Mohammed." Oliver sat up, and for a moment his head swam. "Get the FBI guys to help. We don't have much time." He dropped to the floor and after an unsteady moment rose to his full five-foot-four inches. "That's better," he said, and with Greg's help began to dress. "Frick and Frack are here," he said as the agents pulled back the curtain. "Load up the wagons, boys; we're going for a ride. We gotta line on terrorists number two and number three."

Frick looked at Frack, and then at one of the flustered ER nurses. "What did you give him?"

"Never mind that," Greg said, annoyed and relieved at the same time. "We've got to go, now."

Thirty minutes later, the four of them were stuck in midtown traffic. Oliver had told the agents everything he knew about terrorist number three, and he hoped that the Boston bureau was having better luck than the one in New York.

"It's the middle of the night and every Tom, Dick and Harry is out driving their car. Let's go; we can walk from here," Oliver said. He opened the car door and slowly climbed out. He was bleeding again, but he still felt okay. "He's leaving his apartment," he shouted to Greg. "He knows what happened to Mohammed, and he has the virus!" Oliver tried to run down the sidewalk. Greg and the two agents abandoned the car and followed the wounded priest for two blocks.

"Oliver, you're bleeding everywhere. Just tell us what he looks like, and we'll take him." Greg had taken his arm and tried to guide him into a storefront. For a second, Oliver resisted, and then he stopped.

"Thank God," he said in a breathless voice. "He's coming this way, about a block down that way." He motioned with his head, but all Greg could see was a sea of faces.

"Did you both hear that?" Greg asked Frick and Frack. They nodded as one, just as they had been doing all day. "He's got the virus with him, so be careful what you shoot."

Oliver sat down on a step, his face pure white. *Okay, so I don't feel so good,* he thought. Terrorist number two was less than a hundred feet away, and Oliver grabbed his mind.

***

Greg heard the scream and saw the telltale disruption in the flow of human traffic. He pulled out his now-defunct police badge and forced his way through the crowd to the stricken man. He didn't find what he had expected. Number two was clean-shaven, mid-fifties, and obviously a woman. Oliver had missed.

A gunshot drowned out the woman's screaming, and people began running in all directions. Greg looked up to see Frack sink to his knees, blood beginning to stain the lower portion of his nicely tailored black FBI suit. Frick returned fire, and a man dressed in a North Face ski parka dropped to the concrete, a shower of blood spraying the overcoat of the man behind him. Greg watched as the whole scene developed before him. Frack was down and bleeding, the North Face man was down and bleeding, and then the man with the stained overcoat looked up at Frick and shot him in the head. Frick had missed as well.

The overcoat man began to turn toward Greg, but then suddenly dropped to his knees, his hands clawing at his head and face. He tried to scream, but fell over backward instead. Greg watched the man go down and waited an eternity until he became still. He waited a second longer and then moved carefully toward the fallen terrorist. He reached down and scooped up the fallen weapon, all the while keeping his eyes trained on the man's oddly shaped head. He moved closer and rifled through the stained overcoat. His fingers found a set of keys and a wad of paper in his chest pocket, but no other weapon. Frack had tossed him a pair of plastic wrist cuffs, but they weren't necessary. The man was already very dead. His eyes had ruptured, his face was swollen, the skin was stretched tight and covered in small petechial hemorrhages, and what looked like bloody brain oozed from both of his ears. In his left hand was a small blue vial.

Greg stood and walked back over to Oliver. The priest was praying, and Greg sat next to him waiting for him to finish.

"I don't know how well it will be received, but I just gave myself Last Rites." The priest's voice was barely a whisper. "Sorry, Greg. I screwed up."

He looked over at the still body of Frick. "It happened so fast. I think I passed out a little and then got so scared that he was going to get away that I grabbed the first mind I could." Oliver was crying. "He shot them, and I couldn't stop him. I tried."

"You did stop him. He's dead. We have the vial." The ubiquitous New York City sirens were getting louder.

Chapter 51

The vial was getting warm. *No, it's getting hot*, Issam Rahim corrected himself. He knew that if the vial was warmed too quickly the yield would be low, so he turned the lamp down. He picked up the instructions for the twentieth time in an hour, but they still didn't tell him anything new. His Arabic was only passable, so his particular set of instructions had been written in English, but something had been lost in the translation.

It started raining again, and the drops drummed on the slate roof and Issam's nerves. It was always raining in Seattle, and he didn't have a clue what the rain would do to the processed paper. Part of the reconstitution process involved immersing the paper in a tub of water for five minutes, but then—and the instructions were very clear on this point—the sheets were to be dried and kept dry. He looked out the window as spring rain turned his steep driveway into a small river. Like Izhan Ahmed in Los Angeles, and the other fourteen fighters, Issam had been chosen for his ability to think independently and adapt to changing circumstances. The special paper would never work here, and with each passing moment, Issam knew that his opportunity for *shahada* was slipping away. For more than three years, he had dreamed of his glorious martyrdom. With one act, all his offenses would be wiped away, and he would find himself sitting close to the throne of the Almighty, living in the most beautiful house in all of paradise, the *dar al-shuhada*, the house of martyrs. Now, the rain threatened all of that.

He stroked the blue vial and found that it had cooled. The quarantine was scheduled to begin in less than six hours, and the streets were filled with Americans hurrying to buy enough beer, potato chips, and DVDs to last a week. His heart told him that the time to act was now, but his mind hesitated. The vial had not had the requisite thirty hours to reach maximum potency.

It will have to do, he thought, and resolutely opened the vial of the Hybrid virus.

***

The death of Oliver had slowed everyone and everything, except for Phil's mind. He kept running scenarios in his head, calculating how many more people would die with each second, minute, and hour delay. It had taken more than a day for the government bureaucracy to decide how to get him safely to Los Angeles, and then another four hours to arrange for secure transport. Phil had become a national risk and a national treasure, both of which required a twenty-car entourage.

"This isn't going to work," he said to Rodney Patton through his face shield as they cruised down the 405 with a police escort. Phil was wearing a level-four contamination suit, complete with his own purified air source and a team of technicians to ensure that it worked. "There's too much going on around me to get a clear picture of what's going on out there."

"What do you need?" Patton screamed back.

"To be by myself," Phil screamed. The cacophony of voices, opinions, and worry flooded every space in his head.

"There's no way anyone is going to let you go out solo. That suit alone requires two people to make it work right."

"No, it doesn't." Phil came very close to swearing from pure frustration. Patton just shook his large head.

"We don't have the time for this," Phil said, and then there was a series of muted explosions. Cars ahead of them and behind them began to careen in every direction. Hoods, hubcaps, and engine parts flew all around them. "Keep driving," Phil yelled to their driver as their black Suburban accelerated through the growing pile-up. "Just another day in L.A. traffic," Phil said to Patton.

"Bullshit!" the big black man said, but his face had broken out into a grin from ear to ear. Ron Benedict looked back at them with a scowl on his face.

"You really shouldn't have done that, Doctor," he scolded Phil. "These bastards have infiltrated every level of our government; and after what happened in New York, you can bet your ass that they know that you're here and what you can do."

"Then let me do it," Phil yelled back at Benedict, who glanced over at Patton and then finally turned back to face forward.

"Keep going," he said to the driver.

It took them forty-five minutes to complete the first of twenty-four grids, and Phil had reached his limit. "This is taking too much time. We need to use a helicopter."

No one had wanted to accept the responsibility of putting Phil in a helicopter that was making slow circuits over America's second largest city. Benedict had pushed for one, but had been overruled at almost every level. "You have to convince them that this is going to take too much time." Phil had to yell to be heard.

"Tell them he forced you," Patton added.

Benedict hesitated for a moment and then reached for his cell phone. After ten minutes of arguing, punctuated by long periods of silence, the assistant director of the FBI closed his phone and took a deep breath. "It's going to take at least an hour for the attorney general to sign off on the presidential order. So while they worry about the niceties, we are going to misappropriate a helicopter." Benedict turned and faced Phil. "This better be worth my pension."

Thirty minutes later, the three men were skimming across the rooftops of East L.A. in a police helicopter.

"He wants you to slow down," Patton said as Phil started to motion with his arms. They couldn't get him a headset without breaking the suit's air seals, so he and Patton had worked out some signals. "Hover, right here."

Phil scribbled a note and passed it to Patton. "Can you drop us any lower?" Rodney asked the pilot. The LAPD pilot nodded and dropped down low enough that grass and dust began to fly through the open window.

Phil listened with his mind—there had been something here, but it seemed remote. *He was here—gone now,* Phil quickly wrote and showed it to Patton.

The big man frowned and the search went on. Seven more times, Phil had them pause and nearly land, but each time the spore had grown cold.

"We're going to need to refuel," the pilot told Benedict after nearly two hours of the yo-yo flying. Patton twirled his finger in the air for Phil, who nodded that he understood.

Phil couldn't shut out his companions' growing frustration and panic. He reached for the pad of paper, which had slipped between his seat and

Patton's. He was just straightening up when he felt it again, only stronger. He grabbed Patton's arm so hard and suddenly that the big man yelped.

"Son of a bitch!" Rodney screamed, trying to pry Phil's gloved hand from his forearm. Benedict looked back at the sudden commotion, and it took him a moment before he understood.

"Stop!" he yelled to the pilot. "Hold this position."

Phil was writing again, and Rodney was rubbing his injured arm.

"That's some grip he's got," Patton said to Benedict as Phil finished his note. "He wants to land there." Phil was pointing at the tallest building in a cluster of tall buildings. A circled H marked a helipad.

"That can't be right. That's the Federal Building," the pilot said.

"Shit," said Benedict.

"Son of a bitch," replied Patton. "This should have been the first place we looked."

The pilot flared the helicopter and bumped to a soft landing. Phil was out a moment after the skids touched down. "He's here," he yelled to Benedict through the roar of the blades.

"Say again?"

"He's here." Phil's voice was still muffled, even though the pair had moved away from the helicopter. Patton trailed behind, blocking out some of the rotor noise. "He works in this building," he said, pulling open a door. A powerful stream of mental energy compelled him down a flight of stairs.

"Dr. Rucker, it's safer to take the elevator," Benedict called after him, but all he got in return was a series of unintelligible noises that under the right circumstances could have been words.

"Yeah, he's always this way," Patton said in answer to Benedict's questioning look. "After you," he said, and Patton followed the assistant director of the FBI down the stairs.

Phil went down seven flights before he started checking the floors individually. At first, he would just open the fire door and stand there for a moment. By the twenty-fifth floor, he was walking the circuit of the floor. When he opened the door to the twenty-third floor, he stopped and turned to his two escorts. "In here," he said, and they followed him into the Los Angeles County Office of Emergency Management with their weapons drawn. A number of people began to stand and challenge them, but they were immediately silenced when Benedict introduced himself.

Phil just kept walking until he came to a small corner office. Phil read the nameplate: *Joseph Rider*.

"Is this the guy?" Patton poked his head into the empty office.

Phil didn't hear him. He had wheeled around and was striding towards a young black woman. He almost made it, but the isolation suit wasn't designed for running. Phil fell face first into a file cabinet and cracked his faceplate. The young woman screamed and dropped the phone. "She's warning him!" Phil yelled, struggling to his feet.

Benedict saw the crack and lifted his weapon. "No one move! Everybody down on the floor, now!" Patton had also raised his weapon, and the two panned across the room. "Dr. Rucker, are you still secure?" asked Benedict.

"No leaks; I'm fine. Lower your weapons. They're not involved." Phil was back on his feet and had picked up the phone. Joseph Rider, aka Izhan Ahmed, had already hung up. "Where is he?" Phil addressed the cowering woman.

Adrienne Mays just stared back at the man in the space suit, shaking. The two men with guns and badges came up from behind the spaceman, and that terrified her even more.

"I am Ronald Benedict, assistant director of the FBI, and we need to find Joseph Rider."

"He j-just left for the airport not five minutes ago," she stammered. The two cops exchanged a look of panic. The woman added, "He's not going anywhere. They're setting up a command center there."

It seemed reasonable, since the airports were going to be empty very soon. "It's awfully coincidental that you just happened to be on the phone with the man they were looking for. What did you tell him?" Patton demanded.

"I just told him that some people were here with guns. He said that he was calling our security force." Adrienne looked terrified. "I wasn't doing anything wrong," she pleaded.

"She doesn't know anything," Phil said to both of them. "Call him back," Phil said to the crying woman.

"What do I tell him?"

"Anything; it doesn't matter. Just get him on the phone."

She looked confused, but it was a relatively easy task, so she moved closer to the desk. Phil obligingly backed away. She picked up the phone with a shaky hand and dialed the number. Benedict reached over and hit the speaker button.

The phone rang, and rang, and rang. "Damn it," Patton said. "Tell us exactly what you told him."

Chapter 52

It was sad but necessary, and on the whole inevitable, but Rider liked his boss, and a part of him regretted that circumstances required him to shoot the man in the head. It had also been fairly messy, and he was glad that he had a different car to switch to.

He wondered how the Americans had discovered him, and he feared for the others. If they could find him after all the extra precautions he had taken, the plan was in real jeopardy. When he first arrived in the United States three years ago, he never met with Avanti's contact, choosing instead to create his own identity. It wasn't difficult, especially in Los Angeles, and especially with a good deal of cash. He had paid well and within a month had seamlessly stepped into the persona of Joseph Rider. He had been a model citizen ever since, so how had they found him? He drove down the emergency lane with his lights and flashers on, soon-to-be-dead faces gaping at him from cars stuck in a hopeless traffic jam.

In some ways he was glad. They were forcing him to revert back to the original plan—at least partially. Even with an anonymous, unmarked vehicle, he had little chance of distributing enough of the complexed paper across the Los Angeles Basin before being caught, so he would adapt. The quarantine was still three hours away, and the grocery stores and malls were still packed. If he hurried, he could hand-deliver the partially reconstituted virus to hundreds and probably thousands of Americans, who would then take the infection home and spread it further. Without the full preparation time the impact would be greatly reduced, but combined with a strategic distribution of the viral-impregnated parchment, Rider was confident that it would devastate Southern California. Professor Avanti estimated less than five grams would infect the entire Basin; the blue vial had more than fifty, and Rider was certain that he could distribute at least half.

He pulled into his driveway, and his neighbor gave him a half-hearted wave as she carried supplies into the house. A toddler, dressed in pink and adorned in bows, followed her in. He left the car running and quickly ran inside. Before the song on the radio had changed, he was backing out of his driveway for the last time, a small crash-proof case sitting next to him.

Chapter 53

It had taken them only a few minutes to get a picture of Joseph Rider and pass it on to the LAPD and the military, which had taken over most of the city. To no one's surprise, Rider and his boss never made it to the airport, and his boss didn't answer his cell phone. Ten minutes later, the LAPD found his vehicle and his body. Several minutes after that, the first of several police cars pulled up at the Rider residence, only to learn from his neighbor that he had just left, five, maybe ten, minutes ago. It took another twenty minutes for a hazmat team to arrive and enter the empty house, where they found nothing of use.

He has at least a thirty-minute head start, Phil calculated as he walked into the house in his own hazmat suit. He could feel Rider's energy all around him; it lingered in his house like a familiar smell. Reisch had known this man, and known him reasonably well, but that didn't help Phil establish a connection.

"Anything?" Patton asked. He was out of his element with this psychic shit, but he was trying to adjust.

"Nothing useful. I know he's not here."

"That much we've already established, Doctor," Patton said sarcastically.

Phil looked back at the large detective, who was wearing his own isolation suit, only his was stretched far tighter. "These aren't my rules, Patton. I know he's close."

"Can you tell how far away?"

"More than five miles." Rucker played with a small lamp on the kitchen table and started to feel a vague sense of Rider's thoughts, almost as if they had clung to the metal. He stripped off one of his gloves, and then the other. He unfastened the seals around his hood and removed that as well.

Patton started to object, but then realized that Rucker had no need for protection. Phil fingered the lamp, and for a fleeting moment found him. It wasn't the lamp; it was Rider himself, who had turned his thoughts back to his house, wondering if the police had arrived yet. It happened so quickly, and it was so unexpected, that Phil didn't react fast enough. "Damn, I almost had him," he cursed for the first time in his life. "He's in an apartment or a house about eight miles that way." Phil pointed at a spot just to the left of Rider's refrigerator.

"Don't move," Patton ordered. Someone found a GPS monitor and calculated the vector.

An LAPD detective mapped it for them and then frowned. "If that's where he's at, he picked a damn good place to hide. There are about ten different apartment complexes in this area, as well as about a hundred low-income houses."

"That shouldn't be a problem. He can track 'em," Patton said, motioning to Phil. "Get us there before he moves again."

***

It was supposed to be an ultra-fine powder, but instead, it was somewhat granular, like big grains of salt. Rider, aka Izhan Ahmed, started to grind the grains into smaller pieces. Time was running out. He had two full hours before all the Americans would go scurrying back to their little rabbit holes. Five minutes of grinding had managed to convert the grains of sand into something approaching a powder. It had also managed to infect Rider, and the warm Southern California breeze had managed to infect the other fifty residents of the Villas Del Mar Apartments with a purified form of the Hybrid virus.

He sprinkled some of the powder across the sheets of parchment and then soaked them for five minutes. They came out of the water looking like very thin linen, but ten minutes later they looked like ordinary notebook paper. That made him happy. He checked his watch and wondered if the police had raided his house yet. It didn't matter. They would find nothing that would lead them to him or give them any idea what he was planning next. He decided that he had another five minutes, so he went back to the mortar and pestle and began to grind up the remaining virus. When he had his fine dust, he stopped. The first blister had started to form on his cheek. It took less than ten minutes to finish his final, special task and leave.

***

It had taken them almost half an hour to travel the eight miles. The roads were packed with cars, and there were some physical realities that lights, sirens, and desperate need could not overcome. It had only taken Phil a minute to find the correct apartment complex.

"Stop! He's already gone," Phil yelled. "Don't anyone get out. Keep your windows up, close your vents, and let's get out of here. He's infected the whole place." The police lieutenant driving their car jerked back into traffic, and the trailing cars followed. The police captain began to radio instructions to their military escort to seal off the area.

"Where is he? Where do we go?" the lieutenant asked nervously, snapping the air ducts closed.

Phil didn't have a clear answer to either question. He couldn't get a fix on Rider. He was close, he knew that, but he couldn't pin him down. "What's down this road?"

"The mall," the lieutenant said. "It's about two miles away, but the traffic . . . I don't think we can get there in time."

"Tell your dispatch people to . . ." Patton started barking out orders, but Phil tuned him out. They were missing something, something critical.

They made it less than two blocks before they were once again forced to stop; it almost seemed as if the lights and sirens were causing more confusion than space. Phil stared out the window, willing himself to find Rider in this mass of humanity. It should have been easy; Rider's energy was so radically different from everyone around him. He was happy, almost blissful, reveling in the chaos that he had sown, but all Phil could feel was the terrorist's proximity and general direction. "Stop the car," he finally said. "We might as well walk." A gap had opened in front of them, and the lieutenant drove as far as the bumper in front and stopped.

"The mall is a few blocks beyond the overpass," the captain said as Patton and Phil climbed out. "I've got as many LAPD units as possible responding. The army is sending their helicopters, and security in the mall is looking for him as well."

The two cops droned on, but Phil began wandering towards the jammed supermarket across the crowded street. Rider had been here; Phil could feel it. Something of his presence remained, and its energy drew Phil into the parking lot. People began running from him, scared by his isolation suit. Two nights earlier, the president had given a second tele-vised address in which he explained the reason for the quarantine. He spoke with unusual candor, and the American public responded with un-derstandable panic. Phil saw himself through the eyes of a middle-aged woman; he looked like a space alien in a B-movie, and people everywhere began to scream and run as he approached.

He caught sight of a small child wearing a surgical mask and realized that a lot of the children were wearing them, but few of the adults. It was a curious situation, and Phil's mind focused on it. He approached the mother of the child, but she snatched her toddler out of the cart and began running from Phil.

"What is it?" Patton said slightly breathlessly.

"The masks," Phil said, without further explanation.

"What about them? A lot of people are wearing them." Patton looked around to confirm what he had said.

"Just the children." Phil suddenly saw a small piece of paper tacked to the community bulletin board just inside the market's doors. He walked closer. Patton started to follow, but Phil put a hand to the large man's chest. "I think you need to stay here." He moved into the entranceway, and the sea of humanity parted and began to flow out the other doors. It was a large piece of slightly yellow paper. Phil took it down, unzipped his suit, and tucked the slip of paper inside.

"This is hopeless. Hundreds of people have walked through those doors in the last half hour," Patton said as he watched Phil zip his suit closed.

A woman walked towards him, and three masked children followed her. The smallest of the three was no more than four years old. She was singing and skipping behind her two older and sullen-faced brothers. "Ex-cuse me, ma'am," Patton said. He took out his gold shield and flashed it long enough for her to see that he was a cop, but not long enough for her to see that he wasn't an L.A. cop. "Can you tell me where your children got those masks?"

"A man was giving them away when we came in." She turned and scanned the front of the store. "I don't see him now."

"Was this the man?" he held up Rider's work ID photo, and managed to keep most of a murderous rage out of his voice.

She studied it for less than a second. "Yes, he was giving them out to all the children. The stores have been out of them for days." A look of terror crossed her face. "Is there something wrong?"

"No, this man works for the county, and the masks he's distributing have a high concentration of fiberglass. We're worried that some of it might get in the children's lungs. You should probably take them off." She stripped off her daughter's mask, and her sons took their own off. "Just drop them here. We have some people coming to collect them. Can I ask that you wait by your car until our medical team checks them out? It should only take a minute." Patton smiled as they slowly walked away. Phil walked up to him. "We're too late," Patton said.

"I know."

Chapter 54

He had more blisters now, but he had a mask to cover the visible ones. They had started appearing across the backs of his hands, so he had donned a pair of gloves. His head was hurting, and he guessed that he had only a few hours left. The purified virus worked a lot faster than the native form, but not this fast. You needed a super-concentrated blast to get this bad this fast. He had almost finished distributing the three hundred special masks, and once he was done, he would stroll around the streets of Los Angeles dropping little pieces of death on his way to paradise.

A pair of security guards walked past him for the third time. He didn't think they were looking for him any more than they were looking for shoplifters, but he didn't want to take any chances. The infected masks would create a local hot spot of infection, but to seal the city's fate he had to get the virus airborne, and that meant finding more places like the supermarket.

He smiled under his mask. The bulletin board had been a last-second decision, and a real stroke of luck. Each time the door opened, a blast of wind would hit it, carrying more of the virus into the air. The military had decided that instead of bringing in enough supplies to feed the entire city for a week, they would in the short run use the local groceries, so even after the curfew started, the military would help spread the virus.

A pair of blond-haired children ran up to him and asked for three masks. Rider bent down to eye level, using them to shield him from a group of heavily armed soldiers who had just marched into the mall. They moved with a purpose, and Rider had a fairly good idea as to what that purpose was. He stayed crouched behind the children as a group of four soldiers passed within arm's reach of them. He jabbered on as to how to wear the special masks and made them promise to pass the masks on to someone else when they left the mall. When three more school-aged children appeared, he extracted the same promise from them and finally handed them four of the "special masks." He straightened up and surreptitiously scanned the area. Four soldiers remained just to the inside of the door, and he could make out at least two more outside. A large group of officials and police breezed through them without as much as a glance. They immediately fanned out through the concourse and started searching the faces in the crowd. Rider felt the net begin to tighten. He crouched down to gather his things as a pair of uniformed officers approached. He had four more masks that he quickly stuffed into his shopping bag and then looked up to find two nuns standing in front of him. He had been so preoccupied with the soldiers and police that he hadn't even registered their approach.

"Pardon me, but we saw you passing out surgical masks to the children and wondered if we could bother you for some. We care for eight foster children. They're over at the . . ." She turned to point at a shoe store, and over her shoulder he saw with alarm that a woman was pointing him out to a group of police. A man in an isolation suit stared directly at him, and an old familiar pain split his head. *The German! He's the one who betrayed us,* he thought. The police began to run towards Rider, screaming warnings and alerts to the rest of the security force. They were at least a hundred yards away, and he figured that he had no more than ten seconds.

"Of course, Sister. I don't have enough here, but if you could help me bring the rest out from their boxes inside, I would be forever grateful." Rider pointed to the doors immediately behind him, and the two nuns started to follow him through the doors marked *Restricted Access*. "I just had an operation on my back and I'm not supposed . . ." Rider tried to distract their attention from the shouts of the approaching cops.

"Sisters, stop!" boomed Rodney Patton's voice, and for a moment, everything in the mall did stop, as every eye turned towards the gigantic black man. He was holding up a large gold police shield in one hand, and a larger chrome handgun in the other. He was breathing hard but had stopped running. A smaller man in a space suit continued towards them.

The pain split Rider's head a second time, but he was able to look through it and see Rucker. An expression of confusion crossed his face. Only the German had been able to do that to him, and only the German had known their secrets. Rider closed his mind, just as he did when Klaus Reisch used to hurt him for fun all those years ago. A young Izhan Ahmed, years before he had become Joseph Rider, had tended to the German through his "illness." He had been away in Rome, with Avanti, on that fateful night seven years ago. Less than a man, but more than a boy, he had come to Libya to learn how to fight, but the sheik himself had felt that young Izhan's talents lay beyond martyrdom. He had become Avanti's assistant and learned the ways of the West as the Ukrainian moved through the United States and Europe.

The pain hit him a third time, and Izhan and Rucker were suddenly sharing the same mind—that strange two-way connection now fully established. Rucker struggled to control him, but he fought back, just as he had done with Reisch. Rucker was stronger, though, a great deal stronger, and Izhan knew that it was only a matter of time before the American had full control. Rider grabbed the closer of the two nuns, pulled the handgun from his jacket pocket, and shot her in the small of her back. She screamed, and Rucker's attention was diverted just long enough for Rider to slip out of the mental stranglehold. Rider pulled the other nun through the doors and slid a crowbar through the handles. It wouldn't stop them for long, and it wouldn't stop Rucker at all. Already he had renewed his assault, but it was the best Rider could do. Through the pain, he grabbed the screaming nun by her habit and dragged her up the stairs.

"Move, damn you. Get up, or I'll shoot you as well!" he yelled into her face after her habit had come off. She climbed to her feet, and he pushed her up the stairs.

Chapter 55

"It's bad," Phil said to Patton as they turned Sister Ellen onto her side. "Definitely kidney, maybe spleen, but I don't think he got the aorta." He was applying pressure to the entrance wound with his silver gloves. "I have to go get him, and you have to take care of this."

Patton was looming over him, sweat spilling off his forehead. They both knew that he was now almost certainly infected. "Go. I'll take care of her." They shared the briefest moment of mutual respect when their eyes met. "Take this and kill that son of a bitch, because if he comes down here alive, I'm going to kill him." Patton tried to pass over his weapon, and Phil could feel the pure hatred in his soul.

"I won't need that," Phil said, then he turned towards the doors. He pushed but the crowbar was securely fixed to the handles. He looked back at Patton and the fallen nun, judged that they were safe, and turned back to the doors. It took surprisingly little effort; Phil imagined the doors flying from their hinges and then, they were. They rebounded against the far wall fifty feet away.

"I guess you don't," he heard Patton say as the echoes began to fade.

***

Izhan heard the explosion of doors and was thankful for the brief respite from Rucker's undivided attention. He had reached the roof, and the nun ran out into the dazzlingly bright afternoon sun. They both shaded their eyes and stumbled forward. The chillers were on, and he followed their loud mechanical strumming. He grabbed the hem of the nun's skirt, and she lost her balance. Izhan dragged her across the stone and tar roof. She wouldn't be much of a shield against Rucker, but against bullets she would do fairly well.

They reached the condensers, and a large column of steam shot a hundred feet into the sky above them. He dropped to his knees, and Sister

Janine tried to crawl away as he pulled out the remaining seven sheets of infected paper. He swatted at her, and she responded with a vicious kick. The heel of her shoe opened a large gash across his still-masked face. For a moment Izhan saw only stars; when they cleared he saw the expression of horror written over the nun's face. He thought she was about to apologize for her savagery, but didn't give her the chance. He took the butt of the gun and hit her hard in the face. Her nose broke with a crack, and she spun around into the gravel.

Rucker was at the door as Izhan tore his first sheet and tossed the pieces into the steam column. They shot high into the air as the mental wrestling match resumed. Izhan tore the second and third sheets, but before he could launch them, he was wheeled around and slammed against the metal wall of the chillers, the fragments of the infected paper inches from the rising column. He tried to release them, but Rucker now had full control. Small pieces of torn paper began to fall from the sky and collect at Izhan's feet.

***

Voices and the noise of heavy footfalls started coming up from the stairwell, and Phil slammed the door shut without taking his eyes off Izhan. The isolation suit was both hot and unnecessary, so he slowly stripped it off. A tiny slip of paper fell out and was caught by a tiny breeze that wafted it towards the pile in front of Izhan.

"That's better," Phil said, after stepping out of the pants. "I would like a moment of your time, so why don't you get comfortable as well?" The mask dropped off Izhan's face and fell into the neat pile at his feet. "I can feel that you want to hurt me; you want it very badly." Phil stared at Izhan while the younger man struggled to free himself from the invisible force that held him. "It's interesting; I don't think I've ever felt anything quite as strong. The depth of your hatred is truly impressive."

"What do you know about hatred?" Izhan sneered.

"Very little," Phil admitted. Izhan could use the mental connection almost as well as Phil. "As you can see, I am capable of experiencing only a narrow range of emotions. The truth is that I can perceive your emotions much easier than my own."

"You are an abomination in the eyes of God."

"Are you trying to anger me?" Phil squatted down, using the chillers to shade himself from the sun as he gently sorted through the life of Izhan Ahmed. Izhan tried to resist, but he had no more luck freeing his mind than he did freeing his arms. "Where does all this hate come from?" Phil asked.

"Your Western society degenerates our faithful . . ."

Phil silenced him. "Yes, yes, our very existence offends the Almighty, and it is your duty to destroy us. It's an excellent sound bite, but it's all very trite and uninteresting." Phil forced him to make eye contact. "You are an educated man, Izhan; you have lived here. Lesser men may actually buy into that nonsense because they don't know better, but you do."

The young man stared back at Phil, anger burning in his eyes.

"I really don't want to hurt you, but I must know."

"Why?" Ahmed asked defiantly, and used every ounce of energy to close his mind.

"Honestly, I can't tell you. I find your willingness to commit acts of extreme sacrifice and extreme violence compelling."

"I'm not going to help you learn how to be human," he spat back.

Phil stood up. "If that's your decision." Clumsily, just as Reisch had done to Phil, he reached into Izhan's mind and sifted through every thought, emotion, and memory. The young man passed out almost immediately, and with his loss of consciousness all resistance disappeared. For the first time in Phil's life, he experienced the joys of childhood, the beauty of innocence, and the wonder of limitless potential. He felt the contentment of being a part of a family, of truly loving, and being loved by another in return. The fulfillment of being a part of something greater than one's self.

He could relate to Reisch's need to feed on the emotions of others; they were a powerful potion, both intoxicating and revolting at the same time. The sensations and passions that defined Izhan Ahmed flowed into Phil, filling a void that until this moment he didn't know existed. Even the negative emotions, the pain and suffering, satisfied Phil's sudden need. He pressed into the young man's mind, trying to drain it faster. An alien desire to completely consume the life of Ahmed began to overwhelm Phil. For the first time in his adult life he was allowing himself to be lost in a self-indulgent desire. He felt the control over his mental equilibrium begin to slip from his mental fingers as he drained something vital from the small man. He embraced the chaos and wondered why Reisch feared it so intensely. A voice in his mind began to roar in ecstasy and with a start he realized that it was his own. He had become one of the Monsters.

He suddenly broke the connection, and both Phil and an unconscious Ahmed fell to the gravel. He stared at the prostrate terrorist with his breath coming in gasps. He had come close to killing this man, and in the process, losing himself. A fear as old as Phil rose in his chest and he imagined a small windowless room with a tall steel door.

"What happened?" said a muffled voice.

Phil jumped in alarm at the unexpected appearance of the nun. Her face was covered in blood, and her nose was misshapen. She stood unsteadily and staggered towards Phil.

"Stop, Sister; stay away from that paper." Phil ordered. He quickly climbed to his feet. The echoes of his greatest fear still resonated through his mind, and he staggered a little as he caught Sister Janine a moment before she lost her balance. "He's unconscious," he said, supporting the nun with his arm.

"He shot Sister Ellen." She started to cry and had to breathe in spasms because of her blood-clogged nose.

"I know," he said, and both of them turned towards the roof's metal door as the SWAT team behind it started to use a battering ram. "Can you go and wait by the door, Sister? I just need a moment more with Mr. Ahmed." Her head swiveled back to the fallen terrorist, who was just beginning to stir, and then back to Phil. "Are you with the police?"

"No ma'am, but they're with me," he said. She stared a moment longer and hobbled across the roof. A helicopter buzzed overhead, and Phil gently pushed it away; he still hadn't finished with Izhan.

"Did you get what you needed?" He was awake and still defiant. Phil had released him, and he quickly reached for the pieces of infected paper.

"Please don't provoke me," Phil said, and then not so gently pushed him into the metal frame that housed the air conditioning coolers. "Sister Janine believes that you are evil incarnate, but I know that you're not." He stared into the dark, hate-filled eyes of Ahmed. "You're just a man, and we don't have the luxury of dismissing you as the devil." Phil sat in the shadow that a nearby building cast across the roof so that he could better see Ahmed. "I have to admit that I am somewhat disappointed. I was hoping that you had had some type of religious or personal epiphany that would drive you to this extreme. But you're more complex than that, and once again, I can't discount you."

"Are you going to be my shrink now, and tell . . ."

Phil cut him off. "I'm sorry, but we don't have a lot of time, and I have no patience to listen to your vitriol." He stared back at Izhan, and a desire to make the terrorist writhe in agony welled up in Phil's chest.

"Go ahead." Izhan read the desire that was building inside of Phil. "You can break my body, but never my soul."

"I have more control than that," Phil answered, suppressing the sadistic craving. "At the moment, I want to understand you more than hurt you. I suggest you take advantage of that." They stared at each other until Ahmed's expression softened an iota.

"You can never understand me," he scoffed, but with less venom than earlier.

"I understand that you are not a religious zealot, and that most of your compatriots are not zealots either. You are devout, I will grant you that, but you are also a group of educated men. To some degree, I can understand the refugees, who have known only squalor, suffering, and hopelessness, strapping explosives to their bodies, but that hardly describes you or any of the others. You were chosen because of your education, because of your ability to adapt and function independent of a group. I can see that in your mind. So why would you subordinate those abilities; why would you blindly follow those who espouse hate?" Phil paused for an answer, but all Izhan had was more derision. "Part of the answer lies in human nature, and in that respect, you are not much different from the man downstairs who wants to kill you. But that only gets you part of the way; your sin is that you never questioned the culture of hate that surrounded you. Instead of examining it, you ignored the responsibility of an educated man and accepted it. You allowed yourself to believe the lies because to challenge them would be to challenge those who spread them, and you were too weak to do that. You are going to die because of that weakness."

"My death is inconsequential compared to the devastation we have brought to your country." He smiled smugly.

Phil slowly nodded his head and allowed Izhan to see the utter failure of all their work and sacrifices. "The truth is that you are dying for nothing. No one will visit your father and tell him of the momentous things you achieved in the name of God." Phil listened as the will and heart of

Izhan Ahmed broke. A small part of him rejoiced at the young man's agony, and he quickly chastised himself. He would not be as weak as Reisch and allow his Monsters to consume him. He would never again come that close to losing himself. Changed or not, he, Phillip Rucker, would always be in control. He would make his own decisions, not his childhood Monsters, and in time perhaps not even the Routine that had ruled virtually his entire life.

The pounding from the other side of the door became more insistent, and now there were two helicopters circling the rooftop. Tears began to flow down Izhan's face, and Phil listened to him pray. He prayed for a righteous death, one that would bring honor to His Holy Name.

Phil reached down and retrieved the small pistol that Izhan had used to shoot Sister Ellen. He turned towards Sister Janine as she let out a scream. "It's all right," he yelled to her over the sound of the helicopters, and then turned back to Ahmed, whose prayers had become more desperate. "I haven't learned to hate yet," Phil said and tossed the gun to the terrorist.

Sister Janine stared dumbfounded at Phil. He walked towards the nun and guided her away from the door. "It's going to be all right. He's not going to hurt anyone."

Phil let the door go and three men dressed in black body armor tumbled onto the rooftop. It took them only a moment to assess the situation, and in that moment, Izhan raised his gun. Both of the marksmen in the circling helicopters ensured that Phil was correct.

Chapter 56

"Father Oliver died," Greg told Lisa over the phone.

Lisa suddenly felt empty. Amanda had come home with the news that Reisch had disappeared, and now this. "How?" she asked.

"One of the SOBs was posing as a cop," Greg paused, and Lisa could hear him try to stifle a sob. "The guy shot Oliver. He was out by himself. If I had been there, I could have done something." His voice was breaking. "We found him in a hospital all shot up, and do you know what he did? He goes out and finds the other bastard and kills him right before the guy shoots me. He saved me with his . . ." Lisa let her husband suffer quietly. "Honey, I have to go. I'll call you later. There are arrangements that have to be made."

Lisa hung up the phone and turned to Amanda. "You heard?"

Amanda nodded and went to hug her mother-in-law. "I'm so sorry, Lisa. Sorry that any of this ever happened."

Lisa cried for several moments and then slowly pulled away. "Your eyes are moist, Amanda," she said, wiping a tear from her daughter-in-law's face.

"I guess I'm not totally made of stone."

"It's terrible, but I wasn't just crying for Oliver. I didn't know him as well as Greg did." She looked into Amanda's eyes. "He's a good man, and he's in a lot of pain. I feel so helpless." She tried to stifle a sob, but it escaped as a gasp. "He won't share it with me; he'll take that pain and hide it in a place that I've never been able to reach, and it will eat away at him. Sometimes . . ." Now her tears were falling again. "Sometimes, I wonder why God has brought so much pain into our lives." Lisa's voice began to rise and her voice broke. "What purpose did it serve to allow John Oliver to die? What purpose did it serve to take the lives of Michael and Jacob? Why does He allow such evil to exist? My soul needs an answer beyond the knee-jerk 'trust in God's mercy,' because I really haven't experienced a lot of His mercy in the last few years." Her voice had turned hard and angry, but her tears continued to fall.

"I had a part in that," Amanda said, and a second tear fell down her cheek.

Lisa wanted to deny it, but there was no point in lying. "Amanda, I thank God every night for bringing you into our lives, and I know that Greg does as well." Lisa smoothed Amanda's hair, and then kissed her forehead. "No matter how much you change, no matter what happens to you, we both love you with every fiber of our being."

Amanda wiped more tears from her eyes. "I know that." She pulled completely away. "Are you stocked for the week?" She said suddenly, changing the uncomfortable subject.

"Yes," Lisa said. "Are you going to stay?"

"For a little while, at least until Greg comes home." Amanda picked up the small satchel that she had brought back from Fort Collins. "He has more of the virus, and he won't stop, no matter how many of his terrorist buddies get killed by priests."

"How will you find him?"

"I have no idea. I've lost all traces of him. I don't know if he's too far away, or dead, or just completely shut himself down." She nervously opened and closed the small bag. "I should turn this in and see if someone else can divine something from it."

"You're sure it's . . . Of course, you're sure it's not infected, otherwise you wouldn't have brought it here," Lisa corrected herself. "He wouldn't stay in Colorado. I'm guessing that he's made a beeline for the nearest border or ocean."

"Costa Rica. He plans to wait out our demise while sitting in a tropical jungle," Amanda said, and Lisa stared back at her curiously. "I saw it in his mind when we were at the hospital," Amanda explained. "I saw everything," she added quietly.

***

The check-engine light was on continuously and the temperature gauge was well past the red line. Reisch let loose a string of profanities in three languages, but his predicament didn't change. He was going to have to find another mode of transportation, but in rural New Mexico, three hours after a nationwide curfew had been established, that was going to be a difficult task.

He had been warned that something like this might happen. Jeser's network of support was virtually nonexistent outside major American cities, but Reisch was supremely confident in his abilities. For more than three decades he had been the ultimate survivor.

"You were a professional then," Pushkin said, appearing suddenly and darkening Reisch's already dark mood. "You followed the rules and did things correctly; you prepared yourself to complete your task and to disappear. Years ago you never would have done anything as amateurish as this."

Reisch wanted to ask what he meant, but the answer would quickly turn into a lecture over his behavior the last two months.

"It's not just the last two months," his mentor said, reading his thoughts. "It's been the last seven years; really your troubles began when you went to that sewer in the desert. You had no business passing yourself off as a security guard for a bunch of Arabs."

"If you remember correctly, it was you who introduced me to Avanti. Besides, I've heard all of this before. Do you have anything constructive to contribute, or did you pop in just to harangue me?"

"You rely more on this mind-reading crap than training and experience, and look where it's gotten you," Pushkin said under his breath. "Turn the radio on," he commanded suddenly.

Reisch glanced at the shimmering form of his old teacher and flipped the knob to the satellite radio with obvious irritation. He changed the channel several times looking for a classical music station, but all he heard were news reports.

"Stop," Pushkin ordered, and for a moment, Reisch didn't know what he meant. "Did you hear that? Go back to the last station." Reisch found the station and listened with horror.

". . . still coming in, but what we do know is that there has been another incident in Los Angeles similar to what happened in New York yesterday. The military is being very cautious about this, but it appears as if another terrorist has been caught or killed in a suburban Los Angeles mall as he was trying to release the virus."

A longer string of profanities drowned out the announcer's next words. Los Angeles and New York were critical to success.

" . . . optimism, and that the threat remains. There are no plans to modify or lift the quarantine, and all noncritical people are to remain indoors. All those caught in violation of the quarantine order are being held in contamination centers throughout the country."

Pushkin listened intently, and when the car engine finally seized he turned to Reisch. "It seems that your difficulties leaving this country may have a purpose after all." White smoke began to pour from beneath the hood. "You should have kept the Mercedes," he said as the stolen sedan coasted to an unscheduled stop.

Reisch climbed out of the car and Pushkin followed. They hadn't seen any signs of life for hours; the high desert was cold, wind-swept, and completely dark. The night sky was alight with a universe of stars, and a full moon was just beginning to rise over the mountains to the east. Off in the far distance, two dark shapes glided through the thin air; a pair of eagles out for a late night flight, completely oblivious to the larger plight of humanity, or the more immediate plight of Reisch. "Three or four miles up the road, there's a farm," he said to Pushkin's ghost, and pointed to a small collection of lights. He was angry, but consoled himself with the fact that he had been tested before and had always prevailed.

"I guess we walk," Pushkin said, staring up the road, and Reisch looked at him questioningly. "We could always wait for someone to carry us, but I'm guessing it will be a long wait."

Reisch retrieved his suit bag, slung it over his shoulder, and started down the dark street. Pushkin started in on him in less than fifty paces.

"Why do you always use German cars?" The steaming sedan had been an almost new Audi A8. Reisch found it in a Pueblo used car lot, and with less than ten thousand miles on it, he could never have anticipated its failure after another hundred.

"Usually, they are quite reliable," Reisch said slightly defensively. "Why do you always speak in English?"

"I speak the language you speak," Pushkin answered.

Reisch walked on, pondering Pushkin's answer. "If they admit to finding two, they probably have found more," he said after a long pause. "It had to have been Amanda," he said simply. "She saw everything."

"You're probably correct. It's possible Avanti told them, or they simply stumbled on to it, but I think she's responsible."

"I'm responsible. I should have listened to you and everyone else. If I had done this in Miami as I was supposed to, none of this would have happened, and I'd be safely away."

Pushkin's silence was accusatory. "What are you going to do?" he finally asked.

Reisch thought quietly. There were still nine more moles out there. The plan could still work, but their margin of error had been erased. "I'll wait, and do what's necessary." The weight of the two vials sewn into his coat became a little more noticeable.

Chapter 57

"Morning, Greg," Linda Stout greeted her mentor. She was the first female detective in the small Colorado Springs detective unit because seventeen years ago Greg Flynn had taken a risk.

"Hey, Stick," he said, swinging his old chair away from the window and facing the six-foot-one-inch senior detective. Linda weighed less than one hundred and thirty pounds, and the nickname had plagued her since junior high. The only person in the world who could use it without the threat of imminent physical harm was her old boss.

"I see the office still fits," she said.

"It's only temporary," he said to Linda and to God's ear. Rodney Patton was in a Los Angeles hospital being treated for the infection he had helped to stop.

"I'm sorry about your priest," she said somberly.

"He was a good man." Greg's voice was just above a whisper. Oliver had been flown home to Chicago to join his sister and parents five days earlier, and both Greg and Lisa had resolved to celebrate his life and not mourn his passing. "What have you got there?"

Linda carried a folder that bulged with police reports. "A hunch about our German friend." Greg waved her into the office and into a desk-side chair. "We found the car he used to run down our officer last week. It was in the garage of an auto repair shop. That same auto repair shop reported that one of their customers had a Mercedes SUV stolen from their parking lot the very next day, just before the curfew started. With all that was happening, no one followed up on it or put the two together."

"It's taken almost a week to make that connection?" Ordinarily Greg wouldn't have been so critical, but the nonstop stress was eating away at his restraint.

"We're down to a skeleton crew. The FBI took the BMW and left the grunt work with us, and frankly, we dropped the ball." Linda looked away and Greg felt bad about his comment.

"So the bastard is probably driving a Mercedes SUV. This is a break, Linda." Greg tried to pump up his deflated protégée.

"I hate to burst your bubble, but the Pueblo police found that car a half hour ago. It was in the long-term parking lot at the airport. It's been there for days. I called the FBI and they're on their way down there." Linda shuffled through the papers in her file while Greg waited for her hunch. "The airport only had inbound military flights, so we know he wasn't leaving. The assumption everyone is going to make is that he stole another vehicle from the lot, but I don't think so. There are cameras on all the entrances and exits, and he knew about them." She pulled out a security photo that showed the black hood of a Mercedes SUV; the interior was obscured by a large starburst of light. "He used some sort of laser to screw-up the image. None of the other photos for the next two days were hit by a laser. I think he stole something within walking distance and, based on his pattern, I'll bet it was from here." Linda had pulled out a satellite map and pointed to what could only be a car dealership. "There's a fence along this road, and that's the only security this place has along that section of the lot."

Greg looked up at Linda. "This is excellent work."

"Good, because I used your name to get the manager of that lot to check out his inventory. It didn't make the feds happy, but I said that you were willing to talk with the assistant director if necessary. We should know something within an hour or two." Linda beamed with satisfaction.

Even with Greg Flynn's good name, it took more than four hours before they heard back.

"We've checked three times and the entire new and used car inventory is accounted for. The only thing that may be missing is an Audi, and I'm not sure it was still here. It's the owner's ex-wife's car, and she pretty much comes and goes as she pleases. She brought it in for an overheating problem about ten days ago," Don Weiland, the general manager of Turner Jeep and Audi, told Greg over the phone. "It will take some time to get her number from our computer, but I do have another option."

"Go on," Greg encouraged. He was chasing down this lead while the FBI traced the seventy-three cars that remained in the airport's long-term parking.

"GPS. I sold her the car myself, and I know that it's got a GPS transponder. I've got the security code right here. You guys should be able to access the locator service and know exactly where it is in about ten seconds."

"This guy is a pro. If he stole the car he would have disabled any transponder in under a minute."

"Yes, he probably would," the car salesman said. "If he could find it. The one we installed in Mrs. Turner's car is brand spanking new and specifically designed to prevent anyone from tampering with it. Just to reach it, you would have to dismantle the steering column. It can be done, if you have two or three hours and a cartload of replacement parts. What this guy probably did was to dismantle the factory-installed navigation system. Trust me, if he's still got it, you got him. Just get on the Net and see."

Chapter 58

They had allowed him to return home and wait like everyone else for the quarantine to be lifted; except no one else, at least no one Phil knew, had a company of the U.S. Army "protecting" him. It wasn't all bad. For six days he hid behind the walls he had grown up with and luxuriated in the mental isolation. The soldiers positioned themselves far enough away that their thoughts were reduced to subtle whispers in Phil's mind, and his biggest challenge was living without the distraction of Monsters in his mind. For the first time in his life, he was alone in his own head. The master of his own destiny.

The day after returning from Los Angeles, he tried to resume The Routine, or at least as much of it as house arrest would allow. He got up exactly on time; made up his bed as he had always done; ran on the treadmill with the same intensity and precisely the same distance as always; and ate exactly what he was suppose to eat, but instead of his life feeling familiar, it felt alien. Yesterday morning, he put sugar on his Wheaties and nothing happened. This morning, he quit running twelve minutes early simply because he was tired, and still nothing happened. He was seriously considering not making his bed, or perhaps getting up late to see how far his luck would stretch.

"Hello," a voice said from his living room.

Phil nearly dropped the glass he was washing and, a moment later, the air around him started to hum with static electricity. A static discharge shocked him as his hand brushed the faucet. He turned to see a snowy Amanda Flynn track wet footprints across his immaculate entranceway floor.

"Good morning. Sorry about popping in on you unexpectedly, and about the mess." She said with a smile. She stripped off her jacket and more snow fell to the floor. She was dressed in a faded pair of jeans and a sweater that would make a high school boy lose sleep.

"Good morning," he stammered, reacting more to her figure and the mess she was making than to her sudden appearance. Not knowing what to do next, he simply stared, a wet glass in one hand and a towel in the other.

She took a step into the kitchen and Phil stepped back. The air between them hummed like a power line. "We have some logistics to work out," she said. "If you stay there, I can swing around you and sit over there."

Amanda motioned to his dinette set, but there was at least ten feet of clean floor between her muddy boots and the chair. "Okay," he said, and closed his eyes as she walked around him. When he opened them, there were six new boot prints on his kitchen floor.

"You did well in Los Angeles," she said, slowly lowering herself into one of his polished kitchen chairs. She stretched out and Phil split his gaze between her long legs and the puddle that was forming under her boots. "Have you heard about Rodney Patton?"

"He's pretty bad; his size makes it more difficult," he said, slightly distracted.

"When do you get out of here?" Amanda said, looking around the pathologically clean house.

"I'm not infectious anymore, so I suppose when they let me," Phil said automatically, but he was struck by the realization that he could come and go just as easily as Amanda did.

"I'm trying not to read you, but some thoughts I just can't avoid." She still was smiling, but her face had become a little more serious. "We're going to need a whole new set of rules, aren't we?"

"There are others besides us." He stated the obvious.

"I know. A generation of mutants, sort of like *The X-Men*."

Phil hadn't seen a movie in decades. "Yes," he said. She made him feel awkward; it was one of his own personal emotions and, in a strange way, it comforted him. Unconsciously, he had started to borrow emotions from the minds around him, but Amanda's presence triggered the old familiar clumsy feeling.

"I would like to try something," she said, and Phil's heart was suddenly in his throat, afraid of what she would say next. She had sealed off her thoughts completely, but he wasn't so sure that he was as successful in hiding his own embarrassing thoughts. "It involves some risk."

"All right," he answered.

"I would like you to walk over here and take my hand. I've worked something out and I want to test it."

"I'm not sure that's a good idea, my skin is already tingling."

"Take a step, a single step, and see what happens," she encouraged, and an unfamiliar feeling stirred inside him. He suddenly wanted to impress her. He was a grown man, and she made him feel like the twelve-year-old boy he never was, puffing out his chest as the pretty girl walked by.

He took a step and the tingling in his exposed skin didn't change. The last time she had been this close, it wasn't a tingling he felt: it had been a stinging, burning sensation. He took another, and still nothing changed. "Alright, what's different?"

He was only about four feet from her, and although the air was still charged, it wasn't dangerous.

"Keep coming," she prodded sweetly. He took another step and they were within easy reach of each other. "Give me your hand." Phil looked down and realized that he still was carrying the glass and kitchen towel; he quickly transferred the glass into his left hand.

If anything, the tingling had abated some, and the only uncomfortable sensation Phil was experiencing was desire. He was starting to breathe faster, but it wasn't out of fear. "Are you sure about this?"

"No," she said and reached for his free hand. There was a slight snap when they made contact, but neither let go.

Phil had braced himself for the searing pain he had felt with Reisch, but with Amanda, all he felt was warmth. It wasn't uncomfortable; in fact, it was rather pleasurable, very pleasurable. He began to experience her physically; the smell of her hair, the curve of her hips, the weight of her breasts. The same primal instinct that had nearly driven him to kill Izhan Ahmed resurfaced. He began to run his hand up her arm; a sudden desire to take her body and possess her soul overwhelmed him. He took a step closer to her and then was flung backwards into his refrigerator. He landed hard and for a moment couldn't breathe.

Amanda got up and the humming of the air resumed.

"Oh my goodness, I am so sorry Amanda!" Phil said, gasping for air.

"It's all right, Phil. I'm used to a little sexual tension, but that was a little more than I was comfortable with." She waited while Phil climbed painfully back to his feet, glass and towel still firmly in his hand. "It's nothing to be embarrassed about." Shame radiated from Phil. "It's a natural human reaction, but you can't let it take control. We have a mutual physical attraction, that's obvious, but that doesn't mean that we have to act on it." Amanda returned to her seat and the humming in the air diminished.

"What just happened, with your, our hands?" Phil stuttered.

"That's what I was trying to test." She looked down at her hand and began opening and closing her fingers. "I think if we anticipate contact, or proximity, and accept it, we pull back into ourselves. Somewhat like a cat and its claws. It's a conscious act, though, because our natural state is to have our claws out." She smiled and Phil could detect the faintest blush in her cheeks. "I sound like an expert, but all of this is just speculation."

"If you aren't an expert, then who is?" He meant it as a compliment, but it fell flat as the name Klaus Reisch hung in the air. "What happened to him?"

"I don't know," she said. "I would like your help in finding him; that's really why I'm here."

"He has more of the virus, more than all the others combined. He plans to . . ." Amanda began to nod her head. "You know this already."

"After he attacked you, we had an encounter. I saw everything that you saw."

"I think he left some of himself inside me." It was a revolting, horrible thought, and it was the first time Phil had admitted it to anyone, including himself.

"Perhaps, or he may have simply awakened something inside you."

"That makes it much worse," said Phil, as that uncomfortable thought circled in his mind.

"No, it doesn't; it makes you human. We're all very messy inside, Phil, even me. We all have dark and secret desires that we would never admit, much less let others see. And for me, that helps put things in perspective. What makes Reisch different is that he believes that his infection gives him license to act on those dark desires."

Phil nodded in agreement. "Before he was infected, Reisch was a strongly disciplined man; he resisted those impulses."

"The infection strengthens them. All of us at some point are faced with the decision to resist or succumb."

"Are you a good mutant or a bad mutant?" Phil said, paraphrasing the line from the *Wizard of Oz*. "So, what are we going to do about the bad mutants?"

"We can't concern ourselves with them until after Reisch is dead."

"He's gone, out of our reach," Phil said. "Or at least out of my reach."

"Greg thinks he may have a lead on him. Are you up for a little fresh air?"

***

"That is a Hispanic male, five foot five, at most," Ron Benedict said, pointing to a satellite photo of a farmhouse in eastern New Mexico. Greg and Amanda both nodded. Don Weiland had proven to be exactly correct. The factory-installed navigation system in Corrina Turner's stolen Audi A8 was dead, but the after-market GPS transponder quietly answered its call.

Amanda stared at the blurry image and accepted on faith that Benedict and his photo analysts knew what they were talking about. "So that's not Reisch," she said, feeling not even a trace of his mental signature.

"No," Benedict answered. Phil chose to remain seated while the other three huddled over Benedict's desk. "Do you want to see these?" the assistant director asked Phil.

"No," he said. Amanda's "fresh air" had turned out to be a six-minute ride in her Jeep followed by a meeting with twenty federal and local officials in the old courthouse building.

Benedict shrugged and turned to Amanda. "Here is the vehicle." He pointed to a small grey dot on a two-lane road that sliced through emptiness. "On this magnified view you can see that he's changed license plates."

Greg stared and finally picked up the photograph. Unlike the previous three pictures, this was amazingly clear. "Those are Denver plates; see the registration sticker?"

"So we've found the car, and know that he's being careful." Ron nodded to one of the technicians, who placed a poster-sized view of the area on an easel. "This is the car." He hadn't needed to point, because a red circle was drawn around a small grey dot and labeled *suspect's vehicle*.

"As you can see, there are thirteen occupied residences within a five-mile radius. We can take number eight off the list, because of our Hispanic male. We doubt he would leave any occupant alive." Benedict paused and turned to Amanda. "Can you tell us anything from this?"

"Nothing," she said, and everyone looked at Phil.

"I have no idea which house he's in," Phil said from the safety of his chair. The air in the room buzzed with his proximity to Amanda, but it was tolerable. "How do you know he's even there? Why couldn't he have moved on to another vehicle?"

"He may have," an agent of Homeland Security said. "But we're hoping that because he didn't swap out the license plate he decided to hold up for awhile."

"He may have swapped out with a different set of plates. He had to know that eventually we would find that car with satellite or just a cop driving by. He didn't even bother trying to hide it," Phil argued.

"We think that the engine failed; there's engine coolant around all four tires, so he would have needed help to get it under cover," Benedict said.

"I think he's in one of these houses," Amanda said suddenly, ending the debate. "It is a calculated risk. He's pulled back inside of himself because he knows I'm looking for him. In fact, he told me to come and find him. If he kept going, eventually he would run across a police roadblock or a military patrol. Under normal circumstances, he would simply disguise himself as an ambulance or some other authorized vehicle, but then I would see him. He's not afraid of you; he is afraid of me."

"So what do we do now?" Benedict asked the room.

For a minute, Amanda simply listened to the options running through the heads of the government officials. "Stop, all of you," she demanded. "No low-yield tactical nukes, or cruise missiles, or any other military responses. We aren't even sure he's there. Yes, I have a suspicion he's in one of these houses, but that's hardly definitive enough to kill dozens of people and lay waste to an entire area."

"He has another vial . . ." said the Homeland Security officer.

"I know exactly what he has," Amanda responded. "He's alone in the desert, and very much alert. If any of you got within fifty miles of him, he would know it in an instant. He would destroy your missiles in the air, or worse, redirect them."

"Do you have any suggestions?" Greg asked, subtly shifting his weight and inserting himself between Amanda and the men behind him.

"Send Phil in," she answered. "Alone."

Chapter 59

It had been the most agonizing week of Klaus's life, and now his hosts were beginning to get on his nerves as well. The Theimes didn't believe in creature comforts, but they did supply him with a television, and with their satellite connection, he had been able to experience the twenty-four-hour news cycle for the first time. He was amazed at how many different ways the announcers could repackage what little they knew and then represent it as "news."

There was little news, however. At this point, if everything had gone according to plan, the American government would have to admit to the growing death toll; it would have been impossible for them to hide the deaths of millions of its citizens. And even if they had managed to completely stifle the domestic sources, there were still international news organizations that would jump at the chance to report on another American tragedy. And then there was the Internet. Certainly, someone, somewhere in the world, would have caught a whiff of what was going on.

Klaus covered his nose; he was going to have to deal with Elmer and Rose Theimes. He had managed to restrain himself for almost two days; it was his way of repaying them for taking him in. But his patience had its limits.

He turned the television off with the remote. CNN was replaying the American president's speech. Klaus had already listened to it three times and didn't want to hear his cautious, but triumphant, tone again. Jeser had failed, and he was beginning to accept that fact. Avanti had anticipated the quarantine and had been certain that it would have only a modest short-term effect, but no lasting impact. Once the virus had been complexed with the microcapsules, it was incredibly stable, and would disperse on the wind, dust particles, or even droplets of water. It would find almost everyone, no matter where they hid. What he hadn't anticipated was that the Americans would find the eleven before they had a chance to disperse their virus.

He carefully put the remote down. The desire to throw and smash things was under control, and he began to feel like his old self. He got up and bumped his head on the exposed wooden beam. Mr. and Mrs. Theimes lived in what some would call a modest house; Klaus called it something different. It was tidy, but cluttered with so many pictures and mementos that he was convinced that they were the main structural support for the ancient house. It had been the family home for five generations, but all eight of their children had moved away. Rose Theimes had assaulted Reisch with stories and photographs of her children for nearly two full days, but now she was silent. Her silence would force him to leave soon. The curfew was lifting in a matter of hours, and at least one family member would be checking in to see why Elmer and Rose had stopped answering their phone.

Despite the fact that the president's speech referred to him indirectly, he was still pleased with his decision to stay in the United States; he probably could have slipped into Mexico without alerting Amanda or anyone else, but then he would have missed the perfect opportunity to reverse Jeser's error. They hadn't failed entirely; they had created the right conditions for Reisch to succeed. The world had closed its borders to the United States and, after a week locked inside their houses, the populace was eager to get outside. For a while, suspicion would be running high, but it would take a good deal more than suspicion to stop him.

It had started to rain, and the sky crept closer to the desert floor. The late afternoon started to look more like dusk, and Klaus wondered if he should leave under the cover of the rare thunderstorm. He had planned on waiting until it was fully dark, but if he left now he could stick to the back roads and still be in Dallas for the morning commute.

The experts said that it would take less than a thousand infections in six major cities to create a self-sustaining epidemic. Dallas would be the first. New York, Chicago, and L.A. would be next. He would spend one to two days in each place and then disappear like a ghost. He hadn't yet decided on his last two cities, but he would before he finished in Los Angeles; right now, he was toying with the idea of Washington DC, followed by Miami. Then at last he could find a boat and make it to Cuba.

He stretched his long arms and listened as the rain pelted the metal roof. He yawned and made the decision to take the small risk and leave before it was dark. The back roads would be patrolled by the local or state police, not by the military, and would be relatively easy to handle. He gathered his things and carried them into the small attached garage. The Theimes owned a Ford F150 pickup that was made in the last century, but despite its age was in excellent condition. The thirty-gallon gas tank was always filled, a fact that Elmer had shared with Reisch the day before he died, so his range was easily five hundred miles. More than enough. He opened the single garage door, bid Elmer and Rose a final farewell, and backed their truck onto the gravel driveway. The rain was coming down in sheets, which presented Klaus with a dilemma: leaving the garage door open would be a sign to anyone who happened along that something was wrong. Closing the garage door meant that he would be soaked and driving for hours in wet clothes, something that was very unappealing to him. He looked around the small cab for an umbrella and found nothing. He waited a minute for the rain to ease up, but the steady drumming continued. It wasn't a small point; someone, either the sheriff or a family member, would be checking on the Theimes soon, and if they found the garage door open and their truck missing, they would be rightly suspicious. However, if they knocked and no one answered, they would check the garage, see that the truck was gone and would have an explanation as to why Elmer and Rose hadn't been answering their phone. He looked at his watch and decided that he would give the rain exactly three minutes to let up and then he would be forced to close the door.

***

"We have a heat signature," the analyst announced. The keyhole satellite platform had just cleared the horizon and turned every instrument it had on a twenty-five mile radius of eastern New Mexico. Its infrared sensors had found a small gap in the cloud cover and downloaded the images to a ground station in North Carolina. "Small engine, probably a car. Give the computers a few more minutes and we'll have a better image." The senior analyst reviewed the live feed and agreed. It took less than a minute to relay the message to Ron Benedict.

"It's either house nine or ten; that's as precise as the techies can be," Benedict relayed to the agent on the scene. "Have him start there." It had only taken two hours to transport Phil, Amanda, Greg, and an entire field support team to Clayton, New Mexico. Reisch was a hundred miles to the west, and everyone was hoping that he still had his claws retracted.

"The roads are clear," the agent briefed Phil. "There's a thunderstorm about seventy miles from here, but it's moving north at twenty miles an hour. I doubt you'll even see it, but it left the roads wet. Drive fast, but get there safely. We think that he may have been in one of these two houses, and is now on the move." He gave Phil a map with two red circles. "If he is, then he has to drive north along this road before he reaches Highway 58. If we're right about Dallas, he should turn east and come right at you."

Phil climbed into the unmarked police cruiser. Amanda opened the passenger door and sat down. "I thought you weren't coming," Phil said, hoping that she had changed her mind. They both had very nearly mastered retracting their own claws, and he felt only anticipation in the air between them.

"I'm not," she said and his heart fell. "Don't try and be a hero, Phil. We don't want a confrontation; otherwise, I'd be going. Draw him out, and then get the hell out of there. Twenty, thirty miles should do it. He should pick you up before you sense him, so when you feel him, use this Police Interceptor engine and put some distance between the two of you."

"He'll know it's a trap," Phil said. From the moment Amanda suggested that they use Phil as bait, he saw the transparency of the plan. "You should just let me take care of him." Phil had grown surprisingly confident in the force that was developing inside him. From a raw power standpoint, he was at least Amanda's equal.

"Thinking like that will get you killed, Phillip Rucker. This isn't about power," she said, answering his thoughts. "This is about harnessing the force and directing it, and right now he can do that far better than you can." Her tone was stern, almost angry. "He will know it's a trap, but it's one he won't be able to resist. It will offend him greatly that you were sent instead of me. He'll want to send a message, and if you approach him full of naïve bravado, he will send that message."

Fully chastened, Phil nodded his head. "As soon as I can feel him, I'll turn around. I sure hope I don't run out of gas, or get a flat tire." Phil tried to be funny.

Chapter 60

Klaus smiled when he first felt the tickle that could only be the mind of Phillip Rucker. "So you survived after all," he said to himself. He glanced over his shoulder for his ethereal companion, but Pushkin hadn't shown himself in days.

They were still much too far apart for Klaus to read Phil, much less control him, but the very fact that he was here was a complication. He was driving in from the east, which meant that they had divined his plan. It probably also meant that Amanda was waiting for him to turn west.

He leaned forward and looked at the thick cloud cover. He wasn't an expert on satellite surveillance, but he was fairly certain that the Americans didn't have cameras that could see through miles of clouds. They must have found the stolen Audi.

"Damn." He had meant to move it to the Theimes', but old Elmer wasn't much help, especially after he was dead. Klaus laughed. He wasn't worried about the pathologist, or anyone who would have sent him. He could deal with all of them.

"Aren't you getting tired of having to adapt your plans because of these irritating Americans?" Pushkin asked.

"I thought you had left for good." Pushkin's sudden and unexpected appearances usually irritated Reisch, but today he was glad to see the Russian.

"Why do you suppose they would send him after you?"

"It's obviously a trap. I'm guessing that they want me to turn west into the lovely arms of Amanda Flynn. Either that, or they have far too much faith in Dr. Rucker."

"It's a little too obvious for my liking." Pushkin was always the voice of doubt and restraint. Klaus had grown up respecting the man, but could never understand this character flaw.

The rain had stopped and Klaus pushed the old pickup to its limit, which was just over the legal limit. He reached Highway 58 and had to make a decision: turn east, kill Rucker and face what waited behind him, or do what they wanted and turn west. He let the truck idle at the intersection and turned his mind west.

"Ah, there you are Amanda." She had shut down her mind, but this close, she could never fully hide from him. Twice they had shared a mind, and he would always be able to find her. "It's not a bad plan," he said to Pushkin. "Only one road for me to take, and they have both ends covered. It's too bad I'm not going to play nice." He turned the wheel and the truck to the east. With Amanda accounted for, Phil and the entire U.S. Army posed no real threat to him.

"Make it fast. This pig of a truck couldn't outrun a snake." Reisch looked at Pushkin. "It's a Russian expression."

"Snakes don't run; they slither."

"It loses something in translation. Pay attention."

Rucker was about fifty miles away, but the distance was closing at a rate of two miles a minute. Amanda was almost as far away, and once he turned away from her, she began to give chase and was slowly closing the distance. "She's at least forty-five minutes behind me, and if she gets too close, I can always slow her down."

There was no sense trying to hide anymore, so Klaus unreeled his mind. Aside from his two friends, no one was within reach. No army lying in wait; no air force waiting to blow him apart with a smart missile. Just the three of them. He focused on Phil, his most immediate threat. Rucker's heart was racing almost as fast as his car, but his mind was frustratingly closed. He would need to close the distance before he could concentrate enough mental energy to break through Phil's pathetic defenses. It really was offensive that they would send a neophyte to draw him out. Did anyone seriously believe that he would be threatened by Phillip Rucker? He was little more than a speed bump.

"Maybe it's a suicide mission?" Pushkin offered.

"Could be, or maybe this is Amanda's way of getting rid of Rucker. Given time, I could see him being a threat to her supremacy. I wish I had a little more time, I could use him." Reisch began to calculate how much time he would need to convert Phil, and how fast Amanda was closing the distance. "Pity," he said. Phil would have to die, but that didn't mean he couldn't enjoy himself.

***

Phil could feel the German's attempt to control him, but the separation made the efforts weak and he easily resisted them. It was time to turn back; he had done his job; Reisch had shown himself. But he still drove on. Reisch drew him on, not the German himself, but his very existence. A little closer and he could reach into Reisch's mind and destroy it.

A blood lust unlike anything he had ever felt overwhelmed reason. Power surged through him as he saw Reisch in his mind's eye twisting in agony as his body was slowly torn apart. He could do it; all he needed was a few more minutes. Amanda would be proud.

No, she wouldn't. The long-lost small voice had returned. *She will think that you were a fool for getting yourself killed and undoing their best opportunity to stop this madman.*

Phil tried to ignore the voice, but like the rest of him, it had grown as well. He slowed the cruiser and turned around.

Now she'll be proud, the small voice said.

***

"Why?" Klaus asked himself and Pushkin.

"Curious," was his only answer.

Phil had turned around and was racing away at twice Klaus's speed. There was no way he could reach Phil now. "Cowardice? Second thoughts? A logical response to an overwhelming threat?" He reached back and found Amanda closing as fast as her car would go. It made no sense.

"Turn around; I don't like this at all," cautious Pushkin said, a note of panic in his voice. Klaus slowed the truck and let it coast down the long straight road. Amanda's car began to coast as well.

"They expect me to turn around. She wants me to come to her." Indecision crawled into Klaus's mind. He could feel Amanda now; she was cool and confident, but still too far away to be a threat or an opportunity.

***

Phil continued to drive, but the farther he got from Reisch, the worse he felt. Amanda didn't understand what he had become. It was true that he was new to this, and she had seven years of experience, but by her own admission, she wasn't an expert. All she had to draw on were her own experiences, which were clearly different from his. His mind had been much more powerful than hers before their infections, and it was only reasonable that after their infections he would be stronger still. She treated him like a fool, and he resented it greatly. His foot slipped off the accelerator, and he began to seethe. He didn't care if she was proud of him or not.

Anger began to pulse inside him, and the car slowed to a stop. Reisch had stopped as well, and for the first time he picked up Amanda's presence. She was west of Reisch and waiting for him to turn around. She wanted to kill him. It was all right for Phil to flush Reisch out, but not all right for him to kill the German. That pleasure belonged to Amanda. Resentment began to mix with anger, and he turned the cruiser around.

"To hell with that," he said. He hit the accelerator and the car leapt forward as all four hundred and forty horses started streaking back towards Reisch. The blood lust returned, and he could feel its energy in every cell of his body. For the first time in his life, he began to giggle with enthusiasm. He was getting closer to Reisch, and he began to tingle all over, and even that felt wonderful. He was more alive than he had ever been. Sparks began to snap loudly in the dashboard and Phil laughed. The radio shorted out in a haze of blue smoke, and before Phil could react the car lurched and died.

***

Now all three of them had come to a stop. Klaus looked at a puzzled Pushkin. "It's a trap," Klaus said. "They want me to turn towards Amanda, and Rucker will sneak up behind me."

"Kill Rucker and get the hell out of here." Pushkin's voice was decisive, but Klaus caught the undercurrent of fear.

"I think you're right. This is getting out of hand." Klaus was losing control of the situation; the behavior of Amanda and Rucker was strange and unpredictable. He scanned the area as he hit the gas, but there were still only the three of them.

Amanda started to follow again, but maintained her distance, which only confused Klaus even more. They drove quietly for fifteen more minutes until Klaus reached the point where he could direct Rucker. He reached for the pathologist, but all he grabbed was metaphysical air. Rucker had deflected him.

"Turnabout is fair play," Klaus said as Rucker reached for him, and was repulsed.

The two fenced back and forth, each effort becoming stronger as the distance between them dwindled. Amanda had chosen to be a spectator and maintained her distance.

Maybe she does want me to rid her of Rucker, Klaus thought as he crested a small hill and finally saw him with his human eyes. He was sitting alone in an unmarked police car. Klaus put on the brakes of the pickup one hundred feet from the cruiser and stared at Rucker. They had stopped their futile sparring and now silently regarded each other.

Klaus could feel the anger and conflicted emotions radiating from Rucker. Maybe he did have time to turn him. Klaus got out of the truck and walked towards the police car. The air began to thicken and buzz. Rucker climbed out as well. Confidence and fear enveloped him.

"So you thought you could kill me," Klaus taunted.

"A speed bump?" Rucker said, with mock indignation. They both did their best at closing their minds to the other, but the proximity limited their success.

Klaus felt the skin on the back of his neck begin to tingle, a reminder that Amanda was closing in on him. Facing both Amanda and a speed bump like Rucker could prove to be challenging. "I'm going to give you a single opportunity to join me, but I'm afraid I'm going to need an answer immediately." It wasn't often that Klaus felt or acted mercifully.

A laughably weak wave of mental energy was his answer.

"They sent you to kill me, and that's the best you can do?" Klaus laughed. Rucker backed away as Klaus began to advance. "Go ahead, run; it will make this so much sweeter."

Rucker walked backwards down the road trying to keep his distance from Klaus.

"Do you think you can entertain me until Amanda gets here? You see, Phil, you have to concentrate your power if you want to hurt someone. Let me show you." Klaus blasted Rucker off his feet. He landed in a clump of sage weeds twenty feet from where he was standing. His left arm crumpled beneath him and snapped on impact.

Rucker's pain filled Klaus's mind, and he began to wonder if he could wait for Amanda. "You know, a couple of weeks ago, I would have been satisfied in just driving you insane, but I think your arrogance needs to be punished." Klaus tried to surround Rucker's mind, but he resisted. "So you do have some talent."

Slowly, Rucker began to push the German out of his mind. "I'm stronger than you, Klaus," Rucker said, panting into the weeds as the two took a break from their mental wrestling match.

"I suppose I'll just have to kill you, then," Klaus said, disappointed his fun had to end so soon. He compressed the air around him and sent a shock wave moving faster than the speed of sound at the prostrate Rucker.

Once again, Rucker was lifted off his feet and thrown high into the air. He struck the barbed-wire border fence and slumped into the dirt, his broken left arm impaled on a post.

"Still with me, Phil?" Klaus walked to the top of the embankment and stared down at Rucker. He was conscious, but all his mental resistance had crumbled. The tingling in Klaus's skin began to take on a burning quality, so he stepped away from Rucker, but not so far that he couldn't watch the pathologist die.

***

"Still here," Phil whispered. "She's coming for you; do you know that?"

"I'll be long gone, and you'll be long dead by the time she gets here." Reisch turned to his left in response to something unseen. "That's plenty of time," he said to the air.

Phil looked at Reisch, confused.

"Before you die, can I ask if you can see my friend here?" Reisch turned and pointed at empty space. His expression changed to surprise an instant before his head exploded.

Phil blinked several times, his brain not processing what had just happened. For more than a minute he stared at the German's mutilated corpse, waiting for it to reassemble itself, and then heard approaching footsteps.

"You forgot your pouch," Amanda Flynn said, dropping a small black bag at the feet of what had once been Klaus Reisch.

Phil stared speechless at Amanda. A faint glow of light framed her.

"I told you not to try and be a hero. I should just let you hang there awhile."

***

It was the second time he had ever been in a helicopter and, once again, he couldn't speak properly. His arm, along with a piece of fence post, was wrapped in a large bandage. Several of his ribs were broken, and by the way he was breathing, he was fairly certain that his left lung had been punctured. There was no doubt that he had also sustained internal organ damage, but on the whole, he felt reasonably good with morphine circulating in his veins. Amanda sat next to him as the rotors began to turn. "How?" he whispered, but it was lost in the whine of the turbines.

She looked down at him, earphones tucked inside a ski cap. "Don't try to speak," she yelled.

Phil looked back up at her and the helicopter lifted off. He thought that she was the most beautiful thing he had ever seen. *An hour ago I hated you*, he thought.

You didn't really hate me then, and you're not really in love with me now, she thought in return. Can you sleep?

No, I want to know what happened back there.

You didn't listen to me and nearly got yourself killed.

I know that part; where did you come from? You were fifty miles away; how did get to me?

My Jeep was fifty miles away. I was only a few miles away, and if you had done what I asked, you would have driven right past me. Phil suddenly saw through Amanda's eyes as she sat alone in the dark desert, waiting first for him and then for Reisch. Frustration, concern, and anger filling her mind as he turned the police cruiser around and closed on Reisch. I almost didn't make it. If you hadn't shorted out your engine you'd be dead now.

God watches out for fools and idiots, he thought, trying to fight the narcotic fog. *What did you do to him?* The memory of Reisch's head exploding replayed in Phil's mind.

Very dramatic, she said, sharing the memory.

Phil was suddenly Amanda again and they were running up a dark and wet highway. From the top of a small hill, he watched as his body flipped through the air crashing into the fence, and then the memory froze and dissipated. *Hey, we were just getting to the interesting part.*

You don't see the rest until you're ready, Phil.

Chapter 61

Emil St. Clair closed the first edition volume of Dickinson and waited for the intruder to come into the light. "I guess I won't be finishing this tonight," he said as the man dressed in black stepped between him and the fireplace.

"You failed, Monsieur St. Clair. More than that, you were exposed." The accent was European, but the language was English.

"Yes, I agree with you on both accounts. Did you find the vials?"

"I have them. Perhaps you should have hidden them a little better."

"I doubt that it would have made any difference. Still, I have appreciated the extra time."

"We are not barbarian, just businessmen, " the dark man said, and he fired two silenced rounds.

***

"So they just dropped him on the steps of the Lincoln Memorial with David Moncrief pinned to his jacket?" the president asked Kyle Stanley.

"Yes," Stanley answered. It was a rather ignominious end to the life of the former French ambassador to Spain.

"I met St. Clair once. He was short and pompous." The president didn't add the word rich; it was an uncomfortable fact that St. Clair had been a financial supporter of his first presidential race. "Do we know any more about him and his seven friends?"

The Cabinet members only stared back at the president, and it was the director of the FBI who answered. "If I may, sir?" Stanley asked the attorney general. "Very little. We have made a formal request to the Russians to interview Igor Nachesha, but it seems that he has disappeared."

"So this Group of Eight may be recruiting more than one new member," the president said. "What do a French diplomat and a Russian oil baron stand to gain by attacking the United States?" He silently polled the room, but no one had an answer they wanted to share. "I'm guessing we will continue to try and answer that question?" All the heads in the room began to nod.

"Well, for now it's over. This Reisch fellow is a red spot on a New Mexican road, and we have the virus and vaccine. There are no more new chapters or twists that are going to keep me awake at night, are there?"

Once again the Cabinet remained quiet, and it was left to General McDaniels to answer, "Yes, it's over."

"Eight dead in L.A., 636 in Seattle and, God save us, more than nineteen thousand in Colorado." The president dropped the report on his desk. "Christ, we've had shooting wars with fewer casualties."

"It could have been a lot worse," the secretary of health added.

"A lot worse," Kyle Stanley whispered to himself.

"So how does this cure cancer?" the president asked the secretary.

"Not all cancers, and not even in everyone. Most leukemia, maybe lymphoma and a few others, but not all. Its biggest impact is going to be on stroke and spinal cord injury. If we can eliminate the lethal aspects of the Colorado Springs virus, we probably will be able to treat, maybe even cure them."

"That is fantastic news. I'll bet Dr. Avanti never dreamed that he would be extending human life instead of extinguishing it." For a moment, he smiled. "We still have an issue, though, don't we?" The president's Cabinet allowed him to take the lead; it was usually the vice president who led the weekly meeting. "A security risk that no one, not even the framers of the Constitution, could have anticipated."

The attorney general and the president's national security advisor exchanged a glance

"Any idea how many of . . . I don't even know what to call them?" The president panned the room for suggestions.

"Dr. Rucker said that the German called them the 'Evolved' and the 'Chosen,'" Kyle Stanley answered.

"So by extension, we are not evolved and have been excluded. I think we should find another term." Everyone in the room nodded their heads." I guess we can figure that one out later. Any estimate on their total number?"

The secretary of health opened up his briefing folder. "We think that this change will occur in about one in four who survived the Colorado Springs virus and in all those who survived the original EDH1 virus."

He turned several pages. "The population of Colorado Springs is about four hundred thousand. About half developed a clinical infection, so that means roughly fifty thousand.

"In Los Angeles and Seattle just under thirty thousand people were infected with the EDH1 virus. Most will survive and probably change as well."

"Somewhere in the neighborhood of eighty thousand potential weapons of mass destruction," the president summed up. The seven men shared a thoughtful and solemn moment. "So how do we control them?"

***

Nathan Martin was busy typing away at his computer. He had enough information about the Hybrid virus—or EDH1, he still hadn't decided what to call it—to fill a computer hard drive. He could spend an entire career dissecting the nano-sized virus and eventually unlock the answers that had eluded him his entire professional life. Adam Sabritas would ultimately finish the work that he had started. When the young man had become as old as Nathan was now, he would probably be awarded the Nobel Prize for the discoveries that would come in time. It was ironic that they had Jaime Avanti's warped vision of humanity to thank for it. It was also an uncomfortable fact that Nathan didn't think that Jaime was all that far from the truth.

"You have to be kidding me. Not again!" His secretary shouted loud enough to pull Nathan out of his thoughts. "Oh, General," a suddenly very different Martha Hays said.

Martin stood, leaned to peek out his door, and found the ever-silent Captain Winston standing next to a large uniformed officer. He listened as General McDaniels thanked Martha for her work and insight over the past month.

"Is he in?" the general asked politely.

"Of course sir; go right in," Martha said, obviously forgetting for whom she worked.

McDaniels walked into Martin's office. "Make yourself at home," Nathan said. He was still standing at his desk, which was covered by hundreds of files and articles. "We've been hard at it," he answered McDaniels's gaze at his desk.

"I was on my way to Chicago and thought I would stop in and say hello."

"You do know that there is a more direct route to Chicago."

"I thought I would give you an opportunity to discharge an obligation."

***

They were going to make him wear an isolation suit, and it took the combined efforts of Ron Benedict and his boss, Kyle Stanley, to convince the CDC that Rodney Patton could be released and allowed to travel to Chicago.

Ron had arranged for a plane to pick up the new Colorado Springs police chief from LAX and fly him to O'Hare. He watched as the large man climbed out of the backseat of a small sedan; Patton had lost a lot of weight, but the pilot would still have to adjust the trim of the plane to account for him. "Uh, I don't mean to be personal, but aren't you black?" Benedict had meant it as a joke, but Patton wasn't in a mode to find anything funny. His face and arms were a painful shade of scarlet and patches of the dark man's face had peeled down to pink skin.

"I was before I went to that damn hospital. They asked me what I was allergic to, I tell them sulfa, and so that's exactly what they gave me. I start blistering up, so now I have the Hybrid infection, and before I could call them 'assholes,' I'm in isolation with three IVs in each arm. I should sue the bastards." He slowly climbed the stairs, ducked his head, and boarded the plane. Benedict imagined that the Gulfstream tilted to his side as Patton sat in his seat. "I hope you brought food; man cannot live by Jello alone."

***

"The president is going to dedicate it personally on Saturday, but I thought we might want to have our own personal ceremony." Greg stood with Lisa, flanked by Amanda and Phil.

A small plaque had been built at the foot of John Oliver's grave. *Thanks from a Grateful Nation* had been etched in marble.

"I'm a little uncomfortable with the sentiment," Francis Coyle said to the group. "I knew and worked with John Oliver for a few years, and I can tell you he would be embarrassed by all of this." By order of the president, a road sign outside the gates of the cemetery had been erected that read *National Historic Site.*

Before anyone could respond, the small group turned as a trio of cars approached. Three black SUVs pulled up in front of the gathering. A very large and red man climbed out of the first one. He waved as Greg Flynn approached him.

"Rodney, I'm so glad to see that you're well," Greg said, with obvious sincerity, pumping the giant man's hand.

"If by well you mean that I look like a stewed tomato, then I'm well." Patton smiled and the effect was nothing short of terrifying to those who didn't know him.

More doors opened and the small group doubled in size. Another large man dressed in full military uniform introduced himself to everyone as William McDaniels.

"I didn't know your first name was William," Martin said. "It's so ordinary."

"My brother's name was William," Amanda Flynn said, addressing McDaniels. She turned and faced the shorter man. "Dr. Martin, it's been a long time." Her voice was anything but cordial. "What are you doing here?" she demanded, and everyone around them froze.

Martin didn't answer, but General McDaniels interceded. "He is here to pay his respects."

Amanda looked up at the large man, held his eyes for a moment, and then turned away.

"Phillip Rucker," he said, first to the general and then to Martin. Nathan had come out of the general's shadow to shake Phil's hand.

"Dr. Rucker, I haven't had a chance to thank you for your help. Everything that you surmised has turned out to be true. We are in the process of serotyping . . ."

Phil politely listened as Martin droned on in his scientific persona. His mind ran through the life and experiences of Nathan Martin and found that he couldn't completely agree with Amanda. Martin was flawed, prone to acts of selfish irresponsibility, but he was no worse than most people. After a few minutes, Phil excused himself while Martin was in mid-sentence, and he felt the man's irritation. *He may not be the devil that Amanda made him out to be, but he certainly is boring,* Phil thought.

The group assembled around the plaque, and Father Coyle led them in a prayer. He then spoke about his friend and colleague, and after a few minutes, most everyone had started to tear up, except for Phil.

"I know I'm being selfish," Father Coyle said as he was finishing. "But I just want my friend back."

Amanda said a few words and then turned away from the group and faced the marker that said simply: John Oliver. Only Phil could hear her thoughts, and he kept them secret.

Greg followed and, while holding Lisa's hand, he spoke of a man who had dedicated his life to something greater than himself and enriched the lives of those he touched. He looked up into the warm spring sky and apologized for ever having doubted him, and then thanked the priest for saving his life. He looked away as Father Coyle gave him a hug, and the two men cried softly.

After a discrete interval, Lisa asked if anyone else had anything to say. To everyone's surprise, Nathan Martin stepped up carrying a case of Guinness beer. He began to hand them out one by one, and when everyone had a bottle, Nathan stood before the grave, opened his bottle, and drained it. "I am a man of my word," he said, wiping the foam from his face. "But this stuff is nasty." He looked up to find that no one had joined him in his salute.

Greg and Francis Coyle began to laugh. Even Amanda smiled. "What?" Martin asked.

"Oliver hated beer," Greg said.

About the Author

Brian O'Grady is the author of three novels, *Hybrid, Amanda's Story,* and *The Unyielding Future.* He is a practicing neurologic surgeon and, when he is not writing or performing brain surgery, he struggles with Ironman triathlons. He lives with his wife in Texas.